PRAISE FOR
Venus in Winter

"A vast panorama of Tudor history, from the viewpoint of a legendary woman who loomed large in it."
—Margaret George, author of *Elizabeth I: The Novel*

"*Venus in Winter* does justice to the extraordinary, powerful, and dangerous Bess of Hardwick. Gillian Bagwell has brought to vivid life one of the great women of Tudor England." —Bernard Cornwell, author of *1356*

"The crushing anxiety of family financial burdens, the marital expectations placed on high-born young women, and the uncertainties of life under Henry VIII and his children are all explored in this richly imagined and beautifully written novel. I think it's Bagwell's best!"
—Patricia Bracewell, author of *Shadow on the Crown*

"Bagwell proves that a Tudor heroine doesn't have to be royal to fascinate us. An eyewitness account of the turbulent reigns of five English monarchs, *Venus in Winter* is a refreshing, engaging, and impeccably researched novel."
—Leslie Carroll, author of *Royal Romances*

"A wonderful portrait of one of Elizabethan England's most fascinating— and most long-lived—women. A great read, rich with detail and story."
—Diana Gabaldon, author of the bestselling Outlander series

PRAISE FOR
The September Queen

"Gillian Bagwell did an exceptional job at writing Jane and Charles's on-the-run romance. Charles not only seduces Jane, but the readers as well . . . Sprinkled with Shakespearean references that add a magical touch to Jane and Charles's romance, *The September Queen* is a love story that will stay with you long after you finish the novel." —*Fresh Fiction*

con

"Bagwell's telling of Charles and Jane's romance is bittersweet and full of passion. This richly detailed story will delight lovers of a hot romance!"

—*Dolce Dolce*

"The real hero in this tale is the ever-patient and admirable protagonist, Jane Lane. Her story—her survival and constancy through unthinkable hardships and impossible circumstances—is one that shouldn't be missed!"

—*Historical Novel Society*

"Bagwell may be one of the newer writers in the historical fiction genre, but she is one of the most talented. Her love and knowledge of the time period shines through as well as her beautifully written words and descriptive details. This novel is guaranteed to be a favorite among historical fiction readers!"

—*Pittsburgh Historical Fiction Examiner*

"An extraordinarily engrossing read! . . . It had everything that I look for in a novel—drama, romance, danger, and adventure. I devoured it in two sittings."

—*Passages to the Past*

"Bagwell reimagines [Jane and Charles's] relationship with insight and conviction . . . A fast-paced, sensual chase and a tribute to a courageous woman who made her mark on England's history."

—*The Misadventures of Moppet*

PRAISE FOR
The Darling Strumpet

"Bawdy and poignant . . . An ebullient page-turner!"

—Leslie Carroll, author of *Royal Pains*

"[A] richly engaging portrait of the life and times of one of history's most appealing characters!"

—Diana Gabaldon, author of the bestselling Outlander series

"Hard to resist this sort of seduction—a Nell Gwynn who pleasures the crowds upon the stages of London and the noblest men of England in their bedrooms. A vivid portrait of an age that makes our own seem prudish, told with verve, humor, pathos . . . and not a little eroticism."

—C. C. Humphreys, author of *A Place Called Armageddon*

continued . . .

"As bawdy and engaging as Nell herself was reputed to be. Bagwell's well-researched novel accurately captures the rowdy, sexy Restoration period . . . Romantics will devour this engaging, sexy page-turner." —*Dolce Dolce*

"Fans of historical fiction or the Restoration era, or simply desirous of an immersive, fast-paced look into another time, will likely find much to enjoy here." —*Pop Matters*

"After this fabulous debut piece of work I cannot wait to see what else Gillian Bagwell has for us historical fiction fans." —*BurtonReview.blogspot.com*

"I loved it . . . I found myself caught up in the story and just didn't want to put it down . . . This is a very enjoyable book on an extraordinary woman." —*Broken Teepee*

"Nell claims her place in history and Charles Stuart's heart, a memorable footnote to an era of flourishing theater and outrageous personalities, ever the people's darling . . . The lusty, good-hearted Nell has secured her place in England's turbulent past, a destitute girl who wins the undying love of the Restoration king. Bagwell does her story justice." —*Curled Up with a Good Book*

"Bagwell delights readers with tales of Nell Gwynn's escapades in historically accurate detail . . . Nell would have given Madonna and Lady Gaga a run for their money had they been around back then! *The Darling Strumpet* is a well-told historical romance that will be enjoyed by Anglophiles and fans of the days of old alike." —*Fresh Fiction*

"This is probably not a book I will ever re-read. I don't need to . . . I will never forget it . . . Gillian Bagwell spent twenty years researching this, her debut book. The wealth of historical detail makes it obvious that the time was well spent." —*Seductive Musings*

Books by Gillian Bagwell

THE DARLING STRUMPET
THE SEPTEMBER QUEEN
VENUS IN WINTER

VENUS in WINTER

GILLIAN BAGWELL

BERKLEY BOOKS, NEW YORK

THE BERKLEY PUBLISHING GROUP
Published by the Penguin Group
Penguin Group (USA) Inc.
375 Hudson Street, New York, New York 10014, USA

USA I Canada I UK I Ireland I Australia I New Zealand I India I South Africa I China

Penguin Books Ltd., Registered Offices: 80 Strand, London WC2R 0RL, England
For more information about the Penguin Group, visit penguin.com.

This book is an original publication of The Berkley Publishing Group.

PUBLISHING HISTORY
Berkley trade paperback edition / July 2013

Library of Congress Cataloging-in-Publication Data

Bagwell, Gillian.
Venus in winter / by Gillian Bagwell.
p. cm.
ISBN 978-0-425-25802-6 (alk. paper)
1. Shrewsbury, Elizabeth Hardwick Talbot, Countess of, 1527?-1608—Fiction.   2. Great
Britain—History—Elizabeth, 1558–1603—Fiction. 3. Biographical fiction. 4. Historical fiction.   I. Title.
PS3602.A3975V46 2013
813'.6—dc23
2013007797

PRINTED IN THE UNITED STATES OF AMERICA

10   9   8   7   6   5   4   3   2   1

Cover design by Lesley Worrell
Cover illustration by Trish Cramblet

This book is dedicated to the memory of my grandmothers

Ruth Hedwig Matilda Herbold Bagwell
June 1, 1911–February 12, 2004

Charlotte Inez Prather Loverde
July 23, 1912–August 5, 1995

PROLOGUE

Twenty-fifth of March, 1603—Hardwick Hall, Derbyshire

S HE STOOD AT THE WESTWARD-FACING WINDOW OF HER BED-chamber. The sun was poised to slip over the horizon, and its rays slanted across the rolling hills and fields as though in a last desperate attempt to cling to the rolling ball of the earth. The sky was shot with pink and gold, the underside of the drifting clouds aflame with the sun's dying glory.

The queen was dead.

Bess found it hard to take in this fact. Since the messenger from her son William in London had arrived that afternoon her mind had seethed with thoughts and memories. Elizabeth, whom she had first met as a grave-faced girl of six, her dark anxious eyes in a pale face beneath the shining red hair—so like Bess's own—standing like a small soldier in petticoats to meet the arrival of the stranger who would marry her father. Elizabeth, her face at twenty gaunt with suppressed terror at what she might suffer at the hands of her sister Mary, newly queen, though no one then could have guessed at the horrors the next handful of years would see. Elizabeth, her face alight with love as she gazed on Robert Dudley. Elizabeth, the wind from the sea whipping her skirts at Tilbury as she sat a-horseback, exhorting her troops. Elizabeth, as Bess had last seen her, in that July more than ten years earlier, the queen about to set off on progress to the West Country and Bess returning to Derbyshire, fleeing the plague that raged in London. The queen had turned then, caught Bess's eye, smiled as she raised her hand in a wave of farewell.

Now Elizabeth was gone, reckoned an old woman, and she had been six years younger than Bess. And it was James of Scotland who would succeed her. Bess's hopes and dreams and schemes of the last twenty-eight years, that it might be her granddaughter Arbella who sat on the throne, had finally been crushed in the dust. Well, what did it matter, when all was said and done? Arbella had broken her heart—only five days earlier Bess had revised her will, cutting out her granddaughter as well as her son Henry—and this news was but the final disappointment.

The sun was gone now, and dark fingers of shadow were reaching toward Hardwick Hall. Bess shivered, despite the voluminous folds of the heavy black wool of her gown, and drew her fur-lined robe tighter about her. She felt the cold so easily now and it seemed she could never get warm. Though today, Lady Day, the start of the new legal year, was deemed to be the first day of spring, the Derbyshire countryside was still wintry. And all this glass—her glorious windows, soaring up to the high ceilings—made Hardwick even colder than it would have been otherwise. What was it Robert Cecil had said about the house? Ah, yes. *Hardwick Hall, more window than wall.*

A discreet cough interrupted her thoughts and she turned to see Robert Crossman, her master builder, who had come at her summons, hat in his hands as he made his bow.

"How may I be of service to your ladyship?"

Crossman had been with Bess for more years than she could recall, working first on Chatsworth, then on the alterations to the old manor at Hardwick, then through the ten years it had taken to build the new house, and then at Oldcotes, and he remained in her employ now, with a quarterly wage and the free lease of a farm. She noted his fingers, their knuckles rough and swollen, and the size of his hands, grown with the decades of hard work.

"Thank you for coming, Rob. I know it's late."

He smiled and gave a small shrug. "There is yet light to see by, your ladyship."

She smiled in return. "So there is."

She went to her writing desk and lifted the lid from the wooden box that sat atop a stack of papers. Suddenly she felt a little shy about the reason she had asked him to come. Shy? That was not an emotion that had visited her in decades. She met his eyes.

"I have these few things that I wish you to—to immure."

"Immure?" He tasted the word cautiously.

"I would have you seal them within the wall."

She reached into the box and hesitated before she lifted out a small shoe, the once-bright crimson of its leather faded and dry. It was not exactly shyness, she realized now. It was that the shoe and the other objects nestled in the box were her, in some way, and that showing them would reveal more of herself than she had done to any person in a long time. But she wanted to see these things once more before they were walled up, and she held the shoe aloft.

"Ah, a witch deposit!" Understanding gleamed in Crossman's brown eyes, a grin creasing his face. "I have you now, your ladyship."

"A witch deposit. I suppose you might call it that. Though I would not have you think that I give credence to sorcery and charms."

"As you wish, your ladyship. But there's no shame in the old ways, and better safe than sorry."

Bess had a sudden recollection of old Joan, the searcher she had met so long ago in London, making the sign of the cross over the tiny bag of cloth tied tight with string, keeping a secret of its contents. That bundle lay within the box beside the other things she had gathered together. If it was not a charm, what was it?

"You're right. I suppose I do wish to guard this house against evil. But it's more than that. It's to leave something of myself within these walls."

She and Crossman both glanced around them. The cold gray stone of the chamber's walls was mostly hidden by richly colored hangings, ceiling to floor, providing a layer of warmth against the bitter chill that settled into the very bones of the vast building and its glittering ice-cold windows, as it did into Bess's own bones.

"Your ladyship is here in every inch of this great house," Crossman said, smiling. "In every one of its forty-six rooms."

Bess didn't answer him. She pulled out each of the objects she had secreted within the oaken box and laid them on her desk. Each of them drew her thoughts back to a face no longer on the earth, a voice long silenced, a moment lost in the rushing stream of time, yet vivid within her memory.

She turned to Crossman. His face was placid, patient, lit by the flickering fire in the hearth as the shadows deepened around them. He, too, was a part of this place.

"You know I was born but spitting distance from where we stand?" she asked. Crossman's eyes followed hers to where old Hardwick Hall stood silhouetted against the darkening sky. "What a long journey I have come, to end so close to where I began."

Part One

DAUGHTER

CHAPTER ONE

Fourth of October, 1539—Hardwick Manor, Derbyshire

BESS HARDWICK LEANED AGAINST THE CHIMNEY, ITS RED BRICKS warm in the afternoon sun, gazing out over the landscape below. She loved the view from the roof of her family's home, and today, on her twelfth birthday, she was treating herself to a short escape from her chores. The house was perched on a high hill, and from this vantage point she could see the sweep of the valley below and hills rising and falling into the distance, the River Derwent rushing between its banks, the meadows dotted with white and black sheep. Every time she climbed up to this secret corner of hers, there was always something new to see, some delightful change. In the spring the fields were vivid green, tiny lambs frisked behind ewes fat in their layers of wool, and ducklings paddled behind their mothers in the mill pond. Now, in the autumn, after the harvest, the fields were golden brown. The dusty scent of the earth rose to Bess's nostrils, bringing vividly to her mind the prickle of the cropped stalks of wheat against her ankles when she ran through the fields, and the tingle of the river's water on her feet. In a few months ice would grow at the edges of the river's banks as if from nowhere, and creep toward the center until on especially cold days there would be a thin clear sheet covering the whole surface of the water, like a sparkling window onto the little world below.

Bess turned her gaze to the north, to the little church in the distance at Ault Hucknall. That was where her father was buried. He had died when she was only a few months old, and a painted glass window commissioned by her mother was the strongest reminder she had that her father had existed. From studying the window on Sundays as far back as she could recall, she had come to think of the Hardwick stag in the painting as representing her father personally, and she had memorized every contour of its haunches, every branch of its antlers, and every petal of the collar of eglantine around its neck, almost believing she could smell the wild roses' petals.

The cackling of hens drew Bess's attention downward and she saw her younger sister Alice come out of the henhouse with a basket of eggs and make toward the kitchen door. Alice looked around, and Bess knew that her sister was probably wondering where she was. She thought of the pans of milk she had set out in the kitchen. The cream would have risen to the top by now, and she must get to the churning. With a last glance at the golden horizon of the fields, she made her way to the little ladder that led down to where she could climb in a window. At the rear of the house, the smell of roasting goose met her and she smiled. Old Annabel, the cook, always made Bess's favorite dishes for her birthday dinners.

THE HOUSEHOLD STILL ATE IN THE OLD-FASHIONED WAY, WITH family and servants alike gathered in the great hall, though today the laborers were working in distant fields and had taken their dinners with them. As Bess's stepfather had been in debtors' prison since the previous year, her fourteen-year-old brother Jem, the nominal man of the house, was seated opposite their mother Elizabeth and said the prayer before the meal. Eleven-year-old Alice sat next to Bess with her head bowed, and across the table their little half sisters, Jenny, Dibby, and Meg, kept lifting their heads to peep at the steaming goose.

The blessing over, Annabel served out the food to cries of delight, and the children chattered happily, the birthday giving the dinner the sense of something special. When the main meal was finished, Annabel presented an apple tart swimming with cream. Bess closed her eyes and inhaled the scent, sweet and spicy. She was savoring her first bite when her mother clapped her hands for silence.

"Bess, I have some good news for you." Bess sensed that some uncertainty lay behind her mother's smile and she felt a prickle of foreboding. "Our kinswoman Lady Zouche has agreed to take you into her household at Codnor Castle as a lady-in-waiting."

Bess's spoon stopped midway to her mouth and she stared at her mother. Her two older sisters were attendants to their wealthy cousins the Wingfields, and she had vaguely known that someday her turn would come, but that someday had seemed far off.

She put her spoon down, the bite of tart untouched. Elizabeth placed a gentle hand on Bess's cheek.

"Sweetheart, it's a wonderful chance for you. There you will learn how to comport yourself in polite company, and how to run a household."

Bess felt panic begin to rise within her. Go from Hardwick? From her mother, from Jem, from her sisters, from the hills and meadows and all she knew? Her throat was tight and tears were starting to burn in her eyes. She strove to keep her voice calm.

"I am learning that from you."

"I mean a great household," Elizabeth said, her eyes pleading. "You'll meet many fine people. Perhaps you'll even go to London."

"London!" Alice squealed in excitement, but at the sound of her voice all Bess could think was that Alice, born after their father's death and less than a year younger than Bess, had been her constant companion all her life and she could not bear to leave her.

"I won't go," she cried.

She swung her legs over the bench on which she sat, knocking into Alice, and bolted out the front door, slamming it in her wake. She ran for the barn, and climbed up into the hayloft, wanting to hide from anyone who followed her. She threw herself onto the sweet-smelling mass of hay, her face wet with tears. Shame and anxiety boiled within her. She knew her mother must have gone to great trouble to make the arrangements, and had nothing but her success and happiness in mind. But the thought of facing a household full of strangers filled her with dread. How would she know what to do? Why did she have to go, when everything she wanted was right here at Hardwick? She gave herself up to sobbing and cried until no more tears would come and her head ached with the weeping.

Just as she was steeling herself to return to the house, she heard footsteps below and peeked through the hatch to see Jem come into the barn. He picked up a saddle and disappeared from view as he approached the boxes where the gray mare Shadow and her colt Moth lived. The horses whinnied their welcome and Bess heard her brother speaking low and soothingly in reply. She wiped her nose on the sleeve of her smock before heaving herself through the hatch and climbing down the ladder. Jem glanced up at her.

"I thought that's where you went." He looked annoyed.

"Is Mam angry?"

Jem shook his head as he cinched the saddle onto Shadow's back. "More sad than angered, I'd say."

Bess felt another pang of guilt. She had disappointed her mother and ruined the birthday dinner for everyone.

"Where are you going?" she asked.

"To Grandfather's. Mam is thinking of selling Moth."

"Not yet! She was going to sell him when he was a year old."

Jem shrugged. Bess noticed how tall he had grown in recent months. He was almost a man now.

"I probably won't be back until tomorrow," he said, leading Shadow out into the sunlight.

Bess went to Moth's side and stroked the colt's neck, marveling at the ripple of the muscles beneath the smooth skin.

"We can't let you go, can we?" she murmured, touching the velvety nose. Secretly she had hoped that her mother would keep the colt, and she was sad to think of parting with her companion. She knew she should go back into the house but didn't think she could face her mother just yet. She scooped a bucketful of oats from a sack and poured it into the colt's feedbox. He came to investigate and buried his nose in the treat, and she ran her fingers through his mane as he ate.

"Where did you get these burrs?" she murmured, picking one out of the coarse black hair.

When Moth had finished eating, Bess brushed him, putting her weight behind her shoulder as she made smooth, rhythmic strokes with the curry comb. Gradually she began to hum as the repetitive movement calmed her. Moth nickered quietly.

"You like the song, do you?" she asked, and sang softly to him.

> *Ah, the sighs that come from my heart*
> *They grieve me passing sore,*
> *Sith I must from my love depart*
> *Farewell my joy forever more.*

The pull of her shoulder muscles and the steady strokes were soothing as she worked steadily down his neck, chest, and body; the resulting shine, satisfying. Moth leaned into her as she worked.

> *Oft to me with her goodly face*
> *She was wont to cast an eye,*
> *And now absence to me in place?*
> *Alas! For woe I die, I die.*

Bess had nearly finished grooming Moth when she was startled by the sound of horses' hooves clattering up the drive from the road. More than one horse, so it was not Jem coming back unexpectedly. And the riders were not approaching with the deliberate plodding walk that would presage a neighbor coming to call, but at a gallop that set the dogs to barking. The sound made her uneasy.

In a few moments she heard voices—men's voices, unfamiliar—though she could not make out the words. And then a shriek and loud wailing—her youngest sister, three-year-old Meg. And now she heard her mother's voice, raised in agitation.

Bess emerged from the barn and saw her mother standing at the door of the house, little Meg in her arms and five-year-old Dibby and seven-year-old Jenny peeping out from behind her skirts as she spoke to two strange men. They were dressed for travel, with cloaks and boots spattered with mud and dust, but their clothes, as well as the quality of their horses and the horses' trappings, marked them as gentlemen. Toby, the little stable boy, held the horses' reins, his face white with alarm. Elizabeth's eyes darted from one man to the other, as if gauging which was the greater threat, and Bess set off toward her mother at a run.

". . . already near a week late," one of the men was saying as Bess came close enough to hear his words. The other man glanced her way as she stopped a few feet behind them, but he did not acknowledge her and turned back to Bess's mother.

"I shall send the money as soon as I am able," Elizabeth said, her attention divided between the men and the crying child in her arms. Bess didn't know what to do. She was appalled by the look of helplessness in her mother's eyes but also frightened of these imposing strangers. She wished Jem was there.

"And when will that be, mistress?" the first man demanded. He advanced toward Elizabeth, and when she took an instinctive step back, Bess's fear turned to rage and she dashed toward them.

"Leave my mother alone!"

Both men swung toward her, blocking her path toward her mother. The one who had glanced at her before was younger, with cold blue eyes and dark hair. The other was gray haired and paunchy. Both looked impatient and annoyed.

"What's the matter, Mam?" Bess asked, looking at her mother so she wouldn't have to look at the men. She hoped they couldn't tell that she was shaking.

"Nothing. Come into the house now."

Bess went to her mother's side but did not go into the house.

"The matter is very simple," the gray-haired man said. "The rent was due upon Michaelmas, which is now four days past."

"And I tell you I haven't got it." Elizabeth clutched the sobbing Meg closer to her.

The man grimaced.

"It is two pounds and eight shillings that must be paid, and if you cannot pay it in coin, we will take it in what form we can." He glanced around. "That cow. We will take the cow."

"And how am I to feed my children then?" Elizabeth cried. "My husband is already in prison for debt, though how imprisoning a man will enable him to pay his debts I don't know." Her voice sounded near to breaking.

"If you cannot pay what you owe, you will have to shift some other way," the older man barked. "Take shelter with family."

The younger man looked toward the barn. "I'll see if there's anything worth the taking." His tone made it clear he was sure there was not, but he strode toward the barn.

Moth—the precious colt! Bess ran toward him, unheeding, and grabbed his arm. He whirled, his arm pulled back as if he would strike her.

"Stay away from there!" she shouted.

He laughed, incredulous. But he had stopped walking.

"There's nothing there," Bess said quickly. "The cow is all we have. And as my mother says, if we have not the milk, my sisters will go hungry."

The man glowered down at her and then looked to his companion, throwing up his hands in exasperation.

"Let it be," the other man sighed. "It's more trouble than it's worth to take a beast."

He turned back to Elizabeth. "We'll give you a fortnight. And then you must pay the rent, whether it be in coin, or grain, or something else of value."

He stalked away, his boots grating harsh on the cobbles of the forecourt. The younger man snatched the horses' reins from Toby. They mounted and swung their horses' heads toward the road. The younger man stopped to stare down at Bess, his eyes hard. Her heart was pounding, but she fought the trembling that shook her and met his eyes.

"Perhaps we'll take the little wench." His eyes raked over Bess's form and she thought her legs would buckle beneath her from fear. Then he laughed, spurred his horse, and both of the king's men set off at a gallop, raising a cloud of dust.

Bess turned sharply at the sound of a shriek from Meg. Her mother had collapsed and was sitting on the ground, her body wrapped protectively around the baby in her lap as the two other little girls stood openmouthed with terror. Bess ran and knelt beside her mother.

"Mam, Mam, whatever the trouble is, we can overcome it."

She sounded more sure than she felt. Her mother's shoulders were shaking with silent sobs. Bess's little sisters grappled themselves to her sides while she watched the king's men galloping away in the distance. Annabel had appeared at the door and scowled after the departing riders.

"They've gone now," Bess said.

Her mother looked so fragile and beaten, sitting with her skirts puddled in the dirt. Bess leaned down and took Meg from her mother's arms and murmured, "Come inside, Mam."

Elizabeth seemed to make an effort to regain control of herself. She hauled herself to her feet, wiped her eyes, and bent to kiss Jenny and Dibby.

"There, girls, I'm sorry, all will be well."

But Bess thought she had never seen her mother so shaken.

Inside the house, Annabel took charge of the younger children and Bess followed her mother into her bedchamber. Elizabeth removed her cap, washed her face and hands in a basin, and smoothed her disheveled hair before she spoke.

"Come, Bess. You're old enough to know how things stand. Let me try to explain to you."

She sat on the bed and, putting her arm around Bess's shoulders, drew her close.

"When a man dies and the son who will inherit is still a child, as was the case when your father died, the crown seizes control of the property until the boy reaches twenty-one years of age."

"Why should that happen? You're still here, and it's your home, too."

Elizabeth shook her head. "Hardwick is the property of your father's family and it is Jem who is your father's heir, not I. A widow is entitled to dower rights—a third of the property only. She may also lease back from the crown another third, and that is what I do."

Bess thought of the men who worked in the fields surrounding the house, and the tenant farmers whose cottages lay farther off.

"Then Will and Peter and the others—do they labor for someone else?"

"They labor for me. But only one third of the profits of the land are mine, and I must use that money to pay for the rent of the other third of the land."

"And the rest?"

Elizabeth blew her nose and pursed her lips.

"The rest goes to John Bugby, who bought your brother's wardship from the Office of Wards."

Bugby was a dour-faced man who made brief visits to Hardwick periodically. Bess had always disliked him and now she understood the strain in her mother's face and voice whenever he appeared.

"So you see," Elizabeth said, "when your father died, at once we had less money to live on."

"It's not fair!" Bess cried.

"No. It's not. And your father tried to prevent just such a thing from happening. When he fell ill and knew that he would die, he made a trust, giving the land to his brother and seven other friends for a term of twenty years, intending that Jem should get it back when he was of age. His father had done the same when he died, leaving your own father only twelve years old."

The complexities of her mother's story tangled themselves in Bess's head.

"Then why is Jem the ward of John Bugby? Why do you not hold the lands for him?"

"Because two years after your father's death there was an inquiry, and the king's men found that the trust was not valid, and that the property had passed to Jem, and not to your uncle Roger and the others. And besides, Roger had died then, too."

Bess thought with resentment of King Henry, far off in London. What right had he to take her mother's security and comfort, and sell the governance of her brother to a stranger? Despite the fire crackling on the hearth, she shivered. If home was not safe, what place would be?

"I could not manage on my own," Elizabeth said. "There was the estate to run—not only the lands and woods here but lands at Owle-cotes and Estwheytt and Heth. And seven little children to care for."

Her voice choked. Bess knew that there had been two little girls older than she who had died before she was old enough to recall them.

"And so I married your stepfather. We liked each other well, and he had a small income from his family and leases on bits of property. But it has always been hard, and it grew harder. Crops failed . . ."

A single tear cut a channel through the film of dust that had not been washed from her cheek, and Bess nestled close against her mother, wrapping her arms around her waist.

"When we could not pay what was due on many accounts, he was imprisoned in the Fleet. And now I must find the money to clear his debts and get his freedom, and also to provide for his food until that shall be possible."

"It's not right," Bess said.

"But it is what is the case. We must make the best of it."

Elizabeth pulled back to look into Bess's eyes.

"And this, Bess, is why I have sought to get you such a place as that with Sir George Zouche. At Codnor Castle, you will encounter a wider circle of acquaintance than you could ever meet here. Powerful people who can come to your aid in times of trouble and introduce you to their friends and kin."

Bess thought of the eyes of the king's man upon her and shuddered. It was from such threats and indignities that her mother was trying to protect her. Elizabeth stroked the tangled russet curls from Bess's face.

"You're twelve years old now, Bess. Time to think of a husband."

A husband? Something else Bess had never considered.

"I want for you what you cannot get here. A husband of position and wealth who will care for you and ensure that you will never face such hardships as I have seen."

"I'm sorry, Mam," Bess murmured, looking down at her feet. Her big toes were near to breaking through the worn leather of her shoes. "I will do as you wish. I will go to Codnor Castle. But, Mam, what will we do now? Will we be cast out of the house?"

"I can sell Moth."

Bess restrained herself from objecting. There was far more at stake than her own desires. She understood that now.

"We won't be cast out. If need be, I will borrow money from your grandparents, though I have done so in the past and do not wish to do it again."

Elizabeth straightened her shoulders and Bess realized how it must wound her mother's pride to have to beg for help.

"You're a good girl," Elizabeth said, kissing the top of Bess's head. "Run and help Annabel now. And after supper I will give you the gifts I intended to give you at dinner."

THAT EVENING, WHEN THE LITTLE GIRLS HAD BEEN PUT TO BED, Elizabeth called Bess to where she sat near the fireplace. Bess went to stand before her mother, feeling tears threatening to spill over once more. Elizabeth brushed a tendril of red hair out of Bess's eyes and Bess leaned her cheek against the warmth of her mother's hand.

"I know it seems a frightening thing, going off so far. But once there you'll soon feel at home, I have no doubt."

"What will I do there?"

"You'll be a companion to Lady Zouche. You'll help her to dress, and perhaps undertake such tasks as mending her gowns, or reading to her, or writing letters, or playing with the children. You will not be a servant, but of the household. You are likely to learn dancing, and perhaps will have the opportunity to improve your music."

Bess felt transported when she played the virginals, and was pleased at the thought of spending more time making music.

"You will learn to be a lady," Elizabeth said, stroking Bess's curls. "You know your father was descended, long back, from King Edward the First and his queen, Eleanor of Castile. You have the blood of a king and queen in your veins and can always be proud of that. Hardwicks have lived in this house for more than two hundred years, and though we are at present cast upon hard times, you are a gentlewoman. And you are a pretty and smart and charming girl, very quick and able at anything you set your mind to. I doubt not that when you are at Codnor Castle you will shine and be taken note of."

Bess raised her eyes to meet Elizabeth's, her mother's praise firing courage within her.

"There's no place for you to grow here, sweetheart," Elizabeth murmured. "But in a great household with important connections— even to the king himself—you will meet gentlemen of good families, possessed of influence and wealth. With such a man as a husband, who knows how high you may rise?"

Bess had never thought of what kind of a man she might marry or where a marriage might take her. How high could she rise, and what would that mean?

Alice sidled into the doorway. "Can we show Bess her things now?" she pleaded.

"Yes," Elizabeth said, standing. "Let's do that."

Alice heaved a basket from under her mother's bed and drew off its cover. There was a mountain of cloth in glowing colors, but Bess was entranced at what lay atop it—a pair of shoes in soft leather of deep scarlet, with bows made of golden ribbon. She took them up reverently, inhaling the smell of the leather—surely they had been perfumed with orange blossoms?

"You are such a lucky thing!" Alice cried, throwing herself onto her knees beside Bess, her eyes hungry.

"Here, you hold them," Bess said, feeling her spirits rise as she turned her attention to what else lay within the basket. She drew out a mass of velvet in a golden brown that made her think of the heavy tassels of wheat waving in the wind when the crops were ripe. She ran her hand along the nap of it, more deep and lush than any cloth she had ever seen.

"Tawny, that color is called," Elizabeth said. "And the height of fashion in London."

Beneath the velvet lay folded lengths of wool in dark green, along with yards of fine white linen and brightly colored ribbons.

"We'll make you two gowns before you go," Elizabeth said.

Bess lifted the soft green wool to her cheek. She had never had clothes as beautiful as what these things would make. And suddenly the thought struck her—this was where the money for the rent had gone—to provide her such finery.

"Oh, Mam," she said, her eyes filling with tears.

"You'll be the finest lady there!" Alice breathed.

"So you will, honey-lamb," Elizabeth said, brushing away Bess's tears. "So you will."

CHAPTER TWO

ON THE SUNDAY AFTER HER BIRTHDAY, BESS SAT IN THE LITTLE church at Ault Hucknall trying to keep her mind on the sermon. But her gaze kept drifting to her father's headstone, set into the floor beneath the arch between the chancel and the aisle. Leaving Hardwick would mean leaving him, too, or as much of him as she had ever had, and that thought made her almost as sad as the prospect of leaving her family.

After the service, when her mother stood talking to neighbors, Bess knelt by the marker, the cold seeping up through her skirts, and ran her fingers over the carved letters of her father's name.

"I don't want to leave," she whispered. "I need you with me. Will you help me to get on in that great place, so far from here?" She almost thought she could hear a murmur of reassurance, and pressed her hand flat against the stone in farewell.

Early one morning a few days later, the Hardwick family gathered to see Bess off. As Jem cinched the saddlebags in place, Bess kissed her little sisters, and then faced her mother. This was the moment she had been dreading, when she must say good-bye to all those she knew and loved. She flung herself into her mother's arms for a last embrace.

"Oh, my darling Bess." Elizabeth's voice was choked. Bess inhaled the scent of her mother—the lavender in which she stored her clothes, the lanoline smell of the salve she used to soothe her work-roughened hands, the particular faint aroma of her hair and skin. When would she see her mother again? She had been trying not to cry but now she could hold her tears back no longer and she could hear that her mother was weeping, too.

"My Bess," Elizabeth murmured. "I will miss you as though I had lost an arm, but I am sure that you will shine in all that you do, and when I hold you to me again I know I will be even more proud of you than I am now."

"You will write?" Bess had asked this and been reassured before, but it was all she could think to say, other than that she didn't want to leave.

"Of course, sweetheart, I will write often, and give you all the news of us here at home. And now you should be off, for you have a long ride ahead of you."

Bess nodded, memorizing the feel of her mother's arms around her before she drew back and wiped her eyes on her sleeve.

Jem swung himself up onto the horse's back and gave Bess his arm so she could mount and seat herself on the sideways-facing pillion behind him. Bess's mother stepped up onto the mounting block and Bess leaned down to kiss her once more. Elizabeth gathered the cloak more tightly around Bess's shoulders before joining the little girls, who stood with Annabel.

"Go with God, Bess!" the cook cried as Jem clicked to start the horse walking, and Bess raised an arm to wave as they set off down the hill.

Codnor Castle lay about twelve miles from Hardwick, farther than Bess had ever been from home, and despite her sadness, her interest in what experiences lay ahead of her grew as they rode. The stubbled fields stretched away on either side of the road, and the crisp autumn breeze rattled the red and gold leaves from the trees. They rode at a walk and could speak easily above the gentle clop of the horse's hooves.

"What are they like?" Bess asked. "Sir George and Lady Zouche, I mean? And the castle?"

Jem had been to Codnor Castle once before, accompanying their stepfather on a visit.

"The castle's very grand," he replied. "And has more than two thousand acres of land about it. It was in the Grey family for hundreds of years, I heard, and only came to Sir George's father twenty years ago or so, when he married a lady of the Grey family."

Two thousand acres—more than four times the amount of land that belonged, in name at least, to Hardwick Manor.

"Very big then," Bess said. "There must be a powerful lot of men to work it."

"Well, some of it's held by tenant farmers, of course. But, aye, the household is probably near on a hundred folks."

The thought of living among so many strangers was frightening, and Bess tightened her arms around Jem's middle.

"You'll be fine, I expect," he said over his shoulder. Bess was grateful for the reassurance and that he had not responded with a characteristic jest.

By late morning, the castle appeared before them, high on a hill.

"That's it," Jem said. From this distance Bess could not make out more than stone walls rising dark against the azure sky, but she felt a surge of excitement. As they rode closer, she could see that the castle's crenelated ramparts ran between several tall turrets with cone-shaped tops, and that a high gatehouse with a drawbridge led across a moat. Outbuildings had grown up outside the castle walls, which Bess guessed must house the brew house, servants' quarters, and other facilities similar to those at Hardwick, but bigger and more numerous.

As they rode across the drawbridge, a burly porter appeared, and Jem halted the horse before the arch of the stone gatehouse.

"Good day, sir, and young mistress," the porter greeted them. "Your business here, if you please?"

"I am James Hardwick," Jem said. Bess felt him draw himself up straighter. "Bringing my sister Elizabeth to wait upon her ladyship."

"Ah, very good, then."

The porter stepped aside and they rode forward into the great courtyard. A swarm of men and boys were busy at various tasks, and a fair-haired boy ran up to them to take the horse's bridle and help Bess dismount. She noted that the porter had sent another boy pelting toward a door into the castle, and in a few moments a grizzled man in dark blue that must be the Zouche livery approached them. Bess felt very small as the man looked down at her and was conscious that her skirts were spattered with mud and dust from the road. She was wearing her workaday dress, her two new gowns carefully packed in the saddlebags, and she wondered if she should have worn what had previously been her best gown, saved for Sundays and special occasions.

"Follow me, if you please." The man's tone was curt and Bess wanted to cling to Jem's arm as they followed the man toward an arched stone doorway, but didn't want to seem afraid. As they passed through the door, Bess caught her breath, for the great hall in which they stood was far bigger and more grand than the hall at Hardwick. It must be forty paces wide and sixty long, she reckoned, and the hammer-beam roof, dark with the smoke of centuries, soared far overhead.

Two long tables ran parallel to the huge fireplace, flanked by benches, and boys and men in livery were gathered in knots there and at benches along the walls. Bess was conscious of their eyes on her and was glad that Jem stood beside her.

The man glanced to see that Bess and Jem were still behind him.

"Wait here," he instructed, and disappeared through another door.

Jem and Bess stood, as they had not been invited to sit and did not know what else to do. Bess tried without success not to think about the fact that she needed to make water. How long could she hold out?

"Have they forgotten us, do you think?" she whispered eventually.

"Someone will come."

Bess thought Jem sounded as though he was speaking with more confidence than he felt. She noted a dark-haired boy grinning at her and nodded to him, hoping she did not appear as small and frightened as she felt. The smell of roasting meat wafted from one end of the hall, where the kitchen must be, and Bess's stomach growled with hunger. She hoped that they would be fed, and then worried that perhaps they had missed dinner.

"Master Hardwick."

Bess turned at the sound of the voice. Its owner was a tall, barrel-chested man resplendent in a suit of dark blue, with a gold chain of office around his neck. He bowed briefly, his eyes sweeping Bess from head to toe as she curtsied. Her hands were dusty, she knew her hair must be disheveled, and she felt very shabby. What if she was found wanting before she had even had a chance to join the household? Would this man send her back to her mother in shame?

"Master Hardwick, and Mistress Elizabeth, you are most welcome." His gaze turned back to Bess. "One of the other ladies will take you to your lodgings and get you settled."

Almost as soon as he was finished speaking, a young woman appeared at his side. She was wearing a gown of a vivid blue that nearly matched the color of her eyes, and a dark curl strayed from beneath a gabled silk hood that showed off the swanlike curve of her neck. Bess wondered if she could fashion such a headdress, and then thought that perhaps her own freckled skin would not produce the same elegant effect. She wished she had not ignored her mother's pleas to take more care to protect her complexion.

"I am Audrey," said the young woman, "Lady Zouche's chief lady-in-waiting. Come with me, if you please. We haven't much time before dinner."

Bess turned toward Jem, anxiety rising within her.

"You're not leaving yet, are you?" she asked, trying to keep the fear out of her voice.

"Your brother will stay to dinner, of course," the steward said, and Bess thought that Jem stood a little taller at his words.

"Come," Audrey repeated. "It won't do to be late."

Bess followed her up a wide staircase. Heavy stone walls rose gloomy and dark, and Bess's heart sank at the thought that she would be living in shadow, cut off from sunlight and blue sky. Would she even be permitted to get outside the castle walls?

She was pleasantly astonished when Audrey led her into a room that glowed with color and comfort. Bright tapestries covered the walls, carpets in rich hues warmed the floors, the ceiling was painted in bright colors, and the fire dancing in the great fireplace chased the shadows from the corners. The center of attention in the chamber, however, was a beautiful lady surrounded by three girls. She was dressed in a gown of deep wine red, and one of the girls was combing her luxuriant golden hair, which fell halfway down her back. Another of the girls was tying embroidered sleeves into the armholes of her bodice, and the third held a little chest in which Bess could see the sparkle of jewelry.

Bess knew this must be Anne Gainsford, Lady Zouche. The lady did not look above thirty years of age, and Bess wondered why she had expected her mistress to be middle-aged. Lady Zouche and the girls turned to Bess and Audrey as they entered the room.

"My lady, this is Elizabeth Hardwick," Audrey said.

Bess dropped into a curtsy, but Lady Zouche only gave her a distracted glance.

"You do have another gown, do you not?" she asked.

Bess felt another pang of worry. She had been entranced by her new green and tawny gowns as they took shape at Hardwick, but now, eyeing the gowns of the other ladies-in-waiting, she feared that her own would seem plain. She had no jewelry to dance and shine at her ears and throat, the stuff of her clothes was not embroidered, and she had only ribbons to dress her hair.

"Oh, yes, my lady! Two gowns! Both new."

"Good," Lady Zouche said, peering anxiously into a hand mirror. "We are entertaining the Duke of Suffolk to dinner. Help her, Lizzie and Phoebe. Audrey, for goodness' sake, see what you can do with my hair."

She waved an impatient hand at the pretty, dark-haired girl holding the jewelry box, and the girl set it down on a table of carved dark wood and beckoned Bess to follow her. Bess made to pick up the bundle of her clothing, which sat on a chair near the fire, but the girl who had been affixing Lady Zouche's sleeves—a slight girl of about Bess's own age, with freckles on her pale face—scooped it up with a shy smile, and followed behind as the first girl led Bess into a smaller room, which contained two beds and several chests.

"I'm Elisabeth Brooke," said the dark-haired girl, dimples forming in her plump cheeks as she smiled. "Everyone calls me Lizzie. This is Phoebe, who is our chamberer."

The pale girl bobbed a curtsy and Bess blinked at the idea that she would have a maid.

"You'll sleep with me, here," Lizzie said, plopping herself onto the high bed to watch as Bess undid the bundle of her belongings. "And your clothes can go in that chest—no, not now, later—you must haste and make ready for dinner."

"Is there—where do I . . ." Bess didn't know how to say that her need to urinate was now urgent, but Phoebe read the anxiety in her face.

"Oh! There is a close stool just in there."

Bess went where the girl pointed. In a tiny alcove off the room stood a chair whose cushioned seat had a hole in it. The bottom part of the chair was boxed in, but as Bess hoisted her skirts and peered in, she saw that a pan lay below. There was even a basket with scraps of colored wool that seemed to be there for the purpose of wiping herself, and another for soiled ones. Much more comfortable than using a chamber pot and straw, as she did at home.

When Bess returned to the bedchamber, the blonde girl who had been helping Lady Zouche had joined Lizzie.

"I'm Doll Fitzherbert," she said. "Where do you come from?"

"Hardwick," Bess said. "And you?"

"Norbury."

Phoebe had unpacked Bess's bundle, and her two new gowns and shifts lay on the bed, her red shoes set neatly below them. With an anxious peek at Lizzie's gown of green silk and Doll's of carnation, Bess wondered if her own would do. And which should she wear? The tawny velvet had been intended to be her best, and she had not expected to put it on so soon, but it seemed the household was in turmoil over the visiting duke.

"Shall I wear this?" she asked, and was reassured by Lizzie's little cry of pleasure.

"Oh, yes! Very pretty. And such a good color for your skin and hair!"

With Phoebe's help, Bess stripped to her chemise. She was ashamed at the state of her shoes, covered with the dust of the road and their soles cracking with wear, and gave Phoebe a grateful smile as the girl took them from her and scurried off. She was dismayed to see that the feet of her stockings were black with dirt, and her legs and smock were mottled gray.

"We'll soon have you more comfortable," Phoebe murmured, bringing in a steaming basin and linen towel. "Sit you down, mistress, and I'll have you ready in a trice."

Bess perched on a trunk while Phoebe washed the dust from Bess's face, throat, and hands, and then knelt to peel off her stockings and bathe her legs.

"Surely you'll be wanting one of your fine new smocks," Phoebe said, shaking out one of Bess's new chemises. She held it up like a screen while Bess pulled her dirty shift off over her head and shimmied into the new one before stepping into the skirt of her new gown. Phoebe tied it at the back of her waist and then laced the bodice over it. Bess wondered what she would do if the household was so grand that she had to wear her best gown every day. Would the green wool be good enough? She flushed with shame, knowing what sacrifices her mother had made to provide her with her new clothing.

She slipped her feet into her new red shoes, turning her feet from side to side to admire them and delighting in their elegance. Whatever else she might lack, these shoes at least would surely be fine enough for any lady.

She had barely finished combing and rebraiding her hair and placing a cap on her head when a horn sounded from somewhere below.

"Come!" Lizzie cried. "To the great chamber! Follow me, and do as I do."

Bess nearly fell as she darted after Lizzie, for the soles of her new shoes were slippery on the stone floor. She followed Lizzie through Lady Zouche's bedchamber and into the adjoining room, which was much larger. Audrey and Doll were already there, taking their places on benches along one of three long tables. At the head of these tables, a trestle table covered with a rich cloth was set parallel to the foot of a huge canopied bed, and beside it a smaller table was laden with gleaming gold-plated cups, bowls, and ewers.

"Why is there a bed in the dining room?" Bess whispered as she seated herself next to Lizzie.

"It's not really a dining room. It's the great chamber. The best chamber in the house—the duke will sleep here. All these tables will be taken down when dinner is done."

Ranks of men and boys in the Zouche livery filled the rest of the table at which they were seated and that on the opposite side of the room. These must be the pages and grooms her mother had told her about, Bess thought, the male counterparts to her position, boys and young men of gentle birth who, like her, were there to learn to take their places in society, and to move up as high as they could.

The tramp of many feet sounded on the stairs. A liveried man bearing a staff swept into the room followed by another carrying a tall, footed gilt bowl of salt and still others with ewers of wine, pitchers of beer, a great basket laden with bread, and a tray of spoons and knives. They placed the items on the head table and stood as the salt bearer stepped forward, bowed three times to an empty tall-backed chair behind the table, and placed the bowl of salt slightly to the left of it.

Bess was dismayed at the lack of any food except the bread. And why were Sir George and Lady Zouche not present at the table being prepared so carefully? She leaned toward Lizzie to ask her, but once more a fanfare sounded from below. Three more liveried gentlemen marched in, one of them bearing a great carving knife and another a golden goblet with elaborate tracery. The man with the knife stepped to the stacked loaves of bread, cut a small slice from one, took a bite of it, and set it aside.

"What is he doing?" Bess whispered to Lizzie.

"Taking says," Lizzie answered under her breath, glancing warily at the man with the staff. "A caution against poison. Not so much danger of that now, but ceremony requires it still."

Bess's stomach growled with hunger, and she hoped that no one had heard it. The steward who had greeted her and Jem marched in, followed by three more men with chains of office about their necks. The three dozen people in the room might have been made of wax, Bess thought, they stood so silently.

Another fanfare rang out, followed by the sound of marching feet, and the tantalizing smell of roasted meat. Bess's mouth watered and she swallowed. Good—food was coming soon.

The steward called out, "By your leave, masters!"

Everyone rose to their feet, the men pulling their hats from their heads. Bess scrambled to stand, catching her foot in her skirts, and only stopped herself from falling by stumbling into the boy next to her. He smirked as she righted herself and she heard other boys snigger.

"Here are Sir George and Lady Zouche and their guests," Lizzie murmured, and Bess turned to see Lady Zouche, on the arm of a richly dressed gentleman.

"That's the duke," Lizzie hissed. He was old, fifty at least, Bess thought, with a beaky nose and bushy, square-cut beard that she thought made his face look blockish. His clothes were finer than any she had seen, and jeweled rings flashed on his hands. He bore himself very upright and had a pompous air that she supposed must go along with being a nobleman. Ten or twelve other men followed in his wake, including Jem, dressed in his finest clothes and looking nervous.

"That's Sir George." Lizzie nodded at the gentleman at their head. Bess's new master was a tall and soldierly man in his thirties, with a strong jaw and bright blue eyes, and she thought him a much finer figure of a man than the duke.

The gentlemen took their places at the head table but made no move to eat. Bess looked regretfully at the roast joint and platters of meat on the table, no longer steaming. She was feeling light-headed with the lack of food and thought suddenly with terror that she might faint. She breathed deeply and willed herself to remain upright.

Another fanfare sounded from below. Her stomach turning over with hunger, Bess cried out to Lizzie under the blaring of the horns, "Will we never eat?"

But the fanfare ended even as she spoke. Her words echoed off the high ceiling. Every face turned to her. The duke, amusement in his eyes. Sir George, glowering. Lady Zouche, her mouth tight with anger. Bess wished she could sink into the floor. She opened her mouth to apologize, but found that she could not even speak. Surely she would be sent home now. She had been given a golden chance and had failed before she had even properly embarked on her new life. Oh, God, what would her mother say to see her come halting back? And how could she help the family if she could not reach to some higher place in the world?

The silence seemed to last forever, but at length a black-gowned chaplain stepped forward, and all bowed their heads. No one moved to cast Bess out, and as the cleric said grace, she thanked God, swearing to redeem herself in her mistress's eyes.

At last the company took their seats and the meal began. Plates of roasted mutton and chicken were placed on the tables, along with baskets of bread and a potage of oatmeal, broth, and herbs. When at last the wooden trencher before Bess was laden with helpings of everything, she was so ravenous she thought she could not get the food into her stomach fast enough, but she tried to eat daintily. The mutton was highly spiced, which she was not used to, but she decided she liked it.

There was little talk among the people gathered at the tables and though Lady Zouche appeared to be in good humor now, Bess had no wish to draw further attention to herself, so she took the opportunity to look around the room, admiring the high windows, elaborately molded plaster frieze above the mantelpiece painted in bright colors, and fine tapestries covering the walls. The people were even more interesting. Bess was surprised to note that she, Lady Zouche, Audrey, Lizzie, and Doll were the only females present.

The gowned steward presided over the table where Jem sat with the liveried men who had carried out the ceremony before the meal.

"Who are they?" she wondered, emboldened to speak now that there was a murmur of conversation.

"Sir George's cupbearer, carver, gentlemen ushers, secretary, and master of the horse," Lizzie said.

"They are gentlemen then?"

"Certainly they are gentlemen!" Doll shook her honey-colored curls impatiently. "And they serve Sir George in places of honor, just as he serves the king."

"But then there are other servants?" Bess ventured.

"Of course, but you wouldn't expect the stable boys and scullions to eat in the great chamber, would you?"

Bess only shook her head, not wanting to seem ignorant, as that was exactly what she did expect, as that was how the household ate at Hardwick, everyone together.

"The lower servants eat in the hall below," Audrey explained, "and those who cook and who serve them eat after that."

"The eating must never cease then!" Bess giggled.

Her belly was comfortably full now, and her head slightly abuzz with ale, so she barely kept from exclaiming when no sooner had the dishes been cleared from the tables but the unseen horns sang out another fanfare, and two men marched to the door, staves in hand, to meet a delegation of servants bearing more dishes of food.

Doll's blue eyes danced at the surprise on Bess's face.

"The second course," she whispered.

The ritual that had greeted the first course was repeated, and more dishes were set on the table between Bess and her messmates.

"I'll burst," she murmured, and Lizzie stifled a laugh.

"You needn't eat any more. Just take a spoonful and toy with it."

But the new offerings looked so tempting—a pie with gravy bubbling up from slits in its crust, smelling of onions and rabbit, and beef with mushrooms—that Bess found herself eating them, her belly rebelling against her tightly laced pair of bodies. By the time the second course was taken away, she was having difficulty keeping her eyes open, exhausted from the long ride and so many new experiences. She feared that when dinner was over her new mistress would dismiss her for her impertinent remark. But at the conclusion of the meal Lady Zouche did not return to her chamber with the girls.

"She and Sir George will be entertaining the duke," Lizzie said. "Which gives us a bit of time to ourselves."

"Yet there is still work for idle hands," Audrey reminded the girls.

She set Bess to mending a tear in a fine linen chemise, and drew up a stool between Lizzie and Doll. A cheerful-faced woman who introduced herself as Rachel, Lady Zouche's wet nurse, joined them, sitting near the fire and humming quietly as she gave her breast to a fair-haired baby. Bess glanced around the circle of ladies, their heads bent over their own needlework. The atmosphere was cozy and relaxed. No one said anything about her indiscretion, and she began to think that perhaps she would not lose her place after all. The food and drink still weighed heavily on her, though, and she struggled to remain awake.

"What news do you think the duke brings?" Doll asked no one in particular.

"Something good, I think," Audrey said. "If the tidings were bad we'd have heard them by now."

"Perhaps the king is to marry again," Lizzie ventured.

"Again?" Bess said, roused by this speculation. "But he's been married three times already! How many wives does one man need?"

Lizzie burst out laughing, but Audrey hushed her with a reproving glance.

"He's not just any man, he's the king, and he must ensure that he has an heir."

"But he has a son," Bess said. "It's just two years ago since Prince Edward was born." She recalled the joyful pealing of the bells of the church at Ault Hucknall, and the service of thanksgiving for the safe deliverance of the prince. And then the tolling of the bells and the mourning for Queen Jane, who had died less than a fortnight later.

"He must have another," Doll said, picking up a skein of scarlet thread and comparing it to the embroidery she had been working. "Lest something should happen to Prince Edward."

"And his daughters?" Bess persisted. "Could they not be queens?"

"No," Audrey said. "Of course a woman cannot rule. The king must have more sons. Besides, the king's daughters are princesses no more, but are called only the Lady Mary and the Lady Elizabeth."

"But why—" Bess began, and then stopped. It seemed as if a cold shadow had fallen over the room. The smiles had faded from the faces of the other girls.

"The king's daughters were removed from the succession," Audrey said briskly.

Bess longed to ask for more information but Audrey had picked up her needlework and her eyes were fixed firmly on it.

"Lady Zouche served Anne Boleyn both before and after she was queen," Lizzie whispered, her dark eyes somber. "She was forced to testify against Queen Anne when the king turned against her, and then served in the household of Queen Jane. Audrey was with our lady then, but she does not like to speak of those times."

Bess was startled to think that she was among people who knew of the doings at court firsthand. One of her earliest memories was her mother crying at the news that King Henry had put aside his first queen, Catherine, and she knew that Queen Anne had been found guilty of treason and beheaded, but these episodes had seemed very remote from her life. Looking around at the girls' faces, pale with anxiety, she realized with a sense of awe that she was now much closer to such great and tragic events.

Lady Zouche swept into the room, two little spaniels yapping at her heels. Bess was struck with fear. She had almost forgotten about her mistress's glare at her over dinner. Now her stomach went cold at the thought that perhaps Lady Zouche had arrived to cast her out and send her back to Hardwick. She jumped to her feet and curtsied, but as she raised her eyes, she was relieved to see that her mistress's face was alight with excitement.

"Such news!" Lady Zouche cried. "The king is to be married again! He has contracted with the sister of the Duke of Cleves."

"I knew it!" Lizzie crowed.

"God help the poor lady, then!" Bess murmured. She felt Lady Zouche's eyes on her, and wished she could bite her words back. But Lady Zouche only looked at her as if seeing her for the first time, and after a moment she nodded.

"Yes. We must pray for the success of the marriage. And for the well-being of Anne of Cleves."

Bess felt she could breathe again.

"Will we go to London, your ladyship?" Lizzie wondered. At that, Lady Zouche's smile broke out once more.

"Yes, certainly. We must be there for the wedding."

Bess felt a surge of excitement. London! The center of the world, from everything she knew. She had never really thought that she might go there, and now she would not only be going to London, but to the wedding of the king himself.

"When?" she cried. "When will we go?"

"Soon," Lady Zouche said. "The marriage will not take place until December, but the new queen must have a household, and her ladies and others will be chosen very shortly."

"Do you think you will serve the new queen, my lady?" Doll gasped.

"It's over early to think about that," Lady Zouche said primly. "But certainly we must be in London when she arrives. And the traveling will only get harder the longer we wait."

THAT NIGHT, WHEN BESS AT LAST CLIMBED INTO BED NEXT TO Lizzie, her head spun with the events of the day. She had been overwhelmed at her introduction to the Zouche household and had feared that surely she had lost her place as soon as she'd arrived. But recalling the look of approbation in Lady Zouche's eyes, she now felt on firmer ground. She would not be cast out. She had been accepted. She realized with a pang that Jem would leave the next day, and she missed her mother and sisters already, and said a prayer for their safety and happiness at Hardwick. But perhaps her being in the Zouche household would enable her to help them somehow. And soon she would travel to London, and would see the king and his new queen.

CHAPTER THREE

Third of November, 1539—London

THE ZOUCHE HOUSEHOLD ARRIVED IN LONDON AFTER A WEEK-long journey from Derbyshire. Lady Zouche and her children and attendants rode in horse litters, surrounded by Sir George and his riding household of fifty men and followed by five wagons of household furnishings, clothes, and personal belongings.

They had stopped to stay the night at great houses along their way, and Bess had been particularly enthralled by Nottingham Castle, but as the sprawl of houses and churches along the river came clearly into sight, punctuated by the towering spire of what Lady Zouche said was St. Paul's Cathedral, she craned her neck in excitement. Finally—London! She was eager to see as much of it as she could. She thought, too, about her stepfather, imprisoned in the Fleet, and wondered where it was.

"The house we have taken is somewhat small, but near the palace," Lady Zouche told her, reaching to take her fretting baby from the nurse's arms.

But when the convoy at last clattered to a halt in a street near the river, Bess thought that the house that rose before her was very grand. Everyone was too exhausted to do much but eat supper and fall into bed on that first night, but the next day Lady Zouche and the girls set to work on the important task of preparing themselves for the king's presence. All of their gowns were pulled from the great chests in which they had traveled and hung to let out wrinkles, and shoes, stockings, hoods, caps, fans, gloves, and the myriad other accessories were tallied and arrayed.

"I had thought to wear my green," Lady Zouche fretted, shaking out the skirts of a gown of a color that made Bess think of new spring grass. "But perhaps the blue is better. What do you think, Bess?"

Bess was pleased to be asked for her opinion and considered the gowns. "They are both wonderful, my lady, but the blue"—she gently touched the velvet of the gown with one finger—"reminds me of the feathers of the peacocks at Codnor. So very beautiful."

"Yes," Lady Zouche said, smiling. "I think you're right. The blue it shall be. You can wear your tawny velvet, Audrey her scarlet, Lizzie her green, and Doll her violet, and we shall look like a collection of jewels. Very fit for catching the eye of the king."

"What is he like, your ladyship?" Bess asked. "King Henry?"

Lizzie and the other girls gathered close to hear, as none of them had been to London or seen the king.

"Well!" Lady Zouche dropped into a low chair and smiled conspiratorially at the eager faces around her. "I've not seen him since the christening of little Prince Edward, and I've heard that he's become stout and tetchy since he injured his leg in a fall from a horse near four years ago. But in the early days when I was at court, he was as fine a man as I've ever seen."

Bess pulled a hassock close to her mistress's side, and the other girls drew up stools and hassocks, all thoughts of work gone.

"He is very tall," Lady Zouche said, "and his frame most excellent. Powerful and yet graceful—he dances wonderfully. He delighted in jousting and tilting, and beat all comers. He never tired of hunting and hawking—it seemed he could live in the saddle."

"Is he handsome, my lady?" Doll asked, her blue eyes alight and pink cheeks glowing.

"Oh, faith, he had the face of an angel! Oh, but no." Lady Zouche laughed and shook her head. "That makes it sound as though he were soft, like a lass. But he was none of that. There was deviltry in those eyes of his. I remember—" She broke off, and blushed.

"What, my lady?" Lizzie clamored.

"Oh, I suppose there's no harm to say it," Lady Zouche said. "I was just recalling a time when I watched him play at tennis. It was when I served Queen Anne, in the days before she was yet queen." A shadow of sadness crossed her face. "It was a warm day, and His Majesty had stripped off his doublet and rolled up the sleeves of his shirt. His shirt was of the finest linen, and damp with his sweat, it clung to his form."

Her eyes were distant, reliving the scene long past, and Bess thought she could almost see the glorious young king, too.

"He won his game, and came to the side of the court to have a drink of water and bandy some pleasantries with Mistress Anne. The neckband of his shirt was untied, so that it fell open, baring his throat and chest, and as he drank, I could scarce take my eyes from him, imagining—well, imagining what it was not proper for me to imagine."

The girls giggled in delight, and Bess felt a shiver of excitement run through her. She didn't quite know what it was she was feeling— she had never heard anyone speak of such sensations—but she was thrilled by Lady Zouche's story.

"He must have sensed my gaze," Lady Zouche continued, "for he lowered the mug and looked straight into my face. And it seemed he had read my thoughts, too, for in his eyes I saw such an intensity of desire and hunger that I nearly swooned."

Bess swallowed, overcome by emotions she had never felt before. Were such encounters what awaited her at court?

"And then?" Lizzie's eyes were big.

"Why, and then nothing." Lady Zouche smoothed her skirts, as if trying to regain her dignity. "It was but a glance and meant nothing. He was besotted with Mistress Anne. And even later, when she lost his favor and he strayed, I would sooner have cut out my tongue than break her heart by dallying with he whom she loved so much. And besides, by then I was wed to my lord."

That evening when Bess got to her knees to pray before crawling into bed next to Lizzie, she could not keep her eyes from her gown of tawny velvet, which hung ready to wear, the glow of the fire in the grate warming its sheen. She could scarce believe that the next day she would be at the palace, and see the king and his court. Now she understood why her mother had so wanted her to go to serve Lady Zouche. If she had stayed at Hardwick, tomorrow would have been a day like any other. But tomorrow, she would move among the highest people in the land.

Take care of them all at home, she prayed. *And let me be worthy of the faith they have in me and help me to do honor to my family.*

THE ZOUCHES AND THEIR ATTENDANTS TRAVELED TO WHITEHALL by boat, and Bess was enchanted by the view of London from the river. Great houses stood along the north side of the Thames, their gardens sloping down to the riverbank, and beyond them church steeples punctured the sky. She twisted to look behind her at London Bridge, crowded with buildings. Beyond the bridge the river was choked with ships, their masts piercing the brilliant blue of the sky, their pennants snapping and billowing in the breeze.

"Isn't it grand?" she cried.

"It is," Lizzie answered. "But do you see those black things?"

Bess peered where Lizzie pointed, on the gate at the south end of the bridge. She could not quite make out what they were.

"Heads," Lizzie said. "Boiled in tar so they'll last."

Bess's stomach heaved.

"Whose heads?" she gasped.

"Traitors. And there's legs and other pieces, too. Because they quarter them, you know, and post the bits as warnings." She lowered her voice to an ominous whisper. "So be careful how you behave at court!"

Lizzie burst into a peal of giggles, but Bess clapped her hand over her mouth, nauseated, and snapped her gaze to the river before her.

Heads and quarters of men hung up like sides of beef in a marketplace? She had never heard of such a thing and wished she didn't know of it now.

Ahead the river swept in a curve to the south, and Audrey cried out, "There's the palace!"

Bess saw great arched stone gates and high-roofed halls lining the river. She didn't see any heads, and hoped there weren't any.

"What is that building?" Doll asked, pointing.

"The abbey," Lady Zouche answered, "and Westminster Hall there, and over there is Lambeth Palace."

The boat scraped against the base of a broad set of stairs coming down from the palace to the river, and liveried men reached down to help the Zouches and their attendants alight. Bess took an outstretched hand, clutching her skirts as best she could with her free hand, lest they drag on the slimy green of the stone.

Sir George strode up the steps, supporting his wife's hand as she swept along beside him, and Bess had to trot to keep up. It seemed she was not the only one excited by the prospect of being at court. They entered the palace and passed through a warren of chambers and halls, their progress slower now as Sir George and Lady Zouche stopped to make their bows to gentlemen and ladies clustered along the way.

They emerged into a great hall, and Bess stood and stared, awed by the splendor of the palace. Every surface, from the ceiling soaring high above to the paneled walls, was painted with elaborate scenes and decorations in bright colors or hung with rich tapestries. A chattering throng of people was gathered, gentlemen and ladies swathed in gleaming satin, heavy velvet, and filmy silk, stiff with embroidery in gold or silver, and their movement and laughter made Bess think of a flock of songbirds in a tree, flying up and settling only to flutter off to some higher branch.

They made their way through the assemblage to a door guarded by stalwart liveried men with halberds.

"The presence chamber," Audrey whispered, and Bess felt her stomach contract with excitement. Audrey turned her attention to Lady Zouche, adjusting her jeweled hood, smoothing the shimmering blue of her skirts. Bess and the other girls tweaked curls into place, straightened caps, shook out their gowns. And then Bess heard someone announce the names of Sir George and Lady Zouche, and she hurried behind them through the doors.

Just inside, Sir George and Lady Zouche sank into bows, and Bess and the girls followed, curtsying to the floor. Bess raised her eyes to the dais before them as she straightened and stared in shocked surprise at the man who sat on the throne. He was old. And he was fat. Little piggy eyes gleamed above flabby cheeks, and the scraggly beard could not hide the heavy jowls. It must be the king, for he alone of all those in the room had his hat upon his head, and who but a king would have fingers so stacked with massive rings?

Bess glanced at Doll and Lizzie and was relieved that she caught in their eyes the same astonishment she felt.

Bess's master and mistress advanced to the foot of the dais, where they bowed again.

"Welcome, good Sir George," boomed the king. "How splendid to see you again. And your beauteous wife."

Bess tried to see in the stocky body the lithe tennis player damp with his sweat who had stirred such passion in Lady Zouche those many years ago, but all she could think was that the idea of any woman taking this man to her bed was repellent.

"I thank Your Majesty," Sir George said. "My lady and I wish to offer you our felicitations on your impending marriage."

"You'll be here for the wedding, won't you, George?"

"Of course, Your Majesty. We'll not miss such a happy occasion."

"Good. Good. You are most welcome to London."

And that was all. Bess followed in Lady Zouche's wake as she and Sir George retreated the way they had come. They tarried in the outer chamber greeting acquaintances and exchanging news and gossip, and Bess stood in a corner with Lady Zouche's other girls, trying to take in everything she saw.

As at Codnor Castle, the vast majority of the people who moved around her were men. Black-robed old men with grave faces; laughing, swaggering young gentlemen in jeweled finery; red-coated guards; and burly soldiers. And everywhere liveried servants, from graybeards to young boys. No wonder country families brought their daughters to London to find them husbands. It would be hard to walk ten paces without bumping into a likely match, Bess thought. And was there one here for her? She glanced around, trying to place where all these men and boys stood in relation to her on the ladder of society.

"Come, girls," Lady Zouche murmured, and with final farewells, they took their leave of the palace.

THAT EVENING BESS SAT DOWN TO WRITE A LETTER TO HER mother, and was overwhelmed by homesickness. Being in London was very exciting, but tears rose to her eyes when she thought about what her mother might be doing at that moment. Sitting near the fire, maybe, with some piece of needlework in her hand, with Alice and the little girls close by. Perhaps Jem was reading aloud. Bess sniffled and wiped her eyes. Rachel looked up from where she was nursing the baby near the hearth.

"All right, young Bess?" she asked.

"Yes," Bess said, embarrassed at her emotion. She picked up the pen and wrote, *My honored Mother,* but got no further. She longed for the comfort of her mother's arms.

"Here, now," Rachel said, coming to her. "What are these tears for, honey? Missing home, I'll warrant."

Bess nodded, trying not to cry. Rachel stroked Bess's hair with one hand, the other easily cradling the infant suckling at her ample breast.

"Well, that's only natural, and naught to be ashamed of. First time you've been away from them all, isn't it? I remember when I left home to go to Codnor, near twenty years ago now. I wept all the first night."

Bess felt comforted by Rachel's warmth, and her accent, exactly that of her own family and neighbors.

"Really?" she asked. "Where do you come from?"

"Wingfield," Rachel said. Baby David had gone to sleep in her arms and she pulled her nipple from his mouth and tucked her breast away. Her apple-cheeked face was placid, her hazel eyes seeming even brighter beneath the white cap that did not quite cover her chestnut curls.

"Wingfield is very close to where I'm from," Bess said.

"Aye, lass, I know. I knew your father a bit—your own father, I mean, who died when you were but a babe. Met him when he visited his cousins the Wingfields, where I was in service then. You have the blush of him, you know."

Bess had been told before that she resembled her father, and it always pleased her to think that some little part of him remained alive in her own appearance.

"When did you stop feeling lonely?" she asked.

"Oh, it took a while," Rachel said, rocking the baby gently. His little lips pursed and worked, as though he was dreaming of suckling. "But when I met my husband—that's when I began to feel that home was with him, and not miss my kin so much."

"My mother sent me to Lady Zouche so that I might meet a husband," Bess said. She thought again of the rooms at the palace, thronged with males of every age.

"And so you will, I make no doubt." Rachel smiled. "A pretty lass like you won't go long without catching someone's eye, and his heart, too. And then soon you'll have little ones of your own, to take back and show your mother."

In bed that night, with Lizzie nestled close beside her, Bess said a prayer of thanks for Rachel, a little bit of home to keep her warm in the great strange city.

Over the next weeks, the king's court was in a frenzy of preparation for the arrival of Anne of Cleves. Bess accompanied Lady Zouche to Whitehall every few days and the buzz of excited conversation and the courtiers flitting from place to place reminded her of a hive of bees. The Zouches entertained many guests and Bess became used to the ceremony accompanying the serving of meals. Now she saw that the pomp proclaimed the family's importance and understood that the outward reminders of one's importance were essential. For here in London everyone was on a ladder, everyone always reaching upward, and someone else was always below. A family's position was proclaimed by the manner in which they dressed and ate and to whom they were connected by blood, marriage, service, patronage, or friendship.

Bess looked forward with impatience to the dazzling day when the future queen would arrive, and could scarcely believe that she would be present for such an important event. "What is the Lady Anne like, my lady?" she asked one evening as she brushed Lady Zouche's red-gold tresses.

"Very comely, they say." Lady Zouche slipped into the loose gown of scarlet velvet that Audrey held out for her. "The king sent Master Holbein to paint her picture, you know, and apparently he was bewitched by the portrait that came back."

A fortnight after their arrival in London, the household was thrown into ecstasies at the news that the king had asked Sir George to become one of his newly refounded company of gentleman pensioners, the select few companions who served as the king's nearest guards both at court and when he went on progress about the country during the summer months.

"It is a great honor!" Lady Zouche cried, beaming. "Only fifty gentlemen have been selected. My lord shall be as close beside His Majesty as anyone and we shall certainly be at court very often."

My dearest Mother, Bess wrote that night. *Here are news indeed! As my lord will wait upon the king, we will stay here in London, and not return to Codnor after the wedding. My lady says I shall have two more gowns in the new year, as we will be frequently at the palace. I will write to you of the occurrents here, which are sure to be many. I pray God that He will grant you so to continue in good health and estate. Your obedient daughter, Bess.*

Bess listened rapt as Lady Zouche repeated to her ladies the news Sir George learned at court each day.

"Four hundred gentlemen are to go to meet the Lady Anne at Calais, and accompany her on her journey to London. And such thrusting of sharp elbows there is sure to be among them and to be one of the fifty ladies who will meet her! Of course my lord will remain here, with the king. But we shall go forth to meet our new queen when she approaches London."

The royal wedding was to be held at Christmas, with twelve days of celebrations, punctuated by the queen's entrance into London on New Year's Day. A deputation of gentlemen departed for Calais in the first week of December, but news came that the weather in the channel was terrible, and that Anne of Cleves's arrival would surely be delayed.

As Christmas approached, cartloads of ivy, holly, and mistletoe arrived at the Zouches' house, and every room was heavy with the scent of bay, rosemary, and laurel and hot spiced wine. A Holy Bough, a hoop of hazel garlanded with evergreens and ribbons, and hung with gilded nuts, was suspended above the door to the street. A great Yule log burned in the enormous fireplace of the hall, and the kitchen issued forth a parade of delicacies for the feasting that would continue until Twelfth Night, the Feast of the Epiphany on the sixth of January. Bess was enthralled with the music and dancing, the games and caroling.

On Christmas night the merrymaking continued into the wee hours. Bess danced until she was out of breath, blushing and giggling as the young gentlemen of the household clamored to partner her. She was particularly taken with a tall, dark-haired young groom named Edmund, and her heart beat with excitement when he took her by the hand and drew her into a shadowed corner.

"Why, look, it's mistletoe," he murmured, pulling her toward him. Bess looked up and saw that a clump of the greenery with its waxy white berries hung above them. Edmund's eyes glowed like coals as he gazed at her. She found that her head was spinning from the wine and the dancing and the air, heavy with the scent of spices and the honey smell of beeswax candles. Edmund kissed her and she felt herself drowning in a rush of sensations such as she had never experienced before. The feel of his lips on hers, the taste of him, the scent of him—all were intoxicating. But at the back of her head a little voice whispered a warning, and she put a hand on his chest and drew herself away from him.

"What's the matter, pretty Bess, don't you like me?" He put his hands around her waist, and she struggled to keep from succumbing to the pull of his eyes, suddenly afraid of what might happen.

"Of course I do, but I—I pray you tell me what's the news from court?"

Edward gave her a catlike smile, and she was relieved that he had halted his pursuit, at least momentarily.

"Apparently this lady of Cleves is not quite what His Majesty has been led to believe."

Bess was shocked at the casual way he spoke of the future queen. "How so?"

"Those who have seen her say she's tall and thin, and of middling beauty at best."

He waved a dismissive hand. Surely he must be wrong, Bess thought.

"But her portrait?"

"Is perhaps not quite true to the life. Holbein may have flattered her a little." Edmund glanced around to see if he was overheard, and whispered in Bess's ear, twining his fingers in her curls. "There's a rhyme going around:

If that be your picture, then shall we
Soon see how you and your picture agree."

Bess was appalled. What would the king do if he found that his bride was not to his liking?

Edmund tilted her face up to his, but just as he bent to kiss her, Audrey's voice brought Bess back to earth.

"Bess!" Audrey grabbed Bess's elbow and pulled her away from Edmund. "Her ladyship is looking for you. Come here at once!" She shot a sharp glance at Edmund. "And you, lad, you know better."

Edmund smirked and inclined his head in a bow that seemed to smack of mockery. Audrey steered Bess away from him, through the chattering and dancing revelers. Once on the opposite side of the room she stared sternly down at Bess.

"Have a care, wench. Your virtue is a precious thing, and your good name just as important. Don't allow a roisterer like that to smirch your reputation."

"No," Bess faltered. "I wasn't—"

But she knew that she had been in dangerous waters, and that she must be on her guard in future.

CHAPTER FOUR

THREE DAYS AFTER CHRISTMAS, WORD ARRIVED THAT ANNE of Cleves had finally been able to set sail and had reached Canterbury, and would be in London within a few days. Bess and the other girls accompanied Sir George and Lady Zouche to the palace for the New Year's Day festivities. The king, at the center of an attentive crowd, appeared in high spirits, roaring with laughter at some jest of his own as he cuffed a page good-naturedly. Bess thought he looked like an apple, the shiny red satin of his doublet stretched across the expanse of his belly, but dared not even whisper this conceit to Lizzie.

"A toast to my new queen!" the king shouted, raising his heavy goblet aloft. "The beauteous Lady Anne of Cleves!"

"Lady Anne of Cleves!" a chorus of voices proclaimed, and dozens of goblets flashed in the candlelight.

Surely he had not heard the rumors about his future queen failing to live up to the promise of her portrait, Bess thought. She studied the faces around her. Had others heard the gossip that Edmund had whispered to her?

"I feel like a lad of twenty, so impatient am I to see my bride!" the king crowed. "In fact—George, where did Cromwell say she is now?"

Sir George Zouche hastened to the king's side. "At Rochester, Your Majesty."

"Rochester! Why, I could be there in two hours! And now the idea takes me, I will be there!" He struggled to his feet and clapped Sir George on the shoulder. "Come, let us ride thither! Let my horse be made ready! I shall visit her!"

A groom scurried from the room as the king's eyes swept the revelers. "You'll come with me, Harry Grey. And you, Francis."

When he had named four or five of his cronies, the king strode from the room, followed by his men, leaving a buzz of astonishment in his wake.

The next afternoon, Bess made her way to Lady Zouche's chamber with a gown she had mended. She intended to lay the garment on the bed but was stopped by Sir George's voice coming from Lady Zouche's closet, the small private room that stood between her bedchamber and the little alcove where her close stool was kept.

"It's a disaster!" Sir George's voice was hoarse with anxiety. "His Majesty accused Thomas Cromwell before the council today of having deceived him in the matter of the queen. He was in such a temper that I thought he would order Cromwell to the Tower, and by God, I'd wager Cromwell thought so, too. He went white and stammered that he had received false reports of the lady's appearance."

"But what happened to bring this on?" Lady Zouche gasped.

Bess was frightened by Sir George's words. She had heard from Lady Zouche of the terrible days when the king had suddenly turned against Anne Boleyn, for whom he had thrown over his queen and defied the pope. She knew that King Henry had appointed Cromwell Lord Great Chamberlain only a few months earlier as a reward for promoting the match with Anne of Cleves. If Cromwell's star had risen with the lady, what would happen if the king cast her off? She thought of the tarred heads adorning London Bridge, the sightless sockets of their eyes staring down on all who entered London. That was what happened to people who displeased the king.

She knew she should leave but she was afraid that they would hear her if she moved, and she felt rooted to the spot by the desire to know more.

"When we arrived at the Bishop's Palace where the lady lay," Sir George said, "the king would not wait a moment, but made haste to visit her. As soon as he laid eyes on her I knew the thing would end badly. He was polite but left as soon as he could without giving offense. He didn't even give her the gifts he had brought!"

"Oh, no," Lady Zouche moaned.

"As soon as we were from her presence he began to rant. 'I like her not! I like her not!' he kept saying. And with a face like thunder, he swore he would not marry her."

Bess felt her heart thud in her chest. What would become of the poor lady? Would he have her put to death?

"And what will happen now?" Lady Zouche sounded as distraught as Bess felt.

"The king stalked out still in a rage, roaring that he would have none of her. But I don't see how he can get out of the match now. If he were to send her back to her brother the Duke of Cleves it would be such an insult that it would likely drive the duke into the arms of the emperor and the French king, and that would mean war."

"And already it's been proclaimed that the wedding will be on Twelfth Night."

"Yes. The crowds are gathering in Greenwich to greet the lady. She'll be here tomorrow."

"And we will be there," Lady Zouche said. "Dear God, let it somehow come right."

Bess sat down to write to her mother that night, but could not find the words. She would only worry her mother if she revealed how anxious and frightened she felt. And perhaps it was best not to put to paper her thoughts about the royal marriage.

Here are no news, she wrote, *but . . .* But what? But that the royal marriage, the subject of so much joy and anticipation, seemed to be like a ship headed squarely for rocks on which it would founder with the loss of many lives. She put the letter away uncompleted.

ON THE THIRD OF JANUARY, BESS WAS PART OF THE ENORMOUS party that set out from Whitehall on barges to Greenwich, every vessel decorated with streamers and banners whipping in the breeze. The riverbanks were lined with people, cheering and waving as they caught sight of the king. His coat was encrusted with jewels that reflected the rays of the sun, casting shards of light wherever he turned.

The king retired to the riverside palace, but Bess, along with Lady Zouche and her other attendants, walked with the throngs of gloriously arrayed courtiers up the hill to Blackheath, where a magnificent pavilion of cloth of gold, surrounded by smaller pavilions, had been set up at the foot of Shooter's Hill to receive the new queen. Bess's fingers were numb from the cold and she wished she could warm them at one of the glowing braziers wafting up scented smoke.

She would not have been surprised to know that every one of the king's subjects was packed onto Blackheath, so vast were the crowds. Hundreds of gentlemen and ladies on foot and on horseback were drawn up in ranks, their silks shimmering in the winter sun, and beyond them the king's humbler subjects thronged the heath as far as she could see.

"Look at the number of people!" Doll marveled.

"Yes," Lady Zouche said. "Every great person in England is here today."

She looked apprehensive, Bess thought, though her face showed a brittle smile.

"There are the king's daughters," Lady Zouche murmured, nodding her head toward the gold pavilion. "The Lady Mary and the Lady Elizabeth."

Bess turned with curiosity to where they waited with their ladies.

The Lady Mary was a pretty, small girl with a turned-up nose, who appeared to be a little more than twenty. The Lady Elizabeth, dressed in a gown of white brocade with skirts that stood out stiffly about her, was about six. Bess noted with a pleasurable thrill that both of them had red hair. The Lady Mary's shaded toward golden, but the Lady Elizabeth's was as fiery as her own, and the girl reminded Bess of herself at the same age, but her face was solemn and grave, and Bess thought she read apprehension in the dark eyes.

"I've seen many grand events," an elderly lady bundled in furs pronounced to Lady Zouche, surveying the scene. "The arrival of Catherine of Aragon to marry poor Prince Arthur. His Majesty's coronation, aye, and his father's before that. But none to touch this."

"What of the Field of the Cloth of Gold?" another old lady in furs queried.

"Aye, of course. But that was in France. I mean here. And why should it not top all? His Majesty has found a queen, and we're not like to see such an occasion again."

"It is a great blessing." The second lady nodded. "Thanks be to God, England can rejoice once more."

Bess glanced at Lady Zouche. Her mouth was a tense line and the tendons in her neck stood out hard under her pale skin. How could England be happy when the king had been trying even the previous night to find a way to escape the coming wedding? What would happen? Bess longed to ask but she had not dared to tell anyone of the terrible conversation between Sir George and Lady Zouche.

Anne of Cleves was traveling from Dartford, and at a little after noon Bess heard drumbeats in the distance.

"She's coming!" someone shouted, and a murmur ran through the crowd. Bess craned with everyone else as the sound of drums grew near. And then she caught her first sight of the future queen, riding in a painted chariot drawn by two white geldings, and followed by a mounted retinue of hundreds. She was swathed in a heavy fur robe, so Bess could not tell what her shape was like, but she thought the lady's face was far more pretty than she had feared.

Her nose was longish and thin, and her chin somewhat sharp, but her cheeks glowed rosy in the winter air and her blue eyes were alight with excitement. Her fair hair was gathered in a silver net, topped by a velvet cap almost completely covered by pearls, and with a coronet of black velvet above all. Surely the king could accommodate himself to such a bride.

"Oh, so lovely," Doll sighed.

The chariot came to a halt before the largest pavilion, and a flock of men presented themselves, bowing.

"The gentlemen of her household," Lady Zouche explained.

A dark-robed man from the Lady Anne's party came forward and made a speech to her. Bess could tell it was in Latin but did not know enough of the words to understand its meaning. Then the future queen inclined her head gravely as each of her servitors was introduced. Next, several dozen richly dressed women made their curtsies.

"The ladies who are to serve her," said Lady Zouche.

Bess wondered if her mistress was relieved not to have been chosen for the new queen's household. The scene unfolding before her seemed unreal. Like one of the masques she had seen at court during Christmas. But when it was over, the participants would not put off their costumes and go home and forget about it. Bess strained to understand what Anne of Cleves was saying as the ladies came forward, but could not.

"She is speaking High Dutch," Lady Zouche said. "My lord says she speaks no English at all."

Poor lady, Bess thought again. Not only was she to be married to a king she did not know and who did not want her as his wife, but she could not even understand him if he spoke to her.

When the Lady Anne had greeted all the members of her household, she alighted from the chariot and withdrew into the great gold pavilion, followed by a dozen of the ladies who had ridden behind her.

After a short while, a fanfare of trumpets rang out and over the crest of the hill came the king, mounted on a sleek gray stallion. He was adorned even more magnificently than he had been for the trip by barge from Whitehall, with a broad collar heavy with jewels and pearls draped over his shoulders and chest and a scabbard and sword likewise glittering with precious stones. He rode well, despite his bulk, and Bess could almost imagine the handsome and magnificent man he had been in his youth.

Just behind him rode ten footmen, their coats shining gold like the king's, and behind them a great train of mounted courtiers.

"There's my lord!" Bess cried out, noting Sir George in the first rank of gentlemen behind King Henry.

"Here comes the queen now!" Audrey whispered, and Bess turned to see that the king's bride had emerged from her pavilion. She had cast off her fur robe and the full skirts of her gown of cloth of gold billowed around her. A footman in livery embroidered with a black lion helped her to mount a white mare, its saddlecloth and bridle shining with gold and silver. Once settled, she rode toward her future husband, attended by half a dozen footmen.

The king had reined in his horse and waited. A broad smile lit his face, and Bess thought that if he truly had no liking for Anne of Cleves, he was hiding it very well. She glanced around her, at the hundreds of people watching with rapt attention as the lady neared the king. Here and there Bess saw a face that betrayed apprehension, but for the most part they were smiling, and the common people gathered farther away on the heath were cheering. They didn't know that it was but a sham they were watching.

The Lady Anne reached the king. He pulled off his velvet bonnet and bowed his head before taking her hand and kissing it. Now all the crowd was roaring, nobles and commoners alike. King Henry held the lady's hand in his, and spoke, though Bess was too far away to be able to hear his words. The lady spoke, too, then she and the king both laughed, as if acknowledging that neither could understand the other. Then the royal pair turned their horses and, followed by a sea of attendants, rode toward the ranks of the nobility and the golden pavilions shimmering in the sun, trumpets blazing their way. They turned from side to side, smiling and waving their acknowledgment of the shouted good wishes and cries of "God save the queen!" that echoed off the frozen ground.

When they reached the pavilions, the king swung down from his horse and helped the Lady Anne dismount, and then handed her into her carved and gilded chariot painted with a coat of arms. Two of the ladies she had brought from her own country rode with her, and behind them came three more chariots packed with her ladies, and then an empty litter of cloth of gold.

"A wedding present from the king," Lady Zouche explained, and Bess thought that she, too, was doing an admirable job of covering her anxiety about the king's opinion of his bride.

The royal couple rode down the hill toward the palace, the glittering crowd of their attendants following in their wake. Bess could see that the river below was even more crowded than it had been earlier with craft of every kind, all of them crammed with people cheering, singing, waving banners, seeming determined to make the most of such a day of celebration as most had never seen in their lives.

The booming of cannon announced that the king and the future queen had reached the palace, but by the time Lady Zouche and her ladies reached the bottom of the hill they had retired inside.

WHEN SIR GEORGE WAS AT HOME OVER THE NEXT DAY OR TWO BESS heard tantalizing bits of whispered conversations between him and his wife, but not enough that she could learn what was taking place at the palace.

The royal wedding went forward on Twelfth Night, the sixth of January, which marked the end of the Christmas festivities, and Bess guessed that the king must have decided he liked Anne of Cleves well enough after all, or reconciled himself to his disappointment. Every time she was at Whitehall, the number of people thronging the chambers seemed to have grown. She was making new acquaintances and kept her ears open for any news of the success of the royal marriage. She sidled closer when she noticed Lady Zouche in conversation with Anne Basset, a pretty, blonde girl of about eighteen years of age who was rumored to have been the king's mistress. Perhaps she knew better than others what was happening.

"I was appointed to be one of Her Majesty's maids of honor in December, yet I arrive only to be told there is no place for me," Anne Basset whispered urgently to Lady Zouche. "I shall write to my mother and see what she can do."

Bess wondered if it would occur to the new queen that her household would contain the king's paramours.

"It's because so many of the queen's German attendants are yet with her," Lady Zouche sympathized. "She should send them home and make way for her English ladies."

By late February, Anne Basset had taken her place in the queen's household, and Bess saw her draw Lady Zouche in as she huddled with others of the queen's ladies, Lady Rutland, Lady Rochford, and Lady Edgecombe. They looked like a clutch of chickens in the yard at Hardwick, she thought, the shine of their gowns reminding her of hens' sleek feathers.

"No!" At Lady Zouche's gasp and shocked expression, Bess edged closer. Perhaps there was news.

"The king has not lain with her," Lady Rutland was saying. "She is so innocent, she didn't even know there must be more than his lying next to her in the bed."

"How could she not know?" Lady Zouche exclaimed.

"I would not credit it if I hadn't heard it myself," Anne Basset whispered. "She told us, 'When he comes to bed he kisses me and bids me "Good night, sweetheart," and in the morning kisses me and bids me "Farewell, darling."' We asked her did the king do no more and she asked, 'Is this not enough?'"

Bess was astonished. How was it possible for a grown woman not to know what passed between a husband and wife? She thought of the animals at Hardwick, rams bellowing as they fought, and then mounting the ewes, and the dogs eagerly climbing atop the bitches. Had the queen never seen such things?

"It's that Mother Lowe," Lady Edgecombe hissed. "The mistress of the maids she brought with her. She keeps the queen ignorant like a child. I told her, 'Madam, there must be more than this, or it will be long ere we have a Duke of York, which all this realm most desires'."

"Alas," Lady Zouche murmured, glancing over her shoulder to see who might be listening. "This comports with what George tells me—that the king mutters that he cannot perform the act with the queen—though he thinks himself capable with others."

The women groaned and tutted and shook their heads.

"Then there seems little hope," Lady Rochford said.

"What said she when you told her this?" Lady Zouche asked, turning to Lady Edgecombe.

"She said she had received quite as much of His Majesty's attention as she wished. But she seemed troubled. I think she understands now that things are much amiss."

In March, Bess overhead Sir George telling Lady Zouche that the king had seized on the idea that Anne of Cleves had had a precontract of marriage with the Duke of Lorraine's son, which would nullify his union with her, and had commanded his council to look into the matter further.

"And some say he's already casting his eye around for another queen. Anne Basset's name has been mentioned."

Bess was startled to think that the king might pluck a new queen from among the ladies of the court rather than seeking out some foreign princess. But of course by choosing a bride he knew he would not be buying a pig in a poke, as he had by contracting with Anne of Cleves, sight unseen.

And yet at Whitehall things continued as if nothing was wrong, at least on the surface. The court celebrated Shrove Tuesday with jousts and feasting. Watching the dancing one evening, Bess's eye was caught by a young man in a doublet of flaming gold. As he danced, his manner was self-conscious, and his eyes flickered frequently from his partner to others nearby. He seemed to believe all eyes were on him, Bess thought. And a moment later, perhaps that was true, for in launching himself into a leap for the volta he lost his balance and fell, stumbling against another couple.

"Serves him right," Lizzie sniffed to Bess.

The king took the floor with the queen for a more stately dance. The slower measures were all that he could manage with the pain of the ulcer in his leg. Bess studied Queen Anne's face and thought her smile seemed stiff and uneasy. No improvement, then, in the state of the royal marriage.

A little later she noted the cocky young courtier approach three ladies of the queen's household, apparently seeking a partner for the next dance. She couldn't hear their words, but it appeared that he was turned down by each of the ladies in turn. Anne Basset lifted her pomander to her nose with a curl of her nostrils, as though she smelled a foul odor, and the young man bowed and turned away, his face burning red.

A giggle rang out that made Bess think of the stream at Hardwick eddying over the pebbled river bottom. The laugh belonged to a small, slight girl with russet hair and brown eyes, clapping her hands in delight. Bess thought she had never seen anyone look so alive with merriment. She was sure she hadn't seen the girl before, but that wasn't very surprising—many new faces had appeared at court with the advent of the new queen.

The girl noticed Bess looking at her and beckoned with the conspiratorial raise of an eyebrow. Bess glanced around. Was this elfin creature really summoning her? There was no one else beside her, so it must be the case. She went to the girl's side. Up close, she noted a gold fleck in one of her eyes, which seemed to complement the dimples in her cheeks.

"That Francis is such a fool, don't you think?" the girl whispered, giggling and cutting her eyes at the young man Bess had been watching.

Bess decided immediately that she liked her new acquaintance, who she reckoned to be about her own age, or maybe a year or two older.

"I do," she agreed. "Always strutting and preening."

The young man seemed to sense that he was being watched. He glanced their way and bowed, his lips pursed in a prim smile.

Bess's new friend curtsied, murmuring, "Self-satisfied prat." She and Bess collapsed in giggles and the young man drew himself up and hustled away.

"Who are you?" the girl asked, snapping her eyes to Bess.

"Bess Hardwick. I serve Lady Zouche."

"Oh. I don't know her yet. I've only just arrived at court, you see. I'm Catherine Howard. Call me Cat."

"Where have you come from?" Bess asked.

"I've been living with my grandmother. Well, my step-grand-mother, really. The Dowager Duchess of Norfolk. At Horsham in Sussex and in Lambeth by turns." Cat wrinkled her nose in distaste. "My uncle Norfolk arranged for me to come to court."

The niece of the Duke of Norfolk? Bess was startled that Cat was of such a high family, even by marriage. There was something very free about the wench. Curls tumbled from her cap, and Bess could picture her cavorting with shepherds in a field of lambs.

Handsome Thomas Seymour passed them, and Cat gazed after him. He seemed to sense her eyes on him and turned, raking her with an appraising glance. Cat shot him an arch smile before turning back to Bess. "Being here at court is so much better!"

"Do you not have parents?" Bess wondered aloud, and then worried that perhaps the question would seem impertinent.

"My mother died when I was a baby," Cat said. "My father married not long after, and I reckon my stepmother didn't want to be bothered with me, for they sent me away."

Bess thought of her own fear that being sent to the Zouche household was a kind of abandonment by her mother.

"Perhaps they just wanted what was best for you," she ventured.

Cat jutted her chin. "I don't think so. They soon had children of their own. And when my stepmother died, my father married again. But he's just died, too, so now I have no one to look to but my uncle."

"It was kind of him to bring you to court," Bess said.

"Yes," Cat said, a speculative look in her eyes as she watched a knot of ladies across the room. Bess wondered what she was thinking and then recalled that Anne Boleyn had also been Norfolk's niece. Did Cat wonder to what heights she might rise?

"Whom do you serve?" she asked.

Cat turned laughing eyes on her. "Why, the queen! I am a maid of honor to Queen Anne."

Bess was astonished. Certainly none of the other ladies of the queen's household had ever been so chatty with her. What possessed Cat to be so friendly? Whatever it was, she was glad of it. She liked the girl and would be glad of a friend at court.

CHAPTER FIVE

IN SPRING 1540 CAME THE FINAL STEPS IN THE DISSOLUTION OF the monasteries with the surrender of the abbeys of Canterbury, Christchurch, Waltham, and Rochester, where the king had had his first glimpse of Anne of Cleves. Bess was shocked to hear that the king had had the corpse of the saint Thomas Becket, who had stood against his king, Henry II, dug up and tossed onto a dunghill, and that he now wore the great ruby that had adorned Becket's shrine at Canterbury.

"Fat pickings, these church lands," Sir George commented to Lady Zouche over supper one evening when they had no guests. "The king is handing them off to his favorites. Cheap for him, and buys a lot of loyalty. Or he hopes it does, anyway."

He suddenly glanced around, as if realizing he had spoken without taking account of who might hear. Bess kept her eyes on her plate, but listened intently.

"Cromwell is tottering," Sir George said, lowering his voice. "The king has his eye on another lady already, I hear. It's only a matter of time until he rids himself of 'the Flanders mare,' as he calls her, and Cromwell will fall with her."

"What will happen to the queen?" Lady Zouche asked, her voice tight with worry.

"If she keeps her head," Sir George pronounced grimly, "she might keep her head."

Bess shuddered and said a silent prayer for Anne of Cleves. And wondered who it was that had caught the king's attention.

In mid-April, the court buzzed with the news that Thomas Cromwell had been made Earl of Essex.

"An empty honor," Sir George muttered. "I don't trust it. And the king has bestowed church lands on—on a certain lady. Something is about to give."

His words raised a swirl of anxiety in Bess's stomach. Lady Zouche had told her how Anne Boleyn's fall had brought down not only the men who were accused of being her lovers but many others around her. Were Sir George and Lady Zouche in peril? And what would happen to her if something befell them?

Lady Zouche's face was white. "Can we go home to Codnor? I don't want to be here when—when whatever is coming happens."

Her obvious fear made Bess even more afraid. *Yes,* she pleaded silently. *Let's go back to Codnor, far from here.*

"Not now." Sir George shook his head. "You know I can't leave without the king's permission, and anyway it would look like we were scuttling from the coming storm if we left now. It won't do to look distressed. We must smile and act as if all is well, whatever we feel."

May Day brought five days of festivities, with jousting at Westminster and banquets at Durham House. Watching the jousts, Bess was both excited and terrified at the sight and sound of the huge horses thundering toward each other bearing the armored knights with their lances. The king's ulcerous leg did not allow him to ride, so he sat in the stands next to the queen, cheering on his favorites and smiling grimly as they bowed before her. Bess thought the lady looked terrified, and her own gut now continually heaved with anxiety about the disaster she was sure was imminent.

Late in the final day of jousting, she heard the king's laugh ring out, and turned to see what accounted for his change of mood. The king had left the viewing stands and halted on his way to the litter that would carry him back to Whitehall. A knot of courtiers hung back silently as he smiled down at a slight figure in scarlet. Catherine Howard. She smiled boldly up at the king, tossed her head, and placed a hand lightly on his sleeve for a moment. Anne of Cleves, next to the king, flinched as though she had been slapped.

So Cat was the lady who had caught the king's fancy, Bess realized with a shock. Why, Cat couldn't be more than fifteen, and was an orphan, to boot. With no one to guide her but her uncle Norfolk. A wave of sick uneasiness struck Bess. Norfolk had come through the abasement of his niece Anne Boleyn with his head on his shoulders. Did he think to make up for her disgrace by providing the king with a mistress?

Oh, have a care, Cat, Bess pleaded silently. *It's a dangerous game you play.*

LADY ZOUCHE WENT TO COURT LESS FREQUENTLY AFTER THE May Day festivities, excusing her absence with the fact that she was with child and frequently feeling ill. She seemed perpetually nervous and unhappy. These uncertain times must remind her of the years she had served as lady to Anne Boleyn, Bess thought, and had seen the downfall first of Queen Catherine, and then of Anne. No wonder she was anxious. Bess and Lady Zouche's other ladies took it in turns to sleep on a truckle bed near their mistress, and one night she woke to the sound of stealthy footsteps and was startled to see her mistress standing at the window of the bedroom staring out into the night. The light of the moon fell on Lady Zouche's face, making silver rivulets of the tears that rolled down her cheeks. Bess was overwhelmed by tenderness for her mistress, and wanted to go to her, to put her arms about her, but felt reluctant to intrude on her mistress's private sorrow.

ON THE TENTH OF JUNE, SIR GEORGE STRODE INTO LADY ZOUCHE'S chamber as she was preparing for bed. His grim expression halted the chatter of her ladies. He glanced around at them, as if deciding whether to send them from the room.

"Thomas Cromwell was arrested in the council chamber today," he said. "He has been sent to the Tower. And the council is preparing a bill of attainder against him for treason and heresy."

Lady Zouche clapped her hand to her mouth, and Bess exchanged a horrified glance with Lizzie.

"Say nothing to anyone," Sir George commanded, his eyes sweeping hawklike from face to face. "And do not leave the house unless upon most urgent need."

It was not an order Bess would have disobeyed. She wanted to bar the door and stay far from court, for fear of what might occur next.

"What will happen?" she cried in fright.

"I don't know," Sir George said.

His uncertainty and Lady Zouche's palpable anxiety increased Bess's fear. They had lived through perilous times, and seemed to believe that another such dark season lay before them.

Events moved swiftly. Little more than a week later Sir George announced that the House of Lords had approved the bill of attainder against Cromwell. On the twenty-fourth of June, the king sent Anne of Cleves to Richmond, announcing that it was to keep her safe from the plague, which had been reported in London. A few days later the Commons passed the bill of attainder.

"The king is rowed to Lambeth daily to visit Catherine Howard," Lady Zouche told her girls, her face gray. "My lord says that Cromwell has written to His Majesty, begging for mercy, and that his life be spared." She shivered and tears came to her eyes. "But I fear he will not get it."

"What will happen to the queen, madam?" Bess whispered.

"I don't know. The House of Lords is investigating whether the marriage was valid."

Bess was confused. "But how could it not be valid, my lady?"

"If indeed she had a precontract to wed another, as the king believes," Lady Zouche said, "that is just as if that marriage had taken place, and she could not legally marry the king."

"And if there was no precontract?" Doll wondered, her eyes wide with fear.

"The privy council will solve that difficulty another way. They will say that the king did not consent to the marriage—it was forced upon him by Cromwell. And then there is the matter of the lack of consummation."

The girls gaped at her.

"I have seen it all before," Lady Zouche said, as if to herself. "It's a blessing I was not given a place in the queen's household." She turned her eyes back to the girls and held out her arms, and Bess and the others huddled close to her. "Keep quiet and keep still, and this storm will not touch us."

There was a palpable sense of relief in the Zouche household at the news that Anne of Cleves had received the privy council in Richmond and agreed to divorce proceedings. On the ninth of July, Lady Zouche called her ladies together in her bedchamber. Bess's stomach fluttered with nervousness at what new tidings there might be.

"The convocation of clergy who examined the royal marriage have found that it is null and void," Lady Zouche said, her face blank. "Just as I expected, they have found that the queen had a precontract, and that His Majesty did not consent to the marriage. And if that was not enough, it seems that everyone in England knows that he has not lain with the lady. Very tidily done."

She spoke sharply, but as she turned away, Bess thought Lady Zouche must be glad the matter had been concluded so quickly and without bloodshed.

"She'll be known as the king's sister," Lady Zouche said, picking up her embroidery and stabbing a needle into the linen. "She'll stay here in England, and will receive an allowance of four thousand pounds a year, as well as the palace at Richmond, the manor of Bletchingly, and Hever Castle."

"Hever!" Lizzie exclaimed. "That was the home of Anne Boleyn's family."

"It was," said Lady Zouche. "And the crown took possession of it when she fell."

"Thank God the queen has had the wisdom to make no fuss," Bess heard Sir George tell his wife a few days later as she brought a newly mended pair of stockings into her mistress's bedchamber. "She has set the king free to marry again, which was all that he wanted."

"And will he?" Lady Zouche whispered.

Who would the king marry? Bess wondered. Cat? Anne Basset? She wanted to hear the rest of the conversation, and dallied by folding the chemise carefully. She sneaked a glance at Lady Zouche and Sir George, but they were not paying any attention to her, so she lingered, making herself busy by straightening the other linens in the chest.

"Of course," said Sir George. "The privy council has most coyly petitioned him to 'find some noble personage to be joined with him in lawful matrimony, by whom His Majesty might have more store of fruit and succession to the comfort of the realm,' but there's no question it will be Catherine Howard."

Cat, to be queen of England! Bess was astonished that it had all come about so suddenly.

"She is noble," Lady Zouche said, her voice full of doubt.

"Though barely literate and as empty-headed a chit as one is like to find." Sir George glanced around and, noticing Bess, frowned, as though to disown the words he had just spoken. "A most graceful and sweet-tempered lady, from all I know," he pronounced more loudly.

· · ·

"THE COURT WILL GO TO THE PALACE AT OATLANDS AT THE END OF July when Parliament is dissolved for the summer," Lady Zouche told her girls a few days later. "Sir George will accompany the king, and we must make ready to travel as well."

"Where is Oatlands, madam?" Bess wondered.

"Surrey. It's lovely—the king acquired it only a couple of years ago and laid out much money on improvements. Preparing it for Anne of Cleves." She smiled wryly. "Well, she'll not get the benefit of it now, but we will. It should be a most pleasant respite."

Lady Zouche was in noticeably brighter spirits since the catastrophe of the Anne of Cleves marriage had been resolved, and was actually humming as she went through her wardrobe with the girls to decide what clothes to take with her to Oatlands.

The court traveled by barges down the Thames, and Bess reveled in the glorious summer weather and the prospect of some time away from London, which had been the scene of so much fear and anxiety over the previous months.

"There it is! It's beautiful!" she cried as the red brick walls rose into view amid the golden meadows.

Oatlands was small, as royal residences went, so the four Zouche children stayed in London, and Sir George and Lady Zouche and their attendants occupied only two rooms: a bedchamber, which also served as withdrawing room, and another room where Bess and the other girls slept. A holiday mood prevailed among the clutch of courtiers surrounding the king, who seemed to have thrown off much of his formality and was even cultivating an air of gaiety.

On the first night at Oatlands, there was dancing in the great hall after supper, and Bess came face-to-face with Cat Howard for the first time in many weeks. She didn't quite know how to greet her, so erred on the side of caution and dropped into a curtsy.

"Mistress Howard," she murmured.

"Bess!" Cat cried, taking her hands and pulling her close so that she could kiss Bess's cheeks. "How lovely to see you here! Is the house not enchanting?"

"It is," Bess agreed, put at ease by Cat's greeting but a little bewildered by her friendliness.

"Who is your pretty friend, Cat?"

Bess's heart skipped at the booming voice. It was the king who spoke. She whirled to find him standing just behind her, leaning on a cane, and she curtsied to the floor.

"This is Bess Hardwick, Your Majesty," Cat said. "She serves Lady Zouche."

"Ah, yes." The king's eyes swept Bess from head to foot. "I recall now. That hair—how could I forget it?"

He stumped closer to her, and tweaked a curl that peeped from beneath Bess's cap. She fought the urge to recoil at his touch. She could smell the foul odor coming from the abscess in his leg, and tried not to breathe as she smiled up at him.

"Just like my daughter Bess," he said. "Another pert redhead."

"And a most learned young lady, I've heard," Bess managed to say. She had heard that, but also that the king did not spend much attention on the little girl, and she worried that she should not have spoken so boldly.

"Yes. Smart as a fox," the king mused. "Wasted on a girl, of course," he added curtly. His eyes moved to Cat. "Come, sweetheart, and sit with me to watch the dancing."

Late that night as she lay in bed, Bess heard Sir George come in to the lodgings and speak in low tones to his wife.

"He's with Catherine Howard every minute he can be. There are rumors she's with child already."

"Any report of when the marriage is to be?"

"No. But he's summoned Bishop Bonner. I'd not be surprised if he weds her quietly."

"Hm. Likely."

"Ah, Anne, come and let me kiss you."

Bess heard murmurs and sighs. Her master and mistress seemed deeply in love with each other, she thought. She wondered what it would be like to have a husband, to look forward to a man's return and a kiss at the end of the day. The feel of Edmund's mouth on hers during that heady Christmas evening came back to her vividly, stirring a longing within her.

Her mother had sent her to the Zouche household so that she might find a husband, but with so much happening, she had scarcely given a thought to when she might meet a possible match. Well, she was in no hurry. If God wanted her to marry, no doubt He would put the right man in her path.

The festive mood at Oatlands was shattered when news swept through the court that Thomas Cromwell had been executed at Tower Hill a day earlier, on the twenty-eighth of July.

"And the headsman botched the job," Sir George told his wife. "He needed a second stroke to finish Cromwell."

"Heaven and earth," Lady Zouche murmured.

The flickering light of the candle on the table cast an eerie shadow on her face.

"But he had it easy compared to some." Sir George lowered his voice and Bess, sitting some feet away near the fireplace, strained to hear, though she was afraid of what he might say.

"The Lady Mary's former tutor, the first Queen Catherine's chaplain, and another were dragged on hurdles to Smithfield to meet their deaths. And Robert Barnes, that Lutheran who helped arrange the Cleves marriage, was burned as a heretic."

Bess felt her throat and chest tighten with fear. She didn't know exactly what it meant to be a heretic. But it was clear that ending up on the wrong side of the king's favor was terribly dangerous. *Keep your head down,* she thought. *Keep a weather eye out, and keep your head down.*

In early August, King Henry removed to Hampton Court, and the Zouches with him. On the eighth of the month, the king dined publicly and in great state with Cat Howard at his side. Queen Catherine. For now the news was announced that he had wed her on the same day he had had Cromwell put to death.

Bess watched Cat as she sat next to the king, and thought the young queen looked like a sparrow next to an old buzzard. But if Cat had any distaste for her husband, she didn't let it show. He basked in her sunny smile, and took up her little hand and kissed it. Bess tried to imagine herself kissing the corpulent old man and submitting to his embraces, and shuddered in revulsion.

The king's daughter the Lady Elizabeth, almost seven years old now, sat near to Cat, watching her with rapt attention. Cat noticed Elizabeth's gaze and reached over to take her hand. She smiled and spoke to her, and Elizabeth at first looked startled to be taken notice of and then smiled shyly at Cat with apparent adoration.

The poor child, Bess thought. She had lost her mother before she was old enough to remember her, and then gained a stepmother only to lose her. She had probably not even had time to get to know Anne of Cleves before the king had cast her off. Perhaps Cat would provide the little girl with motherly attention.

The next fortnight was given over to celebrations of the royal marriage, with daily hunting parties and nightly banquets, masques, and dancing to honor the king's bride. Cat was not exactly beautiful, Bess decided, watching her dancing with one of the many handsome young men of the court who buzzed around her, but she certainly drew all eyes toward her. And was likeable as well, somehow seeming to convey to each person to whom she spoke that she had a real interest in them. Watching Cat glitter in some of the shower of jewels that King Henry had lavished upon her, surrounded by the covey of high-born noblewomen who were her ladies-in-waiting, it was jarring to Bess to realize that it had been less than seven months earlier that she had stood among the cheering throngs at Blackheath to welcome Anne of Cleves. It was almost as though that marriage had never taken place, she thought, except she knew that the king had ridden to visit Anne at Richmond, and had heard that he had even given permission for his daughter Elizabeth to spend time with her as well, at Anne's request.

Prince Edward and the king's daughter Mary arrived to meet their new stepmother. Little Edward was a golden-haired, pink-cheeked mite of just three years old, and solemnly bowed to his father and Cat Howard before retreating to the arms of his nurse. The Lady Mary, her skin pallid against the black of her gown, bowed to the new queen with rigid correctness that Bess thought did little to hide her disapproval.

"My father has written that he is coming to court," Lizzie told Bess one evening as they prepared for bed. "He said he had a surprise for me. I wonder what it can be? I can hardly wait until he gets here!"

Lizzie's father, George Brooke, Baron Cobham, arrived the next day. He was a tall, stern-faced man with high cheekbones, and Bess saw that it must be from him that Lizzie got her piercing dark eyes.

"What do you think?" Lizzie cried when she returned to Lady Zouche's chamber from a visit with her father. "I am to become a maid of honor to the queen!"

Bess felt envious of Lizzie's sudden elevation. Whatever her own position, Lizzie always seemed to float a little above her, unmatchable in every way.

"I'm so pleased for you," she told Lizzie. "A well-deserved honor, and I wish you joy of it. And I'll miss you."

Lady Zouche's baby was to be born in November, and soon she would return to Codnor along with the rest of the household, although Sir George must remain to attend on the king. Bess was not sorry that she would be out of the king's presence for some months. Although the only time he had spoken to her he had seemed good-natured on the surface, she was afraid of him. She had a sudden image of the king as a brightly burning fire, drawing people to his heat and light like fluttering moths. But those who forgot the danger and drew too close singed their wings, fell into the flames, and were consumed.

Twenty-seventh of May, 1541—London

Spring had draped a haze of greenery over London of a sudden, and Bess's spirits rose as she gazed out a window of the Zouches' London home. She had enjoyed the months at Codnor, especially since she had been able to visit her mother and family at Hardwick. But it was exciting to be back in London, where something was always happening. Below, the river sparkled in the afternoon sun, and even from this distance, she could hear two boatmen calling to each other and laughing.

"I wish we could cast off all our duties today and go where our fancy takes us," she said, turning back to look at Doll and Audrey, who were mending and brushing clothes.

"Perhaps tomorrow—" Audrey began, but she was interrupted by a terrible shriek from Lady Zouche's chamber. They dashed into the room to find their mistress facedown on the bed, weeping and groaning, with Sir George kneeling by her side.

"Oh, Jesus, it cannot be!" she cried.

Bess had never seen anyone so distraught and was terrified. Had one of the children been killed? But Rachel arrived at a run with baby Edmund in her arms, and she looked as perplexed as Bess was.

"What has happened, sir?" Bess asked.

Sir George raised his eyes and stared at the girls.

"Lady Salisbury," he said, and then clamped his hand over his mouth as though to stifle a sob.

Bess's mind struggled to make sense of what Sir George was saying. She recalled that when they had first come to London, Lady Zouche had told her with outrage that the previous year, the king had imprisoned Margaret Pole, the old Countess of Salisbury, and the last of the Plantagenet dynasty, because her son had plotted against him.

"She has been attainted and sentenced to death at the king's pleasure," Lady Zouche had told her. "He'll never have her executed. She's an old lady of near seventy years and has no designs on the throne. But still it's a cruel thing to lock her in the Tower."

Now a terrible suspicion arose in Bess's mind. She glanced at the other girls. They looked as horrified as she felt.

"Has something befallen the lady?" she asked.

"May God damn him!" Lady Zouche wailed.

"Anne, hush." Sir George stooped to his wife. "You'll do yourself harm crying so." He raised haunted eyes to Bess. "Lady Salisbury was executed this morning."

"Butchered!" Lady Zouche cried. "Like an animal. Dragged to the block and hacked to death, begging for mercy. A dozen strokes of the axe it took."

Bess clapped a hand to her mouth, willing herself not to vomit.

"But why?" Doll asked, her blue eyes pools of horror.

"Because of an uprising," Sir George said. "The king feared . . ." He stopped as if he could not go on.

"The rising had nothing to do with her!" Rachel snapped. "How could it? An aged lady like she was, locked away and powerless. She was lady-in-waiting to the first Queen Catherine and governess to the Princess Mary. How could he have served her so?"

Lady Zouche was sobbing so hard that Bess feared she would choke.

Sir George shook his head as if to clear it. "I don't know. I don't understand why she should have been put to death." He looked around at the girls and Rachel. "But it is not a matter to be discussed."

Bess felt as though she had been forced into a box and a lid closed over her. How could there be such horrors? And being forbidden to speak of it somehow made it worse.

CHAPTER SIX

Thirtieth of October, 1541—Hampton Court Palace

I SEE THEM!" DOLL CRIED, TUGGING BESS'S SLEEVE. THEY HAD BEEN peering out a second-story window at Hampton Court Palace since the advance rider had thundered up with the news that the king and queen would arrive shortly, returning from the progress that had taken them through Berkshire, Oxfordshire, Northamptonshire, Bedfordshire, and Hertfordshire.

"He doesn't look best pleased, does he?" Bess murmured, as the royal party rode through the palace gates. The king was stouter than ever, and seemed to dwarf the gray gelding beneath him. Cat Howard rode beside him, sidesaddle on a dappled mare, shrouded for travel in a gray cloak and veil. "Of course, they've been traveling for three months. That would be bound to wear on anyone's patience, I would think."

"Lady Zouche had a letter from Sir George," Doll said, "that His Majesty was put into a most foul temper when the King of Scotland failed to meet him as arranged."

"His sister Margaret died but a few weeks ago," Bess recalled, "and of course little Prince Edward has been ill, which must worry him."

"I wonder if it worries Cat," Doll whispered.

Bess looked at her in shock. "Why, what do you mean?"

"Well, if the prince dies, any son she bears would be king instead."

Bess shivered, both at the thought of anyone wishing so calculatedly for the death of a child, and because it seemed ill luck to suppose Cat would have a son. Catherine of Aragon and Anne Boleyn between them had not managed to produce a living boy, though they had each been with child and brought to childbed many times, Lady Zouche had told her, proudly fussing over her own new baby boy.

"Too soon to be counting those chickens," she murmured.

"True," Doll agreed. "But Cat must be keeping him happy. He's ordered a service of thanksgiving for the marriage, to be said in every church in England day after tomorrow."

"Better her than me," Bess whispered.

The king and queen kept to their apartments that evening, no doubt exhausted from their travels, but the next day they dined in state, in the seemingly endless ritual that Bess had first witnessed at Codnor Castle. Cat, beside the king, was wearing a gown Bess hadn't seen before, of deep green silk, with outer sleeves turned back to reveal inner sleeves heavily embroidered and studded with pearls, and with starched frills of lace at her wrists. She seemed to sense Bess's gaze and turned her head to scan the lower tables. She smiled when her eyes met Bess's, and Bess bowed her head in acknowledgment.

Bess and Doll managed to catch a few minutes' visit with Lizzie, who they had not seen since the king and queen set out on their travels at the end of July.

"How did you find it going on progress with the queen?" Doll importuned her.

Lizzie hesitated before answering, glancing over her shoulder as if to see who was nearby, and Bess thought she looked nervous.

"Exciting, of course," she said. "But wearying. I'm glad we're back."

"Such beautiful earrings," Doll said. "Did the queen give them to you?"

She reached a finger toward the pearls that hung from Lizzie's ears but Lizzie stepped backward and all but swatted her hand away.

"I must go," she said, and abruptly turned and left.

"Well," Doll faltered, staring after her. "What's got into her? Too grand to speak to us now, do you think?"

"Perhaps she's just tired," Bess said. But she thought there must be something more behind Lizzie's manner.

The next day the court gathered in the palace chapel for the service of thanksgiving. Bess, seated with Lady Zouche, Audrey, and Doll, glanced up to the royal gallery where the king sat, with Cat at his side in a sober black gown. The chaplain stopped speaking, and the king stood and raised his arms to salute the crucified figure of Christ before him.

"I render thanks to Thee, O Lord, that after so many strange accidents that have befallen my marriages, Thou hast been pleased to give me a wife so entirely conformed to my inclinations as her I now have."

Accidents? Bess thought. She wondered if God viewed the fate of the king's marriages as accidents, and then felt guilty, though whether for having critical thoughts about the king or for thinking of the Almighty in such glib terms she wasn't sure.

"Amen," intoned the assembled court.

The king turned to Cat, raising her small dimpled hand to his lips with a meaty paw, and she tilted her head to smile at him. Bess was uncomfortably warm and longed to scratch her leg, and found it hard to concentrate on the rest of the service. She noticed Archbishop Cranmer enter the gallery and genuflect before he made his way to the king's side. King Henry glanced at him, and the archbishop held up what appeared to be a letter and laid it beside the king before departing as silently as he had come. It was odd, Bess mused, that whatever business he had could not wait.

When the service was finished, the congregation rose as the king struggled to his feet and departed the chapel with a flock of gentlemen in tow. The fullness of his robes, standing out from his shoulders, made his legs look even more spindly than they really were. The contrast with the grossness of his body made Bess think of a swollen tick.

As she passed through the hall with Lady Zouche, she saw that Cat had not followed the king, but stood listening to an old woman in shabby clothes who was speaking and gesticulating urgently, though Bess could not hear the words. Lizzie hovered by Cat's side.

"Alas, what ill happenings!" Cat cried, and clasped the old woman's hands in hers. "I will see that something is done, I promise you. Send to me tomorrow."

She prevented the supplicant from falling to her knees on the stone floor, and gestured to two of her ladies to help the old woman to her feet.

"Make sure that she is fed," Cat directed, "and given somewhere to sleep if she has nowhere to go." Turning, she caught sight of Bess.

"Bess Hardwick!" she cried, smiling. "Lizzie told me much about you during our travels, and I long for your better acquaintance. Come to my chambers—there is just arrived a dancing master with the newest steps from France!"

"Gladly, Your Majesty," Bess stammered, looking to Lady Zouche for consent and relieved to find that her mistress was nodding and shooing her toward Cat. Bess felt a pang of sorrow at Doll's envious expression but could only throw her a look of apology as Cat took her arm.

"Come, walk with me and tell me all your news," Cat said, and Bess, astonished, obeyed, trying to think of what to say as they walked.

"My mother writes that my sister Moll—Mary, that is—is to be wed to Robert Wingfield." That had been good news, indeed, as the Wingfields were wealthy and well connected.

"Excellent! I will have to send her a suitable gift," Cat said, drawing Bess along with her as they mounted a grand staircase.

"That would be exceeding kind of you, Your Majesty," Bess murmured, wondering why the queen showed her such favor. She had thought she had met a kindred spirit in Cat when they had first spoken at Hampton Court, but it surprised her that Cat's liking for her remained so strong. What had Lizzie said about her? Or perhaps the queen just wished to have more friends of near her own age, surrounded as she was by so many older women.

The queen's apartments had been newly decorated, Bess recalled as she and Cat swept into a great chamber, followed by Cat's chattering retinue. The walls were hung with glowing tapestries and the paneling of the walls gleamed in the firelight. The dancing lesson had apparently been planned, for half a dozen musicians arrived in moments, along with a sprightly young man in blue hose and an extravagantly feathered hat.

There were about forty ladies in the queen's entourage, enough to form three long sets of dancers, and they twittered and giggled as the dancing master strode among them, correcting posture here, pinching a cheek there, rapping his staff on the floor to silence the noise when he wished to make himself heard.

There was a pause after the first dance had been learned, and the queen's guests partook of spiced wine and little cakes. Bess was feeling giddy with the drink and the warmth of the room, and she hung back against the wall, wishing she could get some fresh air. She was in awe at the company surrounding her, recognizing some of the most noble ladies of the land, some of whom had been in the service of Anne of Cleves only a few months earlier. The dancing master pounded his staff on the floor and the dancers formed into two rings, one inside the other.

Clack, clack, smack, smack went the tambourine and the dancers' hands as they clapped high, then low, turning, jumping, circling. The noise in the room rose so that it seemed deafening. Bess caught sight of Cat across the circle, shrieking with laughter, tossing her curls, now freed from their headdress, and twirling and stamping.

And then suddenly everything was wrong. There were guards in the room, many of them, armed with halberds, their faces stern, surrounding the dancers. The musicians faltered to a stop, a flute giving a last flat little bleat.

"Why, what is this?" Cat demanded, turning a pouting face upon the captain at the head of the guards. "Why have you interrupted us?"

"Now is no more the time to dance, Your Grace," he said. He didn't bow, and Bess's stomach went cold.

"You must all be gone," the captain ordered, turning to the queen's ladies, now silent and fearful. "And you, madam, must remain here, with but Lady Rochford to attend you."

"What . . ." Cat stared up at him, her eyes dark pools.

"It is so ordered by His Majesty."

There was an instant of stunned silence. Cat looked to her ladies as if for help. Her eyes met Bess's, and Bess's guts lurched to see her terror. She wanted desperately to help Cat, but what could she do? If the king had ordered whatever was happening, there was no one to turn to for help.

"Ladies, you must be gone," the captain barked.

Lizzie grabbed Bess's hand and pulled her toward the door, and Bess nearly tripped. When she glanced back Cat's eyes were closed, as if to shut out what was happening.

Cat's attendants fled in a flurry of skirts. It seemed to Bess that they moved in silence. She made not a sound until she and Lizzie burst into Lady Zouche's room. Lady Zouche, Audrey, and Doll were sewing by the fire, but started to their feet in alarm.

"The queen . . ." Bess began. She didn't know how to say what had happened, didn't know, even, what had happened or was about to happen.

Lady Zouche hastened to her and shook her by the shoulders, fear in her eyes.

"What? What's amiss?"

"Guards came," Lizzie said. "The queen is confined to her room with only Lady Rochford."

Bess suddenly recalled Lizzie's strained awkwardness when she had spoken to Bess and Doll the day before, and wondered if Lizzie knew something that she had not wanted to speak of.

"For what reason?" Lady Zouche pressed as the other girls crowded around them. Lizzie remained silent, so Bess spoke.

"I don't know." Bess felt colder than she had ever felt in her life. She shook her head. "I don't know."

THE NEXT DAYS SEEMED LIKE SOMETHING OUT OF A NIGHTMARE TO Bess. Lizzie, suddenly without a queen to serve and terrified about where to turn, begged Lady Zouche to let her stay in their lodgings, and she and Bess and Doll huddled together in one bed.

"I heard," Lizzie whispered, "that Bishop Cranmer told the king that before Cat married him, she lay with Francis Dereham."

"What, her secretary!" Bess gasped.

"Yes, and he says that's why she took Dereham on, so she could play the strumpet with him more easily. The bishop is investigating, I hear, but I'm sure he'll only find what he wants to learn." She looked at Bess with haunted eyes. "What if he calls me to be questioned?"

Bess recalled again Lizzie's odd evasiveness when she had returned from progress. "You don't know anything," she whispered. "Do you?"

Lizzie didn't answer, but her fearful look shook Bess.

A PALL OF DREAD SETTLED OVER HAMPTON COURT. BESS COULD NOT keep from thinking about Cat, confined to her rooms, and how frightened she must be. Several times, Bess found Lizzie weeping and trembling, and her attempts to comfort Lizzie failed. She was sure now that Lizzie knew something that preyed on her mind, and gave up trying to get her to talk.

ON A GRAY AFTERNOON, BESS WAS SITTING WITH LIZZIE AND DOLL in Lady Zouche's room, sewing and trying not to think about what dreadful things might happen, when shrieks of sheer animal terror rose from somewhere outside.

Bess felt as though her heart had stopped beating. She looked to Lizzie and Doll. Both were sitting motionless, their needlework in their hands, their eyes wide with fear.

"That sounds like Cat," Bess whispered.

"It didn't even sound like a person," Doll said, her eyes filling with tears.

Lizzie said nothing, but clutched her needlework with fingers white with tension.

That night, bundled in bed between Lizzie and Doll, Bess listened as Sir George told Lady Zouche what had happened.

"The queen managed to escape from her chambers and ran down the long gallery, trying to reach the king, who was in the chapel. She got as far as the door and beat upon it, but the guards seized her and dragged her back, shrieking for mercy."

"Dear God. It's worse than with Queen Anne. Poor girl, she knows what is like to happen to her."

Bess shuddered, and prayed for Cat's salvation as she and Lizzie and Doll clung to each other, trying to stifle the sounds of their weeping.

A few days later, Bess again listened to Sir George and Lady Zouche talking quietly late at night.

"Cranmer told His Majesty that he believed the allegations against the queen. The king broke down and wept before his council."

"I wouldn't have thought he pitied her so," Lady Zouche said.

Sir George snorted. "I think it's himself he pities, not the queen. He doted on her, and now she's made a cuckold of him and made him to look like a foolish old man. He went staggering out of the chamber and rode off to Oatlands with a few cronies."

"And how does the queen?" Lady Zouche asked anxiously.

"She's in a pitiable state, I hear. She weeps incessantly and neither eats nor sleeps."

"Alas, poor creature."

. . .

THE NEXT DAY, LIZZIE SOUGHT OUT SOME OF THE QUEEN'S OTHER ladies and reported back to Bess and Doll what she had learned.

"They say that Bishop Cranmer told the queen that His Majesty would be merciful if she would confess her guilt."

The hairs rose on the back of Bess's neck. She wouldn't trust the king's word for anything, she thought. Certainly not to be merciful or to keep such a promise.

"And did she confess?" Doll asked.

"First she told him that she and Dereham had been sweethearts and they had dallied, but she had only done so because she expected they would be wed. But then she called him back and said that Dereham had forced himself on her."

Which accusation would surely cost Dereham his life, Bess thought. But would it save Cat's?

"If it were found she had a precontract with him," Sir George said to Lady Zouche that evening, "her life might be spared, for if she was never truly married to the king, she could not commit adultery."

"Adultery?" Lady Zouche cried. "What she did when a girl in her grandmother's house was not adultery."

"No. But what she has done since is. For there are most vile rumors of suspicious doings during the progress. One night the king went to her chamber and found it locked. He was kept waiting for a few minutes before the door was opened, and heard scuttlings within. The queen passed it off at the time with some excuse, but now the incident looks much blacker."

"Oh, no, the little fool," Lady Zouche moaned.

Bess was in anguish. She wanted to beg Lizzie to tell her that the rumors were lies, but Lizzie had slipped out and Bess didn't know where she had gone. And she recalled how frightened Lizzie had been at the thought that she might be summoned to tell what she knew.

How could it be true? Bess wondered. How could any woman

who knew of Anne Boleyn's death after being charged with adultery risk her life by playing the king false? Cat's face rose to her mind, Cat as she had been the evening when they met—those merry laughing eyes, the impish and provocative grace with which she moved. *Oh, Cat, Cat, you've dug your own grave.*

THE NEXT MORNING LIZZIE CREPT OUT TO SEE IF SHE COULD learn any news and soon dashed back into the lodgings, her face white with terror.

"Oh, dear God, Bess! Dereham has been arrested, and many of the household of the Duchess of Norfolk."

The dowager duchess was Cat's step-grandmother, Bess knew.

"They've been taken to the Tower," Lizzie cried. "What will I do if they come for me?"

She threw herself onto the bed and pulled the curtains shut.

What could Lizzie do? Bess thought with horror, as she climbed onto the bed next to Lizzie. There was no one to turn to if the king's guards came. No one could protect Lizzie or hide her without endangering his own life.

"Her own family have turned their backs upon her!" Lizzie wept, clutching a pillow to her chest.

Of course they had. The Duke of Norfolk had survived the fall of one niece, Anne Boleyn. He must feel the shadow of the axe, and would do whatever he could to save his neck.

"THE QUEEN HAS CONFESSED THAT SHE LAY WITH FRANCIS Dereham," Lady Zouche told Bess and the other girls a few days later. "And Bishop Cranmer judges that they had a precontract of marriage."

Bess's hopes rose. "So the king can annul the marriage, and let Cat live!"

"Pray God that it may be so," Lady Zouche said.

. . .

THE KING RETURNED TO LONDON, AND THE COURT FOLLOWED. As the barge rounded the bend in the river and Hampton Court disappeared from sight, Bess stared behind her, thinking of Cat locked within her chamber, and prayed that she would see Cat safe and happy again. A few days later, Lady Zouche told her ladies that Cat had been sent from Hampton Court to Syon Abbey, where she would be kept under house arrest, still considered a queen, but with only a few ladies.

"But she had to leave all her clothes, all her jewelry, everything that denoted her a queen," Lady Zouche whispered. "She was provided only a few gowns, of plain design."

Bess pictured the blood-red garnets she had seen trembling at Cat's earlobes, the pearl-encrusted sleeves, the jeweled hoods. All gone. What would happen to them, she wondered? But what did the loss of clothes and jewels matter, if Cat could live?

AS THE WINTRY COLD SEIZED LONDON, THE NEWS GREW WORSE.

"I hear that Catherine Tylney and Margaret Morton have been questioned," Lizzie whispered. Bess thought Lizzie looked a year older since the queen's arrest. Her beautiful face was gaunt, her usually merry brown eyes shadowed and dull.

"Who are they?" Bess asked.

"Two of the queen's chamberers who were with us on progress. Surely I will be next."

No guards arrived for Lizzie, but Sir George Zouche came home that night with a face even grimmer than it had been over the past weeks.

"The queen's maids said that during the summer's progress, she lay with her cousin Thomas Culpepper at Lincoln. His rooms were searched, and a letter found in the queen's own hand that leaves no doubt of her guilt, for she signed it 'yours as long as life endures.'"

And now that life would be short indeed, Bess thought. *Cat, Cat, would that I could help you somehow.*

"What will happen now?" Lady Zouche asked.

"It has already happened. It is proclaimed that she is queen no longer, and will be proceeded against by law."

Please, God, Bess prayed, *let the king be merciful and grant that Cat may be only beheaded.* She knew that for a woman, a traitor's death was to be burned alive.

"She's wounded his vanity and pride," Rachel told Bess later, shaking her head as she rocked little Edmund's cradle. "And a wounded lion is a most dangerous beast."

"There are horrors going on at the Tower," Bess heard Sir George say. "Torture, betrayals, all doing and saying anything they can to save their own skins. Dereham and Culpepper have been found guilty and the queen declared a common harlot."

Lizzie was summoned to court, not to be arrested, but to bear company with the king.

"The king is acting like a young swain in springtime," she told Bess. "He goes out hunting daily, and when he returns he surrounds himself with the prettiest ladies of the court, and flirts and jests. He chucked me under the chin and asked what gift I would most value." Her eyes shone with tears. "Oh, Bess, I'm so afraid. If I hang back I may offend him. And if I behave as though I welcome his attentions..."

The consequences could be just as bad, Bess thought.

On the tenth of December, Dereham and Culpepper met their deaths. As Culpepper was a gentleman, he was mercifully beheaded after being pulled through the streets to Tyburn lashed to a hurdle. Dereham was spared nothing, but suffered a traitor's death, being hanged only to be cut down from the scaffold to be disemboweled and have his heart cut out before he was beheaded and his body chopped into quarters.

Numerous Howards escaped the headsman but were clapped into the Tower and sentenced to life imprisonment and the loss of their lands.

Bess shivered in the Zouches' London house, feeling like an animal at bay. No place was safe. The king could do what he pleased, and no one could stop him. She prayed for Cat to be reprieved somehow, and for the king to turn his attentions away from Lizzie. And she prayed for the king's death, knowing it was a black sin to do it.

On Christmas Day, Bess recalled the excitement and gaiety of the previous Christmas. That seemed a lifetime ago. It was hard to imagine that she would ever feel joyful again, when death and terror hung so heavy in the air.

The New Year brought no joy, but only the reconvening of Parliament, which took up the matter of the bill of attainder against Catherine Howard. Sir George was daily at the palace and reported what was said of Cat.

"She is calm now," he reported. "Now that she has accepted she will die, she wants to die well and leave a good impression in the minds of the people."

Lizzie was called to the palace to attend a banquet with the king and sixty other ladies. She dressed in her best finery, but the vivid colors only emphasized the pallor of her face.

"I felt like a lamb in a pen with the rest of the flock, hoping that his eye should light on someone else," she told Bess and Doll, shuddering. "And from what I could tell, the others felt the same."

A few days later Sir George strode into Lady Zouche's chamber looking more angry and distressed than Bess had ever seen him.

"What is it, my love?" Lady Zouche went to him in alarm.

"When the council members arrived at Syon and told the queen that she would be taken to the Tower, she would not go, and was at last grappled into the barge by main force." He thrust Lady Zouche away from him and paced, running his hands through his hair distractedly. "Oh, God, the thought of it. Poor girl. She is a silly thing but has not deserved this fate."

Lizzie clutched Bess's hand so tightly that Bess thought her fingers would break.

"Is she to be burned?" Lady Zouche cried.

Bess's stomach rose in nausea and terror. *Oh, please, God, no.*

"No," Sir George said. "He will spare her that. It will be the headsman, and on Tower Green, not on Tower Hill, for all to see."

Lizzie let out a strangled cry. Bess felt her knees turn to water beneath her and she slumped to the cold stone of the floor. Only the axe, thank God. But—the axe. She thought of what Cat must be feeling, locked away in the Tower, knowing that she would emerge only to mount the scaffold.

Late on the night of Sunday, the twelfth of February, Bess heard the terrible sound of a man weeping. She crept on bare feet to the door of Lady Zouche's chamber. Sir George was huddled on the bed, his head on Lady Zouche's lap.

"She asked that the block be brought to her chamber," he sobbed. "So that she might practice laying her head upon it so she would not falter and look foolish as she goes to her death."

Bess felt her heart rend and stifled a cry of horror.

"She dies tomorrow then?" Lady Zouche asked, cradling her husband.

"Yes, God save her."

What was Cat doing at this very moment? Bess wondered. She recalled that Queen Anne was said to have chattered and laughed on the night before she died. Was Cat trying to banish her fears in such a way? Was she weeping again, distraught and terrified? Perhaps she was praying. Bess hoped she was praying, and that the prayers brought her comfort and courage.

The next morning Bess stared out the window, looking east toward the Tower. A bitter wind whipped the leafless trees, and a silver frost covered the ground. She started as a cannon boomed in the distance. Cat was dead.

I will never marry, she swore silently. *I will never put myself at the mercy of a man. Better by far to die in poverty, to join a nunnery, to go back to Hardwick in shame. But I will never marry.*

Part Two

WIFE

CHAPTER SEVEN

Seventeenth of December, 1542—London

GIRLS, SUCH WONDERFUL NEWS!"

Lady Zouche swept into her bedchamber, her eyes alight, and Bess and the other girls looked up from their sewing. Bess was surprised but pleased to see her mistress so happy.

"The king has invited us to the masque at court on New Year's Day! This promises a happy start to next year!"

"I hope so," Doll muttered to Bess. "It would be hard to have a year start more dismally than this one did."

"His Majesty's spirits must be improving," Audrey said, bringing a cup of spiced wine to Lady Zouche's seat by the fireside.

"Yes, indeed." Lady Zouche's cheeks dimpled as she smiled. "Of course he was much pleased at the defeat of the Scots at Solway—not even three weeks ago—and now we learn that the Scottish king has died, leaving a newborn girl as queen."

"How can a baby girl rule Scotland?" Doll wondered.

"That's just the point; she can't!" Lady Zouche exclaimed. "Her mother, Mary of Guise, will serve as regent, but she will have much to do to contend with the nobles, who will be fighting like a pack of wolves to see who shall wield real power. Scotland has been dealt a blow." She set down her goblet and jumped to her feet. "Now, what can we give the king for a New Year's gift?"

"Jewels?" Lizzie suggested.

"Perhaps. But the gift must be more than sumptuous. It must be unusual; it must delight him."

"What about a dwarf?" Doll cried. After a moment of astonished silence, Bess and the other girls hooted with laughter.

"Well, what's wrong with a dwarf?" Doll asked, flushing.

"Nothing, dear heart, it's an excellent idea," Lady Zouche soothed her. "But His Majesty already has that fool—what's his name?"

"Will," Bess said. "Will Somers."

"Yes, Somers. And besides, a gift like that would only give the king another mouth to feed and another body needing lodging."

"Not a very big lodging," Doll sniffed.

"No, perhaps not." Lady Zouche smiled.

Bess's mind was churning. She had been enchanted by a table she had seen at Dorset House when she had accompanied Lady Zouche there on a recent visit to Frances Grey, the Marchioness of Dorset.

"Lady Dorset has a most wonderful table," she ventured. "Inlaid with wood in different colors, in a pattern of knots and rings. There was a chessboard on top of it."

Lady Zouche frowned and Bess wished she had not spoken. Of course a mere table would not be a grand enough present for the king.

"I noted it, too; it is exquisite," Lady Zouche said, and Bess's hopes rose. "And what if it were not just any table? For you have given me such an idea, Bess! A tabletop with two sides, one with some pattern—birds and flowers, perhaps, with the king's initials worked among them—and the other a chessboard!"

"And the table could open to hold the pieces!" Bess cried.

Lady Zouche clapped her hands in delight. "You have hit upon it! A chess set in a table!"

"And perhaps," Bess ventured, wondering if her new idea was too silly, "perhaps the pieces could be Englishmen and Scots? With His Majesty as the English king, and the baby Queen of Scots on the other side?"

Lady Zouche practically whooped with laughter, and Bess grinned in delight that her idea had proved so good.

"Yes! His Majesty as the fair-haired king, and as the dark queen, little Mary, Queen of Scots!" Her face suddenly became somber. "But New Year's Day is only a fortnight away. Could such a thing be made in that time? It must be, that is all. Ah, my dear Bess, you are a marvel of inspiration!"

LONDON WAS BITTER COLD, AND COUGHS AND CATARRHS SPREAD rapidly through the court. As the light faded on Christmas Eve, Bess sat at the bedside of a boy named Robbie Barlow as he sipped a warm posset. He had joined the Zouche household a few weeks earlier as a page, and since he had grown up not far from Hardwick and was desperately homesick, he had sought Bess's companionship. He was shivering, though he was weighed down by quilts and coverlets, and her heart ached for the sad expression on his pale face.

"Do you know, I think I might have met you when you were still in petticoats," she told him, smiling. "For I was with my family at the fair at Chesterfield and I recall my father greeting yours, and your mother standing by with a sweet little boy."

Robbie sniffled and flushed. "You needn't make out you were a grown girl. You are not much older than I."

"Two years," Bess said, pulling playfully on his foot, which was peeking out from the covers. "Not much of a difference now that you are a great boy of thirteen, but all the world when I was six and you were four."

"That's so," Robbie conceded, apparently mollified by her words. "Do you think I will be able to eat Christmas dinner?"

"If you're feeling well enough, I'm sure you'll be allowed."

The thought of Christmas made her think of her family, so far away. It had been three years since she left home, and she missed them intensely. Letters brought news and assurances of love, but were not the same as being able to feel her mother's arms around her. She thought Robbie was beginning to look a little tearful, and tried to shake off her own longing for home.

"Come," she said. "Tell me what you like best to eat at Christmas."

"Mince pies," he said without hesitation. "And Twelfth Night cake, and wassail to go with it."

"Mm, me, too! And marchpane, and Christmas pudding, and a nice fat goose."

"Will they have those here, too?" Robbie queried.

"All those and more," Bess assured him. "For Sir George and Lady Zouche will entertain many of their friends from now until Twelfth Night."

"I'm glad there are twelve days to Christmas," Robbie sighed, putting aside his empty cup. "Surely I will be well enough to have fun on some of them."

ON NEW YEAR'S DAY, AS THE ZOUCHES AND THEIR ATTENDANTS made their way to the presence chamber of Hampton Court, Bess was very excited. For on this day the king would be presented with his gift—the splendid table and chess pieces, which had been completed in time and had traveled from London swaddled in layers of wool.

The mood at court was lighter and happier than at any time Bess could recall. Anne of Cleves was present, companionably chatting with King Henry, and the shadow of Catherine Howard was almost dispelled by the warmth and light from the hundreds of candles, which made the air redolent of honey. A band of musicians played jaunty dance tunes, and the walls were hung with garlands of holly and ivy. Near the king, a table was stacked with gifts of such magnificence that it staggered Bess. Golden goblets, engraved silver coffers, books in richly ornamented bindings, jeweled collars and belts, furs of deep and gleaming pile, which she longed to touch. But nothing like the chess table the Zouches had brought.

Rich pastries and savory morsels were piled on platters, and great bowls of punch perfumed the air with their steam. The room rang with laughter and chatter. Bess, Lizzie, and Doll took up a position near the door where they could watch each new arrival while Audrey trailed Lady Zouche as she made her way around the room greeting her friends.

"There's Anne Basset," Doll said. "I like her. She always makes me laugh."

"Lady Latimer is looking very pretty, don't you think?" Bess asked, eyeing the lady's emerald silk gown with envy. She didn't recognize the handsome dark-haired man next to her, but knew it was not Lord Latimer. "Her husband must be too ill to be here."

"Small wonder, as old as he is," Doll whispered. "That's Sir Thomas Seymour with her."

Bess looked more closely at the gentleman. "The brother of the late Queen Jane? So it is."

"Yes," Doll said. "People say that he's already wooing Lady Latimer."

"Have you seen her brother, William Parr?" Lizzie asked in an excited whisper. "Look, there he is, over by that table."

Bess looked and saw a tall young man with vivid blue eyes and a russet beard. He was handsome, she thought, but there was something a trifle arrogant about him that she didn't like.

"Oh, I'd like to dance with him!" Lizzie giggled. "And do more than that, too!"

"Lizzie!" Doll cried, shocked. "He's married!"

"Barely! His wife ran off with a church prior and has borne him a bastard!"

"And from what I've heard," Doll said, "he's been working his way through the maids of honor at court since then."

"Sounds like one to avoid," Bess said. "Heartbreak is all he'd bring."

Lizzie tossed her head, dislodging a dark curl from her cap. "I wouldn't be so sure. I've heard that the king might let him divorce his wife. And he's to be made Earl of Essex."

Doll raised her eyebrows at Bess. Yes, Bess thought, Lizzie certainly seemed to be quite smitten with the comely William Parr. And as beautiful as she was, especially this evening, her full breasts barely contained by her bodice, her rosy skin glowing in the candlelight, she would no doubt succeed in capturing his attention, if she wished to.

Soon the dancing began. Bess was wearing a new gown of a deep blue that made her eyes sparkle and set off her fair complexion. She had been rigorously following Lady Zouche's instructions about caring for her skin, keeping her face and bosom shadowed from the sun, bathing them in milk, and applying a rich cream of honey and almonds at night. Now her freckles had faded and her skin was a glowing alabaster. Catching sight of herself in a mirror, with the flicker of candles behind her, she thought with satisfaction that she looked very pretty. Though she could never look as lovely as Lizzie, she thought with a sigh.

"Mistress, would you honor me with a dance?"

Bess's head snapped around to find a handsome fair-haired gentleman smiling down at her. His glinting eyes seemed the same color as his dark green velvet doublet. He was probably not yet thirty, but he was a man, no boy. And he was treating her as a lady, not as a little girl. She felt caught off guard and felt a surge of self-doubt, such as she had experienced when first she had arrived at Codnor Castle. She shook off her nerves. How silly—all he wanted was a dance, after all, and she was quite a good dancer now.

"I shall be most pleased, sir," she said, placing her hand in his upturned palm and smiling a farewell to Lizzie and Doll.

He led her to the center of the floor where other couples were forming sets. Bess caught a glimpse of Lady Zouche with a knot of other ladies and noted her approving smile. The music began—a lively galliard. Bess knew she was dancing well and was glad of the dancing lessons she and the other girls had been having.

"I am Christopher Winters," her partner said, leaning close to her as he swayed in the steps of the dance.

"And I'm Bess Hardwick."

"I know who you are. I wasted no time in finding out as soon as I saw you."

His eyes were bright and Bess felt herself blushing. She found it difficult to catch her breath while they danced, but decided it was better not to talk much, anyway. The dancers were at the center of attention and she felt conspicuous. If she could just smile and dance she would not make too much a fool of herself.

The dance finished and Christopher led her back to where Doll still stood. "I thank you, Mistress Bess."

"I thank you, sir." Bess sank into a curtsy as he bowed his farewell.

"He's lovely," Doll breathed as he disappeared into the throng. "And he looked smitten with you. Never took his eyes off you once."

"Well, what was he supposed to do?" Bess said. "It would have been quite rude to be staring around the room while we danced, wouldn't it?"

Doll laughed. "You are funny. Do you not know how pretty you are? It won't be long afore you've a husband and are set up in a house of your own. And what will I do then?" She pouted playfully.

"Silly goose," Bess said. But her thoughts were whirling. She felt intoxicated by the attention from the young man, which seemed to hold the promise of excitement beyond anything she had felt before. But with romance came marriage, and with it danger. Could she not just enjoy an evening's dancing, without being trapped?

No, not and fulfill her duty, spoke a voice at the back of her head. Her mother had sent her to the Zouches so that she might find a suitable husband, and by a good marriage she would help her family. And the beginning of any match was sure to be very like that dance. No action she took was without consequence. She wanted to ask what Lizzie had thought of Christopher Winters but didn't see her.

"Where's Lizzie?" she asked.

"Dancing," Doll said. "With William Parr." She nodded her head toward the center of the room. Lizzie was hand in hand with Parr, gazing up into his face with adoration.

"Oh, of all loves," Bess sighed. "I hope she hasn't got into deeper waters than she can navigate."

Bess danced with many others, but Christopher Winters returned to her twice more, and she felt his eyes on her throughout the evening, and his gaze made her recall the feel of his hands on hers, the scent of his hair, the sound of his laughter. His attention was intoxicating.

Late in the evening it was time for the gifts, and the entire glittering company gathered to watch as the king admired each new offering. He was very pleased with his table.

"What a cunning thing!" he exclaimed, flipping the table top back and forth. "Look at this, madam—is it not beautifully wrought?"

It was Lady Latimer to whom he spoke, and she left Thomas Seymour's side to hasten to the king and curtsy swiftly before running a hand over the elaborate inlay.

"It is most fine, Your Majesty. So smooth. Like satin."

"This is undoubtedly the most splendid gift I could have asked for!" the king exclaimed. He held up the white king, his own face and figure carved in pale maple wood.

"George, Lady Zouche, I compliment you on your most excellent taste and judgment."

Lady Zouche beamed as she curtsied deeply to the king.

It was my idea, Bess thought, gratified that the king had been so pleased with the gift that had been her inspiration. Even as she thought it, Lady Zouche turned to her with a smile, took her by the hand, and drew her forward.

"It was Bess's conceit, Your Majesty."

Faces turned toward Bess. Smiles, murmurs, applause from an older gentleman nearby.

The king's eyes flickered to Bess. She fancied she saw menace in their depths and fear swept over her.

"Indeed?" His voice was cold. Perhaps he was recalling the other time he had spoken to her, she thought, when Cat had been at his side. He looked like a boar about to charge. Bess's palms were damp with sweat. She curtsied to the floor, dropping her gaze so she would not have to meet the king's eyes. He snorted, piglike, and she heard the rustle of his clothes as he turned away. It was a long time before her heartbeat slowed.

The next day Sir George called Bess to him when he came in after supper.

"You have an admirer, my girl," he said, smiling. "Christopher Winters inquired most keenly after you today, wishing to know more about your situation and your family. He wanted to know if your parents would entertain his suit."

The formality of his words confused Bess for a moment.

"You mean . . ."

"I mean he is considering you as a wife. And it would be quite a match for you. He is a rising man at court."

Here it was, and so suddenly. Bess found that her stomach was churning. Christopher was a comely man, to be sure. The touch of his hands, the heat of his gaze, had enchanted her. And for all she knew from their bits of conversation, he was pleasant enough. But marry him? Now that the prospect was real rather than imagined, alarum bells were sounding in her head. She didn't want to marry anyone. It had been almost a year now since the death of Cat Howard, but Cat's terrified eyes haunted Bess's sleep still sometimes. *Cat, Cat, you should have run before you thought ever to wed.*

"I told him that I would write to your mother," Sir George said. "You have no objection, I take it?"

He fixed her with a sharp gaze and she was hesitant to speak. But speak she must, before matters proceeded further.

"It is most flattering that the gentleman shows me such interest, sir," she said carefully. "But I do not think that I wish to marry."

Sir George goggled at her and shook his head as if he had not understood her.

"What?"

"I do not want a husband, sir."

"By God!" His bellow seemed to rattle the windows and Bess flinched. Rapid footsteps sounded in the hall and Lady Zouche dashed in, her face full of concern.

"What is it, George?"

"I have told her of Christopher Winters's interest and she throws him back in my teeth."

Bess was frightened at the look of outrage on Lady Zouche's face.

"Oh, no, sir! No, my lady, I do not mean to do so. It's only—I fear what might happen to me."

"Oh, that." Sir George guffawed. "Sure, every young maid is nervous about her wedding night."

"My dear Bess," Lady Zouche said, putting her hand on Bess's shoulder. "If that's all, don't let those fears stand in the way of a good match."

Bess thought of the procession of queens that King Henry had cast off, into disfavor, despair, and death. He had set a precedent, the rumors flew. Divorce was not enough.

"It's more than that, madam," Bess said. "I saw what happened to Catherine Howard. Anne of Cleves was lucky, but Anne Boleyn— and Queen Catherine before her . . . It seems a dangerous thing to be a wife."

Sir George and Lady Zouche exchanged a glance, and Bess recalled all the whispered night discussions she had heard between them over the last few years.

"Being a wife is not the same as being queen," Lady Zouche said. "It is true that a husband is lord over his wife, but surely you don't think that every man has the power to cast off his wife and put her to death if she displeases him?"

Bess thought back to Lizzie's fevered whisperings the previous night as they'd returned home from the palace.

"Does he not?" Bess asked. "Lizzie told me that William Parr will soon be rid of his wife, accusing her of adultery, and that he has asked the king that she be punished with death."

"But that's—surely she will not be put to death." Sir George seemed to be trying to flounder onto more solid ground.

"Bess, why do you suppose your mother sent you to us, if not so that you might find a husband?"

At Lady Zouche's words, Bess had a vivid image of her mother weeping after the confrontation with the king's men at Hardwick. She had vowed then that she would do whatever she must to make things easier at home. She must keep her vow. But not yet; she wasn't ready yet! *Take it one thing at a time,* she reminded herself, breathing deeply to steady her nerves. *A letter to my mother is not a promise that I will wed. Surely I can find a way out if need be.*

"You are right, sir, and madam. Of course you must write, and I will heed my mother's counsel in this matter."

She curtsied and hurried from the room before she began to cry, and nearly ran into Rachel.

"Why, lamb, what's the trouble?" Rachel cried.

"I don't want to get married!"

"Why, what's brought this on?" Rachel drew Bess to her and peered into her eyes.

"A young man I danced with last night has spoken to Sir George about a marriage."

"And did you not like him?"

"I did, but . . ." Bess tried to order her thoughts and put them into words. "I liked him well. I would like to be someone's beloved. But the idea of marrying frightens me. Look at all the queens . . ." Her voice choked.

"Ah." Rachel nodded. "Aye, it's terrifying enough. But not all men are like the king. And we women are not made to be on our own. You'll want to marry when it's the right man, sweetheart."

Bess felt steadier on her feet at the calm confidence in Rachel's voice. "Do you think so?" she asked.

"I do. And if you've had one offer, sure there will be more."

That night Bess lay awake into the night, images of Christopher Winters and the king and Cat Howard swirling in her mind's eye. Surely her mother wouldn't want her to enter into a marriage she dreaded. But perhaps Rachel was right, and the idea of marrying would not always frighten her. She prayed for the willingness to do as her mother wished, and the strength to go through with a marriage to Christopher Winters if that was what she was bidden to do.

But please, God, she asked, *isn't there some other way?*

Before Sir George's correspondence could have reached Hardwick, however, Bess received a letter from her mother that took her even more by surprise than Christopher Winters's interest.

I have had a letter from Arthur Barlow. He tells me that his son Robert has been most grateful and comforted by the friendship you have shown him, and he sets forth a proposal that you should wed the lad.

Marry Robbie! Bess was amazed. He was still a mere boy, and she thought of him like a little brother.

Arthur Barlow is ill, and he is endeavoring to do just as your own father did when he knew that he would soon die, leaving a young heir. Such a plan would not stop the Court of Wards from taking charge of the estate until Robert comes of age, but if he were married to you he could not then be forced to marry a bride chosen by the man who held his wardship.

It was like a chess game, Bess thought, seeing in her mind the sleek wooden pieces of the king's New Year's present. Robbie's father looked across the board and sought to make a move that would block approaching danger. And she and Robbie were the pawns.

There would be much benefit to you from such a match, the letter continued. *When young Robert is twenty-one he will inherit Barlow Manor, which brings with it about two thousand acres of farmland, meadow, woods, and heath, and rents from properties in five or six villages nearby.*

A vast amount of land, Bess thought. She pictured the green hills rolling away from Hardwick and wondered if Barlow looked the same. She would like to live at Barlow, close enough to Hardwick that she could probably see her mother several times a year. She thought about what it would be like to be married to Robbie. Her heart did not thrill with excitement, but neither was she frightened at the prospect. He was a golden-haired angel child, gentle and affectionate. He could never do her harm and would never want to. And the thought of having her own home, being lady of a manor someday, was very pleasing.

"Well!" Lady Zouche exclaimed when Bess showed her the letter. "You have suitors coming out of every corner, it seems." Her eyes became serious. "Choosing the right marriage is a most important matter. Christopher Winters would not bring you such an estate as young Robbie would, but there is no doubt he has more interest at court, which is not to be sneezed at."

"No," Bess agreed. But the image of the king, his piggy eyes nestled above his lardlike cheeks, rose to her mind and made her shudder. She could not look at him without images of death and blood rising to her mind. Marrying Christopher Winters would take her closer to the king, would likely keep her in London with its noisome air and constant hubbub.

Marrying Robbie, on the other hand, would let her return to near home.

Bess sought out Rachel and found her in the nursery chamber. She found the homey smells of wood smoke and lavender comforting.

"What do you think I should do?" she asked, plopping herself onto a stool near the hearth.

"Well," Rachel answered, swabbing the mess from the bottom of little Edmund Zouche, "if the time has come to wed and you're leery of a husband's power, sure the thing to do is pick the one who is more gentle?"

"That's what I have thought," Bess said. "But surely I should choose a husband who will benefit my family. If I marry Robbie, my parents will give his father my dowry, and also forgive a debt he owes them. So they will gain nothing, and be no better off than if I had not married."

"Perhaps not now," Rachel said, tying a clean clout onto the baby. "But when your young man comes of age, you'll be mistress of a fine estate. You can bring your younger sisters into service, and help them find husbands." She hefted the baby up into her arms. "Nothing needs to change for the present, you know. You would likely both remain in the Zouches' household for now, as you're both so young."

"Then we could live like brother and sister," Bess said.

"Just so." Rachel came closer and put a gentle hand on Bess's cheek. "He's too young to lie with you, you know. So no fear of that for now. And I warrant in another two or three years you'll not mind the thought."

CHAPTER EIGHT

IT WAS A GLORIOUS AFTERNOON IN LATE MARCH, AND BESS AND Robbie were strolling amid fields that were hazy green with the first shoots of spring. They stopped to watch a clutch of brown bunnies emerge from a hole in the ground and tumble together in the sunshine as their mother crouched nearby, her nose twitching as she watched her little ones at play.

"Look at them," Bess laughed.

"I had a pet rabbit when I was a little boy," Robbie said. "I found him all alone in the woods, naught but skin and bones. Something must have become of his mother, I suppose. He looked so frightened, but he let me pick him up and carry him home, and went straight to sleep when I put him in a little nest of straw in the kitchen."

"What was he called?" Bess asked.

"Nubbin," Robbie said, grinning. "He was no more than a nubbin when I found him. He never did get very big."

Bess smiled back at him. She was relieved that he had recovered completely from his illness, which had lingered throughout the winter. It was he who had suggested a walk, and he didn't seem tired, though they had come quite a way, walking up Tottenham Court Road and out into the countryside.

"You know why Lady Zouche sends us out together," Robbie said, tilting his head inquisitively.

"Yes, I know," Bess said. "She is encouraging us. To wed, I mean."

"And what do you think?" Robbie dropped his gaze and bent to pluck some tiny blue flowers.

Bess felt silly telling Robbie that she thought of Cat Howard and feared marriage. What harm could come to her from this boy, with his sunny ways and fond recollection of his rabbit?

Robbie stood and offered her the little nosegay of flowers. "Marry me, Bess. Each of us must marry someone. Why should it not be each other? We like each other well enough."

Bess lifted the flowers to her nose and inhaled their scent before meeting his look. The blue of his eyes was just the shade of the blossoms. The color of a baby's eyes. She loved babies, and the thought of having one of her own, with sweet Robbie its father, made her happy. Robbie was gazing at her with shy hope. Her heart swelled with affection for him, and she made up her mind.

"I like you very well, indeed," she said. "I would be most pleased to be your wife."

"Oh, Bess." His whole face radiated relief and joy, and he stepped close to Bess and gently kissed her cheek. "You make me so happy."

Bess and Robbie were married on a brilliant May morning, the spring sunshine spilling through the colored glass of the church windows. Bess glanced sideways at Robbie as he recited his vows, his clear, high voice not yet broken into a man's lower register. When they stood, she was taller than he was, but kneeling side by side as they were now, they were of a height. His eyes met hers and his fair cheeks flushed. He put out his hand, scarce bigger than her own, and grasped her fingers. Yes, Bess decided. Marriage to Robbie would be what she made of it. And she would make of it a happy thing.

The Zouches feted Bess and Robbie with a wedding breakfast, attended by the household and a few friends. Neither Bess's nor Robbie's family was present. Robbie's father was too ill to travel and his mother was at home with him and the younger children. Bess's mother had written that she could not leave her girls at home for the fortnight it would have taken to travel to London and back, but that she sent her love and would be thinking of Bess on her wedding day and looked forward to seeing her, for Robbie and Bess planned to make a visit to Derbyshire soon after their marriage.

Bess wished her mother could have been there, thought how proud her mother would be to see her in the new gown that Lady Zouche had provided for her, white with embroidered undersleeves of pale blue, which matched the embroidery in the delicate handkerchief Robbie had given her that morning. It had been two and a half years since she had visited Hardwick. Sometimes now she found it hard to call her mother's face to mind, and she knew that her younger sisters would have grown up so much she would scarce recognize them.

"Look at you, a bride!" Doll sighed, as she helped Bess adjust her clothes before joining the wedding guests.

"You'll be one yourself, soon enough!" Bess reminded her, for Doll would shortly wed Sir Ralph Longford.

Bess noticed that Lizzie was suddenly looking sad. "What is it?" she asked.

"Nothing," Lizzie said, tossing her glossy brown curls back before settling her cap back in place. "It's just that so far the king has done nothing to let William divorce his wife."

Each time they had been at court since New Year's Day, Bess had seen Lizzie in the company of William Parr, and each time Lizzie had come home seeming lost in a world of her own, sighing and smiling to herself.

"He kissed me," she had told Bess on the fourteenth of February, "and called me his valentine!"

"Be careful, Lizzie," Bess had warned, worried that Lizzie was so careless of her heart, and was putting herself in peril by longing for a man who had a wife.

But today was Bess's wedding day, and not the occasion to reason with Lizzie, so she simply squeezed her friend's hand. "Perhaps he will be free before long."

Bess and Robbie were excused from their duties for the rest of the day, and Bess read to Robbie in the afternoon, sitting in Lady Zouche's withdrawing room. That night they went separately to their own beds, just as they had before.

"You'll go to Barlow to live in a year or two," Lady Zouche had told them. "There's no hurry, after all."

Bess and Robbie had not been married a month when what his father had feared and prepared for came to pass. A letter arrived from Robbie's mother with the news that his father had died on the twenty-eighth of May. It broke Bess's heart to see her young husband struggling not to cry. Somehow it seemed even sadder that Arthur Barlow had been buried before Robbie even learned of his death.

"It's all right," she told him, pulling him close to her. "You would not have much of a heart did you not weep for your father."

"My poor mother," Robbie sniffled. "I should be there to comfort her."

"She says that it might be just as well if we wait to visit until the inquisition post mortem," Bess reminded him, "and she does not yet know when that will take place."

Bess's life didn't change much once she was a married woman. She was welcomed into the gossiping circles of ladies when she accompanied Lady Zouche to court or to the homes of her friends. And all the talk that summer was the king's apparent interest in Catherine Parr, the recently widowed Lady Latimer.

"Poor lady!" Lizzie sighed. "No sooner does her aged husband depart this earth, leaving her free to follow her heart with Thomas Seymour, than the king casts his eye in her direction and sends him off to Brussels."

"Aye, her husband was barely cold before her brother was made a member of the privy council and a Knight of the Garter," Doll agreed. "That certainly looks like he intends to marry her."

"What will she do?" Bess wondered. "If the king wishes to marry her?"

"She'll bid farewell to hopes of Thomas Seymour," Lizzie said. "It doesn't do to cross His Majesty."

ON THE FIRST OF JULY BESS HEARD THAT THE KING HAD succeeded in arranging a match between the five-year-old Prince Edward and the seven-month-old Scottish Queen Mary.

"How can they betroth a mere baby?" she exclaimed in dismay. "The path the poor mite must tread is laid out for her before she can walk."

"Of course they'll not be married for years," Lady Zouche said. "But the arrangement will secure peace with Scotland in the meantime. And my lord says that now that's settled, it won't be long before the king weds."

CATHERINE PARR MUST HAVE DISGUISED HER DISAPPOINTMENT and put on a brave face, Bess thought, for on the twelfth of July she was married to King Henry at Hampton Court. Bess thought of Cat Howard, and wondered if Catherine Parr was afraid.

Lizzie was in a position to observe the royal marriage at close range, for she was now the lover of William Parr, the queen's brother, though he was still married, and he had secured her a position as one of the queen's ladies-in-waiting.

"She's a different kettle of fish altogether than Cat Howard or Anne Boleyn," Lizzie whispered to Bess. "Married and widowed twice, and not a breath of scandal. I'm sure that's what the king wanted above all else—no nasty surprises."

CHAPTER NINE

August 1543—Hardwick Manor, Derbyshire

BESS CLUNG TO HER MOTHER, BURYING HER HEAD AGAINST HER mother's shoulder and breathing in her familiar scent.

"Oh, my darling Bess," Elizabeth repeated, cradling Bess's head and then pulling back so she could look into her daughter's eyes. They were both laughing and crying at once, as Robbie, Jem, and Bess's younger sisters stood by awkwardly. Meg was seven now, Dibby was nine, and Jenny was eleven.

"I can't believe it's been more than two years," Elizabeth gasped, dabbing at her eyes with a handkerchief. "But come in, come in. I mustn't keep you standing here outside. Alice and Francis will be here for supper."

"My sister is recently married as well," Bess reminded Robbie as they entered the house. "To a nephew of my stepfather's. I wish my older sisters could be here, too."

She turned to Jem and shook her head in amazement. "Look at you, a grown man now."

"I've been doing a man's work for years," Jem reminded her a little gruffly.

"I know, but now your height has caught up with you." She put her arms around her brother and smiled up at him. "I'm so glad to be with you again."

Annabel came out of the kitchen, in a cloud of delicious scents, and pulled Bess into an embrace, then stood back, beaming.

"I shouldn't handle you so. You're a real lady now."

"I'm the same as I always was," Bess said, pulling off her gloves. But it was true that her hair was dressed in the latest London style and her gown was of finer material than could be had anywhere near to Hardwick, in marked contrast to the homespun her mother and sisters wore.

"Tell us what it's like at court!" Alice urged Bess over supper. She had blossomed into a beauty with curling red-gold hair, and if Bess hadn't been sure of Robbie's adoration, she might have felt jealous that he had been tongue-tied when introduced to her younger sister.

"It's not like what you might think," she told Alice, digging into the steaming pie on her plate. "You never know quite where you stand or what is the truth. It's not like here."

"It's good to be back home," Robbie agreed.

They were exhausted by the journey from London and would stay at Hardwick for a week before making the day-long trip to Barlow Manor. Bess felt a little overwhelmed by the prospect of meeting Robbie's family and seeing the estate of which she would one day be mistress. She was pleased that he looked comfortable here with her family and that they had already taken a liking to him.

THE INQUISITION POST MORTEM INTO THE DEATH OF ROBBIE'S father did not take place until December. The court confirmed Robbie's inheritance, but the Court of Wards would control the estate until he reached the age of twenty-one. Godfrey Boswell, soon to be the husband of Bess's older sister Jane, bought Robbie's wardship for sixty-six pounds.

"Thank Heaven there was no objection to that," Robbie's mother,

Emma, exclaimed when all was settled. "It is iniquitous that the control of a family's property may be put into the hands of a stranger with nothing but his own interest in mind." She hugged Bess to her. "I'm so grateful to your good-brother, and to your mother for managing it. And so pleased that she has good news—in her latest letter she said that your father was soon to return home."

"Yes," Bess said. She suspected that Godfrey Boswell and her sister Moll's husband Richard Wingfield had provided the money that would shortly free Ralph Leche from debtors' prison.

She was happy to be at peace in the countryside. Elsewhere, all was in turmoil. The Scots had revoked the Treaty of Greenwich, and the king did not take kindly the rebuff of his plans to marry his son to the little Scottish queen. He had sent an army to Scotland, and Leith, Edinburgh, and Holyrood had been sacked and burned.

The Auld Alliance between France and Scotland is now revived, Lady Zouche wrote to Bess. *The Scots have sent the baby queen to France to keep her safe from King Henry's armies. It looks like war with France is coming. But here in London, all is well. The Lady Mary and the Lady Elizabeth have been restored to the succession, it is said, and thanks to the intercession of the queen, will be at court for Christmas.*

Lady Day, the twenty-fifth of March, marked the start of the new legal year, and provided the opportunity for Bess to be introduced to the tenants and villagers of Robbie's estate, come to the manor to pay their rents.

"A pleasure to meet you, mistress," said a big farmer, appropriately named Bullock, as he pulled off his hat and bowed to her. "It were a sad thing to lose the squire, but a kind and pretty young wife has surely cheered up young Master Robert." He smiled at Robbie, seated proudly in the yard before the house with a ledger before him, and surrounded by a growing accumulation of rents paid in the form of bushels of wheat, young goats and sheep, bales of wool, and a cackling flock of chickens, ducks, and geese.

Robbie's mother had welcomed Bess into the household and was steadily imparting to her all that she would need to know when it came time for her to run the estate.

"Robbie told me how kind you were to him when he was ill in London," she said as they worked in the herb garden one sunny afternoon when the arc of the sky rose a cloudless blue above them. "I'm sure that in that grand house and in the city there was neither the need nor the opportunity for you to learn much about physic, but I expect your mother taught you some before you went away?"

"Yes," Bess said, "but I would like to learn more and would be grateful for your tutelage."

"Well, then," Emma said, beaming, "this is the mint that I've always brewed for Robbie when his poor belly is troubling him, and it never fails to give him ease. I always say that it's best picked when the leaves are the size of a little rabbit's ears."

Every month or so, Jem rode the ten miles to Barlow to fetch Bess back to Hardwick for a few days.

"I'm so glad to be near enough to visit," Bess told her mother as they sat by the fire one autumn evening, Elizabeth mending a shirt of Jem's and Bess working on a piece of embroidery. "I have missed you so much. I never want to go so long without seeing you again."

"It's good to have you close to home," her mother agreed, embracing her. "I wish your sisters weren't so far off."

Jane had married Godfrey Boswell and was now in Yorkshire, and Moll and her husband Richard Wingfield were in Suffolk, a journey of several days.

"At least Alice is nearby," Bess said.

"Do you hear from Lady Zouche?" her mother asked.

"Yes, I had a letter the other day. Sir George is preparing to go with the king to battle in France. The king can scarce walk, she says, his leg is so bad. But he can still sit a horse. And Doll Fitzherbert is married to Sir Ralph Longford now. Just think, I shall have to call her Lady Longford!"

It would be fine to be called Lady Barlow, Bess thought, and then felt disloyal to Robbie. His sweet affection was enough for her; she needed no titles.

Bess did not tell her mother the other news that Lady Zouche had written: Lizzie was living openly with William Parr.

I don't know what her father can be thinking of, not putting a stop to it, Lady Zouche wrote. *I suppose that since Lord Parr is the brother of the queen, he thinks the king will free the man from his wife and he will marry Lizzie. It seems a terrible gamble to me, but Lizzie is accepted at court and treated more or less as Parr's wife.*

Bess thought of Lizzie's giddy happiness whenever she had been around William Parr, and hoped that things would all turn out well for her friend. But she knew that she could never risk her reputation and future in that way. Only a husband provided a bulwark against the future and protection in times of trouble.

BESS'S FIRST SIGHT OF HER STEPFATHER, RALPH LECHE, UPON HIS return from debtors' prison was a shock. He was so thin he appeared brittle, and his face seemed to have aged more than ten years in the six he had been gone. She thought he looked bewildered, and no wonder. He had left a house full of small children, and now they had grown beyond recognition. Bess's younger sisters didn't recall their father, and treated him with careful and distant courtesy as they might a stranger.

"Let us never get ourselves into debt," Bess exhorted Robbie when she was back at Barlow and they were taking a stroll through the orchard. "Whatever happens, we must never put ourselves in the power of the law like that."

"No," he agreed. "It doesn't make much sense to me, though, how a man who is in debt is expected to resolve his problems if he's locked away."

"It makes no sense at all."

Robbie broke into a fit of coughing and Bess looked at him anxiously.

"It's nothing," he assured her, but she was concerned at the paleness of his face. She had hoped that getting away from London and back to the country would make him hardier, but he seemed to have grown more delicate.

"Let's get inside," she said. "The air is too cold for us to be out walking for so long." The sun shone brightly, but a haze hung over the hills and the barren fields had a grayish cast. "Winter is coming on early this year, I think."

In late September, Boulogne fell to King Henry's army, and Queen Catherine, who had been left as regent in the king's absence, proclaimed a day of thanksgiving throughout the country for the English victory. Lizzie wrote to Bess that the queen had convinced the king to let his daughters join her household and was supervising the education of young Elizabeth. Catherine Parr must be a wise lady, Bess thought, that the king had such confidence in her that he would leave the reins of the kingdom in her lap and give her such influence over his children.

Bess was looking forward to Christmas at Barlow, homier and quieter than the festivities in London. The court seemed another world now that she was away from it, and one she didn't miss. In any case, she had had a letter from Doll, telling her that Sir George was no longer a gentleman pensioner to the king, and that the Zouches had returned to Codnor around the time that Doll and her husband had left London.

I am just as glad to be away from court, Doll wrote. *Life is so much calmer back here in Derbyshire.*

In mid-December, Robbie's health took a turn for the worse. He had grown thinner and was perpetually tired. Now he took to his bed with a fever and chills, his narrow chest racked with coughs that left his handkerchiefs spotted with bright blood. Bess sat with him into the night, reading to him by candlelight or simply holding his hand until he fell asleep.

"You'll get well soon," she murmured. But the dark shadows around his eyes frightened her, and when she went to him in the mornings she found him drenched in sweat.

As Robbie got worse, a mood of despair enveloped the house. More than once Bess found Robbie's mother weeping in the kitchen, and they comforted each other with an embrace, as neither could find any words of solace.

"He's always been delicate," Emma sobbed.

Yes, Bess thought, Robbie had never been hardy as long as she had known him. Still, she was astonished by the swiftness of his decline.

He lacked any appetite, and though Bess tried to tempt him to eat, making him warm possets and bringing him his mother's mince pie and his other favorite foods, he couldn't seem to manage more than a sip or a bite, and his slender body wasted away. Dark smudges shadowed his eyes, and he seemed to be drifting, wraith-like, away from her and the corporeal world.

As darkness enveloped the frozen earth on Christmas Eve, Robbie's labored breathing grew slower and finally ceased. Bess felt numb with shock. How could Robbie be gone?

"My poor child," Emma cried, her tears falling on his ashen face.

Bess sat with Robbie, staring at his still, pale form and holding his hand in hers, watching as his fingertips turned to waxy ivory. Then she wept, clutching the delicate embroidered handkerchief he had given her as a wedding present, desolate at the loss of her sweet companion. She grieved that his life had been so short and that she had not been able to make him whole.

CHAPTER TEN

Twenty-fifth of April, 1546, Easter Sunday—Dorset House, London

Bess was sitting on her favorite window seat, luxuriating in the sunbeams and the view over the Thames. A bevy of swans floated at the foot of the landing stairs, ignoring the ripples in the water caused by the arrival of a wherry. On the south side of the river, green fields stretched away into the distance.

For nine months now she had been in the household of Henry Grey, the Marquess of Dorset, serving his wife, the former Frances Brandon. The Greys, like the Zouches, were distant relations to Bess. After Robbie's death, Bess had returned home to Hardwick. Her mother had been happy to have her there, but, mindful of Bess's future, had urged her to accept Frances Grey's offer to join her as lady-in-waiting.

"You're not yet sixteen, you can't stay a widow forever," she had said. "And serving Frances Grey would be a step up from your place with the Zouches. Her father, Charles Brandon, the Duke of Suffolk, was one of the king's oldest friends, and her mother was the king's sister Mary, you know."

And her mother had been right. From the day that Bess joined the Grey household at their magnificent Bradgate House in Leicestershire, she had been dazzled by the stream of their friends and relations, the highest-born people in the land. She was even enjoying being back in London, after an interlude of nearly two years in the country.

"Listen, Bess, I want to read to you from my translation of the queen's book!"

Bess turned to see Frances Grey's eldest daughter, Jane, her eyes shining with excitement. She found it hard to remember that this elfin child was only nine years of age. Jane Grey had the mind of a scholar and the fortitude of a soldier, concealed in a tidy little body and behind a delicate complexion of pink and white.

"Very well, I'm listening."

Jane smoothed the paper before her and declaimed in a clear high voice. Bess recognized that it was Latin, but she couldn't understand more than a few words. When Jane came to the end of the page she threw an anxious look at Bess.

"What a clever girl you are," Bess said, opening her arms. Jane nestled against her, her hair smelling faintly of violets. "Not only to understand such a learned work, but to put it into another language."

"Do you think so truly? My mother and father never seem pleased with me, no matter how I strive. When I read it to my mother, she only said that the Lady Elizabeth had also translated the book into French and Italian."

Bess considered how to answer. Frances Grey was warm and affectionate to her, but she was dismayed at the cold disapproval with which she and her husband treated their daughter. She longed to comfort Jane, but didn't want to encourage her to resent her parents.

"They expect a great deal from you," she said, stroking a red-gold curl from Jane's forehead. "For as they have no son, you are the heir and repository of all they have."

And that was much, she thought. Through her mother, Jane Grey was King Henry's grandniece and the granddaughter of Mary

Tudor, who had been queen of France. On her father's side, she was the great-great-granddaughter of Elizabeth Woodville, queen to Edward IV. With so much royal blood and such close ties to the crown, Harry and Frances Grey considered Jane to be a princess.

Jane sighed. "My mother wants to take me with her to court tomorrow."

"That should be enjoyable, shouldn't it?"

"It would be if she would just let me play with my cousin Edward, but she must always be instructing me."

"Well, she is a lady of the privy chamber to Queen Catherine, and someday you will be a maid of honor. No doubt she wishes to prepare you well for that privilege."

"I suppose. But it's much more fun when they leave us to ourselves. We like to pretend we are shepherds looking for our lost lambs."

Bess smiled to think of Prince Edward, the nine-year-old heir to the throne, rambling through the shrubbery at Whitehall in search of imaginary sheep.

"It will all be easier when you are older," she assured Jane. "For someday His Highness will be king and can command your company."

Jane laughed. "You always know what to say to cheer me, Bess. Promise you won't ever go away?"

The smile faded from her face as quick footsteps sounded outside the door. Frances Grey put her head into the room and Jane stiffened under her mother's cold gaze.

"There you are. Don't forget you must look your best tonight, as William Cavendish—Sir William, as he will be by this evening— will be here for supper. And many others also, to celebrate his elevation."

"Yes, madam," Jane said, her face carefully blank.

"Bess, you may wear my sleeves with the pearls," Frances Grey said, turning to go.

"Thank you, my lady," Bess said, surprised but pleased at the offer.

"And see that Jane is presentable." Lady Dorset disappeared in a flurry of crimson skirts.

"I think she would prefer it if you were her daughter," Jane said, her eyes sad. Bess's heart flooded with an aching sympathy for the girl.

"Nonsense. She's just busy, and wants to ensure that all is as it should be for tonight."

BESS COULD TELL FROM THE EXPRESSION ON FRANCES GREY's face that the supper had been a success. Most of the guests had left, and now Harry and Frances Grey sat at ease in the withdrawing room with only a few close friends. Bess knew many of them, but still, she was surprised when the guest of honor approached her. She could not recall having spoken to Sir William Cavendish before. Certainly he had never sought her out, and she wondered what he could want. He was an important man, the treasurer of the king's chamber and the Court of General Surveyors, and had just become a member of the privy council, as well as being auditor to great men such as Edward Seymour, the Earl of Hertford.

"Mistress Bess." He inclined his head, and Bess curtsied.

"I wish you joy of your knighthood, sir."

"I thank you."

"Good night, Will!" A departing guest hailed Sir William, and Bess studied his face as he turned away from her. He was in the later part of his thirties, she guessed. A tall and sturdily built man, the broadness of his face was emphasized by the square cut of his beard. Like the king's beard, Bess thought. But Sir William's gray eyes, when they turned back to her, were kind.

"Your mistress tells me that you are experiencing some difficulty in connection with the estate of your late husband, and asked if I might counsel you."

"Oh!" Bess said. "Yes, sir, it's most kind of you to ask. When Robbie died, his younger brother inherited from him, and as he is only a boy, Sir Peter Frecheville bought his wardship and gained control of the property."

"And now he will not give you your widow's dower?"

"No, sir. He claims in the first place that part of the land doesn't belong to the Barlows at all, but is only leased. But the greater difficulty is that he says I am not entitled to anything because we were not truly married. That is . . ." She broke off, blushing.

"Because the marriage was not consummated?" Sir William's voice was matter-of-fact, with no tinge of bawdry or humor, and Bess relaxed.

"Exactly. Last autumn Sir Peter offered me a yearly sum if I would waive any claim to my widow's third of the property, and though I had misgivings, I agreed out of necessity, for I was then back under my parents' roof, and their means were stretched already."

"Which of course he knew," Sir William said, "and wished to take advantage of your hardship."

"Yes. But then Robbie's uncle objected to even that settlement, so now I have nothing and am like to get nothing. Not even my dowry."

Bess felt her anxiety rising at the thought that she would be left penniless and powerless. What could she do then? No man would take her without a dowry, and it would strain her parents' resources to have her return home.

"Well, we'll see about that." Sir William shifted so that his feet were set firm and far apart, as if preparing for a fight, and he seemed to stand a little taller. "They won't get away with it if I have anything to say about it, and you may have heard that I am known as a man who does not easily back down from a fight."

Bess's hopes rose. "You would fight for me?"

"I would and I will. I will file a suit on your behalf, and call upon my patron Edward Seymour for his assistance, and they will find that they cannot bully you as they thought."

"Oh, I thank you, sir! I thank you so much."

Sir William smiled and Bess felt as if rays of sunlight shone on her.

"You are most welcome, my dear. I will be pleased to be your champion, and I warrant all will come out right."

"It's so kind of him!" Bess cried to Frances Grey the next day.

Lady Dorset glanced up from her dressing table with a speculative look in her eyes. "What do you think of Sir William, Bess?"

"Why, what should I think? He will help me to get my money! I think he's wonderful!"

"Yes, yes, but I don't mean that. It's been several months now since his wife died and he's sure to be looking to marry again."

Bess blinked in astonishment. Did Lady Dorset mean that Sir William might look upon her as a possible wife?

"His wife died after giving birth to a dead child," Lady Dorset continued, "and both of their other babies died as well, but he has three little girls by his first wife, and they need a mother."

Bess's heart filled with pity at the thought of the motherless girls. She loved little children. She had eased her heartache at being parted from her younger sisters by spending time with the Zouche children, but she had fallen in love with the three little Grey girls. Jane, impossibly smart and yet endearingly vulnerable. Six-year-old Kate, sweet and beautiful. And poor little baby Mary, who had something wrong with her spine so that she was growing crooked.

"Sir William is a man of keen intelligence," Frances Grey said. "Much respected and growing apace in power and influence. It would be a brilliant match for you."

Sir William would make quite a different husband than poor Robbie, Bess thought. He was old enough to be her father, probably twenty years older than her eighteen years of age. He was a man of property and with powerful connections. As his wife she would be well cared for and comfortable. She would not have to endure hardships or fear the future. And he had already shown that he was kind, and would fight for her and protect her.

"Give the matter some thought," Lady Dorset said. "You'll spend time in his company when he helps you with your suit, and have the opportunity to get to know him better."

CHAPTER ELEVEN

May 1546—Whitehall Palace, London

BESS KEPT PACE WITH JANE GREY, WHO WAS TROTTING IN AN attempt to keep up with her mother. Far ahead, Frances Grey's skirts billowed out behind her as she sailed toward the queen's privy chamber.

When Bess and Jane entered the queen's domain, Frances was already curtsying to the queen. Catherine Parr, in scarlet silk and at the center of a dozen or more ladies, looked up and smiled to see Jane, but Frances's eyes were cold when she looked back at her daughter.

"Your Majesty," Jane murmured as she sank into a curtsy.

"Dear Jane," the queen said. "I'm so glad you've come."

Frances Grey's young stepmother, Catherine Willoughby, the Duchess of Suffolk, her blue eyes and pale skin set off by her gown of dove gray, came forward to embrace Jane.

"I know your uncle will be pleased to see you," the queen said to Jane. "He and the prince are at their lessons just now, but be sure to visit with him before you go."

Bess recalled that Henry, the ten-year-old Duke of Suffolk, had been sent to join the household of Prince Edward when his father had died the previous summer. The queen smiled at Bess and Bess curtsied as she passed, catching a faint scent of roses and cinnamon in the movement of the queen's gown.

"I thank you, Your Majesty." Jane bowed to the queen again, and Bess followed behind her as she made her way around the room, greeting the queen's attendants. She had seen many of these ladies at court before, but had never been among them so closely. Many of them were the wives of the most powerful men in England, she knew. She held them in awe and was impressed by Jane's easy grace as she made small talk. Jane Dudley, who had long been a friend of the queen, was wed to John Dudley, Lord Lisle, a member of both the king's privy council and his privy chamber. Anne Seymour's husband Edward, the Earl of Hertford, was the elder brother of the late Queen Jane, and still inward with the king.

And there was the Lady Elizabeth, the king's younger daughter. She must be about twelve now, Bess thought, and no longer looked like a little girl, but was on the cusp of womanhood.

"My dear cousin," Elizabeth greeted Jane. "It has been too long since we have seen each other."

Lizzie was there, too, and embraced Bess. "I hope we have a chance to talk before you go. I've missed your company so!"

There was one man in the room, a black-robed cleric, and soon the queen called to her attendants to gather and listen. "We're honored to have Dr. Crome to speak to us this afternoon."

The queen sat, and her ladies settled around her in a multicolored sea of silk. A little black spaniel frisked toward the queen, barking, and put his paws on her lap.

"Gardiner!" the Duchess of Suffolk called sharply, clapping her hands, and the dog guiltily returned to her side.

"Gardiner?" Bess whispered to Lizzie. "Like the archbishop?" Lizzie only smiled mischievously.

Bess did her best to follow the preacher's words, but she found what he said to be convoluted, and what she did understand alarmed her slightly. Was he really saying that Purgatory did not exist? And that Christ was not present in the consecrated bread and wine of the communion?

After Dr. Crome had left, the queen took up a sheaf of papers and read aloud. She spoke of King Henry, likening him to Moses, leading his people out of captivity and bondage.

Jane must have caught Bess's frown of concentration, for she leaned close to her and whispered, "Freedom from slavery to the pope, she means."

When the queen had finished reading, she led the ladies in discussion. Bess felt herself far at sea. She gathered that the words the queen had read were her own. She had never heard of a lady writing a book before, much less holding forth at length in a learned manner as the queen did. She felt herself nodding off and roused herself. It would never do to fall asleep in the queen's presence.

Lizzie caught her eye and motioned her head toward the doorway, and Bess rose, moving as unobtrusively as she could.

"That's quite enough of that for me!" Lizzie said with a laugh when they were outside the queen's chamber. "It's such a beautiful day, let's go outside."

"Why do the other ladies take such an interest in it?" Bess asked as she and Lizzie made their way down a stairway and out into a garden. "Or do they only feign to do so, as it's the queen's writing?"

"Oh, some of them are very earnest in their beliefs," Lizzie said, squinting at the sun. "Me, I don't care too much."

A tall, dark-haired man wearing deep green velvet entered the garden, in conversation with an older man. Lizzie noted him and raised her eyebrows at Bess.

"Thomas Seymour," she whispered.

Bess recalled thinking him handsome when Doll had pointed him out to her at court three years earlier, and she thought he was even more so now. He broke off the conversation with the other man and walked toward where she and Lizzie sat, moving with arrogant assurance.

"Mistress Brooke." He stopped before them and bowed, smiling down at Lizzie with more heat in his gaze than Bess thought seemly, and then turned his eyes on her. "And who is your pretty companion, Lizzie?"

"Elizabeth Barlow," Lizzie said. "An old friend, for we served Lady Zouche together. Now she is in the household of Lady Dorset."

"Ah, then you are well placed," he said to Bess. His gaze drifted down her body, and though she was modestly dressed, she flushed, feeling as though he saw through her garments. He roused in her the same feelings she had experienced when she danced with Christopher Winters and when Edmund had kissed her at Lady Zouche's house, and she dropped her eyes in confusion. He laughed, his voice deep and rich, and he wandered on.

Bess recalled that before Catherine Parr had married the king, she had been in love with Thomas Seymour. "I wonder if she finds it difficult to have him around," she said, speaking her thoughts aloud.

"She may yet be his wife." Lizzie spoke quietly, but Bess sensed a world of meaning behind her words and turned to her in surprise.

"The king is old," Lizzie said, glancing around to be sure she was not overheard. "But perhaps things will change sooner rather than later."

Whatever Lizzie was implying could not be good, Bess feared.

"The king wearies of the queen, some say," Lizzie murmured. "And she has not got with child."

"Oh, no, not that again." Bess was aghast. Surely the aged king would not cast off yet another wife. "Is not Prince Edward enough to reassure him of the succession?"

Lizzie shrugged. "William says that the king is no longer making daily visits to the queen. And he has been paying especial favor to the Duchess of Suffolk." Frances Grey's stepmother was only twenty-six, and was very beautiful, Bess thought. But surely she would be canny enough to avoid being caught in the king's snares?

. . .

AS THEY WERE ROWED HOME FROM THE PALACE LATE THAT AFTER-
noon, Bess's mind was awhirl with anxiety over what Lizzie had told
her. She had thought the days of plotting and fear were done at
court, but perhaps that was not so.

Jane, who had spent the entire visit in the company of the queen,
was full of admiration for her and all that had been discussed
that day.

"It is her second book from which the queen was reading," she
said, breaking in on Bess's thoughts. "After she published the first,
last November, the universities at both Oxford and Cambridge
begged her to become their patroness! It is a wonderful thing she
does, to take up such weighty matters."

"Does she argue, as Dr. Crome does, that the Lord is not in the
sacred bread and wine? Is that not contrary to what the Bible tells us?"

"That is not meant to be taken in literal terms," Jane said. "Christ's
meaning in that passage is similar to the meaning of those other
places of Scripture. When He says, 'I am the door,' 'I am the vine,'
'Behold the Lamb of God,' 'That rock was Christ,' and other such
references to Himself, you are not in these texts to take Christ for
the material thing which He is signified by, for then you will make
Him a very door, a vine, a lamb, a stone, quite contrary to the Holy
Ghost's meaning."

"So He is not those things?"

"Yes, all those indeed do signify Christ, even as the bread signi-
fies His body in that place."

"I don't understand," Bess said, "why these things should matter
so. Or why anyone would die for what they believe."

"Do you not?" Jane asked. "I do."

CHAPTER TWELVE

Only a few weeks after the visit to Whitehall, the Duchess of Suffolk arrived at Dorset House, visibly distressed. Bess accompanied her to Frances Grey's withdrawing chamber and offered her refreshment, but the duchess waved her off silently, then pulled off her gloves and dropped them onto a table and paced until Frances Grey arrived.

"Why, Catherine, what's amiss!" she inquired as she embraced her stepmother.

"Have you not heard? There have been a spate of arrests for heresy. Including Edward Crome and Anne Askew."

"Dear God." Frances went white. And no wonder, Bess thought, for Edward Crome was the preacher who had been in the queen's privy chamber when they were there. And Anne Askew had visited Frances Grey at Dorset House. Bess recalled her well, a spirited and attractive young woman only a few years older than she was. Jane had told her that Mistress Askew had been cast out by her husband for disobedience, and then come to London where she had become some kind of preacher or reformer, and had been arrested for distributing evangelical books that had been banned.

"Both were questioned about evangelicals on the privy council and in the queen's privy chamber. Frances, they were asked about me." The duchess's eyes were dark with fear. "And they put Anne Askew to the rack!"

Bess's stomach gave a lurch of terror and revulsion.

"The rack?" Frances gasped. "B-but she's a gentlewoman. Surely the privy council did not authorize such barbarism?"

"No, but it was done, nonetheless. The Lord Chancellor and solicitor general ordered the lieutenant of the Tower to rack her. He would not, and went to the king to object. So they did it themselves."

"Thomas Wriothesley." Frances spat out the name. "He would do it. And Richard Rich, too, I would believe it of him. But how came you to learn this? What happened?"

Bess felt rooted to where she stood. She felt exactly as she had when the horror of Cat Howard's downfall was unfolding—afraid to hear what terrors she would learn of next, but unable to stop herself from wanting to know. For only by knowing what was happening could one hope to guess what way to run, where safety lay.

"She managed to smuggle out an account of what was done to her," Catherine Willoughby said. "Wriothesley and Rich stripped to their shirtsleeves, and stripped her to her shift. They tore her on the rack. They tore her sinews and cracked her bones. The wife and daughters of the Lord Lieutenant of the Tower heard her screams, where they were walking on Tower Green." The duchess was weeping now, and Frances Grey took her in her arms. "They racked her so that she fainted. And then they revived her to do it again."

Bess found that she was holding herself, wrapping her arms around her chest and shoulders, as if she could feel her own arms being pulled from their sockets. She could imagine only too well Anne Askew's face, contorted with agony, her soft voice raised in a wordless shriek under her torment. Jesu, if they could treat Mistress

Askew in that way, they could do it to anyone. She wondered wildly if she could flee from London and return to the safety of Hardwick.

"Sweet Christ, would no one stop them?" Frances cried.

"Who was to stop them? At last they laid her on the floor and crouched by her for another two hours, demanding whether the queen or any of her ladies believed as she did, and whether they had aided her."

Was the queen in danger then? Or Frances Grey? Or Jane? Or Lizzie, or Bess herself? They had all been at Whitehall to hear Crome. Bess found that she was trembling.

"And who is behind all this?" Frances whispered.

"Who else but Bishop Gardiner and the Duke of Norfolk?"

Norfolk. Why was he always at the heart of trouble and terror? Bess wondered.

IN THE MIDST OF THE PANIC SURROUNDING ANNE ASKEW, SIR William Cavendish came to Dorset House to discuss Bess's suit with her.

"I have filed what is needful," he said, "and Edward Seymour has said that he will put in a word on your behalf."

"Thank you, sir. And how kind of Lord Hertford," Bess said. "When will the matter come to court?"

"It could be weeks or months, but that's all to the good as it gives us time to prepare. You will surely be called to testify, and that can rattle the nerves of anyone." Sir William smiled at Bess, and in his presence, she felt more calm and safe than she had in a fortnight.

"May I ask you something, sir?"

"Certainly."

"This business with Mistress Askew . . ." Now that she had begun, Bess didn't know what to say.

"Shocking and terrible." Sir William's face was grim.

"It all makes me feel so frightened. I wonder who might be next, to be questioned, to be . . ."

Bess was shaking, and Sir William put a steady arm around her shoulders.

"Of course you do. Who would not?"

"Do you mean that you worry, too?" Bess whispered, looking up into his warm gray eyes.

"I do more than worry. I fear, sometimes."

Bess stared at him. "You do?"

He nodded. "When sands are shifting as you walk, it is hard to know where to put your feet."

"Then what do you do?"

"Keep your head about you. Keep your counsel. Speak your mind to no one that you do not trust utterly."

"How am I to know who to trust?"

"Let them prove themselves to you."

Who did she trust beyond question? Her mother and the rest of her family. Lizzie. Jane, of course. She looked back at Sir William, his face gentle and patient, and recalled Frances Grey's admonition that she think about Sir William as a possible husband. Yes, she trusted him, too. And that, more than anything else, was important to her in a man she thought of marrying.

"Thank you, sir," she whispered. "You are a good friend to me."

He smiled. "I cherish those words, Bess. And I will strive to be the best friend to you that I may be. Always."

A FEW DAYS LATER BESS HEARD HARRY GREY TELLING HIS WIFE that the queen's sister and two more of her closest friends, Lady Lane and Lady Tyrwhitt, had been arrested.

"They searched their rooms for heretical books, or aught else they could find to do them damage."

Bess thought of Jane's translation of the queen's book. What other works might she own that could be considered dangerous? Would Frances Grey hide their books? Was she safe from the reach of such inquiries?

"What has become of them?" Frances Grey asked.

"They were set free again, but there may be more attacks to come. And Anne Askew has been condemned to burn as a heretic."

Bess felt herself grow faint, and held fast to the chair she stood behind.

"She was offered mercy if she would recant her beliefs," Harry Grey said, "but she refused."

"Then she will die?" Frances's voice was little more than a whisper.

"Aye. The only question now is who else may be brought down. For Gardiner and Norfolk and their faction greatly fear and resent the queen's influence on the king and the prince, and I fear would do anything they can to harm her. It is like Cromwell and Anne Boleyn all over again."

Bess thought of Queen Catherine's warm smile. And she thought of Cat Howard, how innocent she had been of the destruction that was about to fall on her. Like a lamb to the slaughter. And she thought of Anne Askew, facing death by fire.

"What shall we do?" Frances cried. "I am to wait on the queen in a few days' time."

"Then you must go," her husband told her. "But for your life, do not discuss anything that could cause the least whisper of suspicion."

IT WAS A BEAUTIFUL SUMMER'S DAY WHEN BESS AGAIN MADE THE journey to Whitehall by boat with Frances and Jane Grey, but a cold lump of fear lay in the pit of her stomach. They made their way through the rooms of the palace to the queen's privy chamber. The mood among the ladies there was vastly different from what it had been on their previous visit, she thought. There was little chatter, and what talk there was took place in lowered voices. The queen was attired in dark gray, and the color seemed to have been drained from her face. There was no preaching and no reading. The ladies worked at needlework, their eyes on the bright skeins of silk in their laps and the lengths of linen stretched in embroidery hoops in their hands.

Bess was relieved to find Lizzie in the queen's chamber, for perhaps Lizzie would be able to tell her more reliable news than she had heard. They had just gone to sit together on a window seat when a man's voice interrupted the quiet hum of conversation.

"Your Majesty, the king commands your presence in the privy garden."

Bess thought the queen went even paler than she had been, and saw her fingers tighten on the arms of her chair, but when she spoke, her voice was calm.

"Then we shall with all obedience attend him."

She rose and her ladies fell in behind her, following her down the stairs and outside like a flock of ducklings after their mother.

The king stood in the garden where Bess had spoken with Lizzie when she had been at the palace last. He was even more stout than he had been when last she had seen him, and it appeared that his head was almost bald under his jeweled cap.

"Madam." He held out a hand to the queen and she went to him, curtsying deeply as she put her hand in his.

The queen's ladies stood uncertainly as the king led the queen away down a path among the bordered flower beds. He was limping, but seemed to be taking care not to lean on the queen for support.

Suddenly Bess heard heavy footsteps, the sound of many booted feet marching. She turned and saw that a party of guards was approaching, the blades of their halberds glinting in the sun. At their head strode Thomas Wriothesley, the Lord Chancellor. The man who had himself turned the crank on the rack, breaking the frail body of Anne Askew. A wolflike smile was on his face, and even from this distance, Bess heard the queen gasp.

This was just what had happened on that dreadful day at Hampton

Court, Bess recalled with vivid clarity. She had been dancing with Cat Howard and her ladies in the queen's chamber when just such a troop of guards had arrived. She and Lizzie exchanged a terrified glance.

The king let go the queen's hand and stepped away from her. She stood all alone, terror etched on her face. Bess wanted to run to her, to protect her. But what could she do, against three dozen armed men?

But the king was advancing on Wriothesley, his face contorted with anger, and now it was Wriothesley who looked confused and afraid. He dropped to one knee and bowed his head as the king snarled down at him. Bess couldn't hear the words, but the king's face was that of a savage animal. Wriothesley began to rise and was clearly pleading with the king, but the king raised a hand as if to strike him, and Wriothesley fell to his knees in complete submission.

"Arrant knave, beast, fool!" the king shouted. "Take your pack of dogs and begone!"

Wriothesley scrambled to his feet, gesturing the guards to follow him, and they retreated in disorder.

Bess looked to the queen and saw the look of intense relief wash over her face, instantly replaced by a careful mask.

The king stumped back to the queen's side and she raised her eyes to his.

"Alas, my lord, what has your poor chancellor done to anger you so?" Her voice and face were all innocence. "I will be a suitor for him, for surely his fault was occasioned by some mistake."

Bess held her breath. What a gamble on the queen's part, she thought, not to let on that she had known Wriothesley's purpose. Would it anger the king?

But the king patted the queen's hand. "Ah, poor soul," he said, a lopsided smile cracking his face. "Thou little knowest, Kate, how little he deserves this grace at thy hands. On my word, sweetheart, he hath been to thee a very knave, so let him go."

. . .

THE KING KEPT THE QUEEN WITH HIM IN THE GARDEN FOR A TIME, but it appeared obvious to Bess that his leg was paining him, and the only reason he did not dismiss the queen and return to where he could be comfortable was to disguise the fact that he had only wanted her there while he played the scene with Wriothesley, for it had indeed seemed like something out of a deadly masque.

When at last the queen returned to her privy chamber with her ladies, she retired to her bed. Frances Grey huddled in a corner whispering with the Duchess of Suffolk and the queen's sister, Lady Herbert. Bess took the opportunity of going to Lizzie, and they retreated to the window seat. Bess gazed at the garden below and shivered despite the warmth of the day.

"She knew it was coming," Lizzie whispered.

"She knew?" Bess was shocked.

"Well, she had known she was in grave danger and that it had passed. Though seeing the guards must have given her a turn."

"I would think so. It did me." As Lizzie shared a pillow with the queen's brother, she likely knew more about what had gone on than almost anyone. "What has happened," she asked, "that she knew she was in peril?"

"A few days ago, one of the queen's servants found a paper on the ground which proved to be a warrant for the queen's arrest. He brought it to her, and she could see that it was real, and signed by the king. Her weeping was lamentable to see."

How terrified the queen must have been, Bess thought. She had the examples of Anne Boleyn and Cat Howard before her, and knew well enough that the king would not hesitate to put her to death.

"Dear God," she cried. "Upon what cause? Surely he does not suspect her of playing him false, like . . ." Cat Howard's terrified eyes came into Bess's mind. She could not speak Cat's name and blinked back tears. Lizzie took her hand and Bess knew that Lizzie, too, must be recalling that terrible day at Hampton Court. And she must have been afraid for her own safety, too.

"No, not that," Lizzie said. "The accusation was heresy."

"Then Dr. Crome, and the books . . ."

"Aye, but there was more than that. The queen has been in the habit of taking the king's mind from his pain by engaging him in learned discourse, debating theology."

"An odd sort of comfort! Why doesn't she just bring him a warm posset?"

Lizzie smiled wanly. "Perhaps she will now. Anyway, when she saw the warrant, she was distraught. Dr. Wendy, the king's new doctor, came to calm her, and he warned her that Bishop Gardiner and the Lord Chancellor were plotting to undo her."

"Thomas Wriothesley again." Bess shuddered.

"Dr. Wendy said that her exhorting the king to further do away with popery had angered him, and that Gardiner had played upon his mind and argued that she was a serpent in his bosom, a heretic who defied his authority and would dissolve the politic government of princes and teach the people that all things ought to be in common. He told the king that all who believed so deserved death, no matter how high they might be."

Bess thought of the queen's face alight with passion as she had read from her book.

"But surely she didn't plot against the king?"

"Of course not. But don't you see—the power of the reformists is growing, and it threatens the conservatives like the bishop. They hate and fear the queen because of her influence with the king, but more importantly"—she glanced around and lowered her voice—"her influence with the Prince of Wales. For he will be king ere long."

"They fear what will become of them if the evangelicals have control of Edward."

"Yes. And it will only get worse, William says. For the king's health is worsening."

Bess looked around to see who was within hearing. She longed to ask what Lizzie knew about the king's decline, and what might happen when he died, but that was a dangerous subject for discussion. She glanced once more down at the privy garden, where the shadows were lengthening across the lawns and flower beds.

"What did she do to save herself?"

"Dr. Wendy counseled her that if she conformed herself to the king's mind he might be favorable to her. But still she wept, and the king, hearing of her dangerous state, himself came to comfort her."

Bess would have laughed if the image of the bloated king sitting at the bedside of the wife whose death warrant he had signed were not so horrible.

"She told him that she feared he was displeased with her and had forsaken her, but he patted her hand and crooned and said it was not so."

The calculating and vicious liar, Bess thought.

"When he had gone," Lizzie whispered, "she bade us get rid of any forbidden books, and told us that pleasing the king was all her care. That night she went to him, and when he sought to trap her, like a cat with a mouse in the kitchen corner, by bringing up matters of religion, she told him that she believed with all her heart that God had appointed him as supreme head of all. 'Not so, by Mary!' he said, and told her that she was become a doctor who thought to instruct him. She told him that her meaning had been misunderstood—she had only sought to distract him from his pain, and that she was but a woman, with the weakness of her sex, and that she happily submitted to his better judgment as her lord and head."

What a cool head the queen must have, Bess thought, to make such a speech, knowing that her life depended on it.

"She told William, and he told me," Lizzie continued, "that then his face broke into a smile, and he cried, 'Is it so, sweetheart? And tended your arguments to no worse end? Then we are perfect friends, as ever at any time heretofore!' Then he kissed her and told her it did him more good to hear those words than news of a hundred thousand pounds coming to him, and he would never again doubt her."

"Then why," Bess asked, "why did the guards come?"

"I expect that was to pay Wriothesley back for his interference," Lizzie said. "He'll be lucky if he doesn't lose his head."

WHEN BESS RETURNED TO DORSET HOUSE WITH FRANCES AND Jane Grey that evening, she felt drained, as exhausted as though she had been laboring in the fields. She was finally beginning to recover her spirits the next day when the Duchess of Suffolk paid a call on Frances Grey, with news that made Bess shiver with terror.

"Anne Askew is to be burned tomorrow," the duchess said. "Along with John Lassels and two other evangelicals."

"And there is no one who can save her," Frances Grey said, dropping into a chair. "For now the queen cannot speak for her, nor any in high places, for fear it will end with them on the flames."

Bess said a silent prayer for Mistress Askew. *And let this horror end there*, she begged. *Let it not touch anyone more. Keep the queen safe, and Lady Dorset and Jane and Lizzie. And me.*

The next afternoon Harry Grey returned from Smithfield to tell his wife what had happened that day. Frances Grey sent away her six-year-old daughter Kate, but Jane would not go.

"I want to hear it," she said. "For surely Anne Askew is a true martyr, and if she can suffer death for her faith, I can hear of it."

"Very well," Harry Grey said heavily, and turned once more to his wife.

"She wore naught but her shift, and she was carried on a chair to the stake because she could not walk, so cruelly had they broken her on the rack. They bound her to the stake with chains."

"Was there a great crowd?" Jane asked, her face white.

"There was. And as the flames were lit, some called out that she deserved her death, but more wept in pity and raised their voices in prayer. Nicholas Throckmorton and his brother were among the crowd, and they shouted encouragement to her, saying that she did not die in vain."

"The queen's own cousins," Frances murmured. "I hope she will not suffer for their words."

"Bishop Shaxton was there," Harry told her, "and preached at the lady, and once she cried, 'There he misseth, and speaketh without the book.'"

"How could she have the heart to do so?" Bess wondered.

Harry Grey met her eyes. "She showed great bravery. She didn't scream until the flames mounted to her chest." Bess's stomach heaved with horror. "Someone had provided her with a little bag of gunpowder, which hung around her neck, and by God's mercy it went off soon, and so she died. The others lasted longer."

A log in the fireplace crackled and Bess clapped a hand to her mouth as nausea gripped her.

"A great lady," Jane said quietly. "I pray that I might show such fortitude were I ever in such circumstances."

"Don't speak like that!" Bess cried, pulling Jane into her arms. "You will never be in such peril!"

"I pray not. But if I were, I would remember Anne Askew, and that would give me courage."

Lizzie and Doll came to visit Bess at Dorset House in early September. Since Bess had last seen her, Doll had been widowed, and had recently married John Port, a justice of the common pleas. Lizzie had been with the queen at Hampton Court Palace, where there had been ten days of celebrations in honor of the visit of the Lord High Admiral of France to ratify the new peace treaty between the two nations.

"Was it like when Anne of Cleves came?" Doll asked. "What a sight that was!"

"Not quite as grand, but still impressive," Lizzie said. "Monsieur d'Annebaut brought two hundred gentlemen with him, and when Prince Edward rode out to meet him, he was accompanied by eighty gentlemen in gold and eighty yeomen of the guard."

"Prince Edward greeted the French!" Bess exclaimed. "Not the king?"

Lizzie shook her head. "He can scarce get around at all now. He has a sort of chair on which he can be carried, and he cannot get up the stairs at all, but must be let up and down by a device. Of course he couldn't let the French see him like that. The Lord Chancellor and privy council welcomed the admiral. The king only received him sitting in his presence chamber on the second day, and then in a pavilion out in the gardens for the feasting."

"I wish we could have gone," Doll said wistfully.

"You'd likely have had to sleep in a tent outside." Lizzie giggled. "The palace was full up. The grounds were covered with tents of gold and velvet that had been set up for the French alongside the banqueting houses. Elegant, but still tents."

"And the queen?" Bess asked. "Does all seem to be well between her and the king?"

"Aye, she is all honey with him."

"No sign of being with child?" Doll asked.

"Not likely," Lizzie said. Even though they were alone in the parlor, she lowered her voice. "I doubt the king could manage it. When they went to Oatlands to hunt, a ramp had to be built to help him mount his horse. And even then, he didn't ride out. They drove a poor stag past him so he might shoot at it from where he sat."

"I have not been at court since—since last I saw you there," Bess said. "Have there been no more plots, no more arrests?"

"I think the failure of the attempt to bring down the queen has settled Norfolk and his crew for the time being. But the battle lines between the factions are drawn, and beneath the surface, tension roils. Little fights break out, and it will only get worse as the king fails. All jostle to control Prince Edward, but of course they must not show that they do it."

"Your William is still greatly in favor with him?" Bess asked. Lizzie had been living with William Parr for three years now.

"Very much so," Lizzie said, with a catlike smile. "He is Edward's favored uncle. And likely to be among the regents."

Regents would only be needed if King Henry died and Edward succeeded him before he had come of age. It was treason to predict the death of the king, so even here among her friends, Bess weighed her words carefully before she spoke.

"So the king is making those plans?"

"He is," Lizzie said. "He must."

CHAPTER THIRTEEN

O N THE DAY IN OCTOBER WHEN BESS'S SUIT WAS TO BE HEARD,
Sir William Cavendish arrived at Dorset House and carried
her behind him on his great bay gelding to Chancery Court. Bess
felt queasy with anxiety, but she knew that she could not have a better ally, for among the positions Sir William held was treasurer of
the court of surveyors, which administered crown lands. He was
used to negotiating about the disposal and administration of estates,
knew the laws in and out, and knew the man who would hear Bess's
case against Sir Peter Frecheville.

The street before the court was bustling with people. Or more
accurately, with men and boys, for Bess did not see any other women.
Prosperous-looking gentlemen with page boys in tow, somber
black-gowned lawyers clutching armloads of papers, grooms leading horses through the mire of straw and mud, their voices rising
and falling in discussion and dispute, a bark of laughter from somewhere.

Sir William helped her dismount and she waited as he handed

his horse's reins to a boy and gave him a coin. She felt very small surrounded by the surging crowd.

"Come, let's get you inside," he said, placing a guiding hand on her elbow. The antechamber was crowded, and here, too, there were no other women. Two or three men greeted Sir William, bowing to Bess, and his assured presence gave her strength as they continued into the court chamber.

Sir William led Bess toward a back bench and she caught sight of Sir Peter Frecheville, glowering at her from across the room. He was a soldierly man in his middle thirties, recently returned from the campaign of destruction against Scotland. Bess knew he had been knighted there by Edward Seymour, and the thought of doing battle with him made her heart race with anxiety. Seymour was Sir William's patron, and Sir William had asked for his help, but had he given it? Perhaps he would be inclined to favor Sir Peter, regardless of what he had told Sir William.

"That's him," she whispered to Sir William.

"Good," he said, inclining his head to Sir Peter with a stern expression on his face. "Then we know all may be dealt with today, and no more waiting."

He was clearly not the least intimidated, and with him standing reassuringly bulky and steady at her side, Bess felt protected.

"Just answer the questions truthfully," Sir William said as they took their seats. "You're entitled to what you're asking for and they've treated you very shabbily."

"Thank you, sir." Bess smiled at him and he patted her hand.

Four men in black gowns were busy at tables at the front of the room, piled with scrolls and documents. At length a clerk called out, "All rise for the Honorable Master of the Rolls," and the hum of conversation ceased and there was a shuffling and scraping as everyone stood. A beak-nosed old gentleman took his seat in the great chair behind the central table and pounded with a gavel, bringing the proceedings to order.

Case after case was called, and the wait gave Bess time to worry. What if the judge found merit in Sir Peter's claim that she was not entitled to her widow's portion, a third of the income from the Barlow estates? Then she would have nothing to live on, nothing to make her attractive to a prospective husband, not even her dowry, small as it had been. Surely no man, and especially not Sir William, would marry her then. And perhaps Lady Dorset would send her back to Hardwick. As much as she had not wanted to leave home, what a failure she would feel creeping back, in no better position to help her parents and with no better prospects than when she had left.

And what would she be required to testify about to prove her case? Her face flushed at the thought of having to speak to this room full of men about whether her marriage had been consummated.

Please, God, she prayed silently, *give me strength to do as I must and the fortitude to bear the outcome.*

And then Bess heard her name being read out and her heart hammered as she got to her feet.

"Speak up so you can be heard," Sir William told her in a low voice. "And don't let any of these old buzzards frighten you."

She returned his smile and walked to the bar, head held high. She felt conspicuous and vulnerable, knowing that so many eyes were watching her, and her palm was damp as she placed it upon the Bible to swear that she would tell the truth.

The master of the rolls in his black cap consulted the papers before him and peered at her from beneath bushy brows.

"Mistress Elizabeth Barlow. You are making a claim against Sir Peter Frecheville for a widow's dower. And yet you previously accepted a settlement offered to you by this gentleman, did you not?"

I had to! Bess wanted to cry. But Sir William had anticipated that she would be asked this question, and she took a deep breath to settle her nerves and calmly spoke the response she had practiced.

"I did, sir. I accepted Sir Peter's offer, though it was not much, on the advice of legal counsel and because I was suffering great hardship."

Bess thought of the lines of worry etched in her stepfather's pinched face when she had last seen him, and the shadows beneath her mother's tired eyes.

"My father had but lately returned home from debtors' prison and he and my mother were striving mightily to manage all and to care for my younger sisters."

"Hmph. I see."

The master of the rolls shuffled through the pleadings before him, muttering as he ran a finger down the pages. Would the fact that her father had been in prison harm her case? She felt ashamed by his imprisonment, and disloyal for feeling ashamed. But surely his troubles would not be held against her. She could not recall if she had asked Sir William about the matter, but it was too late now.

"And what say you, Mistress Barlow," the master of the rolls asked, "to Sir Peter's claims that you have no right to a widow's dower, as you were not truly wed?"

Here it was, the issue she had dreaded. But she remembered Sir William's admonition. She was asking for no more than was her right.

"His claim is groundless, sir," she said. "Robert Barlow and I were married more than a year and a half before he died. We stayed at first in the household of Sir George Zouche, whom we both served. Then we went to Barlow and lived with my husband's family. My husband was very young, sir. I cannot help that. But I cared for him and he for me and had he lived we would have been master and mistress of the place. We were truly married, sir."

"Hmph." The master of the rolls took up one of the papers before him. It appeared to be a letter, written closely and with a heavy red seal. He raised his eyebrows as he read through it again. Bess fought the urge to turn around and look to Sir William for reassurance.

"Very well. You may step down."

The master of the rolls waved a dismissive hand and Bess curtsied and returned gratefully to her seat, taking comfort in Sir William's stalwart presence and approving nod.

Next Sir Peter Frecheville was called forward and argued his case. He was elegantly dressed and spoke eloquently and persuasively, and as Bess watched the master of the rolls nod in seeming agreement, her hopes fell. Who was she to stand against such a powerful man? He would trample her underfoot, keeping all for himself, and she would be left with nothing.

Sir Peter returned to his seat, a supercilious smile on his lips. The master of the rolls conferred in whispers with his clerks, frowning and muttering as he reviewed the documents before him once more. Bess hung her head and twined her fingers in her lap and waited in silent misery. At last one of the clerks called out.

"Come you forward, Sir Peter Frecheville. And come you forward, Mistress Barlow."

The gray-bearded master of the rolls glowered at Bess as she went forward, and she knew she had lost. Her heart was in her throat but she determined that whatever happened she would not cry. She would not let Sir Peter Frecheville see that he had frightened and humiliated her, even though he had succeeded in keeping her money.

"I find," the master of the rolls announced, "for the plaintiff, Mistress Elizabeth Barlow."

Bess restrained herself from gasping aloud.

"The defendant is ordered to pay Mistress Barlow, throughout her lifetime, one third of the revenues of the manor of Barlow and its dwelling houses and cottages, its fields, meadows, pastures, woods, furze, heath, and forests, together with the rents from its sundry properties in the villages of Barley, Barley Lees, Dronfield, and Homfield."

There was a low murmur of voices. Perhaps others listening to the evidence had also not expected her to win, Bess thought.

"Moreover," the master of the rolls continued, turning piercing eyes on Sir Peter Frecheville, "we award to Mistress Barlow additional compensation of half a year's rent for suffering the said most apparent wrongs and injuries since the death of her husband, without the succor or comfort of the said lands."

Bess felt as if life and warmth were flowing back into her again.

"Thank you, sir! Oh, I thank you most heartily!"

The master of the rolls smiled, and Bess wished she could kiss him. Sir Peter Frecheville, white with rage, blew out his breath like a bull, as Bess returned to the safety of Sir William's side. She wanted to throw her arms around him, too, but restrained herself, shaking the hand he offered and curtsying to him instead.

"You did it!" she exclaimed. "I cannot thank you enough, sir!"

"I am pleased that I was able to help. And I don't doubt that my Lord Hertford's letter helped your cause. But the part you played was just as important, Bess," he said. "You showed great courage in going through with this, and it was your speaking on your own behalf that won the court's sympathy and the additional compensation for the trouble that Frecheville put you to."

ONLY A FEW DAYS AFTER BESS'S SUCCESS IN COURT, SIR WILLIAM Cavendish had come to call at Dorset House, but it was Bess's company he sought, and Frances Grey had left them alone in the cozy little parlor with spiced wine and cakes, giving Bess an arch smile as she shut the door behind her. Since then, William had returned two or three times a week, and it was clear to Bess now that he was courting her.

He smiled at her as she refilled his wine cup, and she reflected that she felt quite comfortable around him, and he no longer seemed as imposing as she had found him at first.

"John Dudley was back at court today," he said, inhaling the rich scent of the wine before taking a drink.

"You said he had been sent away, did you not?" she asked.

"Yes, after he struck Bishop Gardiner before the full council a month ago. Had the king been present, his action would have called for a sentence of death. It's a mark of how far in favor he has risen of late that he was not banished for much longer."

Bess thought of Gardiner contriving the terrible death of Anne Askew and attempting to send the queen to the flames.

"Then the bishop has fallen in His Majesty's eyes?" She tried to keep her voice neutral, but a glint in William's eyes told her that she had spoken with more vehemence than she intended.

"Yes. His fall began with the failure of his plot against the queen, and even as he and his faction have fallen, so have his enemies risen."

"Of whom John Dudley is one?"

William nodded. "And my Lord Hertford another."

Edward Seymour, the Earl of Hertford, was William's patron. "As Seymour rises, so will William Cavendish," Frances Grey had said.

"And William Parr is also Gardiner's foe," she said, thinking of Lizzie. "And who else?" William raised his eyebrows. "I don't mean to be impertinent, sir, but I wish to understand."

"You're wise, Bess. It is well to know who stands where. It helps to know where to plant your own feet. William Paget, William Herbert, William Clerk, John Gates, all of the king's privy chamber. And now more than ever, Anthony Denny."

"Why him and why now?"

"Because he is His Majesty's chief gentleman of the privy chamber, and as the king grows more ill, his world grows smaller, until it is bounded by the walls of his privy chamber. The men who attend him there are ever within sight and hearing of him; they know his moods, his thoughts. Denny keeps the gates that shut others out. And he is keeper of the king's privy purse, as well."

"And you are treasurer of the privy chamber."

"Yes. And in that role I come within Denny's realm, and that of the king. But I don't rely on Denny alone. I am fortunate to have the ear of my Lord Hertford. And he is not only favored by the king, but by the Prince of Wales."

Who would be king, Bess thought. When that time came, Edward Seymour would fare well, and so would William.

The next time William came to visit, Bess played for him upon the virginals.

"Upon my soul, you have a rare talent," he congratulated her. "My daughter Kitty plays well, but not as well as you, I think!"

"How old is she?" Bess asked.

"She is eleven. Polly is seven and Nan is just six."

Bess thought William's eyes were sad as he named his daughters. "You have not seen them in some time?"

"No, they are at Northaw. London is no place for them, without someone to care for them, and I am so busy here. But I do miss having them about me."

"What is the news at court?" Bess asked, as they moved to sit before the fire.

"Gardiner has done himself further harm, I think. He refused His Majesty's request for the exchange of some episcopal lands, and now it seems he is barred entrance from the privy chamber."

"And that is important?"

"That is very important, for it means being close to the king's person. Every man fears his enemies will try to poison the king's mind against him, and bring him down, and only by being near the king, or having friends near, can he defend himself."

"Gardiner has earned himself many enemies," Bess said. "Does he still have friends?"

"He has allies still, though they are growing fewer, and their power is growing less. Self-interest and fear bind men together, but as the ground shifts, so do their allegiances. Wriothesley can tell which way the wind is blowing, and now he seeks to ally himself with Edward Seymour and John Dudley, who lately he sought to destroy." William smiled grimly. "Even Norfolk is courting Edward Seymour's favor now. He has got the king's permission to wed his daughter, the Duchess of Richmond, to Thomas Seymour."

Bess thought of Thomas Seymour flirting with her and Lizzie in the privy garden. She had felt a thrill of excitement and danger when he looked at her that she never felt when she was with William. Such spice was alluring, she thought, but was not a dish for every day. She tried to imagine being married to Thomas Seymour. She would always wonder where his eyes were roving. William had got up to poke the fire into life and she studied his face. Intelligent, kind, calm. Life as his wife might lack passion, but with him beside her, she would feel the earth steady beneath her feet.

WHEN WILLIAM CAME TO VISIT BESS ON THE EVENING OF THE thirteenth of December, she could tell even before he spoke that he was agitated. He kissed her in greeting but then paced instead of sitting.

"What's amiss, William?" she asked.

"Great changes are afoot. Norfolk was arrested yesterday. And his son, the Earl of Surrey, today, as he dined at Whitehall. Both are taken to the Tower."

Bess was astonished, and fear rippled up her spine.

"On what cause?"

"Surrey has been making trouble all along, contriving how he may secure the regency and control of the prince when the king is dead. And now that time is coming closer, and it seems likely that Edward Seymour will be given that position, Surrey hatched another plan—to replace the queen with his sister."

"The king's own daughter-in-law!" Bess cried. Mary Howard, the Duchess of Richmond, was the widow of King Henry's bastard son Henry Fitzroy. "Besides, I thought she was to marry Thomas Seymour."

"That was Norfolk's plan, but she would have none of it, nor would Thomas Seymour. Surrey erred gravely in counseling her to angle for the affections of the king."

"Come, sit," Bess urged him. He let her guide him to a chair before the hearth and took her hand and kissed it as she brought him wine.

"Now tell me all," she said, when she had got her own cup of wine and was seated beside him.

"The king is at Oatlands, as you know. A few days ago he fell ill of a fever." William lowered his voice. "His life is feared for. The council has been meeting at Edward Seymour's house, which may tell you in what ascendancy he is. I think he and Dudley thought to make hay while the sun shone, or to strike against Norfolk and Surrey while the iron was hot, to mix my figures of speech. For they accuse Surrey now of seeking the throne himself."

"And does he?"

"Likely not, but was ill advised enough to replace the coronet on his coat of arms with a crown. Of course he says he bears them by right of descent from Edward IV, and it may well be, but the appearance is all in these things, and it looks very bad. His sister has hurt him, too; she says he declared that if God called away the king the Seymours should smart for it. The implication was that he would be in a position to do them ill, for he would have governance of the prince. But what has finished him is that his friend—well, friend no longer—Richard Southwell has given the council information that is enough to convict him of treasonous plots against the king. And the king hasn't trusted Norfolk since the Catherine Howard mess. It's a wonder he hasn't found reason to be rid of him before now."

Bess was afraid at the thought of yet another plot, more men swept into the maw of the Tower, more heads upon the block. But it was William's patron Edward Seymour who had the upper hand, she reminded herself. And others who were friends of his and friends of the Greys. Surely this danger would not touch him or her.

"What does it mean?" she asked. "What will happen?"

"It means that Gardiner and Wriothesley and all their faction are down and will stay down. And for Norfolk and Surrey, it will surely mean death."

THE TWELVE DAYS OF CHRISTMAS HAD BEEN SUBDUED, FOR THE king was very ill, sequestered at the palace in Greenwich and attended by doctors. Only the queen, the Lady Mary, and a few members of the privy council were let into the king's bedchamber.

Now the Grey household and a handful of friends were gathered for Twelfth Night supper. "You should have heard the king speak when he prorogued parliament on Christmas Eve," William told

Harry Grey, "chastising them like a schoolmaster over unruly boys. 'Discord and dissension rule in every place,' he roared, and 'the Word of God is disputed, rhymed, sung, and jangled in every alehouse and tavern.'"

"I fear me that the lion has roared for the last time," Harry Grey said quietly. "Let us hope that the cub is sharpening his claws."

"The prince will be safe enough, and with wise heads around him," William responded. "There are no more wolves, snarling and nipping at each's heels now that Norfolk and Surrey are penned in."

After supper, Bess and William retreated to the parlor where they had spent so many companionable hours together over the past months.

"Is the king really dying, then?" Bess asked.

"He can't last long," William said, nodding.

Bess hated the king for Cat's death, for how he had frightened kind Queen Catherine, for his murder of the old Countess of Salisbury, and for the pall of terror that he had cast over England for so long. She imagined him as he must be now, his great bulk mounded over with bedclothes in a dark bedchamber, listening to the whispers of his doctors and councilors, and knowing that the one enemy he could not vanquish was hovering at the door. But as long as he breathed, she would fear him.

"God keep His Majesty," she whispered. "And grant him comfort if not longer life."

CHAPTER FOURTEEN

Thirtieth of January, 1547—Dorset House, London

BELLS WERE TOLLING ALL OVER LONDON. STANDING AT THE parlor window, Bess could hear the bells of the churches near Dorset House and the discordant tones from farther away, making the very air seem to echo with the clangor. King Henry was dead. As she gazed out over the city, she could feel nothing but relief and a slight sense of bafflement. How would England get on with a ten-year-old king?

She heard voices outside the room—Lady Dorset, and surely that was William talking to her. She smiled as they entered.

"I must see to some things," Frances Grey said. "Bess, come see me when Sir William has gone."

"Of course," Bess said, but Lady Dorset was already on her way out of the room. William stood for a moment, looking slightly awkward, it seemed to Bess, before he came to her and kissed her. She gestured to the chairs before the fire where they had sat so often.

"Edward Seymour has gone to Hertford Castle to bring young Edward back to London," William said after a few moments. "The prince will be proclaimed king tomorrow."

"God save him, and grant him long life."

"Amen to that prayer." He took her hands in his. "Bess, Edward Seymour is now Lord Protector, and he assures me that I will be reconfirmed as treasurer of the king's chamber."

"I'm so pleased for you."

"Yes, I'm very well placed now with his support. The young king likes me well, and God willing, I will prosper in the new reign. Which brings me to the reason for my visit. Bess, will you consent to marry me?"

Bess had known that William was likely to ask for her hand before long, but now the moment was here the proposal left her speechless for a moment. Marrying William would sweep her into an entirely new life, one she could not have imagined for herself only a few months earlier. She would be Lady Cavendish, wife to a man esteemed by the king and the men closest to him, stepmother to his children, and mistress of her own household. More than she had dreamed possible. William was watching her, and she noted with a surge of tenderness that his gaze held hope and also perhaps a little uncertainty.

"Oh, William. You do me much honor. I will happily be your wife."

William kissed her hands, and then sank onto the chair beside her and, taking her face in his hands, kissed her deeply, in a way that he had never done before. His beard tickled her lips and she found that she liked it.

"Oh, my dearest," he said at last. "I am so glad."

Bess felt touched at the happiness shining in his eyes. A new world was opening before her and already she was sure she had made the right choice.

"When will we be wed? And where will we live?"

"I must be in London some of the time, and I will rent a house that will be comfortable for you, as now I only stay in lodgings. But I would like us to make our home in Northaw, where my girls are. They'll love you, I'm sure."

Bess smiled to think of becoming a mother to William's daughters.

"As for when, perhaps in the summer? There will be much to do over the next months, as the young king's council sets about their business. And of course there will be the coronation. So I thought better to wait until things are quieter. What say you to that?"

Bess had a sudden pang as she thought of leaving young Jane Grey and her little sisters. That would be a difficult parting. Northaw was a day's ride from London, and she would be busy managing the household and estate. Perhaps Jane could come to stay, she thought.

"That suits me well," she said. "It will give me time to plan and make myself ready for all that awaits me." She had a sudden vision of her mother's joy on learning the news and smiled at William. "I must write to my mother. She will be so happy. I cannot wait for her to know you."

"NORFOLK HAS CHEATED THE HEADSMAN," WILLIAM TOLD BESS on a cold evening a month after the king had died.

They stood side by side in the parlor, watching a late flurry of snow drift past the windows.

"He will not die, then?" Bess asked. The Earl of Surrey had been beheaded on Tower Hill only a week before King Henry's death, but though his father, Norfolk, had been condemned, he had not yet been put to death.

"No," William answered. "He was to be executed on the morning of the day that the king died, but the order was never given to send him to the block. I think they don't know what to do with him now. No one dares send him to his death, lest taking that step should one day lead to his own. Not even the Duke of Somerset."

On the day of King Henry's funeral, Edward Seymour, now Lord Protector, had made himself Duke of Somerset. The other regents were ennobled, too. Seymour's ally John Dudley was created Earl of Warwick and William Parr was made Marquess of Northampton.

Thomas Wriothesley, who had successfully negotiated the perilous tides in which he had swum and come safe to shore under a new king, was now Earl of Southampton. King Henry had refused to include Thomas Seymour among the regents, but he, favored uncle of the new king, was now Baron Seymour of Sudeley Castle.

"Events are moving fast," William said. "Already the heresy laws are repealed. King Edward is a reformer."

Bess thought of Anne Askew and the other evangelicals who had died so recently for their beliefs, which were now quite legal.

"And it's an odd thing," William said, "but the prophecy caught up with King Henry."

Bess turned to look at William. His face looked eerie in the flickering candlelight. "Prophecy?" she asked.

"During the king's great matter, as it was called, a friar preached a sermon to the king that if he cast away Queen Catherine to marry Anne Boleyn, dogs should lick his blood, as they had done Ahab's. Well, on the way to Windsor, the king's funeral procession stopped for the night at Syon, and the king's body lay in the abbey overnight."

Bess felt gooseflesh shiver over her body. Syon Abbey was where Cat Howard had last been free, before she was bundled shrieking into the boat that would take her to the Tower and her death.

"In the morning," William continued, "it was seen that the lead coffin had ruptured and dark fluid had pooled upon the floor. A plumber was sent for to seal the coffin. His dog came along with him."

"No—!" Bess gasped.

"Yes. When the guards came back into the abbey, they saw that the dog was licking the blood from the floor."

CHAPTER FIFTEEN

Sixth of July, 1547—London

It was a glorious day and Bess turned her face upward to the unbroken brilliant blue of the sky.

"Not a cloud in sight," Jane Grey cried happily.

The tide was going out and the wherry moved swiftly in the sparkling water. They were returning to Dorset House from Whitehall, where Jane had delighted in an unfettered two-hour visit with her cousin King Edward. Bess had been touched to see Jane throw off the cares that usually seemed to weigh her down as she laughed and played. It was the first time she had seen the young king, usually so somber and stiff, behave truly like a boy. He had looked pale and fragile, though, and she had felt a tug at her heart at the thought that he reminded her of her poor Robbie.

Jane put her hand in Bess's. Her eyes were anxious.

"Will you come to visit me in Chelsea?"

"Of course," Bess replied. "It's just down the river, not on the moon." But she felt a pang of sadness that she would no longer be living in the same house as Jane.

In May, London had been shocked to learn that the widowed

Queen Catherine Parr had secretly married her former suitor Thomas Seymour. They were living in Seymour's manor house in Chelsea, with his mother and the queen's stepdaughter the Lady Elizabeth. Harry and Frances Grey had recently agreed to Seymour's proposal that Jane should become his ward and soon she would take up residence in the Seymour household.

"My father says that Thomas Seymour wants me to marry the king," Jane said. "But Edward Seymour wants me to marry his son, Edward. What do you think of that?"

What Bess thought was that Jane would have little say in the matter. She had heard Lord and Lady Dorset discussing the struggle for power and growing animosity between Thomas Seymour and his brother Edward Seymour, the Lord Protector. The news that old King Henry's will had placed the Grey girls in the line of succession to the throne after his own children had increased Jane's value in the marriage market. She was now regarded almost as a princess, just as her parents had always treated her.

"I think," Bess said, pulling Jane into her arms, "that either of the gentlemen would be lucky to get you. I'm sure your parents will make a wise decision. But fortunately nothing needs to happen for the present."

"When are you leaving London?" Jane asked. Her voice was sad and Bess felt a lump form in her throat.

"In August. Your mother has most generously offered that we should be married at Bradgate, you know. And then we'll go to Northaw."

"I wish you weren't going so far away."

"I do, too. And of all the people I'll be leaving behind, I'll miss you most. Perhaps you can come to visit."

The clamor of steel striking stone rose over the water and they both turned to look at the north bank of the river, where a small army of men was at work on the grand new house that the Earl of Somerset was building.

"He tore down a church," Jane said, shading her eyes against the sun. "It scarcely seems right, even though it was a Papist church."

"No," Bess agreed. King Henry's break with the church and the dissolution of the monasteries had resulted in church properties all over England being turned over to private hands, but it made her sad to think of the destruction of so many beautiful buildings that had stood for so long.

"You won't forget me, will you?"

Bess turned back to look at Jane. There were tears in Jane's eyes, and Bess could not hold back her own tears now.

"Of course not. You're like a little sister to me, sweeting." She took Jane's face in her hands and kissed her forehead. "Now listen to me. I want you to remember this when I'm not near to remind you of it. You're a smart, loving, brave girl. No one who has met you could help loving you. Certainly they could never forget you. You'll be at my wedding, and we'll see what we can do to arrange for you to come stay at Northaw later this year. But even when we're apart, you'll be at the center of my heart."

CHAPTER SIXTEEN

First of August, 1547—Dorset House, London

BESS STARED AGHAST AT HER MOTHER'S LETTER AND READ IT through again.

> *It grieves me greatly to tell you of a matter involving your sister that touches me to the heart, and which I pray may not cause harm to you. Alice's husband accuses her of playing him false, and has cast her out of his house. I hoped that once his temper cooled, all could be resolved. But he is not only adamant that he will not take her back, he has sold his family's old lands, "rather than let bastards be his heirs," as he says.*

How could Alice be so stupid? Bess wondered. To risk the loss of husband and home by committing adultery—what could she gain by it but shame and grief, not only for herself but for all her family? Two families, for Alice's husband Francis Leche was related to Ralph Leche, stepfather to Alice and Bess.

Bess threw the letter down and paced, her mind whirling. Was it really true? Perhaps Alice's husband was wrong. But if it were true, what would William think? Would he fear that if her sister could deceive her husband, so might Bess? She felt trapped, afraid to tell him, but fearing that if she didn't tell him and he later learned of the matter he would know she had done as much as lie to him, which would look as if she had something to hide. No, she would have to tell him, and pray that it did not cause him to reconsider marrying her. She cursed Alice for putting her in such a position, and took up the letter again.

The land that Francis sold has been in the Leche family for genera-
tions, and adjoins lands that your father owns, so the family is suing
to overturn the sale and have the land returned to them. Unfortu-
nately, Thomas Agarde, who bought the lands, has connections with
Thomas Seymour, the Lord High Admiral, who has taken up his fight.

If Thomas Seymour was involved, Bess thought, it was very possible that William would hear of the matter. On the other hand, perhaps William would be able to convince Seymour that the Leches should have their land, which Francis Leche, in his anger, had sold at a bargain price.

"I SEE." WILLIAM'S FACE WAS GRAVE WHEN HE LOOKED UP FROM THE letter from Bess's mother, and Bess watched anxiously as he paced.

"I would never . . ." she began, but could speak no more, and wept with frustration and fear.

William came swiftly to where she sat and stooped to look into her face. "My Bess, dry your tears. Of course I don't doubt that you would be ever faithful. You are not your sister."

"I can scarcely believe it's true, what they say of her," she said. "But I thank you. For understanding, and for not . . ." She buried her face against his chest, comforted by his familiar scent—wool and soap, cedar from the chests in which he kept his clothes, and a faint whiff of horse.

"No, I don't question you. I was just pondering how to put this question before my lord."

"You mean that Edward Seymour might concern himself with whether the lands should be returned to the Leches?" Bess's hopes rose. Just then sunshine falling through the windows grew brighter as the cloud covering the sun drifted away, and she smiled and wiped her tears.

"I think he will. And if his brother is representing the other party, perhaps it can all be dealt with without the need of going to court."

Nineteenth of August, 1547—Bradgate House, Leicestershire

Today was the day that Bess and Sir William Cavendish were to be married at the Greys' home, but the king had unexpectedly summoned William to London a week earlier to deal with urgent treasury matters.

"I will be back by the nineteenth of August," William had assured Bess as he leaned down from the saddle to kiss her good-bye. "Were it not His Majesty who calls, you know I would not go."

"I know," Bess said. "I know how important it is."

William had told her that when he had become treasurer of the chamber the previous year, the accounts had been in wild disorder. With diligent work he had done much to right them since then, and for his pains he was more than twenty-five thousand pounds richer than he had begun the year. It was a vast amount of money; enough to buy or build a grand home, furnish it, hire the needful servants, and run the household into the bargain. Bess was astonished to hear him talk of such sums, and amazed all over again at his having taken the care to help her secure her dower rights of thirty pounds a year, an amount which at the time she had thought would stand between her and ruin. Her own father had gone to debtors' prison over a few hundred pounds.

She stood gazing out a window of the upper floor of Bradgate House. From here she could see the road on which William would approach, stretching away into the distance and disappearing at the horizon. No cloud of dust or hint of movement heralded his arrival.

At the dawn of day, she had not worried that William was not yet come. But now, when the sun was past the mark of noon, a shred of doubt crossed her mind. Suppose he had changed his mind? What if he had been thrown into doubt by Alice's unfaithfulness to her husband? Or perhaps there was another lady in London who had caught his eye, and even at this moment he was with her, or debating whether to proceed with the marriage.

Bess's gaze fell on the gown in which she was to be married. It was laid out on her bed, its deep blue set off by inner sleeves embroidered with a pattern of leaves and flowers, beside it a new chemise, soft and fine as a cobweb. On the floor lay a pair of new slippers, in buttery kid leather. How many times over the past weeks had she pictured herself in her wedding clothes, standing by William's side? Should she shut them away again? She didn't think she would be able to bear it if the sun rose the next morning and still he had not come.

She thought of what a crowd of friends and relations had gathered for the wedding. Her parents, Jem, and her younger sisters had all come from Hardwick—even Alice, repentant and sheepish—and her older sisters and their husbands had traveled from farther afield. Lizzie was here, with William Parr, glorying in his new position of influence as regent and uncle to the king. Doll had come with her husband, a cousin of hers whose mother came of an old Derbyshire family and knew the Hardwicks. Jane Grey had journeyed from London, and she and her seven-year-old sister Kate were Bess's bridesmaids. And of course the rest of the Grey household was present, including Frances's stepmother, the Duchess of Suffolk, and her boys.

Two of William's daughters, twelve-year-old Kitty and seven-year-old Nan, had arrived the day before, pleased to be included in the festivities and shy about meeting their new stepmother. His other girl, Polly, was absent, for she had been simple since birth, and had spent the years since her mother's death in the close care of the wife of one of William's tenants, not quite of the family and not quite apart from it.

Bess felt that she must be as nervous as her new stepdaughters, for she wanted them to love her. She thought they had got off to a good start, for they were delighted with the little gifts she had brought them, ribbons and fine lace from London for Kitty and a little doll she had made herself for Nan. And the Grey girls had done their best to welcome the girls, Jane conversing with Kitty, and Kate Grey pleased to meet Nan and have a new friend of just her age.

A host of William's friends and associates from London had come. His brother George, who had prospered in his long service under Cardinal Wolsey, was an important man, and had helped William rise in the world. Sir John Thynne was steward to William's patron, Edward Seymour, the Lord Protector. Bess immediately liked young William Cecil, Seymour's secretary, and understood why her William valued him as a friend. He was another rising man, but warm and plainspoken, a man to be trusted, she thought. His new wife, Mildred, was only a year or two older than Bess herself, and seemed a little shy at the exalted company.

If William failed to come, Bess thought, she would be embarrassed before this host of people. She couldn't imagine having the strength to face down such shame.

"Ah, Bess." Frances Grey entered the room and came to Bess's side at the window. "You're not to worry, my dear. I have every confidence that William will be here. If not today then tomorrow."

Frances took her hand, and Bess thought how fortunate she was to have her patronage and support. More than that, her love. She smiled.

"Thank you, my lady. I know you're right. It's just that I still wonder sometimes what he sees in me."

"You don't give yourself the credit you should. You're a very intelligent and capable girl, as well as lovely. When Sir William began to work with you to prepare for your court case he told me he was mightily impressed with you in every way. You'd make a fine wife for any man."

Frances's words reassured Bess, and that afternoon she distracted herself with a walk with her mother and the Grey and Cavendish girls, luxuriating in the summer sunshine. The entire company of family and friends gathered for supper, a more sumptuous meal than Bess had ever eaten. It was all in her honor, but she was keenly conscious that she was a bride without a bridegroom.

After supper there was music and dancing. As Bess passed down the middle of a laughing and clapping set of dancers on the arm of Harry Grey, she recalled how dazzled she had been during the Zouches' festivities on Christmas night that first year in London. She remembered the thrill she had felt when Edmund had pulled her off into the shadows with him under the mistletoe, and the intoxicating feeling of his lips on hers and the heat she saw in his eyes. She had never felt like that in William's company. Of course, he was old enough to be her father, twice widowed already, and he did not behave like a roistering boy. But she hoped that perhaps she might feel some spark of passion and excitement when once he took her in his arms. *If he ever did*, whispered a voice at the back of her head.

The candles were burning low now, and Bess saw that Frances Grey was directing the servants to take away the tarts and sweetmeats, the cold roast and cheeses. The evening was at an end then, and still no sign of William.

"He will come, my darling." Bess started at the sound of her mother's voice and hoped she had not been looking forlorn, for she had striven all day to be cheerful.

"I know," she said. "At least I think he will. He's a good man, Mother. You'll like him."

"Bess!" Frances Grey was hurrying toward them. "William's secretary Bestenay has just arrived."

"Without William?" Bess's heart pounded. Was he not coming, then?

"He brings word, he says, but he will speak only to you."

Bess glanced at her mother in agitation.

"Come," her mother said, taking her hand. "Surely Sir William is on his way."

They found Bestenay in Harry Grey's office, his cloak heavy with dust and his boots spattered with mud.

"Mistress," he said as he bowed, "my master bid me tell you that he will be with you this night."

A surge of relief swept through Bess.

"But where is he?" she cried. "When did he leave London?"

"I left two days ago," Bestenay said, mopping his ruddy face with his handkerchief, "and he purposed to leave the next morning, as soon as he had finished his business. He bade me tell you that it couldn't be helped, but that he would make up for his tardiness by what he brought you."

"I thank you," Bess said. "Go to the kitchen. They'll feed you and get you settled."

Frances Grey nearly collided with Bestenay as he turned to leave. He bowed his apology and hustled away.

"Well, now at least we know when to expect him," Frances said. "All is in readiness." She came to Bess's side and kissed her. "I'll leave you to your mother's care."

"Why don't you lie down for a while, dear heart?" Bess's mother urged when they were in Bess's bedchamber. "I'll wake you the minute he arrives. After all, you want to be rested for tonight." She came closer to Bess. "Is there anything you wish to ask me? Perhaps I should have spoken to you sooner about matters between a husband and wife."

"No," Bess said, blushing. Robbie had died leaving her a virgin, but as a married woman and a widow she had been privy to many whispered conversations among the giggling ladies at court and in the Zouche and Grey households and she knew what to expect on her wedding night.

"From all that you and Lady Dorset have told me," her mother said, "Sir William is a kind man and loves you well. I have no doubt he'll be gentle and patient."

As it turned out it was near midnight before Bess's mother woke her with the news that William had arrived. Bess threw on a loose gown and ran barefoot down the stairs. He stood in the great hall, bundled in a traveling cloak, his hair awry. When he saw Bess, he hastened to her and clasped her to him.

"I'm so sorry, my own love. I couldn't help the delay. I didn't mean to worry you."

His arms were tight around her and his body was cold from the night air, but Bess felt happy and safe now that he was with her.

"We can wait until tomorrow for the wedding," she assured him. "You must be ready to drop with exhaustion."

"No," he said. "I don't want to wait a minute longer than I must. Give me but time to wash and put on clean clothes, and let us be married."

"Very well," she said, kissing his stubbled cheek. "Nothing would make me happier."

"I will give you my wedding gift now," he said, "because I would have you wear it while we are wed."

He pulled a small packet of wool from within his clothes and handed it to her. Bess's fingers fumbled with the ribbon that tied it, and she gasped as the little bundle fell open. Within it lay a teardrop-shaped pearl on a gold chain.

"Oh, my love," she whispered. "I've never seen anything so beautiful."

He fastened the chain around her neck and looked down at her, eyes alight with tenderness and joy.

"Even more lovely than I had imagined."

THE SAVORIES AND SWEETMEATS WERE BROUGHT OUT AND THE aroma of spiced wine drifted into the great hall. Frances Grey and her daughters, and Bess's mother and sisters, gathered around her as she was helped into her wedding gown. Her mother brushed her hair and settled a wreath of flowers atop her head. And at two in the morning of the twentieth of August, Bess became the wife of Sir William Cavendish. Lady Cavendish, she was now, though she could hardly believe it.

What had been intended as the wedding breakfast was served up as a predawn supper, the dozens of candles in their branched holders casting a magical glow on the darkened hall.

"We'll have dancing and more festivities tomorrow," Harry Grey said. "I know you've had a long day, Will. And I'm sure you're eager for your bed."

He cuffed William Cavendish on the shoulder and kissed Bess's cheek.

William took up a candle and held out a hand to Bess, and they made their way up the stairs to Bess's bedchamber. In their absence it had been prepared for their nuptial night. The air was sweet with the scent of the great bundles of roses that stood in bowls and vases and the rose petals that dotted the bedclothes. A fire burned cheerfully on the hearth.

The door closed, and they were alone at last, man and wife.

William bent to kiss Bess. She felt shy at the thought of giving herself to him as she knew she was about to do, but his warm hands were gentle on her skin and she was not afraid.

"May I undo you, my love?" he asked.

"Sure, I could never be undone as long as you are with me," she said, smiling.

He unlaced her bodice and unhooked the fastenings of her skirts and helped her step out of them. She stood in her snowy chemise, her hair tumbling around her shoulders, the wreath of blossoms still on her head.

"You are so very beautiful," he murmured, hands caressing her shoulders.

Then he picked her up and carried her to the big soft bed. She watched as he threw off his doublet and breeches. Clad only in his shirt, he climbed into bed beside her and took her into his arms.

DINNER THE NEXT DAY WAS ANOTHER CELEBRATORY MEAL, AND with William at her side, Bess felt truly happy.

"Lady Cavendish." Harry Grey grinned at Bess across the table. "How like you married life?"

He winked and the other guests laughed. Bess felt herself go pink, but didn't mind his teasing.

"Oh, fie, Harry!" Frances Grey exclaimed. "Don't embarrass the girl."

"Never mind, my lady," Bess said. "Sir, with such a husband as I have, I like married life very well."

She turned to William and he reached out for her hand and kissed it.

"There was no time for gifts last night," Frances said, "but I have something for you."

She placed a little gilded box on the table before Bess. Inside it was a brooch of heavy gold set with a piece of polished black agate. Bess held it out for William to see.

"It's stunning," she said. "I cannot thank you enough, madam."

"A jewel fit for the jewel you are. I had it made for you in London."

Bess touched William's necklace at her throat. "How rich I am, both in finery and in love."

"I have something for you, too!" Jane cried, presenting Bess with a little bundle of cloth tied with ribbon. Bess undid it and found that it contained a miniature portrait of Jane.

"How marvelous!" she exclaimed, hugging Jane. "The painter has got you exactly!" She touched a finger to the rosebud lips of the portrait. "Now I can have you with me even when you're far away."

She looked around the table and felt overcome with gratitude for all that Harry and Frances Grey had done for her.

"I thank you both," she said. "You have been more kind to me than I could ever have hoped, and have helped me to such a life as I never dreamed possible."

"And now that life is just beginning," Frances said. She raised her goblet in a toast to Bess and William. "And may it be long and happy."

Part Three

MOTHER

CHAPTER SEVENTEEN

Sixteenth of June, 1548—Northaw Manor, Hertfordshire

BESS GAZED DOWN AT HER BELLY, SCARCELY ABLE TO BELIEVE how big it was. She had conceived soon after she and William had been married, and she would be brought to bed any day. She had already spent the past month immured in the birthing chamber, its walls and ceiling heavily hung with carpets and tapestries.

"It's so dark!" she had protested as the windows had been covered over. But the midwife had insisted that it must be so, that ladies near their time must be sequestered, away from worries and foul air.

"At least leave me one window that I may open," Bess had begged, and in that she had prevailed. So now she stood at the one unobstructed window, a golden square of light in the gloom of the chamber, hands clasped across her burgeoning middle. Below her on the old abbey grounds, the farm was busily carrying on with its daily round beneath the afternoon sun. A cackling rose from the poultry house as a kitchen boy entered. Cattle lowed as they were driven out to pasture. In the meadow beyond, two lads were gingerly beginning the task of drawing bees from one of the hives so they could gather the honey.

Just below Bess, in the kitchen garden, her younger sister, Jenny, was plucking sprigs of lavender to brew in hot water for Bess to bathe in. Bess had been pleased when Jenny had accepted her invitation to join her household as a lady-in-waiting, both because she was fond of her sister and took pleasure in her company, and because she was gratified at being able to offer Jenny opportunities she lacked at Hardwick. Jenny was fifteen, already worried about her prospects for a good marriage, whereas Bess had been only twelve when she went to serve Lady Zouche.

Leaving home had been easier for Jenny than it had been for her, Bess reflected. After all, she was going to live with her sister, and not among strangers. And their aunt Marcella Lynacre, a widow, had come at the same time, bringing with her a complement of a dozen servants, girls and lads from near Hardwick, happy to have good positions in service in Bess's house.

As if she felt her sister's eyes on her, Jenny looked upward and broke into a grin to see Bess looking down at her.

"That's all you do, is stand in that window!" she teased.

"It's all I can do! I can find no comfort in any position when I lie down."

"Soon it will be over, and all worth it."

"Yes, please God." Bess said a silent prayer that both she and her baby would come safely through the ordeal of childbirth.

"There you are, Mistress Jenny!" William's secretary, John Bestenay, came around the side of the house. "There's a letter come for Lady Cavendish."

He handed the folded square of paper to Jenny and retreated toward the kitchen door.

"I'll bring it up directly," Jenny called. "Is there anything you lack?"

"More water, if you please," Bess said. "With some lemons. And some of those ginger cakes if there are any left."

Jenny appeared at the door of Bess's room in a few minutes with the refreshments and the letter.

"It's from Jane Grey!" Bess cried as she broke the seal. "Written from Sudeley."

She sat on a chair in the sunlight and read, smiling her thanks as Jenny handed her a glass of water with lemon.

"She's left London with Queen Catherine and Thomas Seymour." Even though Catherine Parr was now the wife of Thomas Seymour, to Bess she would always be the queen that had outlived King Henry.

"And are they all well?" Jenny asked, gathering up some petals that had fallen from the big jar of roses that stood on a table near the bed.

"They are in health," Bess said. "But alas, heavy hearts all around, from the sound of it. The queen endeavors to be cheerful with her husband, but is sad to be parted from the Lady Elizabeth, and distressed at the reason for the parting, Jane writes. And, oh, dear, she says that poor Elizabeth wept most bitterly when she left Chelsea a month gone by, heartbroken and unable to bear her stepmother's coldness."

"A sad business," Jenny said.

Jane Grey had written to Bess regularly since joining the Seymour household, and Bess had been appalled to hear of the tumult that had taken place in April. Catherine Parr had walked in on her husband and Elizabeth in an embrace that was far from what was proper between a man and his stepdaughter. When Bess had learned the news, she had thought back to the day at Whitehall when she had met Sudeley, how she had felt the color rise to her cheeks as he looked down at her. It was easy to imagine that he might have had the same effect on the fifteen-year-old Elizabeth.

Catherine Parr had been beside herself with rage and hurt, and despair at the knowledge that as much as she loved both of them, she could no longer trust either of them fully, and her household could not contain them both.

She feels herself a fool, Jane Grey had written, *because only now does she learn that Thomas Seymour courted the Lady Elizabeth before he turned his attention to her, which of course many people knew at the time.*

"Is the queen not shortly to be delivered of a child?" Jenny asked.

"Yes," Bess said, laying the letter on her lap and letting her hand caress the bold signature of Jane Grey. "But not for another month or two, I think. Poor lady. She little needs more grief at such a time."

On the evening of the seventeenth of June, Bess's pains began. Through the night she gasped and shrieked as she labored to bring forth her child. All the windows were covered now, and she no longer knew whether it was day or night. It seemed she had been in that room forever, the sweat drenching her nightdress and her hair, the still and heavy air causing her head to pound and stifling her as she gasped for breath, the flickering candlelight making her think she was in a tomb as she fell into a few moments of uneasy sleep only to be torn into wakefulness by another wrenching pain.

She lacked for no care or company, attended by the midwife, Aunt Marcella, Jenny, and all the female servants of the household by turn. At last, shortly after three o'clock on the afternoon of the eighteenth of June, she gave a last shuddering heave and felt the baby leave her. She closed her eyes and wept with relief, and in a few moments cried out with joy at the sound of her baby's cry and at the miraculous slippery, red-faced being that was placed in her arms.

"A girl," the midwife said. "And as bonny and healthy a baby as I've ever seen."

CUSTOM DICTATED THAT A NEWLY DELIVERED MOTHER MUST NOT rise from her bed for a fortnight, but Bess, though tired, was eager to be on her feet and doing again. She was up and about a few days after her daughter's birth, and making plans for the christening.

"Look how many letters are come today!" Jenny exclaimed, bringing Bess a handful of sealed packets.

"Oh," Bess cried. "This is from Frances Grey. She and Lord Dorset and the girls will be here, as well as her stepmother the Duchess of Suffolk and her sons. Lady Dorset and Lady Suffolk are to be godmothers, and the young Duke of Suffolk will be godfather. And this from Lady Zouche. And this from Lizzie—I've told you of Lizzie, have I not?"

At last came Bess's upsitting, when she was officially permitted to sit in her bed and even to stir from it, though not too far. She insisted now that the windows be uncovered, and as Frances Grey and her daughters, Catherine Willoughby, William's daughters, and other of her friends joined her and Jenny and Aunt Marcella for refreshment and happy gossip, the room was full of sunlight and warm summer breezes.

When Bess emerged from her chamber for the christening, bearing her little daughter dressed in a flowing white gown, she felt like a queen. William's eyes were alight with joy. He had lost five children born to his previous two wives, and looking at her daughter's perfect little face, Bess wondered how anyone could survive such losses.

The house was full of Brandons and Greys and Cavendishes, come to honor Bess's child, little Frances.

"Of course she could be christened for no one but you, my lady," Bess said to Frances Grey. "For it was you who gave me such love and so many wonderful opportunities while I was in your service. Not least the introduction to my dear husband."

She held out a hand to William and he came to her side and kissed her cheek.

"It is I who am blessed to have you by my side, my love. I thank God for your safe deliverance and that of the child."

It was a glorious afternoon, fleecy clouds scudding across the azure sky and the scent of ripening fruit in the air. Bess smiled as she watched golden-haired Henry, the twelve-year-old Duke of Suffolk, and his younger brother, Charles, race around the lawn, their dignity cast off for the moment.

CHAPTER EIGHTEEN

Fifteenth of August, 1548—Newgate Street, London

W ILL TWO SWANS BE ENOUGH?" BESS ASKED THE COOK.
"I think so, madam. After all, there will also be roast beef, oysters, eels, a great pie of venison, and fricassee of chickens. As well as the kickshaws, salads, fruit, sweets, and nuts."

Bess was huddled in the kitchen with her steward and cook, reviewing the list of the dishes and wine to be served, the silver plate to be polished, and the servants needed to wait at table. The preparations for the supper had been going on for days, and she was exhausted. She had been alternately exhilarated and anxious since she and William had begun to make plans for the evening. Everything must be perfect. It would be the first London social event that she would preside over as Lady Cavendish, and though the guests were not many, they were some of the most powerful people in the kingdom.

They had talked carefully over whom to invite. Of primary importance were William's patron Edward Seymour, Lord Protector of the young king, and his wife Anne.

"The king begins to chafe at how strictly Edward Seymour keeps him," William said. "And there is much resentment against him by the people. The dissolution of the chantries and all they supported has done much harm, including reducing the value of properties held by the guilds. And since the heresy laws were struck down, there has been such an outbreak of preaching and teaching by every sort of hedge-priest and wild-eyed evangelical. But the fact remains that Seymour is king in all but name."

"And he has just settled that matter of the Leche lands in our favor," Bess reminded him. "So of course we must have him and his wife."

"Of course," William agreed. "And close behind Seymour in power is John Dudley. And between us and the fencepost, it would not surprise me if Dudley elbows Seymour out of his way before long."

"Then they must be here," Bess said, carefully adding to her list John Dudley, Earl of Warwick and Lord Great Chamberlain, and his wife Jane. "The king much favors his uncle Thomas Seymour, does he not?"

"He does. But Thomas is much out of his brother's grace still, after wedding Queen Catherine without his leave. And fortunately, they are at Sudeley, awaiting the birth of their child, so we need not worry about them."

"I cannot stomach the thought of entertaining Thomas Wriothesley," Bess had said with a shudder. She could never think of him without envisaging him turning the wheels of the rack himself to torture Anne Askew.

"We may safely leave him out," William said. "I think neither Seymour nor Dudley trusts him entirely, and without either of them, he has no power."

"Of course we must have Harry and Frances Grey and Catherine Willoughby," Bess suggested.

"Certainly, for love and old friendship as well as for their importance."

"And Lizzie and William Parr?"

"Yes, Parr is one to keep on our side. He is much beloved by the king, and the council might just give him leave to divorce his wife, so Lizzie may yet become Marchioness of Northampton."

"Good," Bess said, adding the two names to the list. "Besides, he's our landlord."

Now, with the guests invited and the supper almost at hand, Bess ran an eye over the list of the items to be bought at market and shook her head as she counted out coins to the steward.

"Jesu, the cost of the spices alone would feed a poor family for a week," she exclaimed, and then wished she hadn't. After all, she was no longer the young girl at Hardwick who had been terrified that the king's men might seize the family's only cow, but the mistress of a substantial household. And she knew that William would not question whatever the entertainment cost.

She stood and straightened the apron she wore over her gown of dark gray wool.

"I thank you both for your care in this matter," she told the cook and steward. "I know I can rely on you to ensure that the evening is a success."

She passed through the dining room, where two servants were ironing table linen, and made her way upstairs to her bedchamber. Her maid Cecily was sewing gold buttons onto the sleeves of the plum-colored velvet gown Bess would wear for the supper, and she felt a thrill at the beauty of the material as its sheen caught the sunlight. It was the finest garment she had yet owned, and when the tailor had delivered it and she had stood before the mirror, the reflection that stared back at her was that of a grand lady, a wife eminently suited to a prosperous gentleman well situated at court.

Bess wished suddenly that Jenny would be there to help her dress on the great night, but her sister, along with Aunt Marcella, was at Northaw tending to baby Frankie, as little Frances had come to be called. Bess's stepdaughters Kitty and Nan, at fourteen and ten years of age, were too old to need a nurse, but William had resisted their pleas to come to London.

"I'll be very busy, and the plague is always a danger in town in the summer."

He had bent to kiss Nan's dark curls as he and Bess took their leave, and Bess thought he must see behind her the shadows of the five little children he'd lost.

AT LAST THE EVENING OF THE SUPPER CAME. BESS WAS NERVOUS beyond measure as the time approached when guests would begin to arrive. Cecily was lacing Bess into her gown when her maid Nell came into the room and curtsied.

"My lady, the Lord Northampton and his lady are here."

"So soon! Well, ask Mistress Brooke to join me while I finish dressing."

"Bess!" Lizzie cried as she sailed into the room. "Oh, you look enchanting! Such a color—perfect for your hair and complexion."

"You are most beautiful yourself this night," Bess said, embracing Lizzie, who was radiant in a gown the color of claret, rich with gold embroidery. She examined the strand of gleaming pearls around Lizzie's throat. "New?"

"Yes. From William." Lizzie's dark eyes were sparkling. "Bess, I have news to tell you. But it's a secret." She glanced at Cecily.

"Oh, Cecily won't tell, will you?" Bess said. "Besides, I need her. Come, sit by my side and tell me all while Cecily completes me here."

Lizzie sat on the edge of a chair and leaned close to Bess. "We are married."

"What?" Bess shook off Cecily's hands and turned to look at Lizzie.

"Yes, it's true! William said he could wait no longer, and now we are man and wife."

Bess sat stunned for a moment, and spoke carefully.

"Lizzie, of course I'm so happy for you. But . . . he is still married to Anne Bourchier, isn't he?"

"In name." Lizzie waved a hand airily, as if that could dissolve the bonds of an inconvenient marriage. "But soon the council will grant him a divorce, and then we can marry again properly and publicly."

"Who knows?" Bess asked, as Cecily placed a pearl-encrusted cap on her head and pinned it in place.

"No one. Well, the priest of course, and William's steward and secretary were witnesses, but that's all. And no one must know, for Edward Seymour would be enraged!"

Bess's heart sank. No nobleman was permitted to marry without the authorization of the Lord Protector, and Seymour had been furious when his brother Thomas had married Catherine Parr without his permission. He hadn't been able to do much but roar and seethe and keep Thomas Seymour from having any influence with the privy council. But this was a different case. Lizzie was not the former queen, and the penalty for marrying bigamously was death.

"Oh, he'd never have William executed," Lizzie said, as if reading Bess's mind. "William is the king's uncle, too, don't forget. But still, William says we must wait until the time is right to make all known."

Edward Seymour had spies all over London, Bess knew. What if he had already learned of the marriage? God in heaven, what disaster would the evening become then? And could she tell William? Warn him, so that he was not caught flat-footed if Seymour did know? She stared at Lizzie in dismay. This night must be perfect, and she had striven so hard to ensure that it was so. And now this.

"Your ladyship, the Duke and Duchess of Somerset are here," Nell said from the door.

Bess said a silent prayer for help and stood. There was nothing for it but to go like a bear to the stake, and hope that all would be well.

"Come," she said, offering a hand to Lizzie. "I'm terrified of the duchess. She likes you, doesn't she? Perhaps you can keep her from eating me alive."

"MY LORD AND MY LADY, YOU DO US HONOR WITH YOUR PRESENCE," Bess said, sinking into a curtsy before Edward and Anne Seymour.

She turned to William Parr, who returned her bow. "And you, my lord. It's a great pleasure to welcome you."

"Lady Cavendish." Edward Seymour smiled down at Bess. His eyes were the same rich brown as those of his brother, but his gaze was respectful. As he bowed to Lizzie, he gave no sign that he knew of the secret marriage, and Bess relaxed a little as she turned to his wife. Anne Seymour had the reputation of being sharp-tongued and domineering, even over her powerful husband, and Bess did her best not to quail under her piercing glance. She was saved from any immediate need to make conversation, though, by the arrival of Harry and Frances Grey, together with Catherine Willoughby.

"Please come this way—wine is waiting!" William said, when the guests had greeted each other. He led them toward the great chamber where the table was laid for supper, and Bess was pleased beyond words when Frances Grey gave her a nod and smile of approval as she surveyed the table draped in snowy linen and laden with gleaming plate.

Soon the rest of the party arrived. John Dudley's arched eyebrows, dark eyes, and forked beard put Bess in mind of the devil. Jane Dudley seemed his opposite, softly pretty, belying her forty years, Bess thought, and with a gentle voice.

The cook had outdone himself, and each dish that arrived at the table was greeted with approbation and murmurs of enjoyment.

Bess had been particularly apprehensive about welcoming the Duchess of Somerset into her home, but Anne Seymour seemed to have taken a liking to her, and this helped to calm her nerves. It was a stroke of luck that the lady had been delivered of a son only a few days before Bess had given birth to Frances, for it gave them a natural topic of conversation.

"I hope you have found a wet nurse who is suitably sweet tempered and fair of face?" she inquired, speaking across Harry Grey and taking a hearty swallow of canary wine. "For of course the temperament of the nurse flows with the milk, and it would never do to entrust your dear child to some foul-tempered slut."

Bess met the duchess's eyes with a disarming smile.

"Yes, madam. We were fortunate that a most amiable woman, wife of one of Sir William's tenants, had recently been brought to bed of the most charming fat little pair of twins I've ever seen, and she gives suck to the three of them in turn most deftly."

"I am pleased to hear it. There are some who think they know all there is to the matter of raising children, though they have never before been mothers."

Bess realized this must be a reference to Queen Catherine, who would shortly give birth to her first child at Sudeley Castle. William had told her that Catherine Parr and the duchess had been at war for some months over the issue of Catherine's request to be sent the jewels traditionally worn by the queen, now sequestered in the treasury.

"Anne Seymour considers herself to be all but queen and wants to keep the jewels for herself until such time as King Edward marries," William had said. "She's most unwilling to give precedence to the wife of her husband's younger brother, queen though she was, and the jewels have become the battleground."

"Do you not think it most peculiar," the duchess went on, "that Catherine Parr should be with child now, with her fourth husband, when she never before conceived in all her thirty-six years?" She gave an arch smile. "Of course, she married the king in his doting days, when he had brought himself so low by his lust and cruelty that no lady who stood on her honor would venture on him."

Bess glanced down the table to see if William Parr had heard the duchess's commentary on his sister, but he appeared to be listening intently to Catherine Willoughby, the Duchess of Suffolk, resplendent in black satin with silver embroidery.

"Sudeley has become like a second court," Anne Seymour pronounced. "Catherine Parr thinks herself the queen yet. Why, when she was at court not long past she demanded that I carry her train!" She gave a scornful little laugh.

Bess was mortified at the thought that William Parr might hear the diatribe and think she had said anything to indicate that she regarded his sister with the same disdain that the Duchess of Somerset seemed to. She glanced across the table and was relieved that Jane Dudley gave her a conspiratorial smile and rolled her eyes. Lady Warwick was a close friend of Catherine Parr, Bess knew, but perhaps she thought it pointless to argue the merit of Catherine Parr's position. Anne Seymour did not observe or took no notice of the reaction, and carried relentlessly on.

"Why, pray you, should I give place to her who in her former estate was but Latimer's widow, and is now fain to cast herself for support on a younger brother? If her husband can teach her no better manners, there are those that will!"

Her voice had risen and the others at the table could not help but hear her. Bess thought that Edward Seymour looked embarrassed, but he said nothing to his wife, only resumed his conversation with Lizzie.

When the company rose from the table after supper, Jane Dudley came to Bess's side.

"You mustn't mind what Anne Seymour says too much," she murmured, with a glance at the Duchess of Somerset. "We were all friends together in the old days, you know, she and Catherine Parr and I. Anne wants power above all else, and got a taste of it when King Henry turned his eyes on her sister-in-law Jane Seymour. Queen Jane's death dealt a blow to Anne's ambitions, but when Edward Seymour became Lord Protector, she thought herself near to a queen indeed. She finds Catherine Parr's continued presence on this earth a mighty inconvenience."

Bess was a little taken aback and didn't quite know what to say, so she just smiled, but Jane Dudley didn't seem to find anything amiss in her response and moved on into the parlor where the sweets would be served.

"Oh, how cunning!" Lizzie cried, examining a marzipan nest containing brightly colored birds cast in sugar. "And sugar plate goblets! Exquisite!"

Bess was gratified at Lizzie's reaction. The banquet of sweetmeats had been the part of the supper over which she had fretted most, and it had cost almost as much as the rest of the meal. The light of the candles shone through the translucent sugar plate goblets and little dishes, their glasslike surfaces painted with flowers and elaborate grotesques.

After the eating was done, the guests settled down to play primero. The drink flowed, and as laughter rose from where William sat with Edward Seymour, Harry Grey, John Dudley, and William Parr, Bess judged that Anne Seymour's spite had not ruined the evening after all.

Lizzie came to her side, a goblet in one hand and a sugared almond held delicately in the fingers of the other.

"Well, Lady Cavendish," she said, nodding toward the table of men. "Have we not both risen since when we first made each other's acquaintance?"

Bess thought back to the day she had met Lizzie upon her arrival at Codnor Castle. How intimidated she had been to be among Lady Zouche's servants, and how awkward she had felt, blurting out how hungry she was during the interminable wait for food during that supper. And now she had been presented at court, and here in her home were the most powerful men in England.

"Yes," she said to Lizzie. "We have both come a long way from Derbyshire."

THE GUESTS HAD ALL GONE, AND BESS CARRIED A CANDLE UP THE darkened staircase to her bedchamber, where William was already undressing.

"Oh, my poor belly," he groaned as he threw off his doublet, and he put a hand to his stomach.

"In pain again?" she asked, going to him and putting a hand to his cheek. "I'll make you a posset."

"Ah, you're the best lass a man could want." He pulled her into his arms and kissed her. "A most successful evening, my dear. I congratulate you. The Duchess of Somerset asked that we join them for supper soon."

Bess laughed. "Then I guess she didn't read my thoughts! I was wishing her at the bottom of the sea when she spoke so about Catherine Parr. And with William Parr just across the table."

"Oh, he knows well enough that she can be a harridan. If he heard what she said, he'll probably just repeat it to his sister, and it'll give her the chance to think up some sharp responses for the next time she sees the duchess." He patted her hand. "No, don't worry, it was a good evening's work. Seymour told me, by the way, that the land at Chatsworth will be on the market soon and can be had for a very good price."

"It would be good to own land in Derbyshire. I'd like to have a place closer to my mother."

"Well, we'll look into it, then."

A little later Bess brought the posset to William, who had already climbed into bed. The steam rising from the cup smelled of ginger and licorice and he inhaled the scent before taking a sip, and then held the warm slipware to his belly.

"Ah, much better."

After Cecily had helped Bess undress, Bess sat in her loose gown at her desk and made an entry in her ledger of the five shillings she had given to the cook for his success in the kitchen.

"How did you do at cards?" she asked.

"Lost," William grunted. "Two pounds, five shillings, and tuppence."

Bess raised her eyebrows and silently entered the amount below the gift to the cook.

William chuckled. "Don't worry, dear wife. It's money well spent when it helps cement friendships with such as those we supped with this evening."

CHAPTER NINETEEN

Little more than a fortnight after the supper party, William came home with the news that Edward Seymour had received word that Catherine Parr had given birth to a little girl named Mary.

"It was a difficult labor, so Thomas Seymour wrote, but both mother and child were doing well."

"God be thanked for that," Bess said.

But within days another messenger arrived in London with worse tidings. Catherine Parr had been taken ill within hours of giving birth, fallen into delirium, and died on the fifth of September. Bess received a letter from Jane Grey, who had been at the queen's bed-side throughout her decline.

Poor lady, Jane wrote, *her brain was fevered, and she seemed to be once more discovering her lord and the Lady Elizabeth in each other's arms. She was distraught, crying out, "Those that are about me care not for me, but stand laughing at my grief." I did all I could to soothe her, but she was far gone and knew not where she was or who I was, I think. I had the sad duty of serving as chief mourner at the funeral,*

walking behind the coffin from the house to the chapel. I will go home
to Bradgate for the present, but I long to see you and hope that it may
be so before long.

"So much sadness!" Bess murmured to William that night in
bed. "The death of the queen herself, of course, but now Jane Grey
has lost the kindest mother she had, and the poor little baby—what
will become of her?"

"And Lord Sudeley bereft of a wife," William reminded her,
stroking her hair.

"Bereft! More like relieved, I would think, having played her such
a dog trick as he did."

"No man could be relieved at the death of a wife. And surely his
conscience torments him."

William gathered Bess to him and, lying close against his chest,
the comforting and familiar scent of him in her nostrils, she felt safe
and happy. He would never betray her with another woman, she was
sure.

"I am blessed to have such a husband as you," she whispered,
reaching up to stroke his cheek.

"And I to have you, my darling Bess."

JANE GREY WAS BACK IN LONDON AGAIN LATER IN THE AUTUMN,
and ran into Bess's arms when they met.

"What a great girl you are becoming!" Bess exclaimed, hugging
Jane tight. "Eleven years old now; I can scarce believe it."

Though small and slight, Jane looked even more like an adult in
miniature than most children, Bess thought. Her fair curls were hidden
beneath a gabled hood, and there was an air of bearing up under
weighty sadness that seemed more suited to someone of far greater age.

"The months I spent with Catherine Parr were the happiest in my
life," she told Bess as they stood at a window watching the bustle of
traffic on the street below. "I think that now I shall never be happy
again."

"My dear little sister," Bess said, pulling Jane close to her side. "You are ever in my prayers, and I am sure a happier time will come."

"I'm happiest when I'm with you," Jane said, smiling up at her.

"I have good news to tell," Bess said, deciding on the instant to confide in Jane. "Do not repeat it for I have not told anyone else yet, even William, but I believe I am with child again."

"Oh, Bess, how wonderful!"

"Will you be godmother to my baby? You can come to Northaw while I am lying in, and stay for a good visit after."

Jane's face seemed to glow with joy. "I will be able to get through anything that may come over the next months, knowing that a visit with you lies at the end of it."

Soon after the New Year, Lizzie's secret marriage to William Parr became known.

"Edward Seymour is aflame with anger," William told Bess. "He's banished Parr from court. And the council has ordered Parr to separate from Lizzie, or face a charge of bigamy."

"Oh, poor Lizzie! Where is she? What has become of her?"

"Gone to her father's house, I think."

Bess could imagine Lizzie's distress only too well. Lizzie had loved William Parr since she had met him, and had stayed with him to her own detriment, for what man would marry her now, when she had been Parr's mistress for almost six years? Bess recalled how she had envied Lizzie when they were in Lady Zouche's household together, thinking that Lizzie seemed to get whatever she wanted with ease. How different things were now! She was happy and secure, lacking nothing, and Lizzie's hopes and dreams were in the dust.

"I must go to see her," she said. "Oh, God, what can be done to help her?"

But only days later, greater upheavals shook Bess's world and threw her into a state of anxiety.

"Thomas Seymour has been arrested!" William's voice was hoarse with emotion as he burst into Bess's chamber, where she sat with her household account books. "On the orders of the Lord Protector, and sent to the Tower!"

"His own brother gave orders to arrest him?" Bess gasped, dropping her quill so that a splash of ink blotted her page. "Upon what charge?"

"Treason." William slumped into a chair, his face haggard. "He tried to kidnap the king last night at Hampton Court—some harebrained scheme gone wrong. He claimed he merely wanted to take his nephew out hunting, but he was armed and had an accomplice with him, and shot the poor king's wretched little dog because it set up a barking when he entered the chamber."

"At Christmas you said there were rumors that he planned to seize the king and the Lady Elizabeth."

"Yes, and since then he has been mighty loud in his criticism of the Lord Protector and fool enough to boast that the navy would back him if he chose to take on his brother and try to overthrow him. The privy council learned that he was trying to raise money to finance an attempt to do just that. Edward Seymour tried to save his brother, giving him a chance to vindicate himself before the council, but Thomas did not appear."

Bess felt a thrill of fear. So much danger and intrigue. These doings brought back all that had happened under King Henry, the undercurrent of terror and uncertainty.

"Is the king safe?" she asked.

"Yes, he is well, but under the circumstances he cannot help but see that his uncle meant him no good. Thomas Seymour has hazarded one throw of the dice too many, and now he has given the privy council all that they need to bring him down."

Bess's heart was pounding. William's words brought back her terror and anxiety in the days when the fate of Anne of Cleves hung in the balance; when Cat Howard had plummeted, helpless, toward disgrace and death; and when Catherine Parr had been in danger of being consigned to the flames for heresy. She strove to remind herself that she and William were safe.

"What did he aim to do?" she asked.

"He probably meant to marry the king to Jane Grey, which he has been trying to do for a long time. Worse, he intended to make himself the husband of the Lady Elizabeth."

"Oh, no." Bess was shivering. "Surely she did not have a part in the plot?"

"Likely not," William agreed. "But she has been taken to the Tower, too, and she will have to convince the council that she is innocent. There are rumors that she is Thomas Seymour's mistress and bears his child."

Bess felt ill at the thought of the princess locked away within those dank walls, and could only imagine how frightened young Elizabeth must be. *Keep her safe, Lord,* she prayed, *and give her strength.*

BESS HAD FELT RESTLESS ALL DAY AND HAD LEFT THE HOUSE IN Newgate Street to take a walk, with no particular destination in mind. She had skirted St. Paul's, finding its towering walls cold and imposing, and made her way past the King's Wardrobe and the church of St. Andrew by the Wardrobe, down St. Andrew's Hill past Blackfriars toward the water, and now she stood at Puddle Wharf, gazing out over the river.

A chill breeze ruffled the water's surface and she drew her heavy cloak tight about her, shivering. The sun was setting bloodred, its dying rays giving the Thames the appearance of a river of fire.

Thomas Seymour was dead. He had been beheaded that morning, his life the price of his reckless ambition.

Bess thought back to when she had seen him at court all those years ago, in the company of Catherine Parr, then the not-quite-widowed Lady Latimer, and on that day in the garden at Whitehall, when he had looked upon her so intently that she blushed. She had thought him a handsome man, and so he had been, with luxuriant dark hair and eyes the color of hazelnuts, his voice deep and honey-mellow. And what had it got him? The love of Catherine Parr, the infatuation of poor Lady Elizabeth, the attention of countless other women. Perhaps if women ruled the land, Bess thought, Thomas might have kept his head. But his strutting like a cock in the hen-house had done him no good with the privy council, nor with his brother the Lord Protector, nor even with his nephew the young king.

Elizabeth had summed him up accurately. William had told Bess that upon learning of Thomas Seymour's death, she had said, "This day died a man of much wit and very little judgment." Bess wondered whether grief and passion stirred beneath the princess's impassive young face. If so, she hid them well. She had learned early that it did not do to give away too much of oneself.

Across the river the bullbaiting house stood O-like near the shore. The carcasses of several bulls and dogs and a few bears were heaped beside it, and four men were dragging the bloody mass of one animal toward the bank where a barge waited. Bess's gorge rose as she thought of Thomas Seymour's body, cold now, congealed with blood. Had his head been sewn back on for his burial? William had said that Edward Seymour had at least seen to it that his brother's head would not be put on a pike to adorn the bridge or one of the city gates.

The baby in Bess's belly kicked, and she felt a pang of guilt. She shouldn't be thinking such gruesome thoughts; they might harm the child. Perhaps a son this time. She hoped it might be; she would like to give William an heir. But he would be happy with another daughter, as long as it was healthy. Her happiness and life didn't depend on the production of a male child, as poor Anne Boleyn's had done, and the first Queen Catherine's before her.

It was time to go back to Northaw, she decided. Back to the quiet of the country, the welcoming company of Jenny and Aunt Marcella, her stepdaughters, and of course the smiling face of baby Frankie. At the thought of her little daughter, Bess suddenly had a desperate longing to be away from London and all its ugliness. She wanted to rise with the sun, to hear the birds in the trees, to caress Frankie's soft fat cheek and have nothing more to do than to see to the workings of the house and farm. Soon there would be lambs and calves and colts at Northaw, energetic life, not shadows of death such as those that clung to the darkening stone walls of London.

CHAPTER TWENTY

May Day, 1549—Northaw, Hertfordshire

THE DAY WAS SO LOVELY THAT BESS WAS LOATH TO GO INSIDE. Soon, all too soon, she would be taking her chamber to await the birth of her child, shut away in darkness. Until then, she wanted to make the most of the gladsome, sunny world.

Servants had carried chairs, hassocks, and carpets out to the lawn before the house, and Bess and her flock of ladies basked in the sunshine as they worked. They were embroidering a pattern of leaves on bed linen that was to be a gift for Jane Dudley, Countess of Warwick, who, along with Jane Grey, would be godmother to the coming baby if it were a girl.

Bess and William had chosen their prospective godparents carefully, with an eye to their child's advancement. Jane Dudley's husband had continued his rise in power since Bess's supper party the previous summer, and some said he held such power over the young king that it was he, not Edward, who ruled. Francis, the Earl of Shrewsbury, a member of the privy council who was a Derbyshire neighbor and patron of Bess's dead father, was to serve as one godfather. If the child was a boy, John Dudley would be the other.

"This is lovely!" Bess's stepdaughter Kitty exclaimed, admiring the yards of creamy cloth swirling over the carpet. She shot Bess a smile, her blue eyes twinkling.

"It is, and I'm sure her ladyship will be well pleased," Aunt Marcella agreed.

Her widowed aunt had been an inspired addition to the household, Bess thought, looking at Aunt Marcella's broadly smiling face. Bess felt completely at ease leaving Frankie in her care, and she provided a welcome touch of Hardwick for both Bess and Jenny. And Aunt Marcella had taken a warm interest in William's daughters, who in turn adored her. She had adult daughters of her own, and Bess relied on her advice and experience in her efforts to be a mother to the girls. It wasn't always easy. Kitty treated her with the courtesy due to a stepmother, but at nearly fifteen, was only seven years younger than Bess, and Bess knew she could never fill the place of the mother the girl had lost. Nan was only nine, and had spent half of her life without a mother. And Bess consulted with Aunt Marcella about William's poor daughter Polly, and whether it would be best to leave her where she was or bring her to join their household.

"When will Jane Grey be here?" Jenny asked.

"About the first of June," Bess replied. "I can't wait to see her. I'm sure you'll all love her as much as I do."

"I feel I know her already, from all you've said," Kitty mused.

"The poor girl writes that she longs to be here," Bess said, tying off a knot and smoothing her handiwork in her lap. "Bradgate is in much turmoil. When the Lady Elizabeth's household was broken up after Thomas Seymour's death, many of her people took refuge with the Greys, and remain there yet, not knowing what to do with themselves."

"It's a shame the little orphan baby couldn't stay there, too." Bess's stepdaughter Nan spoke up. "It wasn't her fault what her father did, after all."

"But it's the way of the world," Aunt Marcella sighed. "Great ones cause trouble, and littler people pay for it."

Baby Mary Seymour, the child of Catherine Parr and Thomas Seymour, had lost more than her parents. Her aunt the Duchess of Somerset had refused to take her, and now the disinherited infant had found a grudging home with Frances Grey's friend and step-mother the Duchess of Suffolk, who had been a close friend of Catherine Parr but was not even kin to the baby.

"Will Lady Jane be able to travel, with all the troubles?" Jenny asked, her eyes anxious.

Thomas Seymour's death had provoked dissatisfaction with his brother the Lord Protector, and angry crowds had plundered houses in the countryside.

"The common folk don't like him," William had told Bess. "They don't like so many changes to the old religion, and though the king supports the reforms, they lay the blame on Edward Seymour. And higher folk don't like him, either. He's arrogant and behaves as though he's the king anointed. I fear what he may be bringing down upon himself."

"Surely things will settle down," Bess said. "The disturbances cannot continue long."

"WHAT A PERFECT LITTLE CREATURE!" JANE GREY CRIED, CRADLING baby Temperance in her arms. "How is it possible that hands can be so tiny and so perfect? And look at her hair—just your color!"

Temperance's eyes, cloudy blue, settled on Jane's face with an air of vague consternation.

"Oh, you sweet poppet, all is well in your world," Jane murmured, her lips grazing the baby's forehead. "Look at all your gifts!"

Temperance hiccupped and Bess laughed.

"Yes, an abundance of riches for such a little mite."

Beside the cradle a table stood heaped with christening gifts—tiny feather beds and bed linens; woolly blankets; a little counter-pane of red silk; embroidered gowns; a porringer banded in silver; five silver spoons from Jane; carpets to hang over the windows in cold weather; a set of bed curtains for when Temperance should outgrow her cradle; two little "milk beasts," pewter jugs cunningly made in the shape of a lamb and a calf; a set of silver cups from the Earl of Shrewsbury; and most glorious, a silver salt cellar, the gift of John and Jane Dudley, who had come all the way from London for the christening.

"Temperance," Jane mused. "Such a pretty name. How did you come by it?"

"It's what the king calls his sister the Lady Elizabeth!" Bess laughed. "And so I honor her without seeming to name the child for myself."

Tamsin, the baby's nurse, took Temperance from Jane and laid her into the soft nest of the cradle, and Bess took Jane's arm in hers and led her back to her own bedchamber.

"I'm glad we have a little time to ourselves before supper," she said. "Pray tell me how things are with you. How are your sisters?"

"My sisters are well and send their love." Jane seemed to speak almost as if by rote.

"And how do you find it being back at Bradgate?"

Jane looked down at her hands in her lap and when she lifted her eyes they were sad.

"It seems always that nothing I do can please my parents. When I'm in their presence, whether I speak or keep silence, be merry or sad, no matter what I do, be it sewing, playing, dancing, or anything else, I feel I must do it even so perfectly as God made the world, or else I am so sharply taunted, so cruelly threatened, and sometimes given pinches and smacks, that I think myself in hell."

"Oh, Jane, no!" Bess could not bear to think of her sweet Jane being as little valued as she seemed to be. How was it possible that Frances and Harry Grey could be so kind to her and so cruel to a girl as intelligent, accomplished, and full of affection as Jane?

"What can I do?" she asked.

"Nothing, I fear," Jane said. "But much of the time I can stay out of their way. You know how they love hunting, and whenever they're in the country they're frequently in the field. Then I am left to myself."

"Do they see nothing of your accomplishments?" Bess asked.

Jane shrugged.

"Perhaps, but whatever I do accomplish, there is always more lying ahead of me. You know they have great ambitions for me."

"Do they still favor Thomas Seymour's plan of marrying you to the king?"

"They have said nothing of late, and certainly I do not raise the issue, as I'm not eager to be married yet."

"Jane, sweetheart, my heart breaks for you." Bess caressed Jane's cheek.

"It's not all darkness," Jane said. "You recall my tutor, Mr. Aylmer? I love him well and spend as much time in his company as I can. He teaches me so gently, so pleasantly, and with such fair allurements to learning, that I think the time nothing while I am with him. And when I am called from him, I fall on weeping. I wish they would just leave me to my books."

"I marvel at the mind that lies within that pretty head of yours." Bess smiled. "Latin, Greek, rhetoric—is there nothing you cannot learn?"

"How to die," Jane said.

Her face was serious and the hairs at the back of Bess's neck rose.

"Why do you say such a thing?" Bess gasped.

"Plato. He writes of the death of Socrates, and how bravely he faced it. 'When I come to the end of my journey,' he said, 'I shall attain that which has been the pursuit of my life.'"

"You are far too young to think of your death," Bess said firmly. "For God's sake, Jane, we must find a way to give you more enjoyment in life."

That evening it seemed to Bess that Jane had taken her words to heart, for the girl seemed almost giddily happy at supper, chatting and laughing with Jenny and Bess's stepdaughters. They were good company for her, Bess thought, for Kitty was less than two years older than Jane and Nan three years younger.

After supper, as Bess sat talking with Jane Dudley, she was pleased to see Jane giggling in a corner with the other girls, her cares forgotten for the time being.

"I am so honored to have you as godmother to Temperance, your ladyship," Bess said to Lady Warwick, "and most particularly that you chose to come so far with such troubles afoot in the land."

A week earlier, on Whitsunday, the day of Temperance's birth, riots had broken out across England upon the introduction of the Book of Common Prayer in English, rather than Latin. The situation had undoubtedly grown rapidly worse, since the week following Whitsunday was by tradition a break in the round of working in farm and field, so laborers throughout the land were free from work and able to gather.

"It is a most pernicious situation," Jane Dudley agreed.

William, flanked by John Dudley and the Earl of Shrewsbury, joined them just in time to hear Jane Dudley's remark.

"No good can come of it," he said. "Where there is any lack of order, there needs must be perpetual conflict."

"Yes," John Dudley said, his face stern. "But Edward Seymour has cast away the treason and heresy laws that now are needed to stamp out the fires that are raging everywhere."

Bess was surprised at Dudley's words. She had never heard anyone speak so bluntly about dissatisfaction with the Protector, except when she and William talked in the privacy of their bedchamber.

"That's true," Shrewsbury agreed. "The lower sort of people are angry at the way they are treated, and rise up. The gentry and the nobility resent Seymour for failing to take control, and for his profiting richly from the dissolution of chantries. All are against him, it seems."

His eyes met John Dudley's, and Bess shivered. In such glances plots were born.

Further serious discussion was interrupted for the moment when

Jane Grey and Kitty dashed over to Bess, excitement dancing in their eyes.

"May we go outside, Bess?" Jane begged. "The evening is so warm and pleasant, and the moon so beautiful."

"Yes, do," Bess said. "But don't stray far, and come in if you begin to feel a chill. I don't want you catching a catarrh."

The girls ran off hand in hand, and Bess noticed that John Dudley's eyes followed them.

"A comely girl, Lady Jane is," he remarked.

"And sweet and good, too," Bess said. "It's a joy to have her here."

"She must be but a year or so younger than our son Guildford," Jane Dudley murmured.

"She's just turned twelve," Bess said.

"What do you hear of plans for her marriage?" John Dudley asked. "Is Edward Seymour still trying to match her with his boy?"

Bess felt a stab of worry and protectiveness. Jane, in the line of succession for the throne, no matter how far down it, could easily become a pawn in a game over which she had no control.

"I don't know," she said. "Whoever marries her will get a prize to be treasured, and I hope her parents will bestow her on someone who will bring her happiness."

"I must get back to London as soon as you are churched," William told Bess that night as he blew out the candle and climbed into bed beside her. "These stirrings pose a grave danger to the stability of the state. The changes to the prayer book have come to stand for all the casting away of the old religion."

"No great surprise," Bess said. "The new communion tells us that Christ's body and blood are not in the holy bread and wine. It upsets people, especially as it is only a few years since that people burned for saying as much."

Bess had listened to the impassioned arguments for the reforms that had been made to the church, but in truth, she cared little one way or the other. She found comfort and peace in being in church, and had a love for the old church buildings that had stood through so much, but she felt that God was present, whatever words were used, and whether they were spoken in Latin or English. And she had seen all too clearly that it was dangerous to hew to strong beliefs.

William, whose rise to power and prosperity had so much depended on his efficient work in the business of the dissolution of the monasteries—the receiving and inventorying of gold, plate, and other goods of the abbeys and friaries—had even less sentiment than she.

"It's more than the rebellion among the people that worries me, though," he said. "I've watched John Dudley eyeing Edward Seymour for a long time. Now Seymour is in a precarious position. His brother's execution did him damage."

"In what way?" Bess asked.

"Thomas Seymour went most unwillingly to the block and on the scaffold he spoke messages for the king's sisters, who the people favor. The king loved him, but could not save him. It all contributes to the impression that the king is but a puppet, and it's Edward Seymour who is pulling the strings."

The old familiar terror gripped Bess. More intrigue. And now, it seemed to her, she and William were in a most delicate position, for both Seymour and Dudley were their friends. How would they know with whom to side? What would happen if they chose wrongly?

"What will happen if Dudley should strike at Seymour?" Bess asked. "Would it make the state of the country any more secure?"

"For a time, perhaps. Or at least it might seem so. But to have a boy king, years away from producing an heir, and buffeted by the opposing forces who would each control him—it makes the ground beneath him shaky for all."

"Purge me with hyssop, and I shall be clean. Wash me and I shall be whiter than snow." Bess liked the words of the churching ceremony, which seemed to sweep away the smothering darkness of the childbed chamber and let in the summer sunshine, and the sprinkling of holy water was like the dew of a midsummer morning.

The journey to the village church near Northaw marked the first time she had been out of the house since near a month before Temperance's birth, and she drank in the blue skies and fleecy racks of cloud drifting above. The grand guests were gone, and the company this day was family. Her sister Moll, who she had not seen since her wedding to William, had come for a visit, and as Bess walked beside her, Jenny and Aunt Marcella behind them with Kitty and Nan, she thought how good it was to be surrounded by family. She felt sad at the prospect of leaving Temperance and little Frankie behind when she and William went to London, but she wouldn't risk exposing them to the close confines of the city, where plague and the sweating sickness stalked during the summer months.

CHAPTER TWENTY-ONE

Second of September, 1549—London

ELY PLACE, THE LONDON HOUSE OF JOHN AND JANE DUDLEY, SAT amid sprawling gardens, and beyond it lay the countryside. Bess rode in a horse litter, a suitable means of conveyance for a lady, which saved her gown and shoes from the mud of London's streets, and her slow progress gave her time to admire the beauty and grandeur of Ely Place. It had been the residence of the bishops of Ely, but, like so many hundreds of other pieces of church property, it was now in very secular hands.

She could understand why the common people were confused by the events of recent years. Time out of mind, the church had been at the center of life. Birth, marriage, death, the eternal wheel, had spun around the axis of the church, and at the center of that church had been the pope. But King Henry had changed all that, and made himself supreme head of the church. Men had gone to their deaths because they would not acknowledge him to be so, Bess knew, though she had been too young to understand what was happening at the time. Besides, nothing much observable had happened at the little church at Ault Hucknall, or in the thousands of little churches all over the land. But now things were changing, in ways that were hard to ignore. The pomp and awe that had made a church feel like a church was being stripped away. Now Jane Dudley was preparing to welcome Bess into her withdrawing chamber, in the house from which the bishop had been cast out, and all across the country, monks and nuns wandered destitute and begged for their bread.

By the time Bess and William had reached London in mid-July, the riots that had begun on Whitsunday had flared into something approaching civil war. Armies of angry workers gathered, tearing down the new enclosures that kept their sheep from grazing on lands that had been in common use for centuries. The wealthy, threatened by the instability below, were outraged at Seymour's inability to stem the tide of rebellion, and had put down the risings with a violence born of terror. The summer wind carried rumors that Papists eager to put Mary Tudor on the throne were behind the riots. Onto this bed of red-hot embers Seymour had cast the new prayer books, all that was needed to breathe the situation into a raging fire.

Bess hadn't heard anyone question that the army of men headed by Robert Kett had been in the wrong or had deserved anything less than they had gotten. But she thought back to the day when King Henry's men had come to demand rent from her mother, and remembered her mother's fear and her own desperation at the thought that the cow might be taken from them, and she understood why the people were angry. They were desperate, pinched by rising prices, and squeezed by harsh new poor laws, and they had had enough. What would she have done if those men had led away the cow? Flown at them, kicking and fighting to take back the beast that kept her family fed? It would have done her no good. But if she were a man, now, surrounded by other men, so angry and frightened that they didn't care what happened to them, what would she do? Pick up a pitchfork or a hoe or a cudgel, or whatever was at hand, and fight for her life.

Yet she could understand how the middling sort of people felt as well. They had worked hard for what they had got, as William had worked to get Northaw and the London house, and to provide for his family. And they feared that Edward Seymour would take the side of the common people against them. So they did what they could to protect their property. And, Bess thought, if a howling crowd threatened Northaw, threatened the safety of her children, would she not do whatever she must to protect them? She would.

The litter stopped before the door of Ely Place, and the steward to the Earl and Countess of Warwick came forward to welcome Bess. Inside, brightly colored tapestries covered the walls, and the ceilings were painted with scenes that Bess supposed must spring from the works of the Greek and Roman writers whom Jane Grey was fond of reading.

The steward led her up a staircase broad enough to accommodate a hay wagon and into a chamber where Jane Dudley sat before the fireplace.

"Lady Cavendish, how lovely to see you again. I trust you are quite recovered from the birth? And that little Temperance and Frances are well?"

"Yes, thank you, Lady Warwick," Bess said. "I'm feeling fine, and I had a letter from Jenny that all is well at Northaw. She writes that Frankie is learning to walk and can go high-lone for a few steps now."

"Splendid." Jane Dudley gestured Bess to where a small table was arrayed with cakes and ale.

Bess reflected that surely Lady Warwick had never wondered where her next meal was coming from or whether she would have a roof over her head come nightfall.

"I trust all your family is well?" she asked, arranging her skirts.

"Yes. I could scarce believe it when I heard that the rebels had taken Norwich, and I was quite concerned, as you may imagine, until I received a letter from my husband, letting me know that he was safe."

"How did they manage to capture it?" Bess wondered. Norwich, with a population of twelve thousand people, was second in size only to London.

"There were more than fifteen thousand of the rogues, and they had sufficient artillery to open fire on the city walls and answer the bombardment from the city through the night."

"No wonder the men that William Parr took were not enough to vanquish them."

"No, fifteen hundred men, even with mercenaries among them—Italians, John said—were not equal to the job."

"Poor Sheffield," Bess said. "Poor Lady Sheffield."

Edmund, Baron Sheffield, had been killed by the rebels in a pitched hand-to-hand battle in the streets of Norwich, prompting Parr to retreat with his men, not stopping until they reached Cambridge.

"When John set off for Norwich," Lady Warwick said, "he took fourteen thousand men with him, a real army—Welshmen, Italians, and those terrible landsknechts—and he wrote that the battle was as fierce as anything he saw in Scotland or France. But of course he won the day."

Bess thought of the families of the poor men who had gone to fight, waiting in vain for their husbands and fathers to return. "William said that many were killed."

"Three thousand of the enemy, John reckoned, and more than two hundred and fifty of his men. He hanged some fifty of the rebels right there, on the oak trees beneath which they had gathered."

Bess could imagine the terrible sight of the men swinging from the oaks, flies buzzing around their corpses in the summer heat.

"John captured Robert Kett and his brother the night after the battle," Jane Dudley said, biting into a chunk of gingerbread. "They'll be sent here to the Tower to be tried."

What chance did they have at trial? Bess thought. Of course they would hang. She was glad her children were at Northaw, with plenty of food and surrounded by loving family and servants. They would never have to know the gnawing fear and humiliation of poverty.

She glanced at Jane Dudley, her face serene as she sipped her ale. No, she had never feared that her children might go hungry.

What people am I got myself among? Bess asked herself. *I'm not like them, whatever trappings I may put on. Do they know that, and despise me for it?*

She adjusted the rope of pearls that draped over the rich sheen of her bodice, a present from William a fortnight earlier on the second anniversary of their marriage. The solid heft of the pearls and the silky feel of them under her fingertips reminded her of how far she had come. She could sympathize with the poor, but do what she must, she would never be one of them again.

CHAPTER TWENTY-TWO

First of December, 1549—Northaw, Hertfordshire

IT WAS ONLY MIDAFTERNOON, BUT ALREADY IT WAS GROWING DARK outside. A rumble of thunder rattled the windows. Bess gathered her robe more tightly about her, shivering, and held Jane Grey's letter closer to the candlelight.

My dear Bess, I was so distressed to receive your news that dear Temperance has been ill.

Bess glanced at the cradle where Temperance slept. The baby's fever was gone now and her breathing was even, but still Bess was worried. Temperance seemed more frail than Frankie had been at the age of five months. Bess had put aside her plans to visit her mother at Hardwick for Christmas, for she was not willing either to subject Temperance to the danger of traveling or to leave her behind when her health was precarious. She closed her eyes.

God, please keep my child safe. Punish me if I have sinned, not my innocent babe, for I could not bear her loss.

She took up Jane's letter again.

Such changes there are. You know that John Dudley has at last knocked Edward Seymour from his place and locked him in the Tower on charges of treason, claiming that he plotted against the lives of the other councilors. Dudley has now made himself lord president of the privy council and has such sway over my cousin the king that my father—now on the council himself—says that Dudley effectively rules.

Bess recalled John Dudley's face in the firelight as he had sat at her supper table the previous summer, his dark eyes watching Edward Seymour like a cat watching its prey. And now he had pounced, and Seymour was mewed up in the Tower like a rat in a trap. One near king had been replaced by another, who had been his friend. *Dudley is our friend*, Bess thought. *But how sure a friend? Must we do something to affirm our allegiance? And if he should fall? What then?*

So many fears made her head ache. She turned back to Jane's letter.

Happier news is that Kate and Mary and I visited our cousin the Lady Mary last week and had a most enjoyable time. She is like a kindly aunt to me, praising my music and my little skill at languages.

Bess was grateful for the Lady Mary's attentions to Jane Grey, who blossomed like a dry flower when it is watered at any show of love and approval.

Dear Bess, when are you coming back to London? I miss you every day and long to seek your counsel in so many things. With love, your little sister, Jane.

As always when she thought of London, Bess was of two minds. She enjoyed the bustle of the place and the feeling of being so close to important things happening. And it was exciting to have a growing circle of friends that included the most powerful people in the land. But when she was in town she longed for her children, the company of Jenny and Aunt Marcella, and the quiet of the country. Yet once there, she itched to know what she was missing, and she and William paid a few well-placed informants to keep them apprised of the doings at court when they were away from London. Money well spent, William said, and she heartily agreed.

Second of February, 1550, Candlemas—Northaw, Hertfordshire

Bess clutched the little bundle to her chest, her face bent so that she could press her cheek against the cooling cheek of baby Temperance. The child had died two hours earlier, slipping away in her sleep, leaving the world as peacefully and silently as the petals of a flower drift to earth.

Bess sat in her bed, propped against the cushions, the flickering light of two dozen candles all that stood between her and the immense blackness that loomed outside the windows, enveloping Northaw Manor and her very soul.

Candlemas marked the middle of winter, halfway between the winter solstice, the longest night of the year, and the coming of spring. The beeswax candles that had been blessed at the church that day gave off the scent of honey, recalling to her mind warm days with bees buzzing amid the clover blossoms, but tonight it seemed that cruel winter with its cold and darkness would never end. And what did it matter? How could she ever smile again, ever hope to rise from her bed again, now that her precious Temperance was gone?

She lifted her head at the sound of footsteps. William came and sat beside her on the bed, and wiped Bess's tears from the baby's cheek and then from Bess's.

"The pain grows less in time. I know it's hard to believe, but it does happen." His voice was gentle.

Bess thought of the five children he had lost, and the two wives who had left him a widower.

"How have you borne it?"

"I don't know." He shook his head. "I suppose I have put my head down and moved forward, one step plodding after another, as I have faced everything in life. For if we do not move forward what is there to do but lie down and die?"

He pulled Bess into his arms, the still bundle between them.

"But don't you leave me, Bess. That I think would be beyond my enduring."

"Never. I will do as you do, and believe that in time the grief will cease to be a searing fire."

"It will. In time it will become only a small flame within your heart, giving warmth and light that never go out."

Bess took comfort in the sound of his heartbeat within his chest and his breathing near her ear.

In the midst of life we be in death, the new Book of Common Prayer said. And, Bess thought, in the midst of death, in life.

CHAPTER TWENTY-THREE

Twentieth of December, 1550—Northaw, Hertfordshire

IT HAD BEEN THREE DAYS SINCE BESS HAD GIVEN BIRTH, BUT SHE still felt as if her insides had been scooped out with a sharp spoon and cast aside. The bearing of her first son had been even more difficult than Temperance's birth a year and a half earlier. William, concerned for her safety and that of the baby, had taken the precaution of engaging not only the midwife but a surgeon. Bess's labor had seemed to go on forever and she had first feared she would die and then hoped that she would, if only the pain would end. But both she and little Henry had survived.

Cecily came into the chamber bearing a covered cup.

"A nice warm posset, my lady."

She helped Bess to sit up against the bank of pillows and bolsters, and tucked the bedclothes snug around her chest before going to the cradle.

"He's sleeping well," she commented. "Calm. No fever or aught like that."

"Yes, the Lord be praised," Bess agreed.

"Will you have no other supper, your ladyship?"

"No," Bess said, holding the steaming cup against her chest. "This is all I can manage now."

She could feel some strength returning to her as the warm liquid went down. Cecily poked at the fire and added another log to it, and drew the shutters closed against the darkness enveloping the land outside.

"Sir William asks if you're well enough to see him."

"Of course, thank you, Cecily. Ask him to come in directly."

William stopped to smile down at the baby in the cradle before he settled himself carefully on the bed beside Bess and leaned down to kiss her.

"How's my brave girl?"

Bess hadn't seen William since the previous evening and had missed him, and his presence made her feel better. "Much better today, my love."

"Good. I have several pieces of news that I think will please you. Harry Grey, John Dudley, and the Lady Elizabeth have all sent word that they will stand as godparents and will be here for the christening."

He looked proud and Bess smiled at him, reaching out a hand to stroke his luxuriant whiskers.

"That's wonderful. Two of the most powerful men in England and the king's sister, honoring our son."

"Our boy is off to a good start. Which brings me to the other tidings. The master mason came today. I told him what kind of house we want to build at Chatsworth, and tomorrow we'll ride over so that he may see the land and begin to draw some plans."

A few months earlier, the Leche family lands that Alice's husband Francis had sold so precipitously had come up for sale, and at a good price, as Edward Seymour had said they would. William and Bess had inspected the property, which included not only the manors of Chatsworth and Cromford with their houses and land, but nearly twenty surrounding villages, and had immediately determined to buy it. Francis Agarde had accepted their offer of only six hundred pounds, and now there lacked only the final signing of documents, which they expected to take place within a few days. The land lay not far from Hardwick, a week's journey from London, through rough and remote country.

"Chatsworth will be our bulwark against the storms," William said, getting up to inspect the baby in his cradle, "and a fitting inheritance for our son."

Bess smiled at the thought of baby Henry a grown man, with children around him. And then thought of those children grown old, with grandchildren of their own. She was pleased at the idea that Chatsworth would be the seat of the Cavendishes down through the centuries.

"Oh, and what think you of this?" William asked.

He fished within his doublet and drew forth a swatch of fine woolen cloth, a deep and vivid blue that made Bess think of cornflowers in a summer field.

"For the servants' livery?" Bess asked, fingers caressing the smooth stuff. "It's lovely."

The number of servants in a household was a measure of its grandeur, and outfitting the household in livery was a mark of even higher rank. Bess thought of how impressive she had thought the Zouche servants in their livery when first she had gone to Codnor Castle.

"Goodness, William, what heights we are risen to!"

William took her hands in his and kissed them.

"I'm glad you're pleased, wife. I'll get the tailor in as soon as may be. Perhaps we may have some suits made by the time of Twelfth Night."

"My mother will be so proud." Bess smiled.

"I'm glad she's coming for Christmas. I hope it will cheer her."

Bess's stepfather's face came into her mind and she said a prayer for the peace of his soul. He had died only a few weeks earlier, never quite recovered in body or spirit from the years he had spent in debtors' prison.

"I wish my father could have seen our Henry," she said.

"I know. But at least he lived to see Frankie, and to know you were well bestowed and comfortable."

"Oh, William." Bess reached out her hand and he came to her and kissed her. "You are my rock and my salvation. Whatever may come, I can face it as long as you are at my side."

CHAPTER TWENTY-FOUR

Fifteenth of November, 1551—Newgate Street, London

MOTHER! THANK GOD YOU'VE ARRIVED SAFELY! AND DIBBY and Meg, just look at you!"

Bess welcomed her mother and sisters to her home, enveloping her mother in her arms, feeling like a little girl again as she leaned her head on her mother's shoulder.

"Oh, my dear girl, look at you!" Elizabeth Leche stepped back and smiled at the sight of Bess's swollen belly. "Another son, I'll be bound!"

"I think so, too, but of course I'll be happy either way." She shook her head in disbelief at how her younger sisters had grown since she had seen them last. Dibby was now sixteen and Meg fourteen. "Goodness, you're both all grown up."

Bess saw her mother and sisters settled into a comfortable chamber at the back of the house, away from the noise of the street.

"I've brought you some honey and jams," Elizabeth said, pulling several small pots from their wrapping.

"Lovely, a little piece of home." Bess lifted a pot to her nose and sniffed. "I almost feel I can smell the blossoms on the trees when I eat Hardwick honey."

Bess thought her mother looked tired, and there was more gray in her hair since she had last seen her. She herself found it exhausting to travel the hundred and fifty miles between Hardwick and London, and glad though she was to see her mother, she wondered if the trip had been too much for her.

"How was your journey? Not too wearing?"

"Nothing more than the usual. It is a long way but I'm always happy to make it knowing you and William and the babies are at the end of it."

"Frankie and little Harry are sleeping now, but you and I can have a good visit before supper. Harry and Frances Grey are coming this evening. I hope you feel up to being in company?"

"Oh, my! Yes, of course. I can still scarce believe they're the Duke and Duchess of Suffolk now. What a terrible state of affairs led to that."

Frances Grey's sixteen-year-old half brother, the young Duke of Suffolk, and his younger brother Charles had died of the sweating sickness within an hour of each other in July. As they were the last of the male Brandons, King Edward had bestowed the dukedom on Harry and Frances Grey.

"Yes," Bess said, sadness gripping her heart. She thought of the two boys laughing and running in the sunshine when they had been at Northaw for Frankie's christening.

"And you were there for the ceremony! You will have to tell me all about it."

"Yes, at Hampton Court. It was very grand, and other friends of ours were also honored. John Dudley was made Duke of Northumberland, the Lord Treasurer William Paulet became Marquess of Winchester, and William Cecil was knighted, along with another secretary and three gentlemen of the privy chamber."

"Oh, my Bess, I'm so proud of you." Bess's mother kissed her cheek. "This is exactly what I hoped for you when I sent you off to

Codnor all those years ago. You're a great lady now, with a fine gentleman for a husband, a grand house, and noble friends who will stand by you in time of need."

My friends will stand by me if they are able to stand themselves, Bess thought.

The face of Edward Seymour flashed into her mind. He was imprisoned in the Tower and even though there was little foundation to the charges that John Dudley had laid at his door, he would likely be executed for treason. Just like his brother Thomas. Who would be next? Bess wondered. How long would Dudley manage to stay atop the heap, with so many contentious dogs nipping at him from below?

"I'm happy to say that all has come out well for Lizzie," Bess told her mother. "Parliament annulled William Parr's marriage in March, so now Lizzie is his true wife, and Marchioness of Northampton!"

"What a triumph for her," Bess's mother said. "I would enjoy seeing her again."

"We'll pay them a visit," Bess promised. "They're living in Southwark, in the old palace of the bishops of Winchester."

"A palace. Think of that."

"She almost holds the place of queen now," Bess said. "As the king is not married, and Jane Dudley dislikes public events, it falls to Lizzie to welcome ambassadors and preside over court festivities."

More turning of fortune's wheel, Bess reflected. Who could have foreseen that Lizzie would rise so high, when only a short time ago, her condition had fallen so low?

THE CAVENDISH HOUSEHOLD KEPT A MERRY BUT SUBDUED CHRISTmas. Bess had taken her chamber and the baby would come any day, but she refused to be sequestered from William, and Christmas dinner was served in her withdrawing room. The walls and windows were draped with carpets and hangings, keeping the cold at bay, and a cheerful fire chased the shadows into the corners.

More of the Hardwick family were gathered together than in some time. Bess looked around at the faces of her mother; her brother Jem and his wife; her older sister Jane and husband Godfrey; Jenny, Dibby, and Meg; Aunt Marcella; and little Frankie, sitting proudly at the table for her first meal outside of her nursery. Jenny's face was aglow with happiness. She would soon be married to Thomas Kniveton, a cousin from Derbyshire. William was telling a funny story to Nan, while Kitty looked on indulgently. Kitty would shortly wed Lizzie's brother Thomas Brooke. It was an excellent match, which pleased Bess and William very much.

The smell of Christmas greenery and spiced cider perfumed the air. Outside, the wintry drafts buffeted the walls of the house and the winds of change raised some at court and blew others down, but all was snug and safe around her.

"What is the latest news from Chatsworth?" Bess's mother asked.

"Work on the house comes along apace," William said. "In a few months we'll begin to move the household and furnishings from Northaw. We'll make our home in the old manor at Chatsworth while the new house is still a-building. By this time next year we shall be living there, if all goes well."

"It will be wonderful to have you so much closer to Hardwick."

"It will indeed," Bess said, taking her mother's hand. "Nothing could make me happier than having you a day's ride from me instead of half the length of the land away."

BESS'S SON WILLIAM WAS BORN AT THREE IN THE MORNING OF THE twenty-seventh of December. He seemed to be having trouble nursing, but with some extra care the wet nurse was able to get him to suck and by the time of his christening ten days after his birth, he was feeding well and putting on weight. Lizzie was to be his godmother, and his godfathers were William Herbert, the Earl of Pembroke, and William Paulet, the Marquess of Winchester.

"The pair of them rule the court," William had said. "We could not ask for better situated men to stand godfathers to our boy."

William Herbert was married to Anne Parr, sister of the late queen, and his son was betrothed to Kate Grey, next after her sister Jane in the succession to the throne. William Paulet had ably served King Henry, and continued as a high statesman with King Edward. He had supported John Dudley against Edward Seymour, and been rewarded with Seymour's position of Lord High Treasurer.

After the christening, the house on Newgate Street bustled with Greys, Parrs, Herberts, and Dudleys.

"Another brick in the foundation of our children's success," William said quietly to Bess, as they watched their guests drink to the good health and long life of the newest Cavendish.

CHAPTER TWENTY-FIVE

Second of February, 1552, Candlemas—Newgate Street, London

BESS CLUTCHED THE BEDCLOTHES AROUND HER AND PUT A hand to her aching head. It was the second anniversary of Temperance's death, and she felt the wrenching grief of the loss of the baby almost as keenly as if it had just happened. She had a bad catarrh, with a pounding headache, running nose, and sore throat, and she felt weak and miserable. And little more than a week before, Edward Seymour had died upon the block on Tower Hill. John Dudley had urged the young king to sign his uncle's death warrant, and Harry Grey had been one of Seymour's judges and supervised the execution.

Bess thought of the three men laughing together around the card table at her supper party three and a half years earlier, and Seymour's kindly smile as he had arrived, probably realizing how anxious she had been about ensuring that the evening was a success. What must it be like, she wondered, to watch the axe fall upon the neck of a friend, and know that you had helped it come to pass?

Whatever John Dudley's emotions, his actions had earned him the further distrust and hatred of the people. The crowds on Tower

Hill had shouted "Rescue!" and "Reprieve!" when a contingent of guards late for duty were seen to rush toward the scaffold.

I will drive myself mad, Bess thought, *if I think on nothing but death and despair. Let me think of something that will make me happy instead. Chatsworth! That is good indeed.*

William had recently visited to inspect the progress of the building, and come back well satisfied. The first wagonloads of household goods would soon make their way northward to Derbyshire. Bess longed to see the house taking shape, the turrets rising stone by stone. She could imagine the scent of spring in the country and longed to breathe it in. Yet the thought of being away from London, from the pulse of what was happening in the land, tugged at some string of anxiety deep within her.

A sharp gust of wind rattled the shutters. The wind was from the north, and bitterly cold. How much depended, Bess thought, on knowing which way the wind blew.

"How does the king?" she asked anxiously when William came into their bedchamber. He had rushed to Whitehall that morning at the news that King Edward was ill.

"He has measles, or perhaps smallpox." William's face was grim.

"Then we must pray for him," Bess said.

"For him and for all of us."

The statement hung heavy in the air. In the quiet and privacy of their curtained bed, Bess and William had spoken often of late of what might happen if the king should perish before he had a son to succeed him.

"Only women would be left behind," William had said. "Mary, Elizabeth, the Scots queen, Margaret Douglas, Margaret Clifford, Frances Grey, the Grey girls unless Frances should have a son before the king dies. By Christ, that it should come to this, after King Henry moved heaven and earth to get a son, casting off poor Queen Catherine and then Anne Boleyn, and breaking with the church."

Yes, what human wreckage Henry had wrought to ensure that he had a male heir. The terrified faces of Cat Howard and Catherine Parr had risen to Bess's mind, and she had shivered despite the piles of bedclothes.

"With a woman on the throne," William had said, "England would be seen as weak, like a rabbit waiting to be taken like a hawk. France, Spain, the Holy Roman Empire—who might strike first?"

"Has there never been a ruling queen of England?" Bess had asked.

"Never. But unless God preserves Edward for a few more years, it is very like to happen now. And there are many who don't want Papist Mary on the throne. I tell you truly I fear what may come."

Bess's mind came back to the present as William banged open the lid of one of the great chests that held his clothes and pulled out his heavy riding cape.

"Parliament has been dissolved," he said, "because of the great prevalence of smallpox in the city. So I'll go to Chatsworth while I may to see how the house comes along, and while I'm there I'll have another look at the other pieces of land."

For months, William had been laboring on a great scheme—the granting to the crown of all the far-flung properties he owned in exchange for a vast amount of land near Chatsworth, as well as better pieces of property in other counties.

"Do you think the king will approve your plan?" Bess asked, making a pile of William's shirts on the bed.

"I think he will. I have been nurturing the idea along most carefully."

Bess suddenly felt breathless with anticipation at the thought of possessing sweeping miles of the Derbyshire countryside. "When will we know?"

"Soon. The royal surveyors will go to Northaw in the next fortnight."

"Then we must send them something while they are about their work," Bess said.

"Not money. Too heavy-handed."

Bess thought of the pleasure she felt whenever she received a hamper of food from her mother, full of the bounty of Hardwick.

"Then some good things to eat and drink. No one can object to that, surely."

William took Bess in his arms and pulled her close to him.

"Perfect. You always think of the perfect idea."

She smiled up at him and smoothed his ruffled hair.

"Such as marrying you? That plan has certainly worked out well."

"Indeed it has, wife. For both of us. I knew I had spotted a good bargain when first I clapped eyes on you."

Fourth of October, 1552—Chatsworth, Derbyshire

"This is the best birthday gift I could wish," Bess said. She revolved in a slow circle, admiring the stone walls of the new house rising around the central courtyard where she stood.

"A fitting monument to your attaining the great age of a quarter of a century," William laughed.

"Mother, whose house is this?" Little Frankie, four years old now, tugged at Bess's skirt.

"Ours, my lamb. But it's not finished yet. So we will live in another house and watch this one grow. That will be something to tell your grandchildren in years to come."

"My grandchildren?" Frankie giggled, tossing her red ringlets. "That's silly. I'm just a little girl; I don't have any grandchildren."

"But you will, sweet thing," William said, scooping her into his arms. "You will. And so will your brothers." The nurse Tamsin held baby Willie in her arms and two-year-old Harry clutched her skirts.

"What about our other house?" Frankie wondered.

"Northaw is not our house anymore," Bess said. "But this house will be much better."

In June, William had signed the papers giving over Northaw and small parcels of land scattered in several counties to the crown, and now he was master of hundreds of acres of land in Derbyshire, encompassing meadow, woodland, mines, and quarries, as well as whole villages. The exchange had been an astonishing bargain, costing little in real money, and providing new sources of income. William had taken care that Bess would never experience what her mother and the Barlow family had gone through. All the properties were held in both his and Bess's names, so that if he died before her, she would not lose them and Harry would not be made a ward of the court.

"We will invite the countryside to the house at Christmastide," Bess said. "I wish to know our tenants, and it will be good for them to know us."

"An excellent thought," William agreed. "And when they know you, they will love you, Lady Cavendish, as who could not?"

CHAPTER TWENTY-SIX

Second of May, 1553—Chatsworth, Derbyshire

HUM! HERE IS MUCH NEWS INDEED," WILLIAM SAID, HIS HAND with a piece of bread poised halfway between plate and mouth.

"What is it?" Bess asked. He looked more worried than usual at the regular reports from London.

"John Dudley's son Guildford will marry Jane Grey."

"Guildford Dudley? But last I heard it was likely she would marry the king."

"Everything's changed now," William said, letting the letter drop to the table and sitting back in his chair. "The king is ill. When he opened Parliament last month many thought he was dying, he looked so pale and sick, and afterward he took to his chamber for a fortnight. John Dudley urged him to write his will, and he did so, excluding his sisters from the succession."

Bess's mind ticked off the list of possible heirs.

"Then who is to succeed him if he has no child? The Scottish queen?"

"No. He passes over the descendants of Margaret Tudor, as did his father. Mary of Scotland is too much a foreigner, and her aunt

Lady Margaret Douglas, too, married to the Earl of Lennox, and raising their children as Papists. Besides, there were always questions about her legitimacy."

A cold knot was forming in Bess's stomach.

"Then that leaves Frances Grey."

"Not quite." William's eyes met hers and he dropped his voice. "Her sons. The king declares that the throne will pass to the sons of Frances Grey."

Neither of them had to state the obvious. Frances Grey had no sons. She was thirty-five. It might still be possible she would have another child. But she had borne no living children in the nine years since the birth of Mary Grey.

"Jane." Bess's voice was little more than a whisper.

"Jane. But Mary Tudor will never stand quiet and let the crown pass her by, and there are many who would fight for her, whatever the king may wish. And that is the reason for all these weddings. For what is needed to battle the claim of an unmarried Papist princess is a lady who is emphatically not a Papist, suitably married, and on the way to producing a male heir."

"Who else is to be married?"

"Kate Grey, to Henry Herbert. And Catherine Dudley will wed Henry Hastings, who has his own claim to the crown."

So the Earl of Pembroke had shored up his position since the death of his wife Anne Parr in February, Bess thought, by betrothing his son Henry Herbert to a Grey. And by marrying their daughter to Henry Hastings, the Dudleys gained yet another grappling hook to the throne.

"And poor little Mary Grey is promised to Lord Grey of Wilton," William said.

"She's only eight!"

"Yet she must down. And two more matches are in store. Henry Dudley will marry the Greys' niece Margaret Audley, and the Earl of Cumberland's girl will be the bride of Dudley's brother Andrew. Do you see the effect?"

"It's like a spider's web," Bess said. "With threads thrown out in every direction, binding every possible successor to the throne to the Dudleys."

"Yes. John Dudley rules in all but name, and he has cast the dice on a mighty wager—that kin of his will be on the throne or very near it when Edward is gone. And what is more, if the new monarch is very young, the privy council will keep control of the country. That means Dudley and William Parr. And Harry Grey, if Jane should be queen."

"But what if Mary . . ." Bess couldn't finish the sentence. For what the Dudleys and Greys were gambling in the pursuit of power was the lives of their children.

"If Edward dies," William said, "Mary will expect to succeed. And it will be a dogfight, make no mistake, with much blood spilled."

Fear rippled through Bess and her hands grew suddenly clammy. "Whose side are we to take?"

William's gray eyes were dark with worry, but his voice was calm.

"We must balance as a rope dancer does, a leg on one side, an arm on the other. And be prepared to jump to left or right, lest a fall in the other direction prove fatal."

Twenty-fifth of May, 1553, Whitsunday—Durham House, London

Bess looked around the chapel of John and Jane Dudley's magnificent house on the Strand. It was crowded with the highest and most powerful people in England. Dudleys and Greys were out in force for the wedding of their children. The entire privy council was present, and it seemed that every noble family was represented. Or at least those who were not Papists, Bess reflected, scanning the faces.

The king was not present. He was at Greenwich, and William had told Bess that despite Northumberland's pronouncements that Edward was recovering, he was gravely ill, and his failure to appear at his cousins' wedding would likely fuel the rumors that he was already dead.

The king's sisters, Mary and Elizabeth, were also absent, though Bess had heard that they had both written letters of congratulations and sent gifts.

The room was warm, and the dozens of feather fans waving made her think of a flock of birds, flapping and rustling their wings as they settled on the branches of a tree. Jewel-bright colors shone in the sunlight that flooded in from the courtyard, and the chatter of voices carried a sense of excitement. Of urgency, almost, Bess thought. For this triple alliance between Dudleys and Greys had been the subject of much astonishment and whispering in the weeks since it was announced.

Lizzie sat next to Bess, gorgeous in periwinkle blue. "Thank God this day has come," she said in an undertone. "It was my idea, you know, marrying Jane Grey to Guildford Dudley." She gave Bess a significant look and lowered her voice to a whisper. "For if Mary comes to the throne, I am undone utterly. She is a friend of Anne Bourchier, you know."

Bess had forgotten that William Parr's first wife was close to the Lady Mary. But Lizzie was not the only person who would be undone if Mary came to the throne, for surely she would return England to the old religion, reverse all the changes that had been made over the last twenty years, and restore the heresy laws. Lizzie's marriage to William Parr would be meaningless, as Anne Bourchier still lived.

There was a stir and a murmur, and Bess turned to see Jane Grey, on the arm of her father, coming down the aisle followed by her sister Kate, ethereally beautiful in silver and gold, and twelve-year-old Catherine Dudley.

Jane looked pale, her pointed little chin and cheekbones standing out sharply, and her eyes sunken and shadowed. Bess thought she looked far older than her sixteen years, and nothing like a joyful bride. Jane managed a smile as she faced handsome Guildford Dudley and he took her hand in his. Young Henry Herbert, the Earl of Pembroke's son, looked ill and as if he could barely stand. William had said that he had been abed for weeks and had been harried from the house to wed the Greys' other daughter.

As the priest spoke the words of the marriage service, Bess couldn't help but glance at Frances Grey. Regal in black studded with pearls, she held her head high. Her expression was unreadable. If King Edward died leaving a child heir, Frances would likely be governor to the young monarch. Did she think to be mother to a queen before long? She had raised Jane like a princess, and Jane had been diligent in her lessons, unwilling pupil though she was. And no doubt Frances and Harry Grey intended to control Jane as they had done throughout her life, regardless of whether she wore a crown. Bess hoped that if Jane did fulfill her mother's ambitions and become queen, Frances might at last show her some love and kindness.

Jane Dudley wore no such mask. She looked like a cat that had eaten a canary bird, Bess thought. Beside her, John Dudley, the ghost of a smile on his lips, simply looked like a man who no one dared challenge.

After the wedding, Bess got a moment with Jane, and kissed her pale cheeks. She began to wish Jane joy but stopped, feeling that the words might loose a flood of tears. From herself, and perhaps from the bride as well.

"What a beautiful necklace," she said, for want of anything better to say.

"Thank you," Jane said, a hand flying to her throat. Her fingers toyed with the pearls and rubies. "A New Year's gift from Princess Mary."

"Where will you live?"

"At Syon."

Bess felt a shiver up her spine. Syon Abbey was where Cat Howard had been taken from Hampton Court, where she had learned that she was to die. Edward Seymour had built a fine house there before he died, now in the possession of the Dudleys.

"I hear it's very lovely," she said to Jane, hating the falseness of her voice. Jane looked up at her and Bess was distressed to see tears in her eyes.

"Oh, Bess. I feel so bewildered. Everything is happening so fast."

How can I help her? Bess thought. She pulled Jane into her arms and held her close.

"Come to visit as soon as you can. I'm with child again. Will you stand godmother? November is when it is like to be born. You could come and stay as you did for Temperance's christening."

Jane's face brightened.

"Yes! I'd like that." A shadow of doubt crossed her face. "If I'm permitted."

"We'll find a way," Bess whispered to her, stroking a russet strand of hair from Jane's cheek. "We must find a way. For I feel I can never be happy again until you are happy, too, dear Jane."

Twenty-first of June, 1553—Newgate Street, London

"The storm is upon us." William had barely closed the front door of the house before he spoke. "Time to leave London."

"Why? What's happened?" Bess asked. She was five months gone with child now and they had planned to stay in town for the birth.

"The king is dying."

Bess recalled William saying the same words when King Henry's life was nearing its end. There had been no doubt who would succeed him. But this time nothing was certain.

"When must we go?"

"Now. See to the packing."

He turned and headed up the stairs and Bess followed him, her mind awhirl with all that would need to be done to depart London suddenly. In the six years since their marriage, she and William had divided their time between London and the country, keeping the lease of the house from William Parr so that they always had a suitable place near the court, where they could entertain old friends and woo new ones.

"But the king has been ill for some time," she said. "Why must we leave so suddenly?"

"His device for the succession, which Edward Seymour pushed him to enact, has been signed and approved. He has named Jane Grey as his heir. Mary is in Norfolk, so it will take some days for the news to reach her. But we're in a race against time—Edward is failing fast. The minute he's dead all stability will be gone."

"Stability? We have been poised at the edge of a precipice."

"And now the earth is giving way beneath our feet." William dropped the riding boots he had taken up. He strode toward Bess and grasped her upper arms as though to plant her firmly before him. "There are only two choices now: Mary or Jane. All men will have to declare where their allegiance lies. And those who wager wrong will pay a heavy price. The farther we are from London the better. It will give us time to know how matters are falling out before we must speak."

"Of course it must be Jane," Bess said. William laid a hand over her lips, and she was terrified by the urgency and swiftness of his movement.

"Shh. We must not speak aloud what is in our hearts, even to each other. And on no account to anyone else. We must be gone before anyone knows we are leaving or has the chance to ask where we will stand."

The words of Job echoed in Bess's head.

The thing that I feared is come upon me, and the thing that I was afraid of is happened unto me.

She clutched to William and held fast, as if he were a rock of safety in a heaving sea.

Fifteenth of July, 1553—Chatsworth, Derbyshire

The rider was a blur in the distance. Bess shaded her eyes and tried to see the face, but it was muffled beneath scarf and hat. No matter. Whoever it was came from London, and the news was not hard to guess.

"William!" Bess called over her shoulder toward the house and turned at the sound of a window being flung open. William spotted the horseman and he disappeared within, coming to her side in a few moments.

"It's Cecil's man, Bowers," he said.

A wave of dizziness passed over her. Her whole body felt heavy and sluggish with her pregnancy, and the summer heat added to her discomfort.

In minutes Bowers pounded past the gatehouse and was calling out before he had dismounted.

"The king is dead. The Duke of Northumberland has proclaimed Jane Grey queen."

Bess's knees felt weak and she put a hand on William's arm to steady herself.

"And where is Mary?" William guided her toward the house as he addressed Bowers. "Has the news reached her? Does Dudley have her within his control?"

"She is in Norfolk," Bowers said, gulping down the tankard of small beer that a serving man brought him. "She was on her way to London but must have learned the king was dying, so she turned around and made for Kenninghall."

"God's blood." Bess had almost never heard William swear, and his words shook her. "There she will raise an army, no doubt. Or perhaps fly to Flanders, and seek the assistance of her cousin the Holy Roman Emperor. What a blunder on Dudley's part. What does he do with this news?"

"He is garrisoning the Tower and has sent his son Robert after her with orders to bring her to London."

William snorted with scorn. "It will need more than Robin Dudley to stop the Lady Mary."

"Northumberland has the promise that France will come in on his side."

Dear God, Bess thought, it was real war that was about to be unleashed. Thank heaven the children were here in Derbyshire, far from London. But Jane . . .

"Where is Jane Grey?" she asked.

"She was at Suffolk Place with her mother, but she was being fetched back to Syon when I left London."

Where the Dudleys could keep her in their grasp, Bess thought, and no doubt try to make their son Guildford king regnant, not just Jane's consort, snatching power from the hands of the Greys. Poor Jane. She had not wanted the crown, would have been content to be left to her studies. Bess turned to William, feeling lost.

"What are we to do?"

"Wait. For as long as we can."

Uncertainty and anxiety ate at Bess for two long days, until another messenger arrived with fresh news from London.

"Mary wrote to the privy council demanding their allegiance to her as Edward's rightful heir," William told Bess. "She's been proclaimed queen in Norfolk, and parts of Suffolk, too. Nobles, gentlemen, and the people in their thousands are flocking to her with arms. Dudley was wrong to dismiss the plans of 'a mere woman.' Now he's got a war on his hands and he's not ready. He's gathering arms and munitions at the Tower, and recruits are being offered ten pence a day to join his army. 'Jane the Queen' may be signing orders to the lord lieutenants of the counties demanding their support, but whether they will obey remains to be seen."

Oh, Jane, Jane, Jane.

"But if Jane has already been proclaimed queen?"

"It doesn't mean the people like it. They don't like Dudley and don't trust him. They think he supports Jane Grey only because he means to put his son on the throne, or even to make himself king.

No matter the proclamations that Mary and Elizabeth are bastards, or the reminders that Mary is a Papist. Mary is the daughter of Henry and Queen Catherine, whom people still love. And the countryside isn't London—evangelicals are rare birds outside of town. I think most folk would rather have Henry's daughter, Papist or no, than let the Duke of Northumberland rule. And here is worse news for Dudley—it's said that he's treating with the French, and is willing to replace Jane with the Scots queen if that will bring him the support of France should the emperor take up Mary's part."

"So England would be the prize to be won by the empire or by France."

"Exactly. And where think you Englishmen will stand on that?"

"But if Mary prevails, then Jane . . ."

"Would be guilty of treason."

Bess felt sick, and clapped a hand to her mouth. The penalty for treason for a woman was burning alive.

"But none of this is her doing!" she cried. "It's all her father and John Dudley. Surely Mary knows that. And she's like an aunt to Jane—she could never harm her."

William's face was grim, but she could see that he was struggling to find words of comfort for her.

"Likely not. As you say, she knows the ambition for the throne does not come from Jane."

Bess felt suddenly exhausted and overwhelmed and sank into a chair. The child in her womb kicked, as if he felt her turmoil. She put her hand on her belly, as if to calm the babe as well as herself. She and William and the children were all safe here at Chatsworth. Perhaps they might ride out the storm and come to no harm.

"Bess." William stooped at her side. "We can stand aside no longer. The time has come for action. I will raise as many men as I can, and go to join John Dudley."

A wave of terror swept through Bess.

"But why?"

"If Mary becomes queen, many will suffer greatly for it. Our friends. All of England. The matter now hangs in the balance. Dudley will need every man he can get if there is any hope of keeping Jane on the throne."

Jane, Jane, Jane.

Bess stared at him, feeling numb. "But what if he fails?"

"Then many will die. I must do what I can to prevent it."

WILLIAM HAD GONE. BESS LAY IN HER BEDCHAMBER, WHERE SHE had retreated with a pounding headache. She took up the little portrait of Jane Grey that stood near her bed and studied it. Those keen, bright eyes, the determined chin with its dimple, the delicate hands. Jane was strong, no question, but surely the threat of civil war and foreign invasion was too great a weight for those slender shoulders. And if Dudley should fail . . .

Bess got to her knees and prayed.

God my Father, let Thy care watch over my dear husband, my only harbor in troubled seas. Grant that John Dudley and his forces may be victorious. And protect my Jane. Jane the queen, if so she be, but most of all my sweet beloved Jane. Give her Thy infinite strength and wisdom, and guide and protect her as she treads this treacherous path.

THE DAYS SEEMED TO DRAG ON ENDLESSLY. HERE IN THE COUNTRY-side, summer was in glorious reign. But Bess knew that even as she went about her daily life, supervising the running of the household and estate, seeing to the dairying and the baking, the brewing and the plans for the harvest, matters of great importance were moving inexorably forward in London and elsewhere.

She had had no word from William, but riders passing carried news that the country was rising to support Mary's claim to the throne. She had been proclaimed queen in Buckinghamshire, and armies of men were rallying to her at Framlingham Castle in Suffolk. Five royal ships had mutinied off Norfolk and now stood at her command.

Bess was both relieved and terrified at the sight of William's secretary John Bestenay pelting down the road to the house.

"My husband?" she cried, before he had dismounted.

"My lady, I have no news of him—I come from London—but I
bring a letter writ to him from Sir William Cecil."

Inside the house, Jenny and Aunt Marcella followed Bess as she
led Bestenay to William's study. Once the door was closed behind
them, Bess broke the seal on the folded square of paper that Bestenay handed to her. A smaller letter fell out of it, and as he bent to
retrieve it, Bess saw that on it was written her own name, in Jane
Grey's writing. Bestenay handed it to her, and she clasped it to her
bosom. Jane was yet well, or had been a few days since. But Bess
could not bring herself to open the letter, for fear of what ill tidings
it might bring. She found no comfort in Bestenay's grim face.

"What is the news?" she asked.

"It is over, is the sum of the news."

Aunt Marcella gasped, and she and Jenny stood arm in arm,
their faces grim. Bess wrapped her arms about herself. Where was
William? He could be dead even now. And what of Jane? She
clutched Jane's letter like a kind of talisman. If she held the letter in
her hands, then Jane was well.

"Read me what Cecil says." She strove to keep her voice calm and
steady.

Bestenay opened the letter and read.

*"The nineteenth of July, 1553. This day the Earl of Pembroke pro-
claimed Mary to be queen at the cross in Cheapside, to the great joy
of the people. Bonfires were lit and the bells of the churches rang forth,
as they had not done when the Lady Jane was proclaimed queen but
ten days ago."*

"So Pembroke turned," Bess said. She thought of William Herbert,
godfather to her newest child, sitting at the christening dinner across
from William Parr, whom he had now abandoned to the uncertain
mercy of Mary Tudor. And so many others would suffer, too.

"Harry Grey knew he was beaten and gave in without a fight.

When the soldiers sent by the privy council came to the Tower, he ordered his men to down their weapons, and went forth to Tower Hill to read the proclamation declaring Mary queen. When he returned he tore down the canopy of state with his own hands and told his daughter Jane that she was queen no more."

Jane's face came clear to Bess's mind, and she longed to be with her and to comfort her. Jenny and Aunt Marcella were weeping quietly.

May God damn Harry Grey, she thought. *His ambition overran all sense. And how many others will he take down with him?*

"Grey and his wife are gone to Baynard's Castle," Bestenay read on, *"to plead with Pembroke that all they did was at the behest of John Dudley. After they left the Tower, the guards had orders to let none else leave. Jane Grey, along with her husband and his mother, are prisoners."*

"Oh, God, no!" Bess gasped, staggering as though she had been struck, and Jenny and Aunt Marcella caught her in their arms.

"Do you wish to lie down?" Jenny asked. "Let me help you to your chamber." Her face was gray with worry.

"No. I am well. The child is well." Bess put a protective hand to her belly. She looked to Bestenay. "Read the rest of the letter."

"John Dudley and William Parr are yet in the field," he continued, *"but if they are taken alive and returned to London, there is naught but death awaits them here. Mary is queen, it is most certain. I enclose for your lady wife a letter from the hand of one who loves her well. Yours in haste, William Cecil."*

Bess looked at the small square of paper in her lap and broke the wax that sealed it. The sight of Jane's writing brought tears to her eyes and she wiped them away so she could read.

My dearest Bess: It is hard to believe so much has happened in the few weeks since I last saw you, at my wedding. I will not recount the events as I am sure you have heard them all from those whose thoughts are clearer than mine. I am here at the Tower where I came as queen and from which, perhaps, I will never depart. I wish you were with me. You ever knew what to say to me to ease my fears and to still my whirling thoughts. My cousin Mary, now the queen, has always been kind to me and I hope will show me mercy. Without that, I am lost. Pray for me, dear Bess. With love always, Jane.

O God, protect her, Bess prayed, *for those on earth who should do so have cast her to the dogs.*

WILLIAM ARRIVED BACK AT CHATSWORTH THAT NIGHT, LOOKING like a ghost.

"Thank God, thank God you are safe!" Bess repeated, burying her face against his chest and holding him tight. She raised her eyes to his face. "You are safe? Your men?"

He nodded. "The news from London came to us before we came close to reaching Dudley. If any have reason to ask, I shall say that I was riding to the aid of Queen Mary. And none can prove that was not my aim."

CHAPTER TWENTY-SEVEN

Twenty-first of December, 1553—London

A STIFF BREEZE WAS BLOWING ON THE RIVER, BUT BESS DIDN'T care. She was on her way to see Jane Grey at the Tower, and her heart felt lighter than it had in months, for Jane expected that Queen Mary would shortly pardon her and send her home to Bradgate, and she was now allowed to walk free in the Queen's Garden within the Tower walls.

It would still some of Bess's frantic worry to see Jane with her own eyes, to be able to touch and speak with her. Sheltering at Chatsworth had kept her family out of danger, but left her desperate to know what was happening in London. Once the trial and execution of John Dudley had taken place in August, William had urged that they return to town and she had agreed.

"We must go back sometime," he had said. "My only livelihood is with the crown. And our surest footing is to stand squarely by the side of Queen Mary. An easy path lies open to us—we shall ask her to be godmother to the babe that is coming."

So back to London they had gone, Bess in her seventh month of pregnancy. As always, the sight of London had brought mixed feelings, but she knew that William was right. They could not hide in Derbyshire forever.

She had nearly fainted when William told her on the thirteenth of November that Jane Grey had been convicted of treason and condemned to die by burning. But he had assured her that Mary would pardon Jane. So a few days after their son Charles was born on the twenty-seventh of November, he had been christened in a Papist service, with Queen Mary as his godmother. In a further step to securing the goodwill of the queen, William and Bess asked Mary's longtime ally Bishop Gardiner to be one of the child's godfathers. Bess wept with rage and shame at the thought of smiling at Gardiner, recalling his plot to bring down Catherine Parr, and his sending Anne Askew to the flames. Only the knowledge that she was securing a safer future for her family steeled her to go through with it. But she had insisted that the second godfather be Harry Grey, whom Mary had pardoned.

"We stand by the queen, to be sure," she told William, "but I will not have the Greys think that all their love and care for me is lost. They are yet our friends."

And now she was ascending the stairs to the warder's lodgings where Jane was kept. A servant opened the door. Voices sounded in the background.

"Bess!" Jane launched herself into Bess's arms, and they clung together weeping. When Bess pulled back to look at Jane's face it seemed to her that Jane was more pale than usual and there were shadows beneath her eyes, making her look far older than her sixteen years.

"Oh, my darling girl," Bess cried. "I feel as though I've been holding my breath these past months. I cannot tell you how relieved I am to see you once more, whole and well."

They walked in the garden, both bundled against the cold, with Jane's three ladies-in-waiting trailing behind. Dark clouds scudded overhead and there was frost on the ground, but Jane insisted that the winter air would invigorate her.

"You can't imagine how it has depressed my spirits to be kept shut up this long while. Just to see the sky overhead, to feel the wind in my face, reminds me that I am alive."

"God be thanked," Bess said.

"And I do thank Him, every day. I pray for the people who are so led astray that they have now returned to the Mass and other Popish ways that had been repudiated."

"But Jane," Bess said in alarm, glancing over her shoulder to hear who might be listening. "The queen decreed the return to the Mass! Surely you do not speak of such things?"

"I do and I must."

"No, I beg you, do not so! Is it not enough that your father is pardoned and you will soon be free? There is nothing to be gained by standing in opposition to the queen."

Jane's face was sad. "Do you not see, Bess, that to fall in, uncomplaining, with those who advocate a return to Rome would be like acquiescing to the will of Satan? Agreement of purpose is not always a good thing. Why, there is unity among thieves, murderers, and conspirators."

Bess felt despair wash over her. How was it possible that anyone could value the form in which faith was practiced more than life itself? What did it matter whether people took communion, or whether they believed that Christ inhabited communion bread and wine? But a glance at Jane's face told her it would be useless to argue further. She took Jane's arm in hers.

"Well, I will pray only that soon you will be back at Bradgate, among your books, where you like best to be."

CHAPTER TWENTY-EIGHT

Twenty-second of January, 1554—Newgate Street, London

THERE HAD BEEN RUMORS FOR DAYS OF PLANNED UPRISINGS IN response to the announcement that Queen Mary would wed King Philip of Spain, and as soon as William burst through the door, Bess knew that he bore bad news.

"Frances Grey's cousin Sir Peter Carew was summoned to court for questioning about these murmurs of rebellion. He did not come or send word, which surely means that he was involved in making trouble and is now a fugitive."

Cold fear gripped Bess's heart, a feeling that had become sickeningly familiar over the past months. What would happen to Jane if Queen Mary thought that the Greys were acting against her?

"But surely the Greys would not be so foolish as to be involved in any more plots," she said, praying that it was true.

"I wouldn't lay money on it. Bishop Gardiner told me not an hour since that Edward Courtenay has confessed a plan to remove the queen and put her sister Elizabeth on the throne, and he named Harry Grey among the conspirators."

Jane. Save her and protect her, Lord, for this trouble is none of her doing.

"Jane must be so frightened. I want to go to her."

William shook his head. "It's not likely you'd be allowed."

Within days, the situation became more dire.

"The queen is raising an army, and from what I hear, she'll need it," William told Bess. "Thomas Wyatt set up his battle standard at Maidstone and read out a proclamation against the queen's marriage, charging all of England to rise to his cause."

"And will they?" she asked, her heart pounding.

"He's in a strong position to be dangerous if they do. He's one of the largest landowners in Kent and during the Kett rebellion he put in place a hand-picked militia for the defense of the country. He could be at the head of an army very quickly."

Jane.

"Where is Jane in all this?"

"In a very ill place. The Earl of Huntingdon told the council that Harry Grey tried to get him to join the rising, saying that Wyatt had promised to put Jane Grey on the throne in exchange for Grey's support."

A few days later, William told Bess that Harry Grey had failed to respond to a summons.

"He's been declared a traitor, as have his brothers. And the Earl of Huntingdon has set off to hunt him down and bring him back to London."

"Huntingdon?" she cried in confusion and despair. "But he supported Jane's succession. Isn't he in the Tower?"

"No longer. Alliances are shifting faster than can be reckoned, for to be in the wrong place when the music stops will bring a most unhappy end."

Over the next days, the rumors flew. Wyatt was said to be marching toward London with five thousand men behind him.

What if he should succeed? Bess thought, her hopes rising. Whoever ended on the throne, it wouldn't be Mary. Perhaps Jane would go free, even if she wasn't queen.

"What if you raised men and went to Wyatt, as you went to fight for John Dudley last summer?" Bess whispered to William in the safety of their bed.

"I have thought of it. I think of it still, but it is a very risky thing. I think the queen will prevail, and Wyatt and his supporters will die."

It became more difficult for Bess not to beg William to join Wyatt when she learned that Wyatt's army had taken Rochester Bridge and seized a fleet of royal ships anchored in the Medway, along with their weapons and ordnance.

"And now?" she argued. "You could go to Chatsworth; there are hundreds of men there who would go if you called them."

"No!" he cried. "I've left it too late! It would be a fortnight before I was back in London. It will all be over then. Besides"—he sighed hopelessly—"this is not like last summer. Then I set out from Chatsworth, and thanks be to God, learned that the cause was lost before I met with Mary's troops. Marching on London is quite a different thing."

Then it's hopeless, Bess thought. *We have no choice but to sit and wait.*

On the third of February, Bess woke to the sound of cannon fire.

"That sounds very close," she said to William, and ran to the window and threw open the shutters. Smoke was rising from the east. When she turned back, William was already half dressed.

"Stay inside," he commanded her, and headed for the door of the bedchamber, strapping on his sword. He was back within a quarter of an hour.

"Wyatt and his men have crossed the bridge and are making for Whitehall. The queen's soldiers are marching toward the city. They're like to meet on our very doorstep. Nothing for it but to batten down the hatches to meet the coming storm."

Bess and a few of the servants closed and latched all the shutters of the house and barred the doors, while William gathered the rest of the servants, and armed them with whatever was to hand.

"Don't go out unless I give the word," he warned them. "But be prepared to defend the house against anyone who tries to get in, whether queen's men or the others."

Soon Bess heard shouts, the tramp of feet, drums. Then the clash of steel on steel, the discharge of arms, screams, orders bawled above the chaos. She sat on her bed, feeling helpless, knowing that what was happening outside the windows must decide the outcome of what Wyatt had started. She remembered that Wyatt was Lizzie's cousin, and wondered where Lizzie was, and if she was safe.

By afternoon, the battle sounds had ceased. William went out with half a dozen men to learn what he could.

"The queen's army turned back Wyatt's men," he told Bess when he came back. "There's a corpse hanging in St. Paul's Churchyard. One of Wyatt's, I think."

"Is it finished, then?"

"I don't know. We'll learn more tomorrow."

The next day he went to Whitehall and returned looking haggard and despairing. "That fool Grey has doomed himself and all around him," he said, sitting on the bed.

Jane.

Bess went and stood before him, praying he would have some words of comfort. He took her hands in his, studying them as if he had never seen them before. He kept his eyes down as he spoke. "The queen has agreed to sign the death warrants of Jane Grey and Guildford Dudley."

Bess was seized by a wave of nausea and panic.

"No! Surely she knows that Jane cannot mean her harm!"

"I don't think anyone knows anything anymore. All is in turmoil. But as long as Jane Grey lives, people opposed to Queen Mary will rally to her."

Bess had a sudden recollection of Jane returning from a visit with

Mary years ago, prattling happily about her cousin's kindness and praise for her. It had seemed then that Mary had provided Jane with the kind of encouragement and affection that her own mother did not.

"When?" Bess asked, her throat so tight with fear she could barely speak.

"Three days from now."

Bess's head swam, and the last thing she saw before she slumped into William's arms was the fear on his face.

THE NEXT THREE DAYS SEEMED LIKE A YEAR. DESPITE WILLIAM'S protests, Bess went to the Tower and tried to see Jane, but she was not permitted, and when she returned home she lay in her bed and wept until her head ached and she thought there could be no more tears left to be shed.

On the day that Jane was to die, Bess rose from bed only to kneel in desperate prayer that somehow Jane might be saved. Were it not for William and the children, she would have prayed to be taken instead, if only Jane could live.

When she heard William's footsteps on the stair, she covered her mouth, steeling herself for the news that Jane was dead.

"The execution has been put off," William told her. "The queen has greater dangers than Jane Grey just now. The rebels have reached Knightsbridge. There are rumors that royal troops fled in the face of the attack and that the Earl of Pembroke has gone over to Wyatt's side."

Bess's hopes rose. "Will you join him? If enough men rally to him, perhaps he may win, and Jane will be restored to the throne."

"I would if I thought that it would do any good, but I think the tide is about to turn against Wyatt. Huntingdon and an army of three hundred men brought Harry Grey and his brother John captive to the Tower this day."

"Perhaps Queen Mary will change her mind," Bess said desperately. She thought of the necklace that Jane had worn at her wedding, a gift from the queen. "Mary loves Jane."

But William shook his head. "There's no going back now." He took her into his arms, and she saw that there were tears in his eyes. "You make it harder for yourself if you hold out hope when there is none."

"How terrified she must be," she wept. "If only I go could to her. She needs me; she has no one to comfort her now."

"She knows you love her. You must cling to that knowledge. The best we can offer her now is our prayers."

On the morning of the twelfth of February, a messenger brought a letter for Bess, addressed to her in Jane Grey's bold handwriting. Bess was trembling as she broke the seal and read.

My dear Bess, I know that you will weep for me, but I beg you to take comfort in the knowledge that I do not weep that God will take me from this vale of misery, for I know that in losing a mortal life I shall find an immortal felicity. As we are told, there is a time to be born and a time to die, and the day of death is better than the day of our birth. I pray you remember me in your heart and in your prayers, and that the Lord that has hitherto strengthened you so continue, that at last we may meet in heaven. With my most constant love to you, dear Bess, your Jane.

A lock of red-gold hair tied with a bit of blue ribbon had been folded into the letter. Bess raised it to her nose and thought she could detect Jane's scent. She kissed the lock of hair and curled it into her hand, as if by holding it close she could draw Jane to her, and sobs racked her.

The sound of a cannon boomed and echoed in the distance, and Bess felt as though the shot had gutted her.

"What noise is that?" she asked, knowing the answer even as she spoke.

The young messenger's eyes met hers and she saw that he was in tears. "It is done. Jane Grey is dead."

CHAPTER TWENTY-NINE

Eighth of March, 1557—Chatsworth, Derbyshire

BESS LOOKED AROUND AT THE FRIENDS AND NEIGHBORS WHO had come to celebrate the christening of her baby, Lucres, who had been born the previous week, on Shrove Tuesday. The mood was relaxed and happy. The godparents were all close friends of Bess and William from nearby, rather than highly placed and powerful Londoners. Bess smiled at Jenny, standing next to their brother Jem and surrounded by a knot of tumbling, laughing children, including her three own little ones and Bess's. Frankie was almost nine now, Harry and Willie were six and five, Charlie was three and a half and always into mischief, little Bessie would be two in a fortnight, and May, in the nurse's arms, was fourteen months old.

It had been the right decision to remove themselves from London, Bess thought. Of course William had to spend time at court, but he returned to Chatsworth as much as he was able, and it was so much more enjoyable to stay at home with her children rather than leaving them in Jenny's care and dashing off to town.

Besides, London was a place of horror now. In early February of 1555, a cleric named John Rogers, the prebendary of St. Paul's, had been convicted of heresy and burned at the stake in Smithfield. It had been impossible to avoid the mood of terror and anger welling up among the people in the days before the execution. Worse, the smoke had drifted down toward the river, and Bess, more than seven months gone with child, had been overcome with nausea and revulsion, vomiting repeatedly with such ferocity that William had called a physician to attend her.

That ghastly execution had been only the beginning, and since that time hundreds more had died in the flames—men and women, the feeble old and boys not yet come to manhood—for no more than cleaving to the religion that had been so stringently imposed by King Edward only a few years earlier.

"I cannot bear it," Bess had wept, holding a handkerchief over her nose and mouth to block out the stench of burning flesh. "Can we not leave?"

They had been in London for the marriage of Frances Grey's niece Margaret Clifford.

"We must go to the wedding," William had insisted. "Margaret Clifford is a relation of the queen, and the nuptials will be celebrated like a royal wedding. We cannot afford to have Queen Mary question why we are absent."

So they had attended the wedding, the feasts, the jousts and masques, and inside Bess had felt as if she were dying by inches. The Lady Elizabeth was there, the whiteness of her face standing out against her black gown, and watching her standing alone in a corner Bess was reminded of an animal, hiding trembling and silent in hopes of being overlooked by an approaching predator.

Just as difficult as curtsying low before the queen, swollen with what had proved to be a false pregnancy, and smiling and chatting, had been coming face-to-face with Frances Grey and her daughters, all now serving in the privy chamber of Queen Mary.

How could they do it? Bess shrieked inside her head. Had they forgotten Jane, whose blood had sodden Tower Green only three years earlier? Did they not recall that it was Queen Mary who had sent her to her death? Seeing the Greys only made Jane's absence a new and tearing grief to Bess. And she had found herself looking for the grinning, ruddy face of Harry Grey, who had introduced her to William those many years ago. But he had gone to the block only a few weeks after Jane, along with John Dudley and so many others, for his part in Thomas Wyatt's rebellion. She had searched Frances Grey's face for signs of sorrow but saw none, and the rage rose within her.

Not long after that dreadful wedding, Frances had married Adrian Stokes, her master of horse, to universal surprise, ending any possibility that she would ever succeed to the throne. Kate Grey's marriage to Henry Herbert had been annulled, and little Mary Grey's espousal to her cousin dissolved, with as much dispatch and cold political calculation as the alliances had been made only months before. Bradgate Park, the house that Bess had called home and loved when she lived among the Greys, had been taken by the crown. Everything to do with the Greys had seemed baffling and heartbreaking to Bess, and she had wanted to be far from the court and all to do with it.

Now, on this prematurely springlike day at Chatsworth, peace and happiness reigned, and Bess felt safe. Her mother came to her side, a goblet of good French claret in her hand.

"The house is looking splendid," she said, tilting her head back to admire the plasterwork of the ceiling. "The furnishings in my chamber are magnificent—such exquisite tapestries! You've done so much work since last I was here."

"And yet it seems it will never end!" Bess sighed. "Outside as well as in. The orchard is coming along well, but come summer I plan to put in a pleasure garden, fish pools, and an entrance lodge. And there's work to be done on the land we acquired last year, as well."

"How is William's health?"

Bess followed her mother's glance to her husband, who stood in conversation with William Paulet, and a shadow of worry darkened her mind as it did so often when she looked upon him. He had been extremely ill during the previous winter, unable to eat because his stomach was in such great pain, and far too weak to ride to London until summer. Even then, they had canceled a planned visit to their old friends John and Christian Thynne at Longleat.

Work was more than half the problem, as far as Bess was concerned. When William had become treasurer of the king's chamber accounts upon Edward's accession there was a deficit of nearly two thousand pounds, and he had struggled with that burden ever since.

Now, with the queen allowing England to be drawn into her husband King Philip's war with France, the press for money was even more acute, for somehow those thousands of foot soldiers and hundreds of horse must be paid for. William had refused to provide the crown with the loan of a hundred pounds that was being demanded from landowners across the country, but the pressure was relentless and he tossed and turned in the night, or got up to pore over account books and write letters by candlelight.

"He is better just now," Bess told her mother, not willing to show the depth of her concern. She sought to turn the conversation to another subject. "What a grief to hear of the death of George Zouche."

"Yes. I sent Lady Zouche a hamper of honey and other things from Hardwick. I will always be grateful for the start they gave you."

Elizabeth placed a gentle hand on Bess's cheek, and Bess kissed her, feeling comforted as always in her presence. Having her mother only a few hours' ride away was another reason she was happy to be living at Chatsworth.

Late that evening, when the guests were gone and Bess had checked that the shutters were closed and the doors locked, she mounted the stairs, ready to climb into the soft warmth of the great bed. William sat in his nightshirt, his feet bare, staring into the darkness before him.

"What's amiss, love?" Bess asked. "You'll catch your death; get under the covers."

He started as if he had not heard her come in and passed a hand over his forehead as though to ease a headache. Perhaps the day's excitement had been too wearing for him, Bess thought, chiding herself that she had not noticed earlier how tired he was looking.

"Are you feeling ill? Shall I make you a nice warm posset?"

"No, it's not my gut." He looked at her and she thought he looked more worried than she had ever seen him. "William Paulet says that my chamber accounts have been audited—going back eleven years!— and I am out by almost six thousand pounds. I will be summoned to report. To explain."

Bess was staggered at the vast amount, and baffled. William was so methodical, so careful.

"But how can that be? And why do they seize on your accounts?"

"It's not just mine. The queen seeks to wring every penny she can from the government, in service of the war. But I fear that she wishes me gone, and will use this as an excuse to remove me from my office."

"Surely you can put your accounts straight if they are out."

"It will be a monstrous task. There have been times when I have paid for needful expenses myself as the chamber accounts had not the money, and other times when I borrowed, only to repay the money shortly. And Thomas Knot kept the books much of the time—all those months when I was ill last year—and Paulet said he disappeared when the audit began. I hardly know how to begin."

Bess's heart ached to see the despair and exhaustion etching his face.

"I will help you," she said. "You have taught me well how to keep accounts. We'll sort it out."

"I hope you're right," he said, as she coaxed him under the bedclothes. "Oh, Bess, that all my work should come to ruin in this way."

If William was required to repay six thousand pounds it would be disastrous, but Bess refused to countenance that possibility.

"No ruin," she murmured, stroking his head and kissing him. "We'll write to the queen. All will be well, you'll see."

Eighteenth of August, 1557—Chatsworth, Derbyshire

The household had been in an uproar since the previous day, when Bess had received William's letter from London. He would shortly be called before the Star Chamber to answer for the errors in the privy chamber accounts, and he begged that Bess would come to him.

I need your clear head, my good Bess, he had written, *and your steady hand and heart with me now in this time of trouble. I have been working day and night to prepare fair copies of the rough journal books of the accounts, but I fear I will not finish and at moments I stop and sit and stare and wonder if all my labor is to no avail. I pray you fly to me as soon as you may.*

Bess wanted to reach London as quickly as possible and so would travel light, but still that meant two footmen, a guide, and nurses for six-year-old Harry, whose presence she thought would cheer William, and baby Lucres. Clothes were gathered, baskets and saddlebags were packed, instructions given for the running of the household in her absence.

"Why can't I go to London?" Frankie pouted.

"Sweetheart, you will come another time," Bess said, stooping to tuck a stray golden curl back into her daughter's cap. "Harry has not been to London since he was a baby. And I must haste to your father and cannot take you all. Besides, I need you to help your Aunt Jenny look after your little sisters and brothers and to make sure that all is well, just like a grown-up lady with her own household."

She was relieved to see Frankie's face brighten. "We will be back as soon as we may," she said, kissing her daughter's cheek. "And your father will be so proud to know what a capable big girl you are."

The party set off at dawn the next day. The journey to London, more than a hundred and fifty miles, could easily take a week but Bess was determined to be at William's side as soon as she could. She had always regarded him as unflaggingly steady and strong, and the fear that she read between his words terrified her. Six thousand pounds. However could they come up with the money if the inquiry didn't go well? And what effect would it have on William's health and state of mind if he should lose his position?

We will prevail, she thought, glancing back at the retinue straggling behind her. *We must prevail.*

CHAPTER THIRTY

Ninth of October, 1557—London

"MY LADY, THE STAR CHAMBER HAS SENT BACK SIR WILLIAM'S books." William's secretary John Bestenay looked apologetic as he put his head in at the door of her withdrawing chamber.

"Have you told Sir William?"

"No, my lady. He is asleep."

Bess went to their bedchamber but at the sight of William changed her mind about waking him. His breath was labored and he was gray with exhaustion. She would look at the correspondence herself and determine how to proceed.

Bestenay hovered nearby as Bess untied the ledgers from their bundle. In the weeks since Bess had arrived in London, William had labored to make the privy chamber accounts for the last decade tidy and clear, setting forth a list of the many allowances he was due and expenditures that had not been clearly recorded. Meanwhile, she had seen to the organizing of the household, laying in stocks of food and drink, candles and soap, all the things that were needed to make the rented house a comfortable haven. But despite her care, William was desperately ill. So much so that he had written to the

Star Chamber that he would not be able to attend the hearing sched-uled for the next day in person and begging them to take into con-sideration that he had been deceived by Thomas Knot, who had apparently taken more than a hundred pounds from William's own purse as well as money from the privy chamber accounts.

A letter lay atop the stack of William's ledgers, and Bess opened it with trembling fingers. Her eyes raced over the greeting and pre-amble, looking for the meat of the matter. Surely, she told herself, the Star Chamber would acknowledge that William was in the right and that his explanations were all that had been needed.

But at the bottom of the paper was set forth a number that made her heart stop: £5237, 5s, ¾d. And the instruction, *If it please you, acknowledge that this sum remains to be paid, entering it in the latest of the ledgers with your signature.* She let the paper drop from her hands.

"Oh, no," she moaned. "Five thousand pounds and more." She and William had an income of about five hundred pounds a year. To repay five thousand pounds would surely mean the loss of Chatsworth, of all they had worked so hard to possess.

"We can still fight it," Bestenay said, reading over the letter. "They write, *'If by reason of your sickness you cannot attend in person to answer the further particulars of the said account, you may send one or two of your clerks, or such other as you think good, by your letter of attorney, to do all such things for you as the case shall require.'* I will go tomorrow. But we must needs put our heads together and prepare an accounting of all the sums Sir William has expended on behalf of the crown for which he has not been recompensed."

"He lost armor and equipment worth more than two hundred pounds that was sent on ahead of him to Boulogne and was never returned when King Henry stayed him from going."

"Good. And surely there is more."

Bess looked at Bestenay in gratitude. He had served William well and faithfully for twenty years, and now he stood with them when they needed him most. "I thank you," she said. "What would we do without you?"

When William woke, Bess showed him the letter, glad to be able to soften it with the battle plan that Bestenay had suggested. The three of them worked into the night, and at length had drafted a letter setting forth expenditures of more than four thousand, five hundred pounds: Fifteen hundred pounds that William had personally paid to servants of King Henry, King Edward, and Queen Mary. More than a thousand pounds of unpaid wages and expenses during his service in Ireland. Three months of pay never received for inventorying the wardrobe of the robes. Money promised by King Henry and King Edward but never paid. And a thousand marks expended to raise men to ride to the aid of Queen Mary against John Dudley.

Bess's stomach fluttered with anxiety at that entry. She recalled William's words of three years earlier. *If any have reason to ask, I shall say that I was riding to the aid of Queen Mary. And none can prove that was not my aim.*

But William's mind was on their present difficulties, and he forged ahead with the letter. He would satisfy whatever amount the Star Chamber would decide he owed, he wrote, by selling properties and goods.

"But they shall know what case I am in," he said, looking more determined than Bess had seen him in weeks. He took up the pen and she read over his shoulder as he wrote on a new sheet of paper:

I, Her Majesty's right obedient servant, ready every hour to take my leave of this world, do in the name of my poor wife and my miserable and innocent children, appeal by your honorable lordships unto Her Majesty, heart in mouth, for her most gracious protection and deference, if my whole house and family are to be saved from submersion. Your right humble, meek, and poor sick man, William Cavendish.

The next day Bestenay returned from the hearing before the Star Chamber hopeful, but with no definite news.

"They will take under advisement all that we have submitted and render a judgment soon."

"Then there is hope," William said. He was overcome by a fit of coughing that shook his body, and Bess pulled the bedclothes higher and tucked them tight against his chest.

"While there is life, there is hope," she told him firmly. "Sure your years of service to the crown will not be forgotten."

THREE DAYS LATER WILLIAM TOOK A TURN FOR THE WORSE AND Bess almost forgot about the Star Chamber in the face of her overwhelming anxiety. She summoned Dr. Bartlett, who had attended her after Willie's birth. He bled William and sent his assistant back with several medicinal compounds, but nothing seemed to help. William writhed in pain and could not keep food down, and first was cold and pallid and then consumed by fever.

On the evening of the twenty-fifth of October, Bess knelt by William's bedside, holding his hand and praying that he would recover. He was unconscious, his face contorted with agitation as he muttered incoherently, as if he were having a nightmare. Terrified, Bess put her hand to his forehead and stroked his face, and was relieved that he became calmer. She could almost believe that he was only sleeping instead of hovering on the edge of death.

Dear God in Thy infinite mercy, give me the patience to submit to what Thou wouldst have be. But I know not how I will live without this man at my side. Help him, Heavenly Father. Restore his health and spirit, I beg Thee.

William stirred and his eyelids fluttered open.

"My own one," Bess whispered.

"Bess." His voice was weak. "I am so tired. Stay with me while I sleep again."

"Gladly, my love." She kissed his hand, and he sighed and closed his eyes. She watched the moon rise outside the window, a golden crescent hanging in the black autumn sky. His breathing was ragged and Bess recalled that poor Robbie had sounded even so just before the end. Fear rose within her, and she tried to tamp it down.

Memories of her life with William flooded her mind. Their first conversation, when he had offered to help her fight for her widow's dower. His counsel as they had prepared for court. The pride and affection in his eyes when she had triumphed. His tenderness when she had given herself to him on their wedding night. His tears of joy when first he held baby Frankie. How they had first stood together at Chatsworth, looking over the land, imagining the house that they would build, a fitting inheritance for Henry, their son and heir. His unceasing work and planning and care on her behalf and that of their children. Step by step, connection by connection, laying the stones of their future just as the laborers had built Chatsworth.

How could she carry on without him?

William's breathing slowed and then stopped. Bess's heart lurched. She rose to her feet and peered at his face. He took another laborious breath but his eyes were closed and she sensed that he was drifting beyond her reach now. She took his hand in hers and pressed it to her cheek as she bent her head in prayer.

Dear Lord, if Thou must take him from me, let him suffer no more but go to Thy bosom in peace.

He exhaled, and she raised her head to look at the beloved face, still of this world, but barely. She kissed his hand, wet with her tears. Another breath, and then he lay motionless. She counted. One. Two. Three. Four. Five . . . Another breath came, but shallower than the last. Once more she counted, longer this time. Another breath, almost no more than a catch in his throat, and then a sigh. And then his chest was still and he breathed no more.

CHAPTER THIRTY-ONE

Tenth of April, 1558, Easter Sunday—Chatsworth, Derbyshire

THE EASTER SERVICE WAS OVER BUT BESS HAD WANTED TO remain in the church by herself and had asked her mother, Jenny, and Aunt Marcella to take the children home so that she could think and pray. Now, on her knees on the prie-dieu, with the chill rising from the stone floor of the church, she realized that she was utterly exhausted in body and spirit. She wondered if she would be able to find the energy to rise to her feet. Perhaps she would just stay there until someone came to find her or she died where she knelt.

The nearly six months since William's death had been the most difficult time of her life. He had not yet been laid in the earth of the churchyard at St. Botolph-without-Aldersgate, near his first wife and dead babies, when she had learned that all his labors to straighten out the privy chamber accounts and his appeals to the queen and Star Chamber had been in vain. On his behalf, she now owed the crown more than five thousand pounds. The only way that she could pay it would be to sell Chatsworth, but that would mean the loss of her children's inheritance, the loss of all that she and William had worked so hard to build. She had tried to think what he would advise her to do.

"Wait. And see what may change." Those were the words she could hear him speaking, and so she waited.

When she was still reeling from the news of the enormous debt, baby Lucres had fallen ill, and after a week that had seemed like an eternity, she had followed her father to the grave. The illness sweeping London had also claimed Bess's old friend Doll Fitzherbert and her husband Sir John Port. And soon after, William's daughter Polly had died. The loss of husband, children, and friends compounded into more than the sum of the individual griefs, Bess had felt. She had lain in her bed and wept wretchedly for days, longing to be home in the comfort of Chatsworth, but unable to face the prospect of the weeklong journey and all its hardships.

And then had come the next blow. Parliament was at work on legislation that would allow it to confiscate property to satisfy a debt to the state. Her case would fall squarely within the law and she stood to lose Chatsworth, after all the care that William had taken to ensure that she would be secure after his death. The only comfort was that their son Harry would not fall under the jurisdiction of the Court of Wards, as her brother Jem and poor Robbie Barlow's brother had.

Bess raised her eyes to the image of the Virgin Mary depicted in the stained glass window above the altar, her white hand raised in benediction, the vivid blue of her gown flowing like water about her. Somehow it had survived the destruction wrought on so many churches throughout the land, and she felt less lonely gazing upon the sad but serene face of Mary, another wife and mother who had survived wrenching losses. Sunlight shone through the glass, falling in brightly colored shards on the gray flagstones.

Mother, help me, she prayed. *And Christ our Lord, I thank Thee for the care of so many friends in my time of trouble, and I am grateful that the rest of my children and family are in health.*

Huddled in the London house, and driven by desperation, she

had written to every friend, every colleague of William's she thought could aid her—Frances Grey, William Cecil, John Thynne. She would not let the crown reduce her and her children to poverty. Her friends had rallied to her side, and the bill had not passed. Part of the reason for that, she felt sure, was that it would harm so many others in a like case to hers. *There be few in the house that they or their friends should not smart if the Act should pass,* she had written to John Thynne.

Bess raised her eyes once more to the grave countenance of the Virgin. A draft gusted through the church and she pulled her fur-lined robe tighter about her. Her feet were numb with the cold even under her heavy skirts, and she wiggled her toes in an effort to regain some feeling. It was time she went back to the house. Easter Sunday or no, she wanted to look over her accounts and see if she could find some sources of money she was overlooking, some unnecessary costs she could eliminate.

She bent her head once more and closed her eyes.

You raised Your beloved son, O Lord, from the tomb. I humbly beg You to take pity on me and my poor children and raise me from this pit of black despair that I may live to honor You and show You my duty through all the days of my life.

CHAPTER THIRTY-TWO

Twentieth of June, 1558—Brentford, Middlesex

UPON ENTERING JOHN THYNNE'S HOUSE IN BRENTFORD, BESS had begun to weep. It was here that she had given birth to Bessie three years earlier, and she had not been in the house since then.

But now, with her belongings unpacked and the children settled, and breathing in the scent of the blooming orchard, her spirits rose. She had rented the house for a year, and its location was perfect— out of the unhealthful airs of the city, but less than ten miles from Whitehall, Richmond, and Hampton Court. She could stay comfortably at home with the children when it suited her and be in London when she felt the need. And there would be need, for things were happening fast. She had kept up the payments to William's contacts at court and corresponded with old friends in London, and rumors blew on the spring winds of great changes coming.

Queen Mary, who had for a second time taken to her chamber in expectation of giving birth, was not in fact with child but was gravely ill. She was now forty-two years of age, and even if she would not yet admit it, it was clear that she would bear no children. Her own husband was urging her to acknowledge her sister Elizabeth as her successor to the throne. And John Thynne had written to Bess that the Spanish ambassador was among the parade of dignitaries who were now making discreet visits to Hatfield House, where Elizabeth waited.

Elizabeth! Bess laughed out loud, turning her face up to the sun's warmth as she walked among the flowering trees of the orchard. How wonderful it would be, after the darkness and fear of the last years, to have Elizabeth Tudor on the throne.

The face of Queen Mary as the young woman she had been when Bess first met her came to Bess's mind, and she felt an intense pang of sadness. Then poor Mary had still had her softness and red-gold beauty, her face tinged with pain and loss but not yet hardened into the cruel mask she had worn in later years. When she had come to the throne there had been such hope, Bess thought. It had been hard for her to feel any hope, as grief-stricken as she had been over Jane's death. But Mary was the daughter of Henry, whom the people had loved, and Catherine, whom they had adored and pitied. She was a Tudor, Papist or no.

But what had begun so bright and shining had turned all to blackness and despair. More than three hundred people had gone to the flames during Mary's reign. England had been dragged into Spain's war with France, and what had it got but the loss of Calais, which it had held for two hundred years. And Mary was hated and feared. Of course such sentiments could not be spoken of openly, but they bubbled just below the surface.

Bess recalled the words of a letter from John Thynne. *I never saw England weaker in strength, money, men, and riches. The queen is poor, the realm exhausted, the nobility poor and decayed. The people are out of order and justice is not executed. Here is nothing but fining, hanging, quartering and burning, taxing, levying, and beggaring.*

Mary was vilified as a traitor to God and the country. The sickness the previous year was a plague sent to punish her, the people whispered. It was easy to think that might be true, and Bess found that knotted up with her grief at the loss of William and Lucres was the hope that Mary would die, though she felt guilty at the thought.

But with Elizabeth . . . Bess hardly dared hope for how much better things could be, once the shadows were chased away by the rays of the sun.

And, the thought struck her, perhaps through her friends she might be able to beg reprieve from the debt that hung over her head.

Twenty-third of September, 1558

Bess read over John Thynne's letter again and then called to her sister. Jenny came bustling in from the next room, her smile disappearing as she took in Bess's expression.

"We must go back to Chatsworth," Bess said, folding the letter and tucking it into her bosom.

"Now? But we've only been here three months! What's amiss?"

Bess beckoned Jenny and lowered her voice as her sister sat beside her.

"The queen is dying. Everyone knows now that Elizabeth will succeed her, but as Mary has not named her as successor, she may have to fight. I am given to understand by friends that there could be much trouble, and that it would be safer to be away from London."

It all seemed horribly familiar, Bess thought. The frightened whispers as death crept up on Henry, then Edward. Surely this time the outcome would be better. But without a husband, and with six children, the oldest just turned ten, she wanted to be safe in Derbyshire, far from tumult and danger.

"We must make ready to depart as soon as we may," Bess said. "Thank God, the weather is dry and clear, perfect for traveling."

"Yes, we are like to be able to make the journey in a week or less," Jenny agreed.

"Perhaps, but I must make a little stop on the way," Bess said. At Jenny's quizzical look she added, "To Hatfield House, to pay my respects to the Lady Elizabeth."

"Ah." Jenny grinned. "A most important visit."

"The most important visit," Bess said, "that I have ever paid in my life."

THE ROAD TO HATFIELD WAS HEAVILY TRAVELED WHEN BESS SET out from Brentford two days later. Her slow-moving entourage was passed by ladies and gentlemen on horseback, many of whom she knew. As the sun rose high in the sky, she heard a familiar laugh and turned to see her old friend Lizzie riding between two other ladies and accompanied by a brace of bodyguards.

How long had it been since she'd seen Lizzie? Too long, however it was, and Bess's heart warmed to see the familiar lovely face, a hood covering the tangle of dark curls that Bess knew so well.

"Lizzie Brooke!" she called.

"Bess!" Lizzie cried, catching sight of Bess and spurring her horse forward.

Bess noted that Lizzie's cloak and gloves looked sadly worn, and thought with a pang of sadness that her friend had fared worse than she over the last five years, when she and William had spent most of their time at Chatsworth. Queen Mary had ordered William Parr to abandon Lizzie and return to his first wife, her friend and lady-in-waiting, with the threat of being executed for bigamy if he saw Lizzie again. And, Bess thought, it could not have helped Lizzie's situation that Thomas Wyatt, who had led the rebellion against Mary that had ended so catastrophically, was her first cousin. She should have looked beyond the occasional letters she received from Lizzie and helped her if she could.

"These are my friends Frances Newton and her cousin Anne Poyntz," Lizzie said, as her companions came abreast of her.

Frances Newton's appearance was much like her own, Bess noted, for the lady was about her age, with the same pale rose complexion and red-gold hair. Frances's face lit with a smile and Bess took an instant liking to her. Anne Poyntz was dark-haired, and some eight or ten years younger than Bess, and she, too, was smiling, with an air of barely suppressed excitement.

"This is my dear friend Lady Cavendish," Lizzie said, introducing Bess. Her eyes swept over Bess's widow's weeds. "I was so very sorry to learn of dear William's death."

"Thank you," Bess said. "And I am most grieved to know of the hardships you have suffered."

"I have hopes that the sun will soon shine brighter," Lizzie said. "And thus am making a pilgrimage toward her blessed rays."

Yes, Bess thought, Lizzie's situation would be sure to improve if Elizabeth came to the throne.

"I, too, am bound for Hatfield," Bess said. "It would please me to visit with you, but I mustn't hinder your progress."

"We intend stopping for the night at an inn and going on to Hatfield in the morning. Why not ride with us and meet your family there, and leave them to rest tomorrow while you make your call?"

"An excellent idea," she agreed, for the prospect of spending time with Lizzie, and of arriving at Hatfield in the company of three friends of Princess Elizabeth, made Bess feel much happier and more confident about the visit.

"I'll see you by suppertime," she assured four-year-old Charlie, who began to look tearful as Bess's saddle was placed on the horse ridden by one of her footmen. "And you shall have whatever special treat we can manage for being such a brave boy."

The day was glorious, the sun high in a cloudless blue sky and a cool breeze rattling the leaves in the trees, now turning to burnished gold and russet.

"Anne has been in Princess Elizabeth's household all this while," Lizzie told Bess as they rode. "She only came to London to seek me out and bid me go to Hatfield at the princess's command, and I may tell you I wasted no time in making myself ready. These years have been truly hellish for me."

"So Elizabeth is forming her household already?" Bess asked.

"Hatfield is become a court in little. Now there is no question she will be queen, only how soon it may come to pass."

As Bess and her friends approached Hatfield House the next morning, Bess saw that what Lizzie had said was very true. The lawns were thronged with chattering courtiers, and at their center, fitting an arrow to a bow and taking careful aim at a target, stood Elizabeth herself, soberly dressed in black but seeming to radiate happiness. Her shaft hit the center of its mark, prompting applause, and Elizabeth threw back her head and laughed with delight. Bess recognized Robert Dudley, the handsome older brother of Jane Grey's poor young husband Guildford, near the princess's side.

Yet there was evidence that Elizabeth knew she had enemies. Three guards stood within sword's length from her. One of them, a tall, strapping man with the bearing of a soldier, looked familiar to Bess. He seemed to sense Bess's eyes on him and looked toward her, and bowed as he met her gaze.

Bess, Lizzie, Frances, and Anne dismounted and went toward Elizabeth on foot, and her face lit with a smile as they drew near.

"By my life, I cannot think of four ladies I would rather see before me than you!" she cried. "My dear cousin," she said, embracing Lizzie, "you are most welcome. And Lady Cavendish, it's been an age!"

Bess's heart sang at the welcome and she curtsied low before Elizabeth.

"It gives me joy to see Your Highness in such good health and spirits."

"I thank you for it, good Bess. In truth my spirits are lighter than at any time since I first met you all those years ago, I think." The princess had just turned twenty-five, Bess realized with surprise.

Bess was pleased to find that William's old friend Sir William Cecil was in residence at Hatfield.

"I grieve the loss of William as much for myself as for you, dear Bess," he said over a goblet of spiced wine that evening. "He was a steadfast friend and a most accomplished man. Were he still with us, I have no doubt the princess would have a place for him, for there will be much to be done when she comes at last to the throne."

"How comes your house?" Bess asked. Three years earlier, Cecil had begun building a grand home modeled on Richmond Palace, and she and William had frequently exchanged letters with Cecil about the joys and trials of construction on such a grand scale as they had worked on Chatsworth.

"Oh, there is fair progress," he said. "Though at times I wonder what possessed me to begin it, and fear that I will not live to see it completed."

"I have much the same thoughts. I think the same when I look upon Chatsworth and know how much remains to be done."

And I wonder if it ever will be done, and if I will lose it. No, I must find a way.

THAT EVENING WHEN BESS ENTERED HER CHAMBER SHE WAS drawn to the sight of the moon hanging bright in the darkening sky and went to stand at the open window. The scent of fruit from the orchard drifted on the breeze and mingled with the aroma from the stubbled fields. It had been a long time coming, this season of harvest, she thought, but once it came, England would be in a better case than it had for many years.

She was exhausted after the previous day's long ride and the excitement of being at Elizabeth's budding court, and she was past ready for bed. She reached to pull the great shutters closed but one of them swung stubbornly outward, pinching her finger.

"God's blood!" she swore, shaking her hand in pain.

"My lady, may I be of help?"

Bess whirled around, startled at the sound of a man's voice. What had she been thinking, to daydream there at the window without closing the door of her bedchamber? The speaker was the tall guard she had noticed earlier, standing just outside her door, and she felt herself flush at his gaze.

"No. Or rather yes, I thank you, sir. I would close the shutters but find they misbehave."

The man came to her side, leaned out the window, and easily swung the heavy shutter into place and latched it. He turned and smiled down at her and Bess realized he was head and shoulders taller than she was.

"The wretch should stay in place now, I think. But I beg you to let me know if you need further protection from wayward shutters or anything else."

He was smiling, but there was not a trace of mockery in his words, and Bess smiled back at him.

"Do I know you, sir?"

"William St. Loe, at your service," he said, bowing. "My father was a good friend of Harry Grey's and I recall you from Bradgate Park."

The mention of Bradgate brought a vivid picture of Jane Grey to Bess's mind and she felt the familiar tug of grief that came whenever she thought of Jane.

"A terrible loss that was," St. Loe said. "Both poor Lady Jane and her father."

Was it safe to openly mourn Jane, Bess wondered, now that Mary was almost gone?

"Yes," she said. "We lost much when we lost them. I miss Jane every day."

The man's blue eyes seemed lit from within as he looked down at her, and she felt at ease with him. Safe, as she had felt with William Cavendish when first she knew him. But there was something more she felt with this man. A flame leapt to life somewhere deep within her and she swallowed.

"I was Elizabeth Barlow when I was at Bradgate. Now I am Elizabeth Cavendish. Though I lost my dear husband near a year ago."

"I knew him a bit as well. A good man. And fortunate to have such a lady as you."

"I have seen you at court, also, have I not?" Bess asked.

He nodded. "I have had the honor to be responsible for the safety of the Princess Elizabeth since I returned from service in Ireland five years ago, and when she was at court, so was I."

Bess was suddenly very conscious that she was standing with a man alone in her bedchamber, and felt herself blushing.

"I thank you for your kindness, William. I am most grateful to have a protector."

She had used the word somewhat lightly, but he did not laugh, and she realized that she did feel grateful, and knew that here was someone who would come to her aid if needed.

"Lady Cavendish." He bowed again. "I hope I will have the pleasure of further conversation before you depart."

"WHAT DO YOU KNOW OF WILLIAM ST. LOE?" BESS ASKED LIZZIE THE next day.

Lizzie gave her a catlike smile.

"He's a handsome one, isn't he?"

Bess was annoyed that she found herself blushing.

"Sir William," Lizzie said, emphasizing the first word, "comes of a good family that's been closely tied to the crown for centuries. He served Henry Courtenay when a young man."

The Courtenays, like the Greys, were near-royalty, as Henry Courtenay had been a first cousin to King Henry. So St. Loe must be well-placed and well-respected, Bess thought.

"His father supported Jane Grey, and Thomas Wyatt's rebellion," Lizzie continued, "but managed to survive. Sir William's daughter Mary is one of Princess Elizabeth's maids of honor."

Bess felt her heart contract and scolded herself for it. Of course such a handsome, personable, and successful man must have a wife.

"He's been a widower for almost ten years," Lizzie said, as though reading her mind. "Though how he has escaped capture until now is a great mystery to me."

"Perhaps he's too busy to marry," Bess said.

"Perhaps. And perhaps he has just not met the right woman. Until now." She raised an eyebrow and smiled.

Bess had not thought of being on the hunt for a husband. "I'm only recently a widow," she faltered, though Lizzie's words echoed what was in her own heart.

"Not so recent. Almost a year now, isn't it? You cannot stay alone forever. I'd not waste a moment, were I you, but ensnare good Sir William with that sweet smile of yours. And wherever Elizabeth is, he is not far away. So you may visit her and kill two birds with one stone."

Twenty-fifth of October, 1558—Chatsworth, Derbyshire

Bess woke from a dream of William so vivid that she turned, expecting to find him in bed next to her. But it was a year ago this day that he had died, and the pillow beside her own was blank and cold. She said a prayer for the repose and salvation of his soul, as she did each morning. How had she managed to get through three hundred and sixty-five days without the comfort of his love and company? *Day by day,* his voice whispered in her mind. *Day by day, and the pain grows less little by little.*

She went to the window. The pink of dawn was fading. The day would be clear and beautiful. The trees in the orchard were nearly bare now, their branches like skeletal fingers against the sky. Heaps of golden leaves drifted around their roots, covering the barren earth like a winding sheet.

She thought of the last time that she and William had walked in the orchard, the previous spring just before he had left for London. Then the trees had been in bud, with here and there a delicate white blossom unfurling its petals. William had plucked a flower and, pulling Bess's coif from her head, tucked it into her curls.

"My queen of the May," he had said, and kissed her. He had seemed sad that day, and Bess had put it down to his impending departure and his reluctance to be gone from her and the children. But he had surprised her when he had taken her hands and kissed them before speaking quite seriously.

"When I am gone, dear Bess, don't keep yourself lonely."

"My love, I'll join you in London soon, and the days will not be long, knowing that you are there waiting for me."

"That's not what I mean," he had said. "I mean when I leave you a widow, as surely I must someday."

"Oh." She had not known what to say. It was true that he was near twenty years older than she, but somehow she had always feared that she would die giving birth, leaving him once more bereft of a wife and with the care of their children on his shoulders. "But why do you speak of this, my heart? I'm sure we have many happy years left to us. And it may be that I am gone before you."

"No," he had said, and she had been shaken by his sureness. "I know that it will not be so. And you will ease my soul if you promise me that when your heart is ready, you will open it to another's love. Promise me, Bess."

"Very well," she had said, her hand caressing his cheek. "I promise, then. But let it not be for a great many years."

And now it had been a year since she had lost him. Many left widowed married sooner than that span of time, but she had always thought to do so seemed callous. Her soul had needed the time to heal from William's loss. But now?

The face of Will St. Loe came into her mind. She had not been long gone from Hatfield, but she had thought of him often, and missed those laughing eyes and the deep growl of his voice with its Somerset burr. And she thought she could hear William's whisper.

It is time. I will always be here waiting for you. But cast the shadows from your heart and let yourself smile again.

"I will," she murmured. "I will. But you will always have your place in my heart, my love."

CHAPTER THIRTY-THREE

Ninth of November, 1558—Chatsworth, Derbyshire

Bess reread Sir William Cecil's letter, her heart beating faster at every line.

> *The queen cannot last the week. She has at last named Princess Elizabeth as her successor, and I do not have to tell you that no one will stand in the way of the joyous occasion of that lady's accession to the throne. Parliament has been recalled in anticipation of the change that will come any day. Hasten you back to London. And a stop at Hatfield House would not be amiss.*

"Jenny!" Bess called, and swept her sister into her arms when she appeared, looking anxious. "See to the packing! We are off to London!"

"The children and all?"

"No, no need to uproot them now. They'll be happier here." The images of Princess Elizabeth, soon to be queen, and Sir William St. Loe rose side by side in Bess's mind. "And I have business to attend to."

. . .

IF HATFIELD HOUSE HAD HAD THE APPEARANCE OF A COURT IN September, there was now no doubt that that was what it was, Bess thought. She had arrived three days earlier to find the house full, and had been fortunate that Lizzie's friend Frances Newton had invited her to share her lodgings, else she would have had to seek a bed in the nearest inn, as more well-wishers were arriving to greet Princess Elizabeth than Hatfield could accommodate.

There was little pretense at sadness over the death of Queen Mary, which must come any day. William Cecil was busy drafting proclamations announcing Elizabeth's accession to the throne and the road from London was choked with courtiers hoping for places in the new queen's household. William St. Loe had obviously been very pleased to see Bess when she arrived, and had been as attentive to her as his duties allowed.

The morning was cool but not cold, and Bess was taking advantage of the sunshine to take a stroll with Lizzie and Frances Newton.

"Look at Her Highness, reading beneath a tree as though she had not a care in the world," Frances commented.

Elizabeth sat with her back against an oak, her russet skirts spread out around her and a book in her lap, but though her eyes were on the page, Bess thought that surely her mind must be awhirl. Bess's attention was caught by the furious pounding of horses' hooves and she turned to see a small party of riders thundering along the road toward the house.

"From London, surely," Frances said, and excitement surged in Bess's stomach.

"Come, let us go and hear the news," she cried.

The horsemen were riding pell-mell across the grass toward Elizabeth, and Bess broke into a run. Others were streaming toward the princess from all directions.

Bess, Lizzie, and Frances arrived near Elizabeth just as the riders were dismounting. Bess recognized the two gray-bearded men hastening toward Elizabeth as the earls of Pembroke and Arundel.

Elizabeth jumped to her feet. Her face had gone deathly pale but for two spots of red flaming in her cheeks, and her fingers clenched the little book in her hand, which Bess saw was the New Testament, as though it was all that kept her standing.

The earls swept their hats from their heads and knelt before Elizabeth.

"Your Majesty," the Earl of Pembroke began, his voice breaking.

"Queen Mary departed this life just before dawn this morning," Arundel said. "You are queen, Your Majesty."

Bess found that she was gripping Lizzie's hand and that tears were streaming down her cheeks.

Elizabeth stood silent, as though struck dumb, and gasped for breath. Then she, too, fell to her knees in the grass and clasped the New Testament to her breast before she spoke at last.

"A Domine factum est illud, et est mirabile in oculis nostris!"

"What did she say?" Bess pleaded under her breath.

"'This is the Lord's doing,'" Lizzie translated, "'and it is marvelous in our eyes.'"

THAT NIGHT THE FEASTING AND CELEBRATIONS LASTED LATE into the night. As she looked around the great hall at Hatfield, Bess thought that of all the royal events she had attended, this was the happiest. There was no sense of the danger of the monarch's sudden switch into calculated cruelty, as there had been with King Henry. No barely veiled partisan jostling to see who would control the king, as there had been with young Edward. No gnawing reminder that scores of people were going to fiery deaths, as there had been with Queen Mary.

There was only Elizabeth, smiling, joyful, and radiant.

"Now the golden days are with us," Will St. Loe said to Bess. He sat next to her at the table, with their friends around them, and Bess felt as though she were in a haze of brilliant light. "I can scarcely bear the thought of being parted from you, Bess," Will murmured, touching a gentle hand to her cheek.

"I won't be absent for much time," she promised. "Only as long as is needed to get the children and my household ready to make the move to Brentford. And you'll have much to do before then."

Elizabeth had that afternoon named Will as captain of her Yeoman Guard, and he would never be far from her side in the coming weeks as she went to London to take the throne.

"Every day that I lack you will seem like a year," Will said.

"And I will feel the same." Bess smiled. "We sound like a pair of young lovers."

He took her hand and kissed it. "I feel like a young man when I look on you. But I am a better man and more fit to be with a woman than I was as a boy."

Bess thought of poor Robbie Barlow, her sweet first husband, who had died before he knew what it was to be a man.

"I would not have you other than as you are," she said.

Later, they stood in a shadowed corner of the hall, the light of a hundred candles dancing around them, and Will drew Bess to him and kissed her. She felt as though she were melting at his touch, his lips soft on hers, his whiskers tickling gently, the taste of him sweet in her mouth. Her belly contracted with a pang of longing, a fierce desire such as she had never known. What marvels the world held, she thought, feeling his arm tight around her waist, his hand cradling the back of her neck as he kissed her more deeply.

"I had not known until now," she murmured when he finally released her, "that it was possible to be this happy."

Fifteenth of January, 1559—London

The bells of London's churches had been pealing since dawn, their joyful clanging reverberating in the biting cold air. Bess's breath blew out in silvery clouds, and her nose felt as if it would freeze. But the rest of her was swathed in velvet and fur, and she was kept warm by walking. Because of Will St. Loe's place in the queen's favor, Bess was among the hundreds in the procession following Queen Elizabeth from Westminster Palace to the abbey for her coronation, the tramp of their feet turning the snow into rivers of slush and mud. But the mud didn't matter; nothing mattered on this glorious day.

Ahead, she could see the horse litter on which Elizabeth rode, the canopy held over her bobbing as its bearers went. She knew that Will was only feet from the queen, as he had been almost constantly since she had left Hatfield. Elizabeth had bestowed upon him for his lifetime the offices of Chief Butler of England and Chief Butler of Wales, which carried an annual salary of fifty marks for overseeing the payment of duty on imported wine and ensuring that the queen's pantry was well stocked with good vintages.

"And," Will had told Bess, laughing in delight, "it is my duty to present Her Majesty with the first cup of wine at the banquet following her coronation."

She had felt so proud of him, and touched at how pleased he was by the queen's doing him such honor.

"She loves you well. Almost as well as I do."

Bess's mind came back to the present as the procession stopped before the abbey. The litter and canopy disappeared from sight and she knew that Elizabeth must be alighting. The cheers of the crowds that lined the streets grew louder and louder.

"God save the queen! God save Queen Elizabeth!" the people roared.

And then there was movement again, and Bess mounted the steps into the abbey to see the dawn of a new reign.

Part Four

LADY

CHAPTER THIRTY-FOUR

Eleventh of July, 1559—Greenwich

Hurrahs went up from the crowds packing the tourna-ment stands in the palace yard as Robert Dudley's lance thrust home into the breastplate of Lord Darcy, splintering with a thunderous crack and nearly unseating Darcy.

"Bravely done, sir!" the queen called out. "It is not for nothing that I made you my master of horse, I find!"

"And Knight of the Garter," Lizzie whispered to Bess. The queen had bestowed that honor on Dudley and the Duke of Norfolk on St. George's Day in April, and some said it was a prelude to further elevation. Dudley had organized the day of tilting and a tourney to entertain the queen, as well as the attendant festivities, which included outdoor feasting in flower-decked pavilions and the masques that would take place that evening.

Dudley circled back to the stands and came to a stop before the queen, his horse dancing as he removed his helm and kissed Elizabeth's hand. Bess thought that she certainly understood what the queen saw in Dudley. She had known him since he was a boy, but there was nothing boyish about him now; everything about him seemed primal, pagan, sexual. His dark hair, damp with sweat, curled around his swarthy brow, making her think of a satyr. The eyes that met the queen's were bright with passion. And not only for the exhilaration of the sport, Bess thought. Dudley was married, but his wife Amy Robsart was far from court at Denchworth and said to be ill, and there were whispered rumors that the queen would marry Dudley when his wife died. Yes, a man with powers to bewitch. Dangerous.

Dudley took the flagon of wine that the queen handed him and drank, wiping ruby drops from his mustache with the back of his hand. Bess suddenly recalled Lady Zouche's tale so many years ago of King Henry, his shirt clinging to him after a bout of tennis, coming to the side of the court to pass time with Anne Boleyn, when she had ruled his heart and soul. Surely to be the object of a queen's love could not be so perilous. Or could it?

But in the next moment Bess had no more thoughts for Robert Dudley, for the herald cried out, "Sir William St. Loe!"

Will rode into the arena, straight and powerful on a huge bay stallion caparisoned in crimson, his tilting armor glinting in the sun. Bess's heart surged with love and pride, for it was her own glove that was affixed to his arm as a favor, and the mate was tucked into the jeweled belt at her waist. Anyone with an eye to see would know that she held his heart.

Will bowed to the queen, then touched his gauntleted hand to his lips and raised it in salute to Bess. She felt heads turning to see where his attention lay and flushed at the scrutiny as she inclined her head to him.

"Ah," Elizabeth said, arching an eyebrow. "So, the captain of my guard is captain of your heart, Lady Cavendish. Well chosen. There is not a better man in England."

"I thank you, Your Majesty," Bess murmured, conscious of the many eyes on her.

Frances squeezed Bess's hand and gave her an approving nod at the significance of the queen's praise.

Will's opponent Ambrose Dudley, Robert's older brother, galloped his horse past the stand and saluted the queen, and then rode to the opposite end of the tiltyard from Will.

Bess's stomach was surging with excitement and nervousness. Will was a skilled horseman and combatant, but accidents did happen. Only a few days earlier King Henri of France had been horribly injured in the lists, when the tip of a lance had shattered and pierced his eye. He lay near death, it was said. And the leg injury that had plagued King Henry and turned him into a cripple as he aged had been the result of a fall while jousting.

The two mounted men faced each other down the long length of the tilt. The visors of their helms were down and Bess wished she could see Will's face. He lifted his lance into position, its impossible length balanced before him. Bess thought about the force with which two such combatants rode toward each other. A horse weighing half a ton, the man himself in a hundred pounds of armor, the heavy wooden lances, pounding toward each other at an unstoppable pace.

The herald dropped his arm, the gold scarf in his hand bellying out in the breeze, and the knights spurred their mounts forward. Bess found that she was clutching Frances's hand as the horses thundered toward each other, the plumes of their helms streaming out behind them. She was not breathing, could not breathe, until it was over.

The tip of Will's lance rose. Surely he was off his mark, and leaving himself open to Ambrose Dudley's weapon, moving arrowlike toward his broad chest. And then Will's lance connected with Dudley's helm, carrying him off his horse and onto the sawdust-covered ground with a sickening crash as Will clattered past in a blur of russet and scarlet.

It seemed an eternity before Ambrose Dudley stirred, and then the crowd roared as Will, helm under his arm now, rode back along the stands, bowing to the queen and being pelted with roses as Dudley was helped to his feet and stumbled from the field.

"Spectacular!" Queen Elizabeth exulted. "By heaven, I've never seen better play!"

Bess was trembling with the pent-up anxiety, and laughed aloud in her relief. It had been spectacular, and she marveled to think that this paragon of manhood loved her as deeply as she loved him. Then she saw that he had come to a halt and his eyes met hers. He pulled her glove from its ribbon on his arm and touched it to his breast, and she was seized with an overpowering need to feel his arms around her, to touch his face, to know that he was real and he was safe and he was hers, and she was on her feet and murmuring an apology to the queen before she knew what she was about.

Behind the viewing stands, stable boys looked up in surprise as Bess darted past them, but she didn't care what they thought, what anyone thought. Where was he? She couldn't find him amid the crowd of men and horses. Her heart leapt as she caught sight of him, two servants removing his armor. He turned as if he felt her gaze, and then he was striding toward her, his eyes alight with passion, and he encircled her waist with his hands and lifted her to him and kissed her.

"Oh, Bess, my Bess," he murmured. "I can never feel happy or whole until I know you are mine. Will you be my wife?"

"Yes, yes, oh, yes," she cried, her hands tangled in the damp locks of his hair, kissing his lips, his cheeks, his forehead. "I will be yours until the end of time, Will St. Loe."

CHAPTER THIRTY-FIVE

I MUST SPEAK TO YOU IN ALL SERIOUSNESS," WILL TOLD BESS THE day after the tourney, as they strolled along in the park above the palace. "You gave me your promise in the heat of passion yesterday, but I must speak to you as I would to your father if he were alive and demanding to know in what fashion I will keep you."

"Very well," Bess said. "I am all ears, sir."

"When my father died in December, Sutton Court in Somerset and Tormarton in Gloucestershire came to me, along with all his wealth but seventy pounds to my brother Clement, a dowry for my sister, and of course the jewelry and plate he left to my mother. I have in addition a lease on a substantial property in Ireland. The income from these, together with what I get from the positions in which I serve the queen, is sufficient that you will never want for anything while I live, and I will ensure that you are provided for when I am gone."

"I thank you, my love," Bess said. "And now must I lay my cards on the table, for it is only right that you know how things stand with me."

She paused, afraid to speak of the worry that weighed on her so heavily. For the debt that she owed on William's behalf was great. Might it make Will think twice about yoking himself to her?

"I have yet my dower rights in the properties from my young first husband," she said, "and I hold for my lifetime all the lands, houses, and other wealth of my other William. But his death left me also a burden so heavy that I lie awake at night and think on it—a debt of near on five thousand pounds to the crown from errors in his accounting while he was treasurer of the privy chamber."

Bess glanced sideways at Will's face as they walked, trying to read his thoughts. His face was somber. Laughter rose from below where flower-bedecked pavilions dotted the green hill, their bright banners rippling in the breeze.

"If the money is owed to the crown, I may be of help," Will said at last, and Bess's hopes rose. "Her Majesty considers herself in my obligation for my standing by her when she had few friends and much to fear, and I doubt not but she may be persuaded to forgive the debt." He stopped walking, and cupping Bess's face in his hands, kissed her. "I will speak to her."

"You would take on my burden as your own?" Bess scarcely dared believe it was true.

"I do, and gladly."

Her heart flooded with gratitude and hope, and she stood on tiptoe to kiss him.

"I will speak to Her Majesty soon, then. I must also ask her permission to wed, though I have no doubt she will grant it happily."

Bess breathed deeply of the summer air, perfumed with the meadow grass and the fresh green scent of the river far below, feeling that a shadow that had hovered in her mind for so long might soon be lifted. Will drew her arm into his and pulled her closer as they resumed their walk.

"I must tell you, Bess, that I have a blot of my own that darkens my soul in the long hours of the night."

What terrible secret could this be? she wondered, alarmed at his deep sigh.

"My brother Ned," Will said. "He has ever been a wastrel and a scoundrel, to the despair of my mother and the ire of my father. In the end, my father left him nothing. And now his resentment has hardened into malignancy against me."

Bess felt a curious sense of relief at Will's admission, both to know that he had problems of his own and that he would bare himself to her by telling her of them.

"That must be a great grief to you, surely," she said. "But no more than happens in many families."

"Yet there is worse to tell, for Ned is the center of a scandal that has greatly discredited my family. Last year one of my father's tenants, John Scutt, who had been a tailor to King Henry, died suddenly and of no apparent cause. It was known that he beat his wife, and there were rumors that she had poisoned him. Suspicion fell on Ned a fortnight after Scutt's death when he bought from the widow—Bridget was her name—the leases of some property."

"Could it not have been that he wanted to help her? Perhaps she needed the ready money more than the leases."

"It might have been thought so, except that only another fortnight later, he married her, and before long she gave birth to a baby that most strongly resembled my brother. Then, only a few months later, this very lusty young woman suddenly died."

A chill went up Bess's spine despite the warmth of the day.

"The whispers that had followed the first death rose to a roar when Ned, six months a widower, then wed Margaret Scutt, the stepdaughter of his dead wife, thereby becoming master of all that Scutt had owned. These troubles were the last straw for my father. He had formerly given Ned the leases of some properties at my mother's entreaty, only to have Ned sell them and waste the profits on loose living. So when he died, he left Ned nothing at all. My brother has been kicking up trouble since my father's death, and I fear it will end in the courts."

"I know such woes all too well," Bess said. "I had to fight for my dower rights when poor Robbie died, and William Cavendish and I bought Chatsworth as the result of legal broils resulting from a scandal that touched my family."

"Then you are not so put off that you will not marry me, my love?"

"Not in the least. Bring on all the ill-tempered brothers you may, but I will be your wife."

Twenty-seventh of August, 1559—Sutton Court, Chew Magna, Somerset

The sun rose bright on the morning of Bess's third wedding day, and she felt giddy with happiness as she dressed, surrounded by her mother, sisters, Aunt Marcella, Will's sister Elizabeth, and his grown daughters Mary and Margaret.

She was nearly thirty-two years old, but the years ahead were full of promise. Her first marriage had been to a boy, her second to a man old enough to be her father, and she had nursed both through ill health and at their deathbeds. But Will was only nine years older than she, in the prime of his vigorous manhood, and with God's blessing, they would have many joyous years together.

"I feel like a thoroughgoing bride today," she mused. She took her mother's hand and kissed it. "I'm so grateful to have all my dear ones near me."

Many of Bess's and Will's friends had journeyed to Sutton Court for the nuptials, including their old mutual friends Sir John Thynne and his wife Christian, and Frances Newton and her cousin Anne Poyntz, who were both distantly related to Will. The wedding party set off on foot to St. Andrew's Church in the village of Chew Magna, led by fiddlers and cheered along the way by Will's tenants and farm laborers, given a holiday in honor of the marriage.

As the priest spoke, Bess listened carefully to the words of the marriage ceremony, which had come into use after her second marriage. The words had been spoken at other weddings she had attended, surely, but it seemed she had never properly heard them before. Or perhaps it was that only now, at the age of thirty-one, did her soul truly understand and crave a marriage that promised the "mutual society, help, and comfort that the one ought to have of the other, both in prosperity and adversity."

"Wilt thou have this woman to thy wedded wife," the priest asked Will, "to live together after God's ordinance in the holy estate of matrimony? Wilt thou love her, comfort her, honor, and keep her in sickness and in health? And forsaking all others keep thee only to her, so long as you both shall live?"

"I will."

Will's eyes were the color of the summer sky, thought Bess, and the feel of his hand holding hers like the home she had always sought. And to promise to obey him, serve him, love, honor, and keep him was all that her heart desired, and she answered, "I will."

BESS STOOD AT THE OPEN WINDOW OF THE BEDCHAMBER, GAZING out on the night sky. The moon had been full the previous night and hung bright and heavy like a pearl on the black velvet field of spangled stars. The scent of fruit from the orchard sweetened the air. The quiet of the countryside was broken only by the distant, mellow *whoo* of an owl, and Bess felt at peace and supremely happy.

She turned at the sound of Will's footsteps.

"All well?" she asked.

"Yes," he said, setting down his candle. "Shutters closed, doors locked, fires banked. And I think all the household is asleep."

He came to her side and took her into his arms and kissed her gently.

"I do love this place. I'm glad we chose to have the wedding here rather than in London."

Bess nodded, sliding her hands beneath his doublet and against his chest, marveling as always at the live firmness of his muscles.

One of his hands caressed the back of her neck, the other held her body close against him, and she felt herself begin to take fire. He kissed her, his mouth opening hers, his lips and tongue soft and warm and sweet, tasting faintly of ale.

He untied the ribbon at the neck of her shift and caressed one of her breasts, the rough skin of his fingers rousing her nipple to hardness, and Bess moaned with desire. She felt the hardness of him against her belly, and threw her head back as his lips traveled to her throat, then down to kiss her breasts, cupping them so that he could bring his mouth first to one and then the other.

"Oh, my love," she gasped. "How I have longed for you."

He lifted her into his arms and carried her to the bed, and she sank into the softness of the bedding, opening her arms to him. His hand encircled her ankle, then moved up her leg, sliding against the smoothness of her skin until he brushed against the soft nest between her thighs. Bess gasped as his fingers caressed her, spreading her honeyed wetness, his touch rousing her to a pitch of desire. She moved against him, giving herself over to the waves of pleasure that built within her as his hand moved over her, in her, his touch like liquid flame. She cried out as she reached a shattering crest, calling out his name as wave after wave shook her.

He took his hands from her only long enough to pull off his shirt and shed his breeches, and then he knelt between her thighs and entered her, filling her, thrusting himself to her very core, and she arched up to meet him, wrapping her legs around him to hold him deep within her. His strokes built from slow and languorous to rapid and powerful, pinning her to the bed, possessing her.

"Ah, my Bess." His voice was a low growl in her ear and she sobbed with the pleasure of the feel of him, nuzzling his neck, and then biting softly as he brought her to another crashing peak. She felt as though her edges had blurred, there was no Bess anymore, only undulating waves of sensation.

Later, much later, they lay entangled in each other's arms, legs entwined, and Bess felt as though all division between them had been driven away by the intensity of their merging, that their skins and souls had melded in the crucible of their passion. She kissed his shoulder, trailed her fingers across the silk of his skin, and drifted off to sleep, conscious that the first pale light of dawn was lightening the sky.

CHAPTER THIRTY-SIX

Twenty-ninth of September, 1559, Michaelmas—London

BESS WAS WELL PLEASED WITH WILL'S HOUSE IN TUTHILL STREET, now that she had spent the week since they had been back in London seeing to the opening of the house. It had been dusty and unkempt, and barren of servants, as before their marriage, Will had usually spent his time in London lodging at Master Mann's house in Red Cross Street, just outside the city walls near St. Giles' Cripplegate. But now the house had been aired and scrubbed and dusted, fresh matting laid down, the kitchen well stocked, and a small army of servants hired, and the St. Loe home was not only comfortable and welcoming to Bess and Will and their friends, but ready for the crucial business of entertaining important guests.

The bustle of London! Bess's heart rose at the thought of it. It had been years since she and her first William had regularly spent time there, and for so long the thought of London had carried with it the recollection of Mary's burnings and the death of Jane Grey and so many friends. But now London was the land of Elizabeth, and England was smiling again.

Bess and Will had intended to remain longer at Sutton Court, where immediately after their marriage Bess had embarked on building an extension of the house to provide a suitable parlor, which the old manor lacked. But King Henri of France had died of his injury from the jousting accident and Will had been summoned to London to serve as one of the four attendant knights at the memorial service at St. Paul's. So Bess had sent her children back to Chatsworth, in the care of her mother and her aunt Marcella, bringing her sisters Jenny and Dibby with her to London as ladies-in-waiting. She was grateful and happy that Will had insisted she use his money to resume the building at Chatsworth that had been suspended upon William's death, and she received regular letters from her steward James Crompe about the progress of construction.

Bess could see the spire of St. Paul's from her window and shivered, reminded of King Henri's death. Had she but known it, on that golden day in Greenwich, when she had watched Will's triumph in the tiltyard, her heart in her throat lest he should be hurt, the French king was already cold and stiff from exactly such a misfortune.

Henri's death had done more than leave a grieving widow and nation, too. For now his son the dauphin was King Francis, and his wife, the sixteen-year-old Mary Stuart, was queen of France as well as Scotland. She had also proclaimed herself queen of England, as her grandmother had been Margaret Tudor, the sister of King Henry.

Bess turned at the sound of Will's footsteps on the stair. Dear God, he seemed more handsome every time she looked upon him, she thought. He took her into his arms and kissed her, smelling faintly of leather and ale and tobacco, for he had taken up the fashionable and expensive new habit of smoking a pipe.

"What's the news at court today, my love?" she asked, standing a-tiptoe to smooth his ruffled hair.

"No news but plenty of gossip," he laughed. "Half of London, it seems, has been daily expecting the queen to announce her betrothal to the Earl of Arundel—the earl expecting it most fervently,

I'm told—you should see the set of plate he gave her when she departed Nonsuch—and yet no announcement comes."

Arundel was the widower of Harry Grey's sister Kate. If Frances Grey's brother-in-law married the queen and they had a child, Frances would be disappointed once again in her hopes of being mother to a queen.

The question of Elizabeth's marriage was not only the subject of gossip, but was uppermost in the minds of her council, for of course she needed a man to rule, but it must be the right man. There must be no repetition of Queen Mary's disastrous Spanish marriage.

"Will the queen instead choose Prince Erik of Sweden, do you think?" Bess asked. Will had told her that the Swedish prince was apparently so desirous of a match with Elizabeth that he planned to visit her in person.

"I'd sooner lay my money on the Earl of Arran," Will said, sitting and pulling off his boots. "He's solidly Protestant and heir to the Scottish throne, unless Mary Stuart should bear a child, and by marrying him Elizabeth would take the wind out of the sails of those who would try to put Mary on the throne in her place."

"And will he come to woo?" Bess asked, climbing onto the bed and watching the play of muscles in Will's back as he shed his doublet.

"He'd better be quick about it if he intends to," Will said, throwing himself down beside her and pulling her on top of him. "Since the queen came back from her progress all the talk has been of how much time she spent in private with Robert Dudley and how free he is with her even in company."

"And how does his wife?" Bess asked. But her mind was not much on Elizabeth's suitors now, as Will's hand was exploring beneath her kirtle, and through his breeches she could feel his hardness against her belly.

"Unhappy, I expect," Will murmured, his lips nuzzling her ear. "But hush now, no more of Robin Dudley for the nonce."

CHAPTER THIRTY-SEVEN

Twenty-first of November, 1559—Tuthill Street, London

WINTRY DARKNESS HAD DESCENDED ON LONDON BEFORE four in the afternoon, and as Bess stood gazing out the window toward the river, winking lantern light here and there was the only illumination in the streets. In the black sky above, stars glimmered beneath a moon waxing toward fullness.

Frances Grey was dead. Bess could hardly believe it, though the cold that seemed settled into her very bones was surely due to more than the weather. Frances's face rose to her mind, as Bess had first seen it upon her arrival at Bradgate Park so many years ago. As always when she thought of Frances, Bess felt gratitude, bafflement, and heartache. Frances had taught her to be a lady, had engineered her marriage to William Cavendish, had lavished her with praise and motherly affection even while she stinted her love to her own daughter Jane.

Bess had last visited Frances a month earlier, when all the household at Sheen House in Richmond was in a happy state of commotion over the recent proposal by Edward Seymour, the Earl of Hertford and son of the late Lord Protector, to marry Jane's sister

Kate Grey. Frances had been hoping to get the queen's permission for the marriage.

"My poor girl loves him and he her," she had confided to Bess. "And moreover, the marriage would strengthen Kate's position as successor to Her Majesty, though God grant there be no need of such a thing for many years to come."

Bess's heart had been wrung to see Frances clearly in pain from troubles in her gut, and looking weak and far beyond her forty-two years of age.

"Surely Her Majesty will agree," she had said, wanting to soothe Frances but doubting her words were true, and inevitably thinking of Jane, and Frances's previous ambitions to have a daughter for a queen.

And yesterday, Frances Grey had died, with her daughters Kate and Mary and her beloved husband Adrian Stokes at her side. Will had told Bess that the queen had already promised to bear the expenses of a great state funeral for her cousin and a tomb in Westminster Abbey, and agreed to a posthumous quartering of Frances's coat of arms with the royal arms.

Yet what good would this glory do poor Frances? Bess thought. The end of all was death and being eaten by worms, whether king or commoner.

Why are you so morbid? she chastised herself. Her life was as happy as she could wish it, with Will's love and constancy in daily evidence and her children all healthy and well on the road to successful lives. Willie and Harry would start at Eton College soon, and Frankie was eleven, almost old enough that it was time to start thinking about a suitable husband for her.

Perhaps it was the season, when the short days and long nights somehow made her feel unreasonably that the sun might fail to rise someday and darkness would overtake the earth. Or maybe it was that she had only weeks earlier turned thirty-two. But that was nothing, surely. Her mother was hearty at close to sixty years of age, and she had every expectation of long life.

But no one knows when their hour will come, she thought, crossing herself reflexively, for she had never lost the habit.

Or perhaps the reason for her sadness was that despite their frequent lovemaking, she and Will had not conceived a child. True, they had only been married three months, but with her first William she had gotten with child almost immediately after their marriage and after every pregnancy, and she was beginning to fear that perhaps she was no longer capable of conceiving. The birth of poor Lucres had been difficult. Perhaps it had damaged her.

She thought of a baby with Will's eyes, of seeing another son grow from babyhood to boyhood and to being breeched, and tears came to her eyes. She knew that Will wanted children, and she longed to be able to give them to him—especially a son. And then she worried that perhaps God might think that she questioned his wisdom, and would take away something that meant much to her.

Give me patience, she prayed. *Give me satisfaction with the manifold blessings Thou hast given me, and let me continue in Thy loving care.*

ONE EVENING IN EARLY DECEMBER WILL CAME HOME WITH A special spring in his step.

"Her Majesty has given you a wedding present, my sweet Bess," he said, his eyes twinkling.

"Indeed?" He was not carrying anything that she could see, and she guessed he was enjoying the suspense. "And what might that be, dear husband? Has she given you a holiday, that we might spend Christmas at Chatsworth?"

"Not this year. But I think you will not mind it. You are to be made a lady of her privy chamber."

Bess had not been prepared for such news and gaped at him in astonishment. Ladies of the privy chamber outranked maids of honor and ladies-in-waiting. Only ladies of the bedchamber, who took it in turns to sleep in the queen's room, held more privileged positions.

"That's—but—" She found she could not speak coherently.

"It is a great honor," Will said. "And a mark not only of her gratitude to me but of her respect and affection for you."

"She hardly knows me," Bess finally managed to gasp.

"It doesn't take much knowledge of you to like you, Bess."

"Then I will strive to fulfill the trust she has placed in me." She sat down suddenly on a chair near the fireplace, feeling faint. "Dear God. When do I begin? What do I do?"

"She has bid you to attend her next week. And I'm sure that any duties she may ask of you will be no more than you performed for Lady Zouche or the Duchess of Suffolk. Attending Her Majesty while she dresses, seeing to her clothes, providing company and amusement. She loves music, you know, and I'm sure would be pleased to have you play upon the virginals."

"Her skill in that is greater than mine, I believe."

"Whatever is required of you, I'm sure you will perform it to perfection."

LATER THAT NIGHT, AS THEY LAY IN BED, THE CURTAINS PULLED shut against the drafts, creating a little haven of love and safety, Bess was still thinking about the queen's honor to her.

"The queen owes you much, I think," she said, her hand caressing the scratchy stubble of Will's cheek. "More than you have let on."

"She thinks so, it is true." His voice was somber, and she sensed that something weighty lay behind his words.

"Will you tell me?"

"It was during the time of Thomas Wyatt's rebellion, in which my father and many of my friends were also involved. I served Princess Elizabeth then, and as you know when Queen Mary insisted on the Spanish marriage, Wyatt's plan was that Elizabeth should be put on the throne in place of her sister and married to her cousin Edward Courtenay, the Earl of Devon. But the plot was discovered and Courtenay was arrested. There was great fear that he would divulge what he knew, which was much, and so Wyatt and his allies were forced to act much sooner than expected."

Bess recalled those terrifying days, when she had secretly hoped that Elizabeth would be queen but had not known whom to trust, and could say nothing.

"Sir James Croft came to Ashridge House where the princess was, to convey Wyatt's urging that she remove to Castle Donnington, where Mary could not so easily get at her. She was very ill and in no condition to go anywhere. But she sent me to Tonbridge to give Wyatt her answer."

The hairs at the back of Bess's neck rose to think of Will putting himself in such danger, for if Elizabeth had agreed, it would have been treason, and Will implicated with her if her involvement was known.

"She supported the plot and would follow Wyatt's plan," she whispered.

"Yes. And had we not been forced to act before all was in place, it might have succeeded. But Wyatt was captured less than a fortnight later, and soon there was a harvest of death. Wyatt's men with whom I had spoken in Tonbridge were among the first to die."

"But not the last," Bess said, her throat constricting with grief. It had been Harry Grey's involvement in Wyatt's conspiracy that had cost Jane Grey her life. Jesu, how close Will had come to dying for Elizabeth.

Will pulled her closer to him and kissed the top of her head.

"Mary ordered Elizabeth to court, ill though she was. The journey took a week, the princess riding in a litter and looking like a corpse. For that cruelty alone if for nothing else Mary should burn in hell."

In the days following Jane's execution, Bess had been so devastated that she scarcely knew whether it was day or night, but she recalled William telling her of Elizabeth being sequestered at Whitehall.

"Many were seized and imprisoned. Harry Grey and his brother, of course. Lord Cobham, Nicholas Throckmorton, Robert Dudley, and many more who were my friends. When I was arrested and taken before the privy council I knew that my only salvation—and that of the princess—was that they had no proof of my involvement or hers, for she was not so foolish as to have put anything into writing, nor was I."

"You must have been very afraid."

"I was. But I could not let them see it. I swore my allegiance to Mary and denied that I had stood with the rebels, even when they took me to the Tower and showed me the instruments of torture, which I knew had been in use on men who had less to hide than I. What they wanted most, of course, was proof that Elizabeth had been complicit in the plot. That was all that was needed for Mary to have Elizabeth put to death. But I would not be responsible for sending her to the block, though it cost my life."

Bess could hardly breathe, thinking of how terrified she would be in such circumstances.

"I told them nothing." His voice was hollow, and sounded near to breaking. "I told them nothing."

"Did they torture you?" She wasn't sure she could bear the answer but could not forbear from asking the question.

"They used me roughly enough." His hand went to a scar on his cheek, his fingers brushing the pale line on his skin. Bess had wondered how he had come by it but had never asked. "They did not put me to the rack or the most severe means of questioning. I don't know why. Perhaps because they thought if they killed me what I knew would be lost. But I think perhaps it was because I had so stoutly set my mind to deny that she knew aught of the plans that I came to believe it myself."

"She was in the Tower, too."

"Yes, and poor lady, she knew what men were suffering on her behalf."

"How long did they keep you?"

"Four months in the Tower. Then I was taken to the Fleet Prison, and I knew that I had passed the greatest danger. It was another seven months before I was brought to a hearing. I was fined and my Somerset lands taken from me, but Queen Mary put me in command of a regiment and sent me away from London, and I had my life."

"Elizabeth knew," Bess said. "She knew what you had done for her."

"Yes," he said. "When I next saw her, not long before you came to Hatfield that day, she wept at the sight of me, and declared that she would be ever in my debt."

"Not only her," Bess said. "But all of England, did they but know it, for preserving her life that she might reign."

CHAPTER THIRTY-EIGHT

Christmas Day, 1559—Whitehall Palace, London

Bᴇss sᴛᴏᴏᴅ ᴏɴʟʏ ꜰᴇᴇᴛ ꜰʀᴏᴍ Qᴜᴇᴇɴ Eʟɪᴢᴀʙᴇᴛʜ, sᴜʀᴠᴇʏɪɴɢ the laughing and chattering crowd that filled the room. It was the same chamber in which she had watched King Henry and his court celebrate Christmas twenty years earlier. How far she had come, she thought. Then she had been merely one of Lady Zouche's attendants, awed at the noble ladies and gentlemen who surrounded her, wearing the only gown she had that was good enough for such company. Now, she was a lady of the queen's privy chamber, a titled lady herself, resplendent in a new gown of forest green velvet, her sleeves and underskirt heavily embroidered with gold, and wearing on her head a French hood of the latest fashion. Ropes of shimmering pearls cascaded over her breast, jewels sparkled at her ears, and her fingers were heavy with rings.

Then she had been a budding girl, still a virgin, hoping that she might find love but wary of what marriage might mean. Now she had been thrice married, had borne eight children and buried two, and had finally found the passionate love that she had not even known that she sought until she met Will.

She picked out his tall figure across the room, in conversation with Sir Robert Dudley. *The two handsomest men in London,* she thought, smiling. *One of them is mine and the other the queen's.*

"Lady St. Loe."

Bess turned to find Sir William Cecil at her elbow. When she had seen him at Hatfield House that autumn, she had noted that the sleeves of his doublet were fraying and his shoes down at heel. Now he wore a handsome black velvet robe, lined with fur, befitting his position as the queen's secretary of state and head of her privy council.

"Sir William, what a pleasure to see you. I was just thinking how it warmed my heart to see old friends who have weathered all the storms and are now standing safe in the sunlight."

"Indeed. And while I miss William Cavendish, I'm most pleased that your new husband is a man who has stood so steady by Her Majesty all these years."

His eyes went to Will, hand on the shoulder of Robert Dudley, leaning in to speak to him above the clamor of voices. The court had been thronged with suitors to the queen these last months, but it was Dudley who was ever at the queen's side. She had recently made him Lord Lieutenant and Constable of the Tower, and many of his friends now held coveted positions at court. The Duke of Norfolk had publicly accused him of interfering in state matters, but the result was that Norfolk had been sent to the Scottish border to serve as lieutenant general, and Dudley was as close to Elizabeth as ever. More so, perhaps. It was whispered that he was her lover. And the rumors that he would find a way to be rid of his wife would not be quieted. Bess wondered what William Cecil thought; he had been the queen's man for years, and though Elizabeth's eyes did not light with love when she looked on him, she relied on his wisdom and advice more than that of any other man, Robert Dudley included.

Bess glanced at the queen, surrounded by Duke John of Finland, brother to the hopeful Erik of Sweden; Baron Breuner, the representative of Ferdinand, the Holy Roman Emperor; the Spanish ambassador Bishop de Cuadra, also pressing the suit of the emperor's son Archduke Charles; and the envoy of the King of Denmark, in his ridiculous doublet of crimson velvet embroidered with a heart transfixed by an arrow.

"The siege continues," she remarked.

Cecil's eyes flickered to the queen's knot of admirers and he sighed.

"Yes, here is a great resort of wooers and controversy among lovers. I would Her Majesty had one and the rest honorably settled."

"Then you think she will pick one of the foreign rulers? And not—someone more near to hand?"

Will and Robert Dudley were now at the center of a laughing knot of men that included Robert's brother Ambrose and brother-in-law Sir Henry Sidney, Sir James Croft, and John Appleyard, the half brother of Lady Dudley.

"I see that your husband is among Dudley's cronies," Cecil said. "I mean no offense," he added, as Bess glanced at him in surprise. "It is only that I am ever thinking who might speak a wise word in the queen's ear."

"On what matter?"

"If she takes my Lord Robert," Cecil said quietly, "she will incur so much enmity that she may one evening lay herself down as the Queen of England, and rise the next morning as plain Mistress Elizabeth."

"But why?" Bess asked. She had always liked Robert Dudley. "He is Protestant, and the queen loves him. It is said his wife is very ill. Surely if they wait until sometime after her death . . ."

"It is not just that he is married. You well know that his father and brother were executed as traitors, as was his grandfather. Yet she made him Knight of the Garter along with the three highest peers of the realm, the Duke of Norfolk, the Marquess of Northampton, and the Earl of Rutland, who have long served England. And he? He rides well and has a handsome leg and whiskers that curl."

Bess giggled despite herself and Cecil gave her a dry smile.

"People mistrust the name of Dudley, and mistrust Lord Robert, thinking that he seeks to gain the throne for himself. If she were to look close to home she would do better to pick Edward Courtenay or Arundel or Sir William Pickering. No, there is not a man who does not cry out on him as the Queen's ruin, and on her with indignation, and yet I have a great fear that she will marry none but the favored Robert."

Cecil's eyes were tired and Bess noticed that his beard was frosted with gray as it had not been before.

"I hope she will listen to your counsel," she said. "For I'm sure you would guide her to what is best for England."

"She will listen. Whether she will act on my counsel is a different thing entirely." He bowed and made his way toward Sir Thomas Parry.

Watching the queen dance with Robert Dudley, Bess took the opportunity of seeking out Mary Grey. Although Mary was now fourteen years old, her tiny height, vivid red hair, and freckles made her appear younger.

"Bess! What a joy to see you!" Mary exclaimed, as Bess bent to embrace her.

"And you. I have thought much of you since your mother's death."

"It is hard, at Christmastime, to be missing her. She would so much have loved to be at court now, and I cannot help but want to turn to her and see her smile."

Kate Grey danced past with handsome Henry Carey, the queen's cousin and a favorite at the new court.

"How stands the matter of Kate's marriage to Edward Seymour?" Bess asked. "Your mother was so hopeful the last time I saw her."

"Alas, it is in a frozen state. My poor mother died before sending her letter to the queen, and now there is no one to speak for Kate, begging permission for her to marry Edward Seymour. He writes that perhaps they can importune the queen when the matter of her own marriage is settled."

The queen's marriage again, Bess thought. So much hung on that urgent question.

"And Kate must tread most carefully," Mary said, "and do nothing to bring the queen's wrath down upon her, for under the will of King Henry the crown would fall to Kate should something happen to Her Majesty, and thus Kate attracts plotters and suitors with their own ends in mind."

As had Elizabeth, when she stood next in line to Mary. And Jane . . . Bess's heart clutched with pain, and from the anxious expression on Mary Grey's face, she knew the poor girl must fear for Kate's safety, with the shadow of Jane's fate hanging over them.

It was ironic, Bess thought, that even as Elizabeth was hindered from being able to wed the man she loved, so the unhappiness was passed down to poor Kate Grey.

"Perhaps it will all come out well yet," she tried to reassure Mary.

"God's wounds," Will swore one cold morning in February, as he sat reviewing a letter. "I would the matter of the queen's marriage were resolved. While it hangs fire I shall have no peace."

"What's amiss now?" Bess asked.

"Here is news of a Spanish plot to kidnap Kate Grey and marry her to King Philip's son Don Carlos, and put them on the throne in Elizabeth's place."

"Surely Kate can have no part in this scheme."

"No, no, but that matters not at all. Until the queen is wed and has a son, there will always be plots and intrigues against her life. But it seems that will be no time soon; she has at last made plain she will not marry the son of the Holy Roman Emperor nor yet Erik of Sweden."

"Every time I am at court I hear that all is the fault of Robert Dudley."

Will looked up at Bess and shook his head.

"I've nothing against Dudley personally, but the rumors that he is the queen's lover echo through the courts of Europe, and people lay the queen's failure to marry at his door. I heard the French ambassador inquire yesterday whether England was so poor in men of courage that no one would assassinate Dudley, and he was but a quarter in jest, I think."

"And yet all strive most mightily to remain in his favor."

"Of course they do," Will snorted. "For it seems like enough he may be king before long. Even Cecil claps him on the shoulder and smiles upon him, though he loves him little enough."

When Bess next waited on the queen she found her tetchy and irritable. Her ladies kept their eyes down and scurried to be out of reach of her fan after she fetched a young page boy a blow with it for bringing her the message that Cecil wanted to see her at the same time she planned to watch Robert Dudley in a shooting match.

"What's amiss?" Bess whispered to Frances Newton when they were out of the queen's hearing.

"I think she's in a temper because she's just made Kate Grey a lady of the bedchamber, much against her will."

"She doesn't like Kate much; why do that?"

"Because she wants to be able to keep a close eye on her," Frances whispered. "Kate is her nearest relative and next in line for the throne until the queen has a child of her own. Better keep Kate nearby than push her away and let her fall under the influence of God knows who."

"Not the Spanish," Bess insisted. "Kate has far more sense than that."

"There are other possibilities than the Spanish. I've heard that Kate might marry the Earl of Arran." Frances raised an eyebrow at Bess.

"Oh." The implications struck Bess immediately. "He's heir to the Scottish throne, and should they have a son . . ."

"The crowns of England and Scotland could be united, exactly. Not a terrible thing for the future, perhaps, but such a marriage now might incite some to remove Her Majesty from the throne in favor of Kate. For she would be married, and soon might bear an heir. I've also heard whispers that Kate might marry the Earl of Huntingdon."

"I doubt that will come to pass," Bess said. "Or a marriage with Arran either. Kate's heart lies with Edward Seymour, last I knew. And besides, there are rumors that Her Majesty will adopt Kate. That sounds as if she means to acknowledge her as her successor rather than the Scottish queen. And surely with that prospect, Kate must be prepared to wait and see, and not take some precipitous and foolish action."

BESS WAS EXTREMELY WARY OF BEING SEEN TO BE PART OF ANY FAC-tion, and when she was in the queen's company she strove to be blithe and sunny, and to speak of nothing more consequential than the latest needlework pattern and whose baby was the bonniest.

She had plenty to occupy herself with at home. James Crompe, steward at Chatsworth, dispatched news of the progress of the building work, the crops, the livestock, and a dozen other matters, and requested her opinion and authorization of a hundred details. He sent lists of the books that Willie and Harry needed for school, and of the clothes they had outgrown or worn out, which must be replaced.

"They might as well be eating their boots," Bess remarked to Jenny as she counted out the money to send to Crompe. She wished she didn't have to worry about costs, but at the back of her mind was always the debt to the crown.

"Better they are healthy and needing clothes than needing none."

"Of course, you're right," Bess agreed, with a silent prayer of thanks that all her children were healthy.

The thought of children brought a trace of sadness to her heart, for she and Will had been married for six months, and no child had taken root within her belly. She was grateful that he had come to love her children as his own, but still longed to give him a son and heir.

As though her thoughts had summoned him, Will came into their bedchamber, a letter in his hand.

"Bess, my brother Ned writes that he will visit at the end of the month, to pay his respects to you as he was not at our wedding."

"Good," Bess said. "If he is as charming as your brother Clement I will be most happy to know him."

"He's not," Will said. "He's never been anything but trouble."

Will's face was stony. Did he believe, then, that Ned had murdered John and Bridget Scutt?

"Well, let him come," Bess said. "Perhaps he wants to make peace, and this visit can be the start of better relations between the two of you."

"BROTHER WILL! AND MY GOOD-SISTER BESS," NED ST. LOE CRIED as they greeted him at the door of the house in Tuthill Street.

But Bess sensed a coldness behind the jovial manner and the smile, and Will seemed wary as his brother came into the house.

"The place is looking much more elegant since I was last here," Ned said, clapping Will on the shoulder. "The influence of your lady wife, I make no doubt."

"She does have a civilizing effect," Will agreed, gesturing his brother to a chair in the withdrawing room. "And how is Margaret?" he added with forced politeness as a servant brought in cakes and ale and laid them on the table.

"Ah. She is less than thriving and joyous, alas." Ned affected a mournful expression, which seemed to Bess clearly calculated to elicit concerned inquiries, but Will remained silent as he handed his brother a flagon of ale. "Actually, brother, it is partly on my wife's account that I am here."

Bess saw Will's shoulders tighten and his jaw clench, and the eyes he turned on Ned were cold. It was an old game between the brothers, she saw. Ned seeking attention and inquiry; Will refusing to be drawn into his snares.

"The fact of the matter," Ned said, "is that my dear wife and I were much surprised to learn of the building works going on at Sutton

Court." He turned to Bess and smiled, but there was nothing pleasant about the smile and she thought his eyes were reptilian. "For shortly before our father died, he promised the house and lands to my Margaret, to be hers for her lifetime."

Bess could see there was nothing feigned about the astonishment on Will's face. It rapidly turned to outrage. Ale sloshed as he slammed his cup onto the table. "The devil he did."

Ned appeared to have been prepared for such a reaction. He merely crossed a booted foot over his knee and took a slow drink of ale.

"But he did, brother Will. And I am here to demand that you remove whatever of your possessions you have put into the house and hand over the keys."

"And just why would Father have done such a thing?"

"Why, it's only fair, isn't it? You have the property at Tormarton, and this fine house. And your lady"—a poisonous smile at Bess—"is possessed of that grand house a-building at Chatsworth, and vast amounts of land besides. What need you of yet another house? Whereas my Margaret and I are crammed into that pitiful poor house at Stanton Drew."

"The house that you bought from Bridget Scutt a fortnight after her husband died in such suspicious circumstances and a fortnight before you married her?" Will asked, his voice dangerously flat. "The house in which she died so suddenly after that marriage? The house in which you then took to wife your stepdaughter? You liked the house and what it offered well enough before. Why do you suddenly set your eye on Sutton Court?"

"Because I've a right to it—my Margaret has a right to it."

"That's a lie," Will said, jumping to his feet so suddenly that he knocked over his chair. "You well know that our father, along with half of Somerset, was aghast at your tricks. He had time enough to change his will if he wanted to leave you something more than the nothing he gave you. Get out."

Ned blinked at him, and Will grasped him by the front of his doublet and hauled him roughly to his feet.

"Get out of my house. Stay away from Sutton Court. And darken my door no more."

LATE THAT NIGHT WILL WAS STILL PACING THE FLOOR OF THEIR bedchamber and practically shaking with rage.

"It's a lie, I'm sure of it," he said. "Father had no use for Ned."

"Why would Ned think you would believe that Margaret Scutt was to have the use of the house?"

"There is only one speck of doubt that gnaws at me; one reason that there might be the faintest stain of truth in what he claims."

He sank onto the bed beside Bess and sighed heavily.

"My father wanted me to marry Margaret Scutt. I had no interest in the wench, though I felt sorry for her, as well as her mother and brother, for it was well known that John Scutt was a brute."

"He beat them, you mean?"

Will nodded. "It is just conceivable that my father told Ned that if I married Margaret, as he wished, she would have the use of the house for her lifetime if I died before her."

"Oh. But surely she has no right to expect it now, since she is married to Ned and not you, and they have a house to live in."

"You would think not. There is one more piece of the puzzle that troubles me. Ned came to me just after John Scutt died. He asked me not to marry Margaret and he persuaded me to buy the wardship of her brother Anthony."

"So that it would not be bought by someone who would take over the property and marry the boy off to his own daughter. I know well enough how that works."

In an instant, Bess was back all those years ago, feeling once more her mother's despair when Hardwick was under the control of the Court of Wards, and when she had had to fight Sir Peter

Frecheville, who had bought the wardship of Robbie Barlow's brother, for her widow's dower.

"Yes, exactly. But if that were the case, why did he not put it into his will? It makes no sense. And the only reason I can see for Ned's claim is that he will get Sutton Court."

"Would your mother know the truth of the matter?" Bess asked.

"I'll write to her," Will said. "But by God, that rogue never fails to set my teeth on edge."

"It is hard that he should have been left with nothing. It must have been a surprise to him when after years of you leaving Sutton Court alone we descended and began making changes. And with you a widower all these years and with only daughters, he no doubt came to expect that he would be your heir. But our marriage and the likelihood that we will have sons has put paid to that hope."

Let it be a likelihood still, Lord, she prayed.

"My father knew Ned too well to leave him with anything valuable," Will argued. "Six or seven years ago he gave Ned the leases of Whitchurch and Felton, and within three years Ned had sold them and spent what he got. If he gets Sutton Court—for it will be he, not Margaret Scutt, that controls it—I have no doubt he'll ruin it or lose it gambling or through mortgaging it."

"Might there be a way to give them the use of the house without the control of it? We must have a steward there; why not let it be Ned? Perhaps it would make him lay down his arms and live in peace."

"Faugh!" Will exclaimed in disgust.

"Well, let us think on it," Bess said, realizing that he was in no mood to make any good decision. "Come, my own, come to bed and hold me close, and let not Ned ruin the night as he has ruined the day."

Will's letter to his mother, and further letters to friends of his father, produced no confirmation of Ned's claim that their father had promised Sutton Court to Margaret Scutt for her lifetime. But he agreed with Bess's suggestion of making Ned steward of the property, allowing him and Margaret to live there.

"After all," he said, "so long as I continue in the queen's service I must be in London, unless she is on progress and then will I be where she travels. And when you go from town you go to Chatsworth. So I suppose it may be the best way out of a bad situation."

The letter was written and Ned replied, tersely, that he would become steward of Sutton Court.

"Does he thank you for it?" Bess asked.

"No," Will growled. "He accepts with little grace and no thanks."

"Perhaps he will unbend in time."

"Perhaps," Will said, balling up the letter and tossing it into the fire.

SOON THEREAFTER, WILL'S MOTHER CAME TO VISIT. BESS HAD taken a great liking to her mother-in-law at her wedding, and was pleased to be able to entertain her and introduce her to her friends. Margaret St. Loe was not yet sixty, vigorous, and good-natured, though with a tart wit. Will's father had been a friend of Harry Grey's, and Bess had seen him occasionally at Bradgate House, but from what she recalled of him, she thought Will had inherited many of his most likeable qualities from his mother.

One night while Will was kept late at court, Bess and her mother-in-law sat by the fire in Bess's bedchamber with their needlework, Margaret St. Loe telling Bess the family's history.

"The St. Loes have served the crown for more than five hundred years," she said. "Will was attendant knight at the recent obloquy for the French king; it was the same service that his grandfathers have performed since time out of mind, watching over the bodies of English kings, alive or dead. They have been warriors, always. My own husband had license to keep a hundred mounted soldiers, ready to do battle for the king."

Bess thought of Sutton Court with its fortified walls and tower, and could easily imagine that it could have withstood a siege in the not so distant days when such things still happened.

"My husband was one of the knights who welcomed Anne of Cleves.

And he was an official mourner at the funeral of poor King Edward, alas, so very few years after we so joyously welcomed his birth."

Bess got up to refill Margaret's goblet, and stirred the fire into fresh life.

"Will you have some of this mince pie?" she asked. "It arrived just this afternoon as a gift."

"I thank you, no," Margaret said. "I do endeavor to limit my sweets. But I will happily indulge myself in a few more of those delicious dates instead."

Bess took the plate of nuts and dried fruits to her mother-in-law and dished herself some of the pie. It was redolent with spices, and looked wonderful.

"Your husband spent much time in Ireland, Will said."

"He did. King Henry sent him there, and valued his service so that he was shortly made marshal and then commissioner. My husband's brother William was there, as well, and Will joined them for a year at the age of seventeen, before he became gentleman usher to the Marquess of Exeter. Of course that came to a sad end."

"Yes, alas," Bess murmured. For Will's patron Henry Courtenay, King Henry's cousin and great friend, had lost his head after Thomas Cromwell convinced the king that Courtenay was plotting a rebellion.

"After that Will was once more soldier in the king's service, first in Boulogne and then in Ireland for another eight years, before young King Edward placed him in charge of seeing to the safety of Princess Elizabeth."

Suddenly agony seized Bess, a twisting, cramping pain in her belly that reminded her of the pains of childbirth. She cried out and Margaret came to her side, her face full of alarm.

"What is it, my dear? Are you taken ill?"

"Yes," Bess gasped. She was awash in perspiration and she felt nauseated and dizzy. "I—oh!—help me to lie down, please."

Margaret took her arm and tried to guide her to the bed, but Bess crumpled to her knees, moaning in pain.

"Oh, dear God, I think I am dying."

A peculiar expression came over Margaret St. Loe's face.

"The pie. Whence did you say it came?"

"I don't know. A gift, the steward said—ohhh . . ."

"I think you are poisoned. Have you an emetic?"

Poisoned? Bess felt panic rising in her along with the overwhelming pain and nausea. Who would want to poison her?

"Yes," she gasped out. "Ring for help."

She felt disconnected from her body as she lay there on the floor, noting a large yellow bloom in the pattern of the Turkey carpet that seemed no less a part of her than her outflung hand with its rings. Poisoned. Surely she was dying. And she would never see Will again, or the children.

Footsteps, alarmed voices. She was being raised to a sitting position, supported by one of the footmen, with the steward and her mother-in-law swimming in a haze before her.

"Drink this, my lady."

Her head was tilted back, a little vial brought to her lips. Terrible, terrible, oh, the vileness of the stuff being poured down her throat. Like a liquefied frog, she thought. And then a powerful surge within, her gorge rising, her belly convulsing with the effort of heaving forth its contents. Vomiting into a basin, helplessly, feeling as if her soul were pouring forth. Would it never stop? Still more, still more. Surely there was nothing left inside her now; surely her very innards had been cast out. She was on her hands and knees now, weeping with pain and despair. Vomit on the fine expensive damask of her gown and on the carpet, on her hands and face. *Oh, God, let me die rather than live through more of this.*

And then blackness surged up and she was falling, falling . . .

BESS'S EYES FLUTTERED OPEN TO FIND HERSELF IN BED WITH WILL looking down at her, his face taut with worry.

"My love, my own, my life." He seized her hand and kissed it, then held it to his chest. "Thank the Lord. I feared you were lost to me."

A rush of memory came back. All had been well, chatting with Margaret, eating pie. The pie.

"What happened?" Bess managed to ask. Her belly felt as if it had been trodden on by horses.

"My mother thinks you were poisoned."

"Will I die?"

"No, thank God we had a remedy to hand. The doctor has been here; you will recover."

"But who would want to poison me?"

Will's face was stony. "Ned."

"Surely not. My death would do him no good."

"But mine would. The pie was meant for me."

Bess was appalled. Could Ned St. Loe be so twisted with hatred that he would poison his own brother over a house?

"I told you there were whisperings of poison when John Scutt died and then Bridget so quickly after him, leaving Ned master of their house," Will said. "I will make most careful inquiries and learn whence that pie came and whether it is possible that Ned had a hand in this mischief. But I pray you, Bess, be most careful. Eat or drink nothing that was not prepared here in the house and bear a wary eye if you must be out of doors until I come to the bottom of this."

"Bess, you must have some protection." Lizzie's eyes, the color of the hard brown shells of hazelnuts, were earnest.

"Why, I do, I have Will. If he can see to the queen's safety, surely he can see to mine!"

"That's not what I mean. If Ned St. Loe has used poison, it may be that he is also employing enchantments and charms against you. You must get something to ward against whatever forces of evil he is recruiting."

Bess stared at Lizzie.

"You think he is using witchcraft to harm Will and me?"

Lizzie shrugged. "I don't know, but it may be. Poison is an underhanded weapon, and if he would stoop to that, why would he not call upon the powers of darkness, too?"

The powers of darkness. Did such powers exist? Lizzie seemed to believe so. If they did, surely it was best to be protected. And nothing lost if there were no dark forces.

"I wouldn't even know where to go to get such a charm."

"But I do," Lizzie said. "I have had need of help in the past years, and have learned where to find it."

BESS HAD NEVER BEEN IN THE NARROW STREET TO WHICH LIZZIE led her. It was close to the river, and a chill wind gusted, making Bess glad of the heavy layers of wool of her gown and cloak. She wore high pattens, to keep her skirts from dragging in the muddy slush, and picked her way gingerly on the uneven ground.

Here were no grand houses, but ancient, ramshackle, half-timbered structures, their stories jutting out over the street, each thrusting farther than the one below, so that the topmost stories almost met, blocking out the wintry sun and creating a murky tunnel.

Lizzie stopped before a house on which a sign painted with an image of a cockatrice swung, creaking. The diamond window panes were obscured with dirt, but Bess could make out a grotesque shape hanging within, which bore a resemblance to the fantastical beast on the sign. It was about the size of a cat, looking somewhat fishlike, with a tail and fins, but with a face that was eerily human, with lank hair falling over it. Bess looked away.

A low arch opened onto a dingy yard strewn with rubble.

"Here?" she asked.

Lizzie nodded and Bess followed her into the yard. Narrow galleries on each story ringed the space. The building was an inn, then, or had been at one time, though it would be a desperate traveler who would seek shelter there, Bess thought.

Lizzie climbed a rickety stairway, its timbers creaking as she and Bess made their way upward, and Bess prayed that it would not collapse beneath their weight. When they reached the uppermost gallery, Lizzie led her to the corner farthest from the street, and knocked at the weathered door.

The door opened a crack, revealing a pair of piercing blue eyes peering out at them.

"Gammer Joan," Lizzie said. "I've brought a friend who needs your help."

"Your ladyship." The voice was that of an old woman. Her words carried no surprise at seeing Bess and Lizzie. She opened the door to admit them, and in the dim light Bess saw a withered form in garments so old and worn that they were shapeless and of no determinate color.

The room was tiny, no bigger than the closet off Bess's bedchamber that contained her close stool. The only furnishings were a small table, a bench, a stool, and a chest. A rolled pallet lay in one corner, and in another stood a waste bucket. Bunches of dried herbs hung on the walls and from strings stretched overhead, permeating the air with their scents. A tallow candle guttered on the table, its flickering light barely breaking the gloom. A tiny fire burned in the grate, but still the room was bitter cold.

Joan waved Lizzie and Bess to be seated on the bench. She remained standing, her gaze sweeping over them. She nodded, as if her glance had confirmed some earlier suspicion.

"My friend Bess has been poisoned," Lizzie said. "She needs something to work against the poisoner, and to protect both her and her husband. Can you provide such a thing?"

"Certainly, my lady." Joan turned to Bess. "Have you anything of the poisoner's own body? Hair? Nail parings? Or perhaps summat he has worn?"

"No." Bess shook her head.

"No matter. We will make do without, have no fear."

The old woman knelt and opened the chest, and Bess saw that within it lay a shallow tray containing numerous little bundles, pots, and jars. Joan's clawlike hands ranged over them, hovering before seizing on a little bundle of rag tied with twine and a tiny cloth pouch. She brought them to the table, worked the bindings of the bundle loose, and drew forth a small white object that looked like a splinter of white wood. She held it up for Bess to see, turning it so that the candlelight shone gold upon it.

"A bit of the horn of the unicorn. The most powerful protection against poison, my lady."

Her face was grave, and in the eerie light, it seemed entirely possible to Bess that what Joan held was indeed a piece of unicorn's horn. She glanced at Lizzie, who only nodded.

Joan put the horn into the pouch, and then gazed around her at the forest of hanging herbs and flowers. She broke off a few leaves from one bunch and desiccated blossoms from another, thrust them into the pouch, and tied the neck of it tight with a bit of twine. She fetched a little bottle from the trunk and removed the cork.

"Give me your hand."

Bess did as she was bid. Joan placed the tiny bundle into her palm, unstoppered the bottle, and poured a few drops of amber liquid onto the bundle. It gave off a pungent scent that Bess couldn't identify. Joan curled Bess's hand shut around the little pouch and made the sign of the cross over it. She closed her own hands over Bess's, and shut her eyes. In the silence, Bess was keenly conscious of the sound of her own breathing, and that of Lizzie and Joan.

Joan opened her eyes. "Wear that close to your heart. It will protect you from poison."

"I will."

"You wish to protect your husband, too?"

"Yes. But he would never—" Bess tried to imagine asking Will to wear a pouch containing the horn of a unicorn. "Have you something that I can use without telling him?"

A faint smile lit Joan's lips. "Certainly, my lady. It is ever the way with men that we must quietly go about things that are for their own good. Take a shirt belonging to your man, and soak it in his urine. Then burn it. That will work against the poisoner. And to protect all in your household, burn sage upon the fires."

Joan turned to Lizzie, then, and looked upon her steadily for a few moments, seeming to read her as she had done with Bess.

"You have prospered since I saw you last, my lady."

"Yes. My fortunes have turned for the better."

"The queen favors you."

Bess glanced at Lizzie, wondering if she had told Joan that she was now serving the queen, but Lizzie looked surprised at the remark, and only nodded.

Bess looked around the room and its meager furnishings, shivering as she drew her heavy cloak tighter about her. Old Joan had a roof over her head, but not much more than that. How did she keep herself fed? she wondered. She took out her purse, drew out two silver shillings, and put them into Joan's hand.

Joan's brows rose, and she inclined her head in gratitude. "I thank your ladyship." She smiled then, showing her few remaining teeth. "I will pray that your bounty will delay the deaths of a dozen souls."

Bess's confusion must have showed on her face.

"I am a searcher," Joan said. "It is my employment to examine the newly dead, and report the cause of the death to the parish clerk. Last year was a good one for me, but a hard one for the parish. Men must die—and women and babes, too—that I may eat."

There had been an outbreak of the plague in London the previous year. That must be what Joan meant, Bess realized with a shudder.

"A hard way to get your living," she said.

Joan shrugged. "Easier than dying." Her eyes flickered from Bess to Lizzie and back. "Though to be sure, in the end, there are none of us escape that."

CHAPTER THIRTY-NINE

THE FRIGHT OVER BESS'S NEAR ESCAPE RIPPLED THROUGH THE
queen's court, already fearful that there might be an attempt on
Elizabeth's life. For she had recently angered the French by sending
ships to blockade Scotland and preventing shipments of arms from
reaching their destination. Now Cecil issued orders that no one but
the inward circle of the queen's attendants should handle her clothes
or anything she would touch. She must not accept gifts of perfume
or objects such as gloves, which could easily be impregnated with
poison. She must eat and drink nothing that had not been prepared
by trusted cooks and brought to her straight from them. Will dou-
bled the guards who attended her and ordered that they be even
more alert to the possibility of danger than usual.

Will's inquiries traced the pie's origins back to an inn at Bristol,
not far from Sutton Court, owned by a man named Hugh Draper,
who had previously been suspected of witchcraft and poisonings. He
was imprisoned in the Tower, and soon some apparent accomplices
were with him, including a St. Loe cousin named Elizabeth. Will's

mother, back at her home in Somerset, was apparently in no doubt about Ned's guilt.

I am sure that Will would not mislike his brother without a great cause, she wrote, *and I am sure he is in the right. Many have said to me they hear say that Edward should go about to poison his brother and you, and I fear that this was the goodwill he bore you when he came up to London to see you, for he liked nothing your marriage. His good friendship to you, as to me, is all one. God defend us from such friends. I know that Will is seeking out the truth of the matter, and I pray you, madam, send me word how this devil's devices began, and how it came to light. Thanks be to God you know about it and can be on your guard. I pray God send you both long life and good health. Yours most assuredly as long as I live, Margaret St. Loe.*

Bess was shocked at the ferocity of Margaret's denunciation of Ned. He must have committed black deeds, she thought, for his own mother to be brought to the point of calling him a devil.

Will was sure his brother was to blame, and that he, not Bess, had been the intended victim of the poison. He continued to pay informants in Somerset and Gloucestershire, and gave orders to his men guarding Ned's cohorts at the Tower to note down any incriminating statements. But infuriatingly, no positive evidence could be found linking Ned to the pie or to poisoning it, and eventually, Ned was freed and Will and Bess could do no more against him.

THE QUEEN WOULD SPEND SOME WEEKS IN THE SUMMER ON PROGRESS, and Will would have to be with her. He still feared for Bess's safety, and the queen agreed with him that Bess should return to the protection of Chatsworth in his absence.

As the house came into sight after the arduous journey from London, Bess felt suffused with joy, knowing that she would very shortly be reunited with her children. She corresponded with them regularly, of course, even four-year-old May laboriously inscribing the letter *M* at the bottom of a letter written by her nurse, but it was a far cry from holding them in her arms, hearing their voices, sharing the joy of each day with them.

And the house! It rose impossibly grand and impressive, its white stone standing out against the green hills, the crenelated roofline and four turrets of the façade echoing those of a castle, and yet somehow the whole was modern and new. Much work had been done since she had last been there, and she fairly ached to inspect the progress.

"Mother!"

Bess saw Frankie tearing across the grass toward her, her cap falling off so that her red hair streamed behind her.

"My darling!" Bess called, waving.

Frankie had grown, she thought, and if she had not been running pell-mell she would have looked like a young lady instead of a little girl. She was twelve now, just the age that Bess had been when she left Hardwick for Codnor Castle. Time to think about finding a suitable lady for Frankie to serve; someone who would help assure her rise in the world.

"My dearest, what a joy to see you!" Bess cried, pulling Frankie onto the litter with her and holding her close. "And plenty of time we'll have together now, for I'll not go back to London until the queen returns."

And maybe she would take Frankie with her then, Bess thought. She could take her to court and let her be seen, for she was a glorious sight as she looked smiling up at Bess, bright and bonny and blithe.

Supper that night was joyous, the children all talking over each other in their eagerness to tell Bess of their doings. Harry and Willie, nine and eight years old, were full of excitement about their enrollment at Eton, where they would go in the autumn, their first foray into the world away from home.

"Why can't I go, too?" Charlie demanded.

"You're too little; you're only six," Harry pronounced, and Charlie's face crumpled.

"You will go soon enough, poppet," Bess said, gathering him onto her lap before tears could erupt. "And when you do, your brothers will be there to keep you company."

"What about me?" asked Bessie, only just turned five.

"You and May will do your learning here at home with me and your grandmother and auntie," Bess said, smiling across the table at her mother and Aunt Marcella. "For one day you will be great ladies, and they don't teach that at Eton."

"I going to be great lady," May echoed solemnly, and put her fingers in her mouth.

"Oh, it's wonderful to be home!" Bess cried. "London is all very well, but nothing compares with home."

THE GREAT HALL WAS READY FOR DECORATIVE PLASTERWORK, and Bess wrote to John Thynne, asking if he would send his plasterer from Longleat. There was still a platoon of men at work at Chatsworth, however, and Will replied to Bess's letter describing the state of the house by addressing her as "chief overseer of my works."

"Ah, dear love, how I miss you," she murmured, bringing the letter to her nose to see if she could catch his scent on the paper. He wrote every couple of days, as the court made its way from Winchester to Basing to Windsor, and Bess faithfully dispatched long letters in return, full of news of the family and estate.

She found it comforting to be back in the country, and felt her body and mind fall in with the rhythms of nature. It gave her joy to watch the lambs and calves and colts grow bigger, to see the wheat ripen in the fields, to oversee the cheese making, the brewing of beer, the harvesting of honey from the buzzing hives, the picking of the orchard's riches. Chatsworth had lost its air of incompleteness and now seemed a part of the land and at one with the seasons.

Jem rode over from Hardwick for a visit of several days. Bess had not seen her brother since her wedding, and then there had been little time for real visiting. When had they last sat and spoken at length? Bess wondered. It must have been two years earlier, when she had retreated to Chatsworth after William Cavendish's death. But then she had been so sunk in grief and despair that she had barely been herself.

As they sat in the shade beside the house sipping cool cider, she noticed for the first time that Jem's clothes were far behind the London fashions and even a little shabby, and then felt guilty for the observation. Why should he trouble with what was in or out in London, after all? His business was the running of the estate, not flattering or seeking to impress with costly apparel.

"Your wife is well?" she asked.

"Aye, faith, well enow," he answered, and it struck her that even his speech was far different from hers. Had she truly sounded like that? She must have, she supposed, and realized that it was she, not he, who had changed. Did he resent her? Regard her as a poseur or superficial time-pleaser?

"So it's all come out well for thee," he said suddenly. "I recall how frighted and nervous you were when I took you to Codnor. But look at you, a grand lady now, inward with the queen and all the high and mighty folks."

"Aye. Mother knew what she was about when she sent me away, reluctant though I was to go."

What would her life have been like if she had had her way and stayed? She would likely have married some boy of a neighboring family and would now be overseer to a manor house and a few acres. Not chatelaine of a great estate such as Chatsworth and the sprawl of land about it. Not mistress to an army of servants in four great houses. Not on intimate terms with the queen and her court, with the highest people in the land, those who determined what happened for all the rest.

Jem coughed into his sleeve and Bess noted how tired he looked.

"You've been ill?" she asked.

"Faith, it comes and goes, but never seems to go completely," he said. "A rackety breathing, I seem to have."

"And how do things go on at Hardwick?"

Jem shrugged. "With difficulty. It's hard to make the place keep itself, and then I must always be riding off to see to the coal mine at Heth or the other bits of property here and there."

Bess thought that it must be even harder since Jem had no sons to help him in the running of Hardwick. He and his wife had no children though they had been married for a few years, but Bess knew from her mother that he had sired at least one bastard child. She wished that she could offer to help him, but until the matter of her debt to the crown was resolved, she worried constantly about her finances. And, she thought, Jem's pride might be offended if she offered him money.

IN EARLY SEPTEMBER, THE COURT WAS AT WINDSOR, AND PREPARING to return to London. Will wrote to Bess that he had visited Eton, where Harry and Willie would begin their studies in the Michaelmas term.

> It is a fair place, and I visited with the almoner, who sends you his compliments, and assures me that no gentleman's children in England shall be better welcome, nor better looked unto, than our boys, so I pray you set your heart at rest about sending them thither. Yesterday Her Majesty spake so fair of my horse—the new gelding that I wrote you thereof—that I gave it to her as a birthday gift, thinking it little enough cost to please her. Things continue much the same with Dudley as before. The queen hunts with him every day from morning until night, and yesternight Sir William Cecil told me that he purposed to retire to the country soon, for as he said, "It is a bad sailor who does not make for port when he sees a storm coming," and he fears that when Dudley's wife is dead, which it seems cannot be long, the queen will marry him, willy-nilly, throwing herself away on him, as he says, and forgetting what she owes unto herself and her subjects.

*I have hopes that once the queen is bestowed in London she will grant
me leave to come to you at Chatsworth soon, which I desire mightily.
Thus wishing myself with thyself, thine who is wholly and only thine,
yea and all thine while life lasts, your husband, William St. Loe.*

Will was no sooner back in London, lodging once more in Red
Cross Street, than he sent word of news that had rocked the court.

*Amy Robsart, wife to Robert Dudley, is dead. Not from the malady
that has long been spoken of, but by mischance, it seems, for her
servants, having gone forth to a fair, returned to the house to find
her dead at the bottom of a pair of stairs with her neck broke. The
queen has ordered that there be an inquest, sent Lord Robert away
to his house at Kew until the coroner shall come to a verdict, and
mewed herself up in her rooms with her confusion.*

"Sure she must have done away with herself," Jenny surmised
when Bess read the letter over to her. "Poor lady, what a grievous
position she has been in so long, with all the world and his wife
speaking of Robert Dudley's love for the queen and the queen's for
him, and that it wanted only her death to make him free to marry."

"Perhaps," Bess said. "But I am positive that though Dudley was
far from his wife, many will say that he had a hand in her death, and
even that the queen did, too."

A few days later Will wrote that the coroner had concluded that
Lady Dudley's death was accidental.

*But this does nothing to still the wagging tongues, and though the
queen has recalled Robert Dudley to her side, there are dangerous
suspicions and mutterings that Dudley sent someone to do his wife
to death. In truth I think the queen will never be able to marry him
now. Lady Throckmorton tells me that her husband writ from
Paris to say that all the talk there is that the queen and her lover
have murdered his wife.*

Bess felt a wrenching sorrow for Elizabeth, imagining only too well how she herself would feel if she had been prevented from marrying Will because of what people would think, because of a duty to put the needs of the country before her own happiness. And Elizabeth was twenty-seven. She could not wait forever to take a husband. Could she afford to delay making a choice, hoping that eventually the furor over Amy Robsart's death would fade and she could marry the man she loved so well?

A month later Will wrote that the queen had finally given him permission to leave court but that something was finally happening with Bess's case against the Exchequer.

I should have been with you this day but for that, he wrote. *I will forbear answering your last letter, for that God willing I will this next week be the messenger myself . . . Farewell, my own sweet Bess, from him who dares not so near his coming home to term thee as thou art, yet thine, William St. Loe.*

THE PREPARATIONS FOR HARRY'S AND WILLIE'S REMOVAL TO ETON had been going on so long that it had seemed inconceivable to Bess that the day of departure would ever come. But here it was, the nineteenth of October, and their trunks were loaded onto a cart, the footmen and guards were milling around the forecourt of the house, and any minute now she would have to kiss her boys farewell.

"How long will the journey be?" Willie asked, looking anxious.

"I've told you ten dozen times," Harry said, rolling his eyes. "A week."

"Perhaps a week," Bess said, straightening Willie's cloak. "Perhaps less, if the roads are good. And you may chance to meet your father on the way, for he will be traveling here from London."

"That would be a fine thing," Willie said, perking up a bit.

Bess thought he must be a little afraid to go so far away, leaving behind everything he knew and venturing among strangers, but she knew he didn't like to seem to be a baby compared with his older brother.

"Yes, it would be a fine thing," she agreed. "And I shall be in London in a matter of weeks, and as soon as I'm there I'll come to see you. You'll be so busy with your studies you'll hardly miss me, I'll be bound."

"But I will miss you, Mother," Willie said, casting aside all pretensions of manhood and flinging himself into her arms. "And Gran and Aunt Marcella and Jenny and Big Meg and Little Meg, and the sheep, and the dogs, and everything."

Bess struggled not to weep, for she thought that if she started now she would never stop.

"And we will miss you," she said, stooping and tightening her arms around Willie. "All of us, most dreadfully. But you will write to everyone here, and to your father and me in London, and let us know how you get on."

"I'm going to serve the queen when I have done at school," Harry declared, setting his hat on his head at a rakish angle. "I will be a soldier like Father."

"And I will be most proud of you," Bess said. "Of both of you."

The entire household was gathered to see them off, and when the boys and their companions had finally mounted, they looked like a small army.

At least they are well guarded, Bess thought. *Please, God, keep my angels safe on the roads.*

She ran forward to give her sons each one last kiss, and even Harry, considering himself grown up at almost ten years old, looked a little tearful as she pressed her lips to his cheek.

TWO DAYS AFTER THE BOYS LEFT FOR ETON, BESS SAW FROM AN upstairs window that a party of riders was approaching Chatsworth. Surely that was Will at the front of the pack, his cape flying out behind him as he came at a run? She gave a shriek of joy and dashed to the stairs.

"My own darling!" she cried as Will alighted and swept her into his arms. "How have I missed thee!"

"Ah, by God, heaven is nowhere but in your arms, sweet Bess." He kissed her deeply, heedless of the tumble of children, servants, and his companions around them. "I met with Harry and Willie on the road near Northampton. We dined before we parted company, and they were fine and in good spirits."

"Ah, the most comforting words to a mother's soul," Bess said, pressing her head to his chest. "They're like to be at Eton by now, I hope."

Will's brother Clement was with him, along with four friends and half a dozen servants, and besides what they carried there were three more horses laden with gifts for Bess and the children and luxuries for the household: oranges and lemons, olives, pepper and spices, and two dozen packets from an apothecary's shop, containing ingredients for remedies and simples.

It was like Christmas, Bess thought, as after dinner the family sat surrounded by opened bundles, their contents strewn across the carpet. Velvet shoes, silk points for tying sleeves to bodices, perfumed gloves, lace and ribbons, furs and lengths of fine fabrics, toys for the children, gifts for the servants.

"And look at this!" Will crowed, unwinding a heavy object from its swaddling of wool. "A knocker for the great gate!"

"You are a marvel!" Bess exclaimed, running a finger over the gleaming brass stag's head. She threw herself into his lap, put her arms around his neck, and kissed him. "Empty-handed you would have been a sight for sore eyes, but you come bearing such a quantity of fine things that I wonder the carrying of them didn't cripple the horses."

"And yet there is more," he said, his eyes twinkling. "Her Majesty has given me some land near Tormarton—I must take occasion to see it before I return to London—and she has granted my request to commission a suit of armor from Erasmus Kerkener."

"Oh, Will!"

Kerkener was the royal armorer at Greenwich, who created masterpieces of armor for field and tiltyard, costly in the extreme and prized not only for their craftsmanship but for their proclamation of the wearer as a gentleman of wealth and high standing. But thanks to Will's salary from the queen and the income from his properties, he could afford to equip himself so handsomely.

"When I return to London I will call upon him and look at his patterns to see what will be most fitting."

"I hope Her Majesty will have another tourney," Bess said, "just so I may see you in your armor and on horseback, conquering all that come before you."

"Tell me of the Exchequer matter," Bess urged Will as they lay close in bed that night.

"Our suit was not granted out of hand," Will said, "nor was it ruled against. It will come to hearing sometime in the next months, I think."

"What if it does not go our way?" Bess fretted.

"We'll skin that bear when we've caught it. No use distressing yourself until the time comes, and when the moment is right I'll put in a word with the queen."

"Ah, my love, my savior. What would I ever do without you?" she murmured, inhaling his scent and sighing in contentment.

"Alas, I also bring news that is not so comfortable," he said. "Ned is up to no good again."

The mention of his brother seemed to bring a chill into the room.

"He has not been sending me the rents," Will said. "I wrote to him to know the cause of it, and he boldly claimed that the rents were his, and if I didn't like it I could come to collect them myself."

"The villain."

"Yes. And he's been holding court and meting out judgment, as though he were lord of the manor there and justice of the peace. I will have to go to Sutton Court to set things straight, and then on to visit my mother before I return to London."

Sorrow seized Bess. "Oh, my love, I cannot let you go from me just yet."

"I'll not be gone for at least a fortnight," Will said. "But as things stand at court I dare not be gone too long."

"Why, what's the news?" Bess asked in alarm.

"More of the same," Will sighed. "The queen's marriage, and Robert Dudley."

"Still?"

"Still, and hotter debated in the last few days now, for the court is out of mourning for Lady Dudley and Robin Dudley is back at the queen's side. He makes no secret that he is courting her. It is all that is talked of. Throckmorton writes from Paris that the courts of Europe take it as fact that Dudley murdered his wife, and think it likely that Elizabeth was complicit."

"But they can't believe it!"

"Many do. It is brazenly claimed that the queen has married Dudley in secret or that she has borne his child. The French are joyous at the prospect that England will not tolerate a whore and murderess on the throne, but will cast her out in favor of the Scottish queen. If these slanderous rumors be not slaked, England's reputation is gone forever. War will follow, and utter subversion of the queen and country."

"War abroad?"

"Aye, with France, or Spain, or Scotland, or all of them together who would do much to put a Papist on the throne."

"And will she not still the rumors one way or the other? What says she?"

"She keeps her own counsel. There is still talk of a foreign marriage, though it seems to me that she has no liking for the prospect but it suits her to keep people guessing. And I must confess I cannot see how any prince will marry her, thinking her to be Dudley's strumpet."

"And if she marries him? Would not that still the poisonous tongues and put the matter to rest?"

Will sighed and shook his head. "I fear that could lead to war within England. Marrying a subject would be beneath the queen's dignity. And to marry a Dudley, and Robert Dudley, of all men! He is not well liked—the court is riven by factions. And though the inquiry cleared him of guilt in his wife's death, there are many who will always believe he killed her. No. Faced with the prospect of King Robert, there might be risings, and she could be swept from the throne."

"And who would they put in her place? Not the Scottish queen?" Bess guessed the answer even as she asked the question and her stomach went cold with fear. "Kate Grey."

"Aye, that's likely."

And would Kate Grey resist such a tide? She who had been raised with the thought that she was near to the throne, and who was next in line according to the terms of old King Henry's will? Surely the example of her sister Jane must warn her to steer clear of plots and intrigues?

"So you see why I must return to London soon," Will said. His words brought Bess back to the present, and she stroked his cheek and kissed him.

"I cannot live without you near me, my love."

He pulled Bess close to him. "And I cannot bear the thought of having you so far from me, either. Come back to London when I return there. The children will be well here with your mother and aunt."

"Yes," she said, though the thought of parting from her children and leaving the peace of Chatsworth made her sad.

"From London you can easily visit Harry and Willie at Eton," Will urged, one hand caressing her breast and the other lifting her nightdress. "Oh, Bess." His voice was husky in her ear, and her loins stirred to feel him hardening against her. "I must have you, now and later, and ever and anon."

CHAPTER FORTY

Twenty-seventh of December, 1560—London

BESS AND WILL'S LONDON HOUSE RANG WITH THE LAUGHTER and chatter of their guests rising above the music. A dozen couples danced the galliard, points and ribbons flying and bouncing as they leapt and skipped. The table at one end of the hall was laden with delicacies—pies and tarts, gingerbread, candied fruits, roasted nuts, sweetmeats in jewel-like colors—and the air was heavy with the scent of spiced wassail.

"A most glorious evening," Frances Newton complimented Bess. "Wonderful food and drink; the house looks so festive; and I don't know how, but you have managed to get everyone worth knowing here."

She tilted her head to indicate Sir William Cecil in deep conversation with George Talbot, who had recently succeeded his father as Earl of Shrewsbury.

"The most powerful man in the country—Cecil, who has the queen's ear—and George Talbot, the wealthiest man in the land and a very prince."

"Ah," Bess laughed. "Well, Cecil is an old friend—he was secretary to Edward Seymour when my husband William Cavendish was his treasurer—and the Shrewsburys have long known my family. The previous earl was somewhat of a patron to my father."

"Well done, nevertheless."

"Do you know what gives me the greatest joy of all?" Bess asked. "Look."

William Parr was leading Lizzie down the middle of a clapping set of dancers, both of their faces glowing with happiness. Their long-enforced separation under Queen Mary had come to an end when Queen Elizabeth had declared their marriage valid, and Lizzie was now accepted everywhere as William's wife and the Marchioness of Northampton.

"They look like newlyweds," Frances said.

"Which you will soon be yourself! Only another few weeks now."

"Oh, that reminds me," Frances cried. "My William wants to have a wedding portrait painted. Yours are spectacular, who did them?"

Bess's eyes went to the twin portraits of her and Will, completed only a few days earlier. She was eminently pleased with them. Will, wearing a black velvet doublet beneath the breastplate of his armor, looked like a warrior king, she thought.

"You look like the queen herself," Frances commented.

Bess had been painted in a black velvet robe with a collar of downlike white fur over her gown of white satin intricately embroidered with gold, the fur lining of the coat perfectly setting off the heavy gold toggles down the front of the robe and at the slashes of its short puffed sleeves. Her hands, stacked with rings, clasped a pair of fine doeskin gloves. And the French hood she wore was set with pearls and jewels. The portraits had cost a fortune, but they had been worth it.

"I'll give you the name of the painter and how you may find him," she said. "I must say I am satisfied with the pictures."

Frances's cousin Anne Poyntz joined them, breathless after the dance.

"What do you think I've just heard!" she exclaimed, fanning

herself. "The Countess of Lennox has sent her son Lord Darnley to France to woo the Scots queen!"

Three weeks earlier, young King Francis of France had died after a serious ear infection, leaving the beautiful eighteen-year-old Mary Stuart a most desirable widow.

"Dear God, does the queen know?" Bess whispered.

"She can't," Frances said. "She'd never have allowed it. For of course Darnley has his own claim to the throne. And a match with the Scottish queen—"

"Who's already calling herself queen of England—" Anne Poyntz broke in.

"Would be far too threatening a match for Her Majesty to contemplate," Bess finished.

"What can have possessed Lady Lennox?" Frances breathed.

"We know well what possessed her," Bess said. "She hopes to put her son on some throne or another. But let us hope she does not pay for her ambition with her head and that of her son."

WILL'S VISIT TO SUTTON COURT IN NOVEMBER HAD NOT GONE well. His brother Ned was not only keeping for himself the rents paid by tenants and holding courts as lord of the manor, he was claiming that in fact he was the rightful owner of the property, using old title documents stolen from his father and new forged documents to support his lies.

"I ordered the wretch to leave, but he would not," Will had fumed to Bess when she had first arrived in London. "There's nothing for it but the law courts."

Bess had groaned at the thought of more lengthy legal proceedings—her fight for her Barlow widow's dower had gone on for years—but agreed that, short of descending on Sutton Court with an army, there was no other way to dislodge Ned from the house that was rightly Will's.

Ned had responded that he had documents proving that his

father had left the house to Ned's wife Margaret Scutt for her life-time, but he had not produced them for Will's perusal. Worse, he had claimed that Bess had used unnatural powers to induce Will to make her heir to all his property.

The charge had frightened Bess, for an allegation of witchcraft was a serious matter. She had burned a shirt of Will's soaked in his piss, as old Joan had directed, though she had felt foolish doing it. And she wore the little bundle beneath her clothes, taking comfort in its presence, whether it had an effect against poison or not. But those actions were not witchcraft. In any case, no one but Lizzie knew of her visit to old Joan, she reassured herself. Unless Ned had somehow learned of it? No, it was impossible. Unless he himself was using unnatural powers. In which case, it was a good thing she had the charms.

Fortunately, Will had been outraged at his brother's claim.

"I'll not stand by and have him make such a dangerous and out-rageous accusation against you," he had fumed. And the judge had not given any more credence to Ned's slanders than Will had.

The battle had raged for months, and now, as spring was turning to summer, came the resolution, which pleased no one. The judge ordered that Ned St. Loe and his wife should continue to live at Sut-ton Court as tenants but that part of the rent they paid to Will would be paid back to them for their care of the place.

"Imbecility!" Will roared, slamming his hand against a wall in frustration when he read the order. "To allow that villain to remain in the place, which he will surely destroy, is not to be borne."

"But what can we do?" Bess asked, fearful that he might give himself an apoplexy, so great was his rage.

"It may be that we cannot change what happens for the present," Will said, yanking a sheaf of paper from his desk and searching for a pen. "But I will see him in hell before he gets Sutton Court when I die. I will make a will leaving all to you—it is mine to do with what I please by the terms of my father's will—and moreover I will make a deed of gift to you."

"For Sutton Court?" Bess asked.

"For everything."

"And what of your daughters?"

"They will be married. Let their husbands care for them. And of course you can give them what you will. But I'll not see Ned inherit a farthing."

CHAPTER FORTY-ONE

Thirtieth of July, 1561—St. Osyth's Priory, Essex

A SEARING WHITE FORK OF LIGHTNING RIPPED THROUGH THE darkening sky, followed a second later by a clap of thunder so loud that Bess felt it in the very pit of her stomach. The spire of St. Paul's Cathedral in London had fallen only a few weeks earlier after being hit by lightning, and Bess feared that the walls of the great house would collapse around her. But the old priory stood, and the only sound that came was the driving rain spattering against the windows and pounding into the dry ground below.

In the courtyard, servants were scurrying to carry the remains of the interrupted feast to safety inside. Platters of delicacies, richly upholstered chairs and benches, painted silk banners were all sodden and forlorn. All afternoon the clouds had seemed pregnant with the threatening storm, the sky crackling with pent-up energy. But not until the queen and her court were in the midst of the evening's festivities had the storm broken.

Bess heard the door of the chamber open and turned to see Will, his clothes and boots drenched, rainwater running in rivulets from his hair and down his face.

"Is Her Majesty well settled?" she asked.

"Yes," he said, dropping his cloak and hat onto the floor and unbuttoning his doublet. "She should be stepping into a hot bath just about now, and the royal nightgown was warming on the hearth as I left her."

Bess went to him and untied the neck of his shirt.

"You're wet to the skin," she said, putting her hands against his chest. "And cold." She stood a-tiptoe and pulled his head down to kiss her.

"And now you'll be wet, too," he said, peeling off his shirt.

"I don't care." She put her arms around him, marveling as always at the smooth hardness of the muscles of his back beneath her fingers, the coiled strength of his arms around her. God, what fire he kindled in her, no matter that his skin was slick with water and cold and that the fine linen of her chemise was now sticking damply to her. His dark hair was sleek against his head, and she reached up to touch it.

"You're like a silkie." She smiled. "A seal from the sea, come to land to steal a lady's heart."

"The land is almost as wet as the sea, and I'll warrant the surf on the rocks would be the death of any silkie seeking the shelter of a lady's bedroom this night."

He sat on a bench by the fire and reached down to pull off his boots, but struggled with them, so heavy with water was the leather.

"Let me."

Bess stooped before him, grasped the heel of one boot in her hands, and tugged, nearly falling backward as the boot came free of his foot. Soon she had the other boot off and before he could stand she moved so that she knelt between his legs and wrapped her arms around his neck. He kissed her deeply, his fingers tangled in her loose hair. She slipped a hand to the front of his breeches, caressing the hardness beneath the cloth, and heard his breath come ragged and hoarse. She threw her head back, arching toward him as his hands danced over her breasts, leaving her skin burning.

In one motion he stood and pulled her up into his arms, and then he carried her to the bed. He struggled to free himself from his breeches with one hand even as he was pulling her chemise up with the other, and then he was filling her with liquid fire, murmuring her name into her ear as he took her.

IN THE MORNING THE SUN ROSE BRIGHT ON A CLEAR DAY, AND THE court resumed its progress through a countryside that seemed to sparkle beneath the summer sky, despite the roads squelching with mud. They would reach Colchester that night and the next day make for the port town of Harwich. Bess was feeling the need of exercise and had elected to ride rather than be borne in a horse litter, and Frances, who since her recent marriage to William Brooke had been Lady Cobham, rode beside her.

"For all the distress of the privy council, I see no signs that the people do not love the queen," Bess remarked.

Since they had left London on the fourteenth of July, the queen's subjects had gathered along her route to stare upon her and to cry out their good wishes.

"There are even more folk along the roads today than when we first came to St. Osyth," Frances said. "No doubt because those who missed the queen's arrival have now come out to see her departure."

Ahead of them, the queen's litter came to a halt, and two tiny red-headed girls, their arms full of flowers, curtsied before the queen.

"Aye, the sight of her works magic upon them," Bess said. "As she well knows."

"Would they cheer so if they knew that she had just given Robert Dudley apartments in Greenwich that adjoin her own and a pension of a thousand pounds?" Frances murmured.

On the fifth of August, the court reached Ipswich, the farthest point of its journey, where the queen would stay for a week before making her leisurely way back to London. Bess was glad of the respite from travel, especially as it meant that Will had more time to spend with her. The chamber in which they were staying commanded a view of the town, and it was flooded with summer sunshine during the day and had a vista of the stars wheeling above the darkened land at night. During the days and evenings, Bess attended the queen, but the nights belonged to her and Will, and as he came into her arms each night, she prayed that their lying together would result in a child.

On the evening of the ninth of August, as Bess prepared herself for bed, she heard a knock on the door and opened it to find Kate Grey standing there, her eyes swollen and her pretty face streaked with tears. Bess's first reaction was alarm, but surely if something had befallen the queen, Will would come to tell her of it.

"Kate, sweetheart, what's the matter?"

She drew Kate into the room and tried to guide her to a chair, but Kate collapsed into her arms, sobbing like a lost child, her golden hair cascading over her shoulders.

"Oh, Bess, help me! I know you'll know what to do!"

"I'll help you if I can, love, but whatever is wrong?"

"I . . . I can't tell you. I'm so afraid."

Bess was baffled. She had seen Kate daily during the weeks they had been on progress and had noticed nothing amiss. What could have changed so suddenly? She stroked Kate's hair, soothing her as she would one of her own children.

"Kate, dearest, I cannot help you if you won't tell me what's wrong."

Kate lifted her eyes to meet Bess's. "You won't be angry?"

"Why would I be angry?"

"Because it's so awful."

"Kate, just tell me."

"I'm with child," Kate whispered.

Bess was staggered. Whatever she had been expecting, it wasn't that. And now that Kate had spoken, she wondered how she could have failed to observe Kate's condition, for certainly the girl's trim waist looked thick, and now Bess noticed, everything about Kate shouted that she was breeding. Well, it was a problem, there was no mistake, but perhaps the situation could be put to rights.

"Oh, honey, why did you not come to me before?" Bess murmured. "And who has got you into this state? Surely the queen will make him wed you."

But that would not fix a new and insoluble problem, she realized as she spoke. For if Kate gave birth to a bastard child, it would remove her from her place in the succession. Neither Elizabeth nor anyone else could overlook such a failing.

"He has wed me already." Kate slumped into a chair and mopped her eyes with her handkerchief. "Edward Seymour is my husband, and the father of the babe."

Bess felt as though she had been struck a blow with a cudgel. A cold sharp knot of terror clenched her belly. For Kate, looking at her so hopefully, must not grasp the seriousness of her situation. Under the Act of Succession put into effect under King Henry, no one of the royal blood could marry without the monarch's consent. And that Kate should have married a Seymour, that family so closely tied to the Tudors by marriage and death . . .

"You didn't marry him—surely you didn't marry without the queen's permission?" she cried.

"I did." Kate jutted out her chin defiantly. "I love him so, and he loves me, and we had waited so long."

Worse and worse!

"When?" Bess gasped. "When did you wed? How on earth did you manage it?"

"We married in November, when the queen was away at Eltham—Edward's sister Jane helped us to do it, and we met in her rooms, but when she died it became difficult to find a way to be together . . ." Kate's face crumpled and her weeping began anew. "And now he's abroad—Cecil sent him to France—and does not answer my letters, and my belly can be hid no longer."

"How far along are you?"

"Nearly eight months."

Bess's mind was reeling. How could she have failed to see what was right before her eyes? Because she was caught up with other things, with Will, the troubles with Ned St. Loe . . .

"I've been lacing my gowns looser, wearing my kirtle higher, draping myself with shawls in hopes of hiding my belly. But now I've got so big it cannot be hid much longer. And people are talking about me, I know it. I see them whispering . . ."

"We must get word to Edward," Bess said, her mind racing. "I'll write to him. Or perhaps I can speak to Cecil and he will bring Edward to heel."

"I fear that he's forsaken me," Kate sobbed. "I even tried to go back to Henry."

Oh, God, the depths of desperation that Kate must be in, Bess thought. Kate had married Henry Herbert, the son of Lord Pembroke, when Jane Grey married Guildford Dudley and Henry Hastings married Catherine Dudley, only for the marriage to be annulled in the disastrous aftermath of the Wyatt rebellion.

"My father-in-law wrote to me; he suggested that Henry and I live as man and wife. At first Henry's letters were full of love, but"— Kate's shoulders were shaking with sobs now—"he must have found out about Edward, and now he writes with such venom, calling me whore and worse. Oh, Bess, I don't know what to do. I know I must confess the marriage to Her Majesty—surely she will understand— but I'm afraid to speak to her myself. Will you not speak to her for me, dearest Bess?"

Bess stared at Kate, appalled at the web of secrets and utterly foolish choices in which Kate was stuck—and in which she herself was now hopelessly entangled.

"But it's—" Bess tried to steady her voice, to speak calmly instead of shrieking in panic. "Kate, you must know—for anyone of royal blood to marry without the queen's consent is treason."

Treason, and for her to connive to keep such a marriage secret was treason, too. For a woman convicted of treason the punishment was death by burning. The smell of the smoke that had drifted from Smithfield to Newgate Street before she had fled London during Queen Mary's reign seemed to flood her senses. Her gorge rose, and with it, panic.

"How could you do such a thing?" she cried.

Kate gaped at her, clearly alarmed and surprised by her reaction. Bess struggled to control her fear and anger.

"I am most heartily sorry," she continued, striving to speak gently, "that you have acted without the consent of the queen's majesty, for I greatly fear how she will take such news."

Now Kate's tears had stopped and it was Bess who was weeping. She paced, wringing her hands in her chemise, her stomach churning. She feared she would vomit and sank to her knees, burying her head in her arms. All she could think was that the wretched girl had put her in such danger as Bess had never been in her life. Cat Howard, Jane Grey, Harry Grey, Edward Seymour, Thomas Seymour, John Dudley—the faces of so many she had known who had died for their folly or someone else's swam before her. She staggered to her feet, took Kate by the arm, and guided her to the door.

"I must think—I must consult my husband"—dear God, this disaster would come crashing down upon Will's head, too—"my mind is whirling."

"But—" Kate gaped at Bess as Bess opened the door. Bess thought Kate looked like an animal about to be slaughtered and took the girl into her arms again.

"Go to bed. Try to sleep." She kissed Kate and stroked her hair. "All will be well. But I must think, I must consult with Will. We'll speak in the morning and find a way to set all to rights."

Bess shut the door behind Kate and leaned against it, gasping for air, trying to clear her head. Immediately she was consumed with remorse. How could she have turned Kate out like that, when the girl had come to her for help? She would go to Kate, bring her to sleep in her own room for the night, make her feel comfortable and safe, promise her that a solution would be found, and pray that she could somehow make it so.

She opened the door to find Will, startled at the door being yanked open.

"Dear God, what's wrong?" He took her into his arms and pulled her into the room.

"Everything. Everything is wrong. Oh, Will."

Bess wept as she poured forth the terrible story. Will's face went white as she spoke and when she had finished, he slumped onto the bed and sat in silence for some moments. His actions alarmed her even more, for she had never seen him less than self-assured.

"I'll go to Her Majesty first thing in the morning," he said at length. "I don't think she'll thank me if I wake her to tell her such a tale." He shook his head. "Poor Kate. But how can she have acted so rashly? And Seymour, too!"

"What do you think the queen will do?" Bess was afraid of the answer.

"I don't know. But she must be told, whatever may follow."

WILL WAS UP EARLY BUT RETURNED TO THE BEDCHAMBER ONLY A few minutes after he had left, his face grim.

"I was already too late. After Kate left you last night she went to Robert Dudley's bedchamber."

"What! Does she crave her death?"

"No, she didn't go with the intention of his bedding her. She confided in him what she had already told you and begged him to speak to the queen on her behalf, thinking that the queen might deal less roughly with her if she heard of the marriage from Dudley."

Oh, poor Kate, Bess thought. She must have despaired when Bess had sent her back to her room, and who was left to ask for help but Robert Dudley, her brother-in-law and the man who might win her mercy from the queen?

"Dudley went to the queen at dawn," Will said. "When I went to her chamber she was already in conference with him and Cecil."

"Cecil was in favor of the marriage; he told me so at Christmas."

"The circumstances are altered. With the queen's permission, the match certainly had its value to Cecil's plans. But this way—he thinks it's part of a plot to murder the queen and put another Grey on the throne."

Bess clapped her hand over her mouth, a tide of horror rising within her.

"The queen cannot believe that," she whispered.

Will sat next to her on the bed and took one of her hands in his. He stared at his boots as he spoke.

"The queen has ordered that Kate Grey be arrested and sent to the Tower. My men have gone for her already."

"Oh, God!" Bess buried her face against his shoulder.

"Bess." Will's voice was hoarse and Bess thought he sounded frightened. "You also must return to London."

"Not now, I don't want to leave you." She sought comfort in his eyes but saw there tears and his own despair.

"My love, it cannot be helped. For the queen has ordered that you are to be taken to the Tower, for questioning."

A wave of blackness rose in Bess's mind and she faintly heard Will's voice calling her name as she fell.

BESS CAME BACK TO CONSCIOUSNESS TO FIND THAT SHE WAS LYING on the floor, with Will kneeling at her side and holding her hand. The full horror of what he had told her just before she fainted flooded her mind and she clutched his hand.

"I am to be arrested, too?"

"No. You are not arrested. But since Kate told you her story, the queen has given orders that you are to be delivered to Edward Warner for questioning."

Warner, lieutenant of the Tower, had attended Bess and Will's wedding and been a guest in their London home. She recalled his smiling face as he kissed her on her wedding day.

"He's married to Lizzie's aunt. And he's your friend."

"Yes, and you have nothing to fear from him. Just tell him what you know—everything you know—and all will be well."

CHAPTER FORTY-TWO

THE JOURNEY BACK TO LONDON HARDLY SEEMED AS IF IT could really be happening, Bess thought. The summer weather was glorious, but she could not shake the dread and terror that hung over her, knowing that each step brought her closer to the Tower. She and Kate rode on separate horse litters and they were not permitted to speak to each other. Bess was not under arrest but she felt that she might just as well be, for she had no choice but to ride onward to London, a guard riding alongside her. Ahead of her was Kate's litter, slung between two horses, flanked by three guards on either side. Kate took no pains to hide her belly now, and wore a loose gown. When they stopped at midday on the first day of the journey Bess caught a glimpse of Kate's face. It was splotchy from weeping and from the effects of pregnancy, and she seemed to have aged ten years in the last week.

Ipswich lay more than seventy miles from London, and the journey would take some days. At the end of the first day's travel, the party stopped at an inn to spend the night. Bess ate supper alone in her chamber and then lay on the bed, feeling more lonely than she ever had in her life. She could hear Kate weeping in the neighboring chamber, and knew that however frightened and lonely she felt, Kate must feel even more so. She rose, took up the candle in its holder, and left her room. A guard stood outside Kate's door. Henshard, his name was. One of Will's men, as were all the men accompanying her and Kate back to London.

"May I go to Lady Catherine?" Bess asked him. "I would like to comfort her, offer her some solace."

Henshard looked uncomfortable. He was young and Bess recalled that Will had told her he was from Somerset, not far from Sutton Court.

"I'm sorry, your ladyship. My orders are that the lady is to have no discourse with anyone."

"I understand. And I'm sure it was my husband that gave that order."

Henshard shifted his weight from one foot to the other and looked as if he would rather be anywhere but there.

"I promise you that I will not speak to her of the matters about which she is to be questioned. About which I am to be questioned."

Henshard glanced toward the stairs that led down to the taproom and Bess sensed that perhaps he would relent.

"You could leave the door open, so that you may hear all that passes between us. I only wish to remind her that she is not all alone in the world with her troubles."

Henshard nodded. "Very well, my lady. But only for a few minutes."

He stepped aside and opened the door so that Bess could enter. Kate turned toward the door at the sound of it opening, and by the light of her candle Bess could see the fear in Kate's eyes, and the relief when she saw Bess.

"There, there, hush now," she murmured, setting down the candle and taking Kate into her arms. "All will come right somehow."

"I don't want to die," Kate whimpered, clinging to her.

"Sure, it won't come to that," Bess said, hoping it was the truth.

"I wish my mother were here," Kate sniffled.

Bess tried to think what Frances Grey would say to comfort her daughter, but found no answer.

"She is with you," she said. "In spirit though not in body, I am sure. And even when it seems that no living person in the world can help you, remember that God's love and protection is with you always."

Please, God, ease this poor frightened child's fears and keep her safe in Thy bosom, she prayed. *And show me the path forward, for I am afraid and cannot see the way.*

"They may not let me speak with you again before we reach London," she told Kate. "But if I am not able to come to you, know that you are in my heart and my prayers until we next see each other."

Kate nodded, sniffling and wiping her eyes.

"And think of your child. You must not wear yourself out with grief, but remember the precious life that lies within you."

"I will. Thank you, Bess. Those words will help me."

"Good night now, lamb. Things will seem better tomorrow."

WILL HAD MADE ARRANGEMENTS THAT WHEN BESS REACHED London she would stay at the home of Thomas Lodge, Sheriff of London, who would accompany her to the Tower for questioning.

"Not as his prisoner," Will had reassured Bess. "But so that no one need know you have left the queen's retinue and returned to London until the matter is over and done with. He knows me well and will make you comfortable."

Lodge, a soldierly man some six or eight years older than Bess, welcomed her to his home, and his wife Anne made her as comfortable as she could be in a neat upstairs chamber. It was a small comfort, Bess thought as she made herself ready for bed, that her friends and household would not hear that she had been sent back to London under a cloud of disgrace. But still it was odd to be back in town, so close to her own home, and yet not there.

The following morning, she rode pillion behind Thomas Lodge

to the Tower. Its dark presence loomed as they approached, and Bess was consumed with dread and terror. How many people had entered within those walls, never to be seen again? How much misery and fear must have seeped into the very stones of the place over the centuries? She tried to breathe deeply to calm herself, and recalled what Will had told her.

"Tell Edward Warner all that you know. You are no conspirator; you knew nothing of Kate's marriage or babe until she confided in you, and you made the story known to me as soon as she told it to you. And when Warner puts his questions to you, try to remember that the shoe has been on the other foot. Thomas Wyatt, who led the rebellion with the aim of putting Elizabeth on the throne, was the son of Warner's wife. He has been in the Tower as prisoner as well as lieutenant. He has a job to do and he will do it, but he will not make your time more difficult than it must be."

As Lodge's horse arrived at Tower Hill, Bess could not help but think of the many who had perished there. Thomas Seymour, Edward Seymour, John Dudley, Guildford Dudley. The reputed lovers of Anne Boleyn and of Cat Howard. Crowds baying for their blood the last sound they had heard, the gray skies above and then the planks of the scaffold their last sight.

The horse's hooves clopped on the cobblestones as they approached the gate, and she drew her cloak close around her, for she was shivering despite the sunshine. She was glad she was veiled and that no one could see her tears.

Once within the walls, Bess was seized with a sense of suffocation. She knew that the green before the chapel was where Jane Grey had died, and Anne Boleyn and Cat Howard before her.

"I will not die." She realized she had spoken the words aloud, and then repeated them inwardly, praying that she would believe them. *I will not die, I will not die, I will live to see my children again, and soon.*

She moved as if in a dream as Thomas Lodge helped her to dismount and led her through a low door and up a narrow spiraling stairway, the dank stone walls closing in around her. A door stood open at the top of the stairs, and Lodge stepped aside to let her enter. Edward Warner stood there, his face grave as the black of his clothes.

"Lady St. Loe." Warner bowed, and gestured Bess to a chair as Thomas Lodge took his leave and the door shut behind him.

Bess seated herself and glanced around the room. There were no instruments of torture, no manacles on the wall. A fire burned in the hearth, and besides the two chairs there was a table with a few books, as well as ink, pens, and paper. It was Warner's office, then, and no dungeon.

"I'm sure you know, madam, that Catherine Grey's marriage to Edward Seymour is a most serious matter. They will be questioned, too, of course, but I am charged to learn all that you know of it."

"And I will tell you truly all that I know," Bess said.

"Good. Then let us make as quick work of this as possible." Warner took up his pen and dipped it in the ink pot. "Did you know beforehand of the marriage between the two?"

"Not of the marriage itself, no. I learned from the Duchess of Suffolk shortly before her death that Catherine Grey and Edward Seymour hoped to marry. Their mothers both favored the idea, and the duchess told me that she planned to write to the queen to ask for her consent to the match."

Warner's pen scratched across the paper. The face of Frances Grey, pale in her last illness, rose to Bess's mind. *Oh, Frances, that you could see how your ambitions have put another of your children in the shadow of the scaffold.*

Warner raised his eyes to meet Bess's, his pen poised. "You are known to be most inward with Catherine Grey. She did not tell you of her plans to marry before she did so?"

"No, truly. I knew nothing until she came to my chamber at Ipswich."

"And what did she tell you then?"

Bess told Warner all that she could recall of Kate's tale of intrigue and heartbreak, and Warner's flowing writing covered page after page. At last Bess came to the end of what she knew.

"And what must happen to me now?" she asked, her voice barely above a whisper. *Please,* she prayed inwardly, *let me not be kept here in the Tower.*

Warner set down his pen and studied her before he spoke.

"I have instructions that I may keep you here for two or three nights, should I think it best."

Oh, God, no, I cannot face it.

"But I believe that you have told me all you know and that you had no part in the unlawful marriage or keeping it secret. So I will release you now. Do you wish to stay with Lodge again until your house can be made ready?"

"No," Bess said, standing. "No, I thank you most kindly, but I will go home. My servants will be unprepared for my arrival, but that is no great matter."

"I can have one of my men take you."

"No." Bess wanted to be out of the room, out of the walls of the Tower, before anything happened that might keep her from leaving. "I thank you again, but it will do me good to walk."

She all but ran down the stairs and hurried toward the gate, her breath coming fast as she strode up Tower Hill, and it was not until she reached the door of her own house that her footsteps slowed. She pounded on the door, glancing behind her, almost expecting to see a party of armed men come to take her back to the Tower. But no one was there save a man leading a pig. And then she slumped to the ground and wept, heedless of the mud dirtying her skirts or anything else but the knowledge that she was free and safe.

"Oh, Will." It had been nearly six weeks since Bess had been parted from Will, and she clung to his reassuringly solid body, breathing deeply of his scent, comforted by the feel of his arms around her. "I was so frightened."

"Hush, my love, all is well, all is well."

"The queen is back in London now?"

"Yes, she is back. You should have seen the crowds at Islington when we came there—the people out in their thousands. And now I will not be parted from you again, my own love."

At supper that evening, Bess could scarcely force herself to take her eyes off Will, and kept reaching out to touch him, as if to reassure herself that he was home and they were safely together once more. The small familiar sounds of the house, the homey scents of lavender and beeswax candles and fresh-baked bread comforted her and anchored her to the present moment. The terrors of the past weeks were over and now that Will was at her side again she could face the future without fear.

"What's the news?" she asked him. "I've been so distressed that I've scarcely stirred from the house in the month since I came back to London."

"Edward Seymour was arrested at Dover and brought back to London a fortnight ago. He and Kate Grey were questioned separately, and their testimony given to the privy council. The council has determined that there is no evidence of a plot against the queen."

"Thanks be to God." Bess put down her spoon and bowed her head to send a silent prayer heavenward.

"But there is also doubt as to whether they were truly married and the queen has ordered a commission to look into the matter."

"Of course they were married! Kate told me all about it!"

"Yes, yes, I know. But Seymour's sister was the only witness, and she's dead. She was the one who procured the priest, and no one knows his name and he cannot be found. Seymour said that before he left for France he gave Kate a will bequeathing her lands worth a thousand pounds a year, but she cannot find it."

"She cannot find it!"

Will shrugged. "It all defies belief, I know. But the result is that there's no proof that any marriage took place."

Bess wanted to weep in despair. "Then the child . . ."

"Will be a bastard, if the queen has her way. Because otherwise, by the terms of King Henry's will, that child will stand next in line for the crown after Catherine Grey. Although the queen's position is that Kate's place in the succession was nullified due to her father's treason." Will shook his head. "The timing could scarce have been worse, in any case. The Scottish queen landed in Scotland a month ago. She's young, beautiful, and seeking a husband—in the same marketplace in which Elizabeth's hand is for sale. Should she marry someone powerful, and a Papist like herself, she'll be a great bait for intriguers who wish to remove Elizabeth from the throne."

"Then surely for Kate Grey to have a child will be good—if it's a boy, there is a Protestant heir if the queen has no child of her own."

"If the marriage was lawful and the baby legitimate, that would be true. And there are those who are pressing the queen to declare the marriage valid and Kate Grey her heir. But to have the validity of the marriage tinged with doubt casts everything into question. Cecil, who supported the idea of the marriage before it happened, now thinks that it is God's will that no Grey should inherit the throne. And meanwhile, this child of Kate Grey's presents a threat, for if it should be a boy, there will surely be those who will want him on the throne sooner rather than later, in place of Elizabeth, who has tarnished her name by this dalliance with Robert Dudley and who may never now wed and bear a child."

"Then we must pray that Kate bears a girl," Bess said.

But two days later, Kate Grey gave birth to a boy, who was christened Edward and given the title of Lord Beauchamp.

"She and Seymour have both been found guilty of fornication," Will told Bess. "He's also been convicted of seducing a virgin of the royal blood. They are to remain prisoners in the Tower, housed separately and kept apart, until it may please the queen to release them."

"Oh, poor Kate," Bess cried.

"This son of hers is a great threat to the queen. I cannot see that Elizabeth will ever let her go free, much less acknowledge her as her heir."

Oh, Kate, you fool, Bess mourned. *Why could you not have waited for the queen's permission to marry? You might have had it all—husband, baby, and crown. And now you will live out your days in the Tower.*

And a further pain twisted her heart. No baby had quickened within her though she and Will had now been married for two years. Why could it not have been she giving birth to a longed-for child, instead of Kate Grey, whose motherhood brought so much trouble to her and others?

CHAPTER FORTY-THREE

Tenth of July, 1562—Chatsworth, Derbyshire

BESS COULD NOT STOP HERSELF FROM CRYING AS SHE WATCHED her fourteen-year-old daughter Frankie marry Henry Pierrepont. The marriage was everything she had hoped for for her daughter, the culmination of years of planning, the achievement of her long-held ambition to set Frankie on the path to a life of comfort and good fortune. Beside Bess, her own mother, Aunt Marcella, and her sister Jenny were also in tears of joy.

"Oh, my darling, I am most happy to see you happy and so well bestowed," she murmured to Frankie after the ceremony, as Will clasped the young bridegroom in an embrace. "It's a wonderful marriage."

Frankie, her copper-colored hair flowing down her back and adorned with a wreath of flowers, kissed Bess. She was practically wriggling with delight, for the marriage was a love match as well as being eminently practical.

"Thank you, Mother. This day is heaven." Her eyes went to her young husband, and he reached out his hand to her.

Bess had negotiated the match with Henry's father, Sir George Pierrepont, but she had been determined that the marriage should only go forward if it pleased her daughter. Frankie had gone the previous year to serve Lady Pierrepont at Holme Pierrepont, within a day's ride from Hardwick, and so had come to know and like the family into which she would marry. And in the spring just past, young Henry had come to London to visit Frankie, and the young couple had immediately become very fond of each other. Though Henry was only fifteen, his parents had been eager for the wedding to take place, as Sir George was ailing. The specter of the Court of Wards must haunt the Pierreponts, Bess knew, but now that her old friend William Cecil was master of the court, its power did not terrify her as it had when she was a girl.

Bess's mother came to her side and slipped an arm around her waist. "Ah, Bess, your girls are getting off to a very good start, indeed. You've done so well."

A few weeks earlier Bess's stepdaughter Nan Cavendish had married Sir Henry Baynton, the younger brother of Will's first wife.

"I am very pleased," Bess agreed. "And it's thanks to you, you know, placing me so well with Lady Zouche and then with Frances Grey."

"The putting you in place was one thing," Bess's mother said, squeezing her hand. "Doing so well once you were there was entirely your own achievement."

During the wedding festivities, talk turned inevitably to the latest gossip from court. The Archbishop of Canterbury had opined that there was no evidence that Catherine Grey and Edward Seymour had ever been married.

"It's what Her Majesty wanted," said Frances Brooke, seated in the shade with Bess and a few of her other closest friends. "But of course now she's under even more pressure to name an heir."

"It could still be the Scots queen," Lizzie said, sipping a cup of syllabub. "Her Majesty smiled like the cat that has eaten the cream at the masques in May at Nottingham Castle, which were all to do with love and friendship between two queens. And she planned to meet with Mary in September."

"But Mary Stuart is fishing for a powerful Papist husband," Bess said. "And sure Elizabeth will never put her in line for the English throne knowing that she would return England to the old religion."

"The Countess of Lennox is a fool," Frances said. "If she had bided her time, perhaps her boy might have married the Scottish queen yet."

There was much truth in that observation, Bess thought. The Countess of Lennox and her son Lord Darnley had no sooner been released from the Tower than the countess was found to be involved in a plot to marry her boy to the Scots queen and depose Queen Elizabeth, and now she was a prisoner again. How much her haste had cost her.

"I think these wars in France between the Papists and Huguenots have truly scuppered any hope that Her Majesty will make Mary Stuart her heir," Lizzie said. "It is Mary's Guise relations who are behind the oppression and murder of Protestants. Her Majesty will never meet with her now."

"Then she had better marry and get an heir of her own," Frances murmured.

"How stood things in London when you left?" Bess asked.

There was a rustle of skirts as the ladies turned to see who was within earshot and moved their seats closer to Frances.

"I think she could still marry Robert Dudley," Frances said.

Bess thought of Elizabeth's face, alight with joy as she looked up at Dudley. Surely if the queen was happy the country would be the better for it.

"He told me at Christmas that she had promised to marry him," Frances continued, "but not this year. And you know at the Garter ceremony in April, Norfolk invited all the other knights to support Dudley's courtship of the queen, and they agreed—"

"Except Arundel and my husband," Lizzie snorted. "They were so incensed that they walked out of the gathering. No, William believes most strongly that the matter of his wife's death will always taint Dudley, and that the queen can never marry him without tarnishing her own honor and that of England."

CHAPTER FORTY-FOUR

Sixteenth of October, 1562—Hampton Court Palace

THE QUEEN IS GROWING WORSE." KAT ASHLEY'S EYES WERE dark with worry. Bess knew that Kat was like a mother to Elizabeth, having served her since she was a toddler. "She has lost consciousness. We must pray."

Though Bess was no longer serving the queen, she had accompanied Will to Hampton Court Palace, glad of the chance to spend time with old friends, including Lizzie and Frances Brooke. The queen had fallen ill six days earlier, and a bath and a walk in the bracing air had not only failed to bolster her strength but had left her with a chill. Dr. Burcot had examined the queen and declared that she had smallpox, but there were no spots, and she had cursed him for a fool and dismissed him from her presence.

Now the ladies hovering in the queen's privy chamber sank to their knees in a sea of dark velvet. Bess caught Lizzie's hand and held it tight. She thought their murmured prayers sounded lost in the high-ceilinged room, and hoped that they would pierce to heaven.

God help us, and all of England, Bess prayed. For surely if the queen died now, childless and having designated no successor, the country would be torn apart by war.

The next day William Cecil arrived from London and the privy council sequestered itself for hours.

"They must decide what to do if the queen dies," Will told Bess that night. "Or when the queen dies, for I fear she is failing."

He slumped forward in his chair, head in his hands, and Bess stooped to wrap her arms around his shoulders and kiss the top of his head.

"What will they do, think you?"

"As you might expect, they cannot agree. Those most given to the new religion want Kate Grey to succeed Elizabeth. After all, she stands next in line according to King Henry's will, and has a male heir."

"But her marriage . . ."

"Could be examined again and found to be legitimate, if it were convenient. But of course others of the council will have none of her."

"Then it will be the Scottish queen?" Bess thought how strange it would be to have a foreigner rule England, for Mary Stuart had lived all her life in France.

"None raise their voice to support her."

"Then who?"

"Some argue for the Earl of Huntingdon."

"Surely he lies far out of the natural line of succession."

"He's descended from Edward the Third," Will said. "He is Protestant. And he is a man. That weighs most heavily now—the council have seen what a troublesome thing it is to have a woman on the throne."

"How will they decide?"

"As there's no clear path set out and no agreement among the council, the matter may be sent to the judiciary to decide. But of course that cannot happen yet, not until . . ." He pressed her hand to his cheek and kissed it. "Let us to bed. And let us pray."

The next day the queen regained consciousness briefly only to lapse into insensibility again, and for two days she continued in that state. Meanwhile, the privy council argued, and the court prepared to go into mourning.

"I cannot believe it," Bess wept to Will. "What a senseless loss it would be, for her to have come through all the troubles that she has, only to have her life cut short like this."

"And I am quite powerless," he said. "Against assassins and plots, I can take action. But against this enemy, all the guards in the world can do nothing."

In the morning Bess made her way to the queen's chambers, through flocks of grave-faced courtiers and diplomats. Lizzie and Frances stood just outside the closed doors of the queen's bedchamber, their faces leaden with sorrow.

"Is there any improvement?" Bess asked.

"None." Frances shook her head. "She looks like the grave."

"But Dr. Burcot is with her again," Lizzie said. "Lord Hunsdon bustled him in there just now."

The bedchamber doors burst open and the black-robed young doctor strode toward Bess and the other ladies.

"Fetch red flannel," he ordered. "Such a quantity that Her Majesty may be wrapped in it from head to toe."

"Red flannel?" Frances gaped at him.

"Yes, yes, do not delay—send someone for it, there must be some in the house—it is the only chance that is left."

Frances turned and ran from the room. Past the doctor, Bess could see the queen's body inert beneath the bedclothes, her face pallid and damp with sweat. Mary Sidney bent over her, sponging her forehead, her beautiful face pale and her eyes red with weeping.

"Let me help you," Bess said, approaching the bed. "Have you been here all night?"

"Aye." Mary nodded and wiped a tear from her cheek. "No, there's no need," she said, as Bess tried to take the sponge and basin from her hand. "We'll bundle her in flannel as soon as it comes and lay her before the fire. The doctor says that will sweat the illness out of her."

Soon Frances was back with an armful of red flannel. She and Mary Sidney helped Dr. Burcot roll the queen in the cloth, swaddling her like a baby so that she was closely wrapped, and then laying her on a pallet near to the hearth.

"Oh, my lady," Mary murmured, kneeling at her side.

Dr. Burcot stooped beside the queen. "Raise her head," he ordered, and Mary Sidney cradled the head with its tumbled red locks in her lap as the doctor poured some distillation from a vial into the queen's mouth.

"Oh, Bess," Mary whispered. "Whatever will we do if it doesn't work?"

"She swallowed it," Bess said. "Surely that's a good sign."

"Yes," Dr. Burcot said. "Keep that fire built up."

He fell to pacing and Bess knelt on the floor beside Mary Sidney. Frances, Lizzie, and Kat Ashley huddled nearby, their eyes bleary with lack of sleep.

A servant had added wood to the fireplace and the room was sweltering. Bess bowed her head over clasped hands and prayed, for there was nothing else to do.

Father, preserve the life of Her Majesty, for surely we are lost if she perishes. Let not England be riven with war and her fields watered with blood, but save the queen and keep the land in peace.

The queen gave a little moan.

"She's stirring!" Kat Ashley cried, dropping to her knees beside the queen's pallet. "God be praised." Lizzie and Frances hovered nearby.

The queen opened her mouth and her tongue quested weakly along her lips.

"She wants water," Bess said. She lifted the queen's head while Mary Sidney put a cup to her lips and poured a few drops of water into her mouth and then more as the queen drank.

In a minute or two the queen opened her eyes. She seemed to

smile a little to see that it was Kat Ashley who was stroking her face, and her eyelids drifted shut again.

"Let everyone leave Her Majesty," Dr. Burcot ordered. "All but Lady Ashley and Lady Sidney. But tell the privy council that Her Majesty is with us once again."

"She asked that Robert Dudley be made Lord Protector if she dies," Will told Bess that night.

"That is better than no direction, surely?"

He shook his head. "They promised it but I'm not sure they would make it so. Dudley has generated such resentment already I don't see how he could control the wrangles that would arise if he were given such a position. And the privy council would be especially loath to give him the salary she directed, twenty thousand pounds per annum."

"Dear God," Bess said. "I could build another Chatsworth for that."

"She also asked that Dudley's man Tamworth, who sleeps in his chamber, be given a yearly pension of five hundred pounds. Of course there are murmurs that it is to buy his silence, even though she swore that as God was her witness nothing unseemly had ever passed between them."

"I wish the poor lady had married him when first his wife died," Bess said. "Yes, there are those who would not have liked it, but she might have had a child by now, and all these troubles prevented."

"If she lives," Will said, "I don't see how she can continue to forestall a marriage. She must have an heir. We cannot come to this brink of danger again."

The next day the queen broke out in spots, confirming that it was smallpox she suffered from. Dr. Burcot assured the queen's court and council that the pustules, though alarming to look at, signified that she was out of danger. But the news struck a chill into Bess's heart, for she had touched the queen when her illness was at its height. Would she now fall victim to the pox as well? She examined her hands anxiously, for that was where the red spots frequently broke out first, but saw no marks.

For another week the queen was confined to her bed, but as her health returned, so did her determination to act as she saw fit, whether her council liked it or not.

"She's made Dudley a member of the privy council—and Norfolk," Will said. "I suppose she thought no one could argue against Dudley as long as she raised his old enemy at the same time."

"I heard that Mary Sidney has fallen ill," Bess said.

"Yes, alas. And sadly there's no mistaking that it's smallpox—the spots are all over her face and hands."

Bess felt a rush of nausea, thinking of how she would feel if she were in Mary Sidney's place. She had examined her own skin anxiously each day, but no spots had appeared.

"Poor lady," she said. "To be rewarded for her care of the queen in such a terrible way."

By the end of October the queen was once more in health. In late November she summoned Parliament, and both the Lords and Commons petitioned her to marry or to designate an heir.

"Kate Grey's name is raised again," Will told Bess. "Maybe the queen will make the girl her successor after all, in spite of everything."

But soon, it became apparent that Kate Grey had lost her final hope for the throne, for she was with child again, and on the tenth of February, 1563, she gave birth to a second son.

"The queen must be apoplectic!" Bess exclaimed. "That is—Edward Seymour is the father, I take it?"

"Aye. Apparently he bribed the guards to let him see Kate, and it appears they could not bridle their passion."

"What will happen?"

"Edward Warner has been dismissed from his post and is made a prisoner."

Bess felt a rush of sympathy for Warner, who had been as kind as he could to her in difficult circumstances.

"Seymour was brought before the Star Chamber," Will continued, "and fined fifteen thousand pounds."

Fifteen thousand pounds? Bess was staggered.

"All the wealth of the Seymours will never be able to pay such a vast sum," she murmured.

"Worse, Kate is to be sent to her uncle John Grey at Pirgo, and the little boys taken from her. The queen swears that she and Seymour will never be allowed to see each other again."

Bess tried to imagine being sequestered forever from Will and from her children. She would rather die than endure such heartbreak. She shivered, for she thought Kate was not strong and might well die of grief.

"Damn Edward Seymour for the harm he has done the girl!" Jane Grey's face rose to her mind and she began to weep. "Why?" she pleaded with Will. "Why could Kate not have learned from Jane's death and been more cautious? If she had only waited for the queen's permission, she might have married Edward, had her babes, been heir to the throne, and lived in happiness. But she has doomed herself to misery, and her children to an uncertain fate."

"She hasn't your sense," Will said, taking her into his arms. "Ah, Bess, if every woman had your wisdom, the world would be a happier place."

CHAPTER FORTY-FIVE

Twenty-fifth of July, 1563—Tuthill Street, London

THE MOOD IN LONDON WAS BITTER AND FULL OF FEAR. AMBROSE Dudley had not only failed to regain control of Calais, but had surrendered the other English-held port, Newhaven. Adding to England's humiliation, he had been shot in the leg during the negotiations with the French. Robert Dudley, in defiance of the queen's wishes, had ridden to Portsmouth to welcome his injured brother. And to top all, the returning English troops had brought plague to London and now the pestilence was raging through the city.

"More than three thousand dead last week," Will said somberly. "The sooner the queen departs on her progress the better."

"I thank God that you will be here to help me in court next week," Bess said. "I don't think I would have had the courage to face it alone."

At last, after six agonizing years of uncertainty, the Exchequer suit over the money that she owed to the crown on William Cavendish's behalf would be heard.

"You have the heart and courage of a lion, my love." Will smiled. "And Her Majesty listened with great sympathy when I begged for lenience in the matter. But I, too, am glad I will be here to stand in your defense."

When they entered the court chamber, memories rushed into Bess's mind of the day she had appeared in court in her fight to get her widow's dower after Robbie Barlow's death. That battle had been the start of William Cavendish's courtship of her, and his steady guidance when she was so frightened had been the foundation on which her love for him had been built.

Bess was not so frightened now. She was no naïve girl as she had been then, clinging to William Cavendish as her only hope in a sea of despair. She knew the judge, and he knew her both as a lady of the queen's privy chamber and as the wife of Sir William St. Loe, on whom the queen relied for her daily safety.

Still, if the court should find against her, she would have to come up with five thousand pounds. She had tried for so long not to let the possibility become too real in her mind, for it terrified her. For the only way that she would be able to raise such a sum would be to sell her beloved Chatsworth, into which she had poured so much work and money, so many hopes and dreams. She thought of the endless wagonloads of furnishings brought from London at such huge expense. A hundred details of the house crowded into her mind—the four dozen tapestries; the rich sheen of the sunlight on the paneling of the walls of her bedchamber in the late afternoon; how luxuriant and lovely the garden Jenny had planted had become. And what the house had seen! There May and Lucres had been born, and Bess had watched with pride as her children grew and thrived.

Her children! She and William had conceived of Chatsworth as the seat of a family growing in power and importance. The grand house and its vast lands were to help secure a great prize of a bride for young Harry when it came time for him to marry. So many times Bess had imagined future generations of Cavendishes, each rising higher than the last. If Chatsworth were lost, that future would be lost as well.

Bess glanced at Will's impassive face beside her. Losing Chatsworth would affect him profoundly as well. Ned St. Loe and his wife were settled at Sutton Court and would hold it through her lifetime. Will's other main house, Tormarton, was leased. She and Will and the children still at home would have nowhere to live but the house in Tuthill Street. The thought of being in London always, not having the refuge of Chatsworth to retreat to, cast an even deeper shadow over her heart.

And Bess thought of her first William. He had planned so carefully and labored so hard to acquire Chatsworth, gradually building its holdings, tending its acres like a vast garden.

Help me, William, she begged silently. *You helped me before, help me now to know what to say that I might not lose our treasure.*

When Bess was at last called to testify, she felt as if William Cavendish's spirit were hovering nearby, giving her strength as he had done in life.

"I know without question," she declared, "that my husband did all that was in his power, through the many years that he served the crown, to oversee accounts that were in a tangle when he took over responsibility for them. I know that he strove to ensure that King Edward, and then Queen Mary, should live comfortably and with never a worry if he could prevent it. I know that he paid for expenses of the privy chamber from his own pocket rather than something that was needed should be lacking, and that he did his best, unfailingly, in circumstances that were always difficult." Tears came to her eyes as she recalled William struggling from his sickbed to prepare the account books that he sent to the Star Chamber when he was too ill to appear himself. "I know that his travails cost him many an anxious night and at the end, his health and his very life. I beg you to accept the records over which he labored in his efforts to clear himself, for they are written with his heart's blood."

She stopped, trying not to weep. Perhaps she had not spoken like a lawyer, but she had told the truth, and if they would not hear her, there was nothing more she could do.

She made her way back to her seat, where Will was waiting. He took her hand in his.

"Well said, my love," he murmured.

They sat in silence while the judge studied a sheaf of papers before him, their cargo the long sad story of William Cavendish's battle to clear his name and his debt and to leave Bess in comfort and security. Atop them lay a sheet from which dangled seals of red wax. Could it be from the queen? Bess hoped. The judge read it over again, his finger moving down the parchment, his lips pursed. At last he looked up.

"Come forward, Lady St. Loe, and you, too, Sir William."

Will took her arm and helped her forward and she tried to keep from trembling as she waited for the judge to speak.

"Taking into consideration all that you have said, and all that your worthy husband Sir William Cavendish did and said, and the recommendation of her most gracious Majesty, I find that it is most like that any shortfall in the accounts was not from dishonesty, but from oversights and errors, many of which, as you say, existed before ever your husband became treasurer of the king's chamber."

Bess let out the breath she didn't know she had been holding.

"Therefore, I do not find it meet that he, or you, should be held accountable for the sum of"—he squinted at one of the sheets of paper—"five thousand, two hundred thirty-seven pounds, five shillings, and three quarters of a penny. However"—Bess's heart plunged into her stomach—"at the queen's pleasure, I am imposing a fine of a thousand pounds. And you, Lady St. Loe, and Sir William, and also Henry Cavendish, the son and heir of Sir William Cavendish, must beg pardon of the queen. And there the matter shall be at an end."

"Thank you, your worship," Bess could barely get the words out and was afraid she would swoon, so great was the pressing swirl of emotions she was feeling. Relief that she would not lose Chatsworth, not have to beggar herself to pay the crown the debt of five thousand pounds. Anxiety at the fine—still a great amount of money. A sense of lightness that at last it was all over, and she was finally free of the burden of worry that had crushed her for so long.

"We can manage that," Will said, once they were outside, and her heart ached to see the relief in his face and to know how afraid he had been as well. "A sharp bite, make no mistake, but then all the trouble will be behind us."

"Yes," she said, seeking the shelter of his arms. "Oh, Will, thank you. I don't know how I would have borne it if I had lost Chatsworth. I wish you could go home with me now."

"I know. But as soon as the queen's progress is done I will join you there." He wiped a tear from her cheek with his thumb and kissed her. "Hush, now, my sweet girl. All is well, and all shall be well. There's not a braver lass in the kingdom."

First of February, 1565—London

"Ah, Bess it is such a joy to have you back!" Frances Brooke greeted Bess. "Come, let us sit by the fire with our needlework, and gossip to our heart's content. At court there is never the time to truly talk."

"Nothing would please me more," Bess said, kissing her, "but first you must let me see the baby. And look, I have made him a little cap."

She pulled the tiny item from the bag of needlework she had brought and held it up. She had worked a pattern of strapwork in crimson on the ivory silk, and little ribbons would tie beneath the baby's chin.

"What an angel you are!" Frances cried. "And how exquisite it is! If he be awake we'll put it on him straight away."

Little Henry, born at the end of November, was awake, and smiled up at Bess as she took him into her arms.

"Oh, what a sweet little lamb thou art. And strong and determined, too!" she laughed, as he pulled at her hand and latched his mouth onto the tip of her little finger.

"Any good news for you, Bess?" Frances asked, bending down to hoist her two-year-old daughter Elizabeth into her arms and jouncing her on her hip.

"No, alas," Bess said, kissing Henry's forehead and inhaling his sweet scent. "I don't know, I think perhaps the birth of my poor Lucres left me unable to conceive. For I never had any difficulty before—I bore eight children in ten years with William. No, I am struggling to accept that I will have no more."

"Oh." Frances's eyes clouded with sadness and she took Bess's hand. "I'm sorry. How sad."

"Yes. But I thank God that all my little ones are well—and not so little, anymore, either. Charlie has joined Willie at Eton, you know."

"Has he! How time flies."

They settled near the hearth in Frances's withdrawing chamber, the light and warmth of the fire warding off the gray of the winter sky outside the windows.

"Have you heard from Lizzie lately?" Bess asked, taking out her needlework. "I've had no letters since I last saw her a fortnight ago."

A few months earlier, Lizzie had told Bess that she was suffering from what her doctor believed was a cancer in her breast. The queen had summoned the King of Bohemia's own doctor to attend on her, she said, and she had great hopes that she would be cured. But during their recent visit, Bess had been shocked at how thin and fragile Lizzie looked.

"I called on her a few days ago," Frances said. "She was very tired and in low spirits. And ashamed over what had happened with that rogue Griffith, though it was none of her fault."

"Is it true, then?" Bess asked. "I heard that the servant of one of the doctors attempted to seduce her."

"Alas, yes. Though to call the man a doctor is a stretch. In my opinion he's little better than a mountebank, giving her false hopes with his ridiculous concoctions."

Bess could imagine only too well Lizzie's desperate desire to find a cure. She might well have fallen victim to such a charlatan herself if she were in similar circumstances.

"Poor Lizzie."

"Well, both mountebank and servant are in prison now, so at least they have got their due."

A sudden gust of wind rattled the shutters and Bess looked up from her needlework.

"It will be snow tonight, I think."

"Aye." Frances's face was sad. "Oh, Bess, tell me some good news. Surely there is some!"

"Did I tell you that Will has been made commissioner for the peace in Derbyshire and Gloucester?"

"No! That's splendid. A reason for him to be able to spend more time at Chatsworth, perhaps?"

"I will certainly make the case for it! Though like his being a member of Parliament for Derbyshire there is more honor than actual work in the position."

"I hear that Kate Grey has been moved to Ingatestone Hall," Frances said, pulling out a skein of bright blue silk and holding it up to the embroidery in her lap. "Do you hear from her?"

"Yes, she writes." The familiar weight of sadness settled on Bess's heart. "There is but one theme to her letters: she misses Edward and her babies most dreadfully, queries whether the queen shows any sign of forgiving her, and importunes me to beg Her Majesty that she be allowed to live with her husband and children, or at least to see them."

"And?"

Bess shrugged helplessly. "I cannot be forever peppering the queen with questions about what she means to do with Kate Grey. I have twice taken what seemed an opportune moment to put in a plea on Kate's behalf, but you know as well as I that pushing will gain nothing."

"You're right there."

They worked in silence for a few moments, the pungent scent of the peat on the fire perfuming the air.

"The queen was so pleased with our New Year's gifts," Frances said. "Let us put our heads together and devise something special for her birthday." She had made a pair of sleeves and Bess had made a matching caul for Elizabeth, with materials that Frances had sent her at Chatsworth.

"An excellent idea. What would suit best, do you think?"

Frances had recently been made mistress of the queen's robes. She cocked her head as she took a mental inventory.

"Perhaps a suite of ruffs for neck and wrists. She has not many of them and the fashion seems to be with us for the nonce."

"I saw the most beautiful white silk—fine as a spider's web."

"Perfect. Perhaps we can use it to catch her goodwill for poor Kate."

A FEW DAYS AFTER HER VISIT WITH FRANCES, BESS RECEIVED A letter from her brother Jem and one from her mother. She opened her brother's first, feeling a pang of guilt that she had not written to him lately, and growing more worried as she read. Jem wrote that he was very ill—still the trouble with his lungs—and in desperate financial condition. In halting and embarrassed language, he asked if Bess could lend him money, with his coal mine at Heth as collateral, or whether she might want to buy a piece of land he owned at Auldwerk. Things must be bad at Hardwick indeed, she thought, for Jem to swallow his pride and come to her, cap in hand. She broke the seal on the letter from her mother.

My dear Bess, I pray that this letter finds you well. The girls and all here are in health, but the same cannot be said for your brother. I know that he has written to you, and I urge that if you are in a position to do so, you buy the land he offers. It is very good land, and it would be worth much to my comfort that you should have it before any other.

"Your mother is a good judge of property," Will said when Bess read him the letters that night. "She put you onto Chatsworth, after all. It would be better to have a sight of the land, though. I hate buying a pig in a poke."

"I don't suppose there is any question that you can go?"

"I wish it were so, but not just now. I'm sure the queen can spare you for a bit, though. Why not go and stay at Chatsworth until the spring?"

"The roads will be dreadful at this time of year. But it would do me good to see the girls."

"You could be there for Bessie's tenth birthday."

Bess's mind immediately turned with pleasure to what delights she could bring her daughter.

"Oh, you know me too well, my heart. Very well, that settles it. I shall go, hard as it is to be away from you."

BESS HAD BEEN AT CHATSWORTH ONLY A FEW DAYS, AND HAD NOT yet had time to inspect Jem's land, when her steward James Crompe came to her chamber as she was visiting with her mother and Aunt Marcella one evening after supper, appearing agitated.

"What is it?" she asked in alarm.

"My lady, I'm most sorry to disturb you, but your husband's man Greves has just arrived from London. He says that Sir William is ill, and that he must speak with your ladyship urgently."

Bess jumped to her feet, her heart pounding with fear. Will had been fine when she had left him less than a fortnight before. It was not the season for plague. Smallpox then? He would not have sent for her if he wasn't seriously ill. She raced down the stairs and to the kitchen, her mother and aunt at her heels and Crompe following behind. Greves paced there, his cloak and boots spattered with mud and his face red with the cold.

"Oh, your ladyship!" Greves bowed hastily when he saw Bess.

"My master fell suddenly ill a few days after you left London and was in a most grave case when I left him. You must come back to London, my lady."

"What happened?" Bess cried. "What signs of illness did he exhibit? A fever? Is it smallpox? Did he send a letter?"

"He was out of his senses, madam, and could not write. The sickness came upon him most suddenly—a griping in the guts, and bloody flux."

"Dear God." Bess turned to Crompe. "I must leave in the morning—see to everything. I'll ride and take only two men with me besides Greves."

"What else?" she demanded of Greves. "Had he doctors? Who is caring for him?"

"Oh, yes, madam. Two doctors, and Sir William's own brother was most solicitous of him, sitting by his bedside into the night."

A wave of terror and nausea swept over Bess.

"His brother?"

"Yes, my lady, Edward St. Loe. He arrived but a day or two after you left and had been in the house some days when my master was taken poorly."

Bess staggered with the shock of it and clutched her mother's arm.

"Oh, dear God. Surely he is poisoned! Ned tried it once before."

"Come, sit," her mother murmured, guiding her to a chair. She turned to Crompe. "Fetch some brandy for her ladyship, if you please."

"Mother, what shall I do?" Bess cried. "How can I wait until morning? Perhaps I should leave tonight."

She threw her arms around her mother's waist, burying her face in her mother's skirt as if she were a child and her mother could make all well.

"You would take your life in your hands to travel these roads by night," her mother said, stroking her hair. "We'll get you packed and you can leave at sunup. Perhaps by the time you reach him he will be quite recovered. We must hope for the best."

. . .

BESS MADE THE JOURNEY TO LONDON IN ONLY FOUR DAYS, EVERY minute of it a torment of anxiety. When at last she arrived at her house she slid from the saddle without waiting for a groom to help her dismount and pounded at the door. The porter opened it, his face wet with tears.

"Your ladyship." His voice choked. "Alas, my master . . ."

"No," Bess cried, rushing up the stairs to the bedchamber. The steward met her at the door, blocking her way.

"My lady, I pray you, don't enter . . ."

She pushed past him and stopped in her tracks, clapping a hand over her mouth in grief and shock. For the face of the figure on the bed was draped and the stench of death was in the air.

"Will!"

She went to the bed and threw back the cloth and then started back and screamed. It was Will's face, but scarcely recognizable, his lips drawn back over his teeth in a grimace of pain, eyelids half-closed over lifeless jelly, skin blackened with decay.

Then Jenny was at her side, taking her by the arm. "Oh, Bess, come from here, come away."

"Oh, God!" Bess keened, collapsing against her sister, sobbing. "How came it so? What was Ned doing here? Why would Will have let him in the house?"

"I will tell you all," Jenny promised, leading her from the room. "Come, the best bedchamber is made ready for you. Let me make you as comfortable as you may be. Oh, Bess, I'm so sorry."

BESS GOT THROUGH THE DAY OF WILL'S FUNERAL FEELING AS IF she were in a nightmare. Surely she would wake and find that this horror was not true. She tried to listen to the priest but his voice seemed to be first loud and then to fade to nothing, to be overwhelmed by the buzzing in her head.

"Man that is born of a woman hath but a short time to live, and is full of misery: he cometh up and is cut down like a flower; he flieth as it were a shadow, and never continueth in one stay . . ."

She watched as Will's coffin was lowered into the ground beside his father's at the church of St. Helen's Bishopsgate, heard the dull thud of the clods of earth on the lid. Around her Will's friends were gathered—so many people, the highest in the land, come to do him honor. But surely he couldn't be gone. It made no sense.

"I shall rise out of the earth in the last day, and shall be covered again with my skin, and shall see God in my flesh . . ." But how was that possible, when his skin was rotted away? "And I myself shall behold him, not with other but with these same eyes." No, not with those dead-fish eyes rolled back beneath their lids.

"Of whom may we seek for succor, but of Thee, O Lord?"

But it is Thou who hast taken my most beloved husband from me . . .

"Thou knowest, Lord, the secrets of our hearts: shut not up Thy merciful eyes to our prayers."

God, help me, for if I cannot turn to Thee, then who can I turn to? And yet I have such rage in me for what Thou hast taken from me. This is a loss more than I can bear . . .

"Earth to earth, ashes to ashes, dust to dust . . ."

God help me . . .

". . . he is able to subdue all things to himself . . ."

If it is so, then make it so, Holy Father. Take my grief unto Thee and show me how to bear it, or take me into the black earth as well, for I cannot bear this pain.

CHAPTER FORTY-SIX

Tenth of August, 1565—Chatsworth, Derbyshire

BESS STOOD AT HER BEDCHAMBER WINDOW, LOOKING OUT OVER the countryside. It was good to be back at home—her whole body seemed to relax and her mind to become more serene once she was at Chatsworth, despite the depth of her grief.

She had remained in London for some weeks after Will's death, but the house was too full of echoes of him—alive and dead—to be comfortable, and being at court, where he had been such a fixture for so long, was even worse. Then poor Lizzie had died in April, and her death had sent Bess into an even deeper feeling of profound loss and awareness of her own mortality and the fragility of life.

She was sure that Ned St. Loe had been responsible for Will's death, and suspected that he had given him poisoned water, but there was no proof, only her suspicions, and no official action had been taken. Besides, Ned had been long gone from London by the time she arrived.

Her rage and pain had only increased when, less than a fortnight after Will died, she received a letter from Ned's lawyer claiming that on his deathbed Will had signed an indenture giving Ned and his wife Sutton Court. Forged, no doubt, but she had not seen the actual document. Then Ned had stopped sending her the tenants' rents, and she in turn had stopped sending him the payment due under the settlement of their last suit. So back to court they had gone, in Somerset once again, with the same judge as before, and once more, a decision hung in abeyance. Bess had taken some satisfaction in the fact that through her connections at court she had managed to have Ned sent to a post in Ireland where he could cool his heels for a time.

Ned was surely also behind Margaret St. Loe contesting the will that left all of her father's property and income to Bess and her heirs. Will had considered that Margaret was well provided for, as her husband Thomas Norton was wealthy, and the will had been upheld, but it made Bess sad to think that Margaret resented her, and that many at court took Margaret's side and thought she had been ill used.

Bess wondered if she would ever be free of lawsuits, and reflected that it was particularly hard that every time she had lost a husband, her grief and pain had been compounded by the need to fight a battle in court. Especially as in each case, her husband had taken pains to make arrangements so that matters would go smoothly if she were left a widow.

The sound of laughter below brought Bess's mind back to the present. Bessie and May, the only children left at home now, were giggling and crying out in delight as they tried to get their two puppies to race. They were well on their way to grown up now; Bessie was ten and May eight and a half, and Bess thanked God for their blooming health, as she did every day.

The thought of children reminded her of Frances Brooke, who was expecting another baby in December, and she took up the letter she had received from Frances the day before and read it over.

The news that the Scottish queen has married Lord Darnley has sent Her Majesty into a rage, Frances wrote. *For of course the fact that his grandmother was the sister of King Henry gives him a claim to the throne to match that of Mary's own, as granddaughter of Henry's other sister.*

Had Darnley learned nothing from the disastrous outcome of the marriage of Kate Grey and Edward Seymour? It seemed not, although the two marriages were in exactly the same case—matches of two heirs to the throne, sure to attract plotters who would rather see them and their heirs on the throne than a childless woman. The Papist rulers of France and Spain would be all too likely to back the Scottish queen's claim to the English throne with their military might, and even Darnley himself might raise an army from the Papist northern counties of England.

They have assured Her Majesty that they will take no action against her, and ask in return that she declare them to be her heirs. But as you may imagine, she will not be dictated to. She has thrown her support to the Earl of Moray, the half brother of the Scottish queen, in what looks like will soon be civil war in Scotland. And she has put Darnley's mother in the Tower again—such is the satisfaction that Lady Lennox has got from her scheming so long to make her son a king! I hardly think Her Majesty will ever make Mary Stuart her heir now. And of course this is the end of her plan of marrying the Scottish queen to Robert Dudley, which seemed to me plain madness, and likely to please no one.

Bess shook her head with grim amusement. No, Mary Stuart had not wanted to wed the queen's own beloved, though he had been made Earl of Leicester to make him a suitable match. Dudley had not wanted the marriage—or to be sent to live in Scotland. And Bess doubted that when it came down to it, Elizabeth would have been willing to part with her dear Robin. She thought of Will and wondered how the queen could even have contemplated marrying Dudley off to someone else.

This marriage of the Scottish queen only serves to make our queen's advisors more frantic in their determination that Her Majesty must be married, Frances's letter continued. *I saw her reduced to tears—a*

sight I never thought to see and that amazed me much, I promise
you—at the combined haranguing of Dudley, Cecil, and Throckmor-
ton that she must have a husband.

Bess recalled that in the wake of Cat Howard's death, the eight-
year-old Elizabeth had declared she would never marry. An under-
standable sentiment, and one Bess had shared at the time. But would
the queen finally evade all plans to have her husbanded? It seemed
inconceivable that she could hope to rule on her own and keep
her throne with no husband or the prospect of children, but so far
she was proving most expert in promising much and doing only
what she wanted. She had inherited her father's strength, that was
certain.

But it would take more than strength to face the prospect of a life
alone, Bess thought. Especially a life fraught with the challenges
that a ruler faced. It would take a shutting down, a walling off, of
some deep-set need for love and emotional sustenance, would it
not? She tried to imagine committing herself to a life of such isola-
tion and could not. Of course a marriage did not promise love,
either, especially if it were a marriage of state such as the queen was
pressed to make. And if she could not marry Robin Dudley, would
it not be an unbearable torment to wed someone else, knowing that
she cut the thread of possibility that bound them, casting him adrift
to be taken up by someone else?

Bess looked out the window again and saw that Aunt Marcella
was with the girls now and had got them back in their bonnets
against the sun. It wouldn't be long before she would need to start
thinking about getting them married. And with the money and
property she had inherited from Will, she was in a better position
than ever to find husbands from wealthy and powerful families, and
to weigh carefully what would make her daughters happy. Soon she
would have to consider wives for Harry and Willie, too. Yes, with
God's help her children would all be raised as high as she could
manage, and never have to worry about money as she had done.

Bess realized that she was pacing rapidly. Thinking of Lord Darnley's marriage to the Scottish queen, and her own children's prospective marriages, seemed to have lit some fire within her, for she suddenly felt more animated than she had since Will died.

What eminent young men were of an age to make suitable husbands for Bessie and May? There was Philip Sidney, the son of Sir Henry Sidney and Mary Dudley—though being entwined with the Dudleys could have its drawbacks. The Earl of Shrewsbury's second son was yet unmarried; she must inquire of Lady Shrewsbury when she saw her next. And Edward de Vere, the Earl of Oxford, had been born only a few months before her own Harry and was of a suitable age for Bessie. Dare she hope for such a match? The young man lived in the household of William Cecil, who was certainly favorably disposed to her.

Perhaps George Carey, the eldest boy of Baron Hunsdon, Mary Boleyn's son, who some believed to be the child of King Henry? He was in the full sunshine of the queen's favor. And he had three or four younger brothers—she would have to look into the possibilities. Yes, there were plenty of young men, now she thought of it. Lord Rutland, Lord Sussex, Lord Wharton . . . Peregrine Bertie! He was the son of the Duchess of Suffolk, and the same age as Bessie.

Or could she aspire even higher for her girls? she wondered. There were young men of the royal blood who were not likely ever to sit on the throne, and so perhaps almost within reach. It was a pity, Bess thought, that the Countess of Lennox had earned the queen's enmity, for her younger son Charles Stewart could have made a good husband for Bessie.

How, Bess mused, could she improve her daughters' prospects? Now she would be able to provide very generous dowries for the girls, and everything about Chatsworth bespoke wealth and status. But what could make it even more grand—a place that would show her girls to be worthy matches for young men of the oldest and most exalted noble families of England?

What was needed was a suite of rooms worthy of the queen

herself—and why could they not be used by the queen herself? Elizabeth went on progress every summer; why should she not visit Chatsworth?

The thought of the queen in residence at Chatsworth took Bess's breath away. Yes, that was what she would do—she would make alterations to the house. Just thinking about it gave her a sense of purpose such as she had not had since the building of the house had been completed the previous year. And now she had ample money to do it.

Bess rang for her steward.

"I wish to see Robert Smythson," she told Crompe. "As soon as he may be got."

"Could we add a third story to the house?" Bess asked.

Smythson, a mason who had supervised the recent work on the house and had also worked on Longleat, Sir John Thynne's grand house, nodded thoughtfully.

"Certainly, my lady, it could be done. It would not be quick nor yet inexpensive, but it could be done."

"What I want," Bess said, "is a bedchamber and withdrawing chamber fit for a queen. Fit for the queen, in fact."

Smythson's brows rose and he grinned. "That would be something, indeed, my lady, to have Her Majesty lay herself down in rooms that I built."

"Indeed it would." Bess smiled back at him. "Come, sit. Let us think about this together."

"Have you any paper, my lady? That I might sketch to catch the ideas as they fly."

"Yes, at my desk here. Draw up a chair."

Two hours later Smythson gathered up the heap of papers upon which, to Bess's amazement, he had made corporeal the fancies that had lived only in her mind, sketching windows, walls, staircases, overmantels, ceiling medallions, and friezes.

"I will have some better drawings for your ladyship in a few days."

"Excellent. How soon can we begin work?"

"Soon, my lady, as soon as you like. We'll need to get the quarry operating again, and recruit laborers, but ready money works wonders."

When Smythson had left, Bess laughed out loud in pleasure at the prospect of resuming work on the house.

"We'll need to do an inventory," she murmured. "So I truly know what is here and what will be needful to furnish the new rooms. Oh, that the building could begin today."

Twenty-sixth August, 1565—Chatsworth, Derbyshire

Bess stared at the letter in numb disbelief and read Cecil's words over again.

> *Here is an unhappy chance and monstrous. The Sergeant Porter, being the biggest gentleman of this court, has married secretly the Lady Mary Grey: the least of all the court.*

"Oh, no!" Bess cried aloud.

> *The offense is very great and the queen in a rage. The Lady Mary is locked up at Windsor with only a groom and a waiting woman and forbidden to see anyone. Her husband, Thomas Keyes, is in a noisome and narrow cell at the Fleet.*

What self-destructive madness was it that seized the Greys? Bess wondered. Could Mary, after witnessing Kate's ruin, truly have thought the queen would turn a blind eye to her marriage? And the timing could not have been worse, for it had finally seemed that perhaps the queen was beginning to soften toward Kate and might let her return to court. Now Mary's actions would likely doom them both.

Jane Grey's face rose to Bess's mind and she wept, grieving once more the senseless loss of that sweet and courageous soul, who had died for her parents' ambitions.

CHAPTER FORTY-SEVEN

A S SOON AS THE CHRISTMAS FESTIVITIES ENDED WITH
Twelfth Night, Bess embarked on her inventory of Chatsworth.

"We will deal principally with the furniture, hangings, bedclothes, and so forth," she told Crompe. "The best will go into the
new rooms, and when I am in London I can buy what is needed to
furnish the rest of the house." She glanced around her bedchamber—
how many articles it held! And all the ninety-seven rooms of the
house were the same, containing acres of carpets and tapestries and
untold numbers of objects. "What a job it will be. But the sooner
begun, the sooner we will be done."

When Crompe had gone, she seated herself near the fire and
looked around the room. Over the years she had made her bedchamber into a comfortable and elegant nest for herself, filled with
her favorite items. The bed curtains were of rich red and trimmed
with silver lace, a red silk quilt overlay the underquilts and down
feather bed, and three velvet bolsters and a pile of pillows made it
easy for her to sit up in bed and read or write.

Gathered near the fireplace around the large chair in green

checked silk in which she sat were a smaller chair upholstered in black velvet and two of leather. Will's portrait stood on a table near the bed, and the portrait of Jane Grey and another of her first William decorated other tables. All the tables were draped in green silk that matched the window curtains. Six large coffers held her clothes and bed linens. This room contained everything she needed; she could have stayed within it for months, lacking nothing from outside but her meals.

No, not quite nothing. Companionship was something she very much needed, and for that, she must sometimes venture out. True, her daughters and Jenny spent much time with her, as did her mother and Aunt Marcella. And other attendants and servants were always within the sound of a bell.

But still something was missing. A man's presence.

Could it be? Bess wondered. When Will had died she had thought she would never again look on a man with love, that no man could compare to he whom she had lost. But now, almost a year since he had departed this earth, she was not so sure. She missed the company of someone—not just anyone, but someone who understood her without her having to explain herself, someone with whom she walked in comfortable yoke, like oxen harnessed for plowing. A husband. She was used to being married, and missed it.

The next day Bess received a letter from Frances, full of the news at court.

I am sure you will not be surprised, Frances wrote, *to hear that all the talk is still of Her Majesty's marriage. On Twelfth Night, Robert Dudley told me that at Christmas he had asked the queen to marry him and that she had promised she would answer him by Candlemas. But the day passed with nothing said, and now I hear he has urged the queen to marry the Archduke Charles, as Cecil and others of her privy council have so long desired.*

But think you she will? I do not. The archduke is most stubbornly Papist and the queen declares that for her to marry one who does not share her faith would cause a thousand inconveniences. Moreover, she reminds the privy council of the disastrous consequences of the Spanish marriage of Queen Mary. She argues—with truth, I must say—that changing laws on the succession and the uncertainty and turmoil over royal marriages have been responsible for many rebellions from the time of her father's reign until that of her sister's. She says that no matter who she marries, many will be displeased, and that any marriage will be likely to incite further revolts.

As to Dudley, I think Her Majesty liked not that he seemed to give her up at last, for she flirted much with her cousin, my lord of Ormonde. She hit the mark she intended, it seemed, for Leicester was in a rage to see the attentions she paid to Black Tom, as they call Ormonde, and he has gone from court.

You will likely have heard that the Scottish queen is with child. God knows how that development will affect what Her Majesty does, but I have heard her say that naming any heir would be an inducement to some to hasten her out of this life, and I do not think her mind is changed. I heard Cecil treat with her on the matter of the succession and she cried, "God's blood, would you have me in my own life set my winding sheet before my eye?"

Bess smiled; she could only too easily imagine the queen's enraged roar when provoked too far by the insistence of her ministers.

But now, Bess, let me talk of you, Frances's letter continued. I wish you would be as great a stranger to Derbyshire as you now are to London. You have been too long away, both from my company and from attendance on the queen. And I must confess to you that of late my mind has been preoccupied with the question of a husband for you. I know how much you loved Will, but you are still a beauty, besides the much else that you have to offer as a wife, and must not waste that precious commodity.

What odd chance, Bess thought, that the matter of her marrying again had been in Frances's thoughts just when it was in her own.

My husband's brother Henry Brooke would make you an admirable husband, and nothing would make me happier than to have

*you as my sister. But there are many other possibilities. You know
that John Thynne's wife died, I am sure. He is a most handsome man
and you are old friends, I know. Would he not be a fine match?*

Perhaps it was a portent, Bess thought, that Frances wanted to
play matchmaker. And whether or not she got a husband there, she
did miss London and the excitement of being at court.

"OF COURSE YOU SHOULD GO BACK TO COURT," JENNY SAID WHEN
Bess told her about Frances's letter, and as Bess looked into her sister's blue eyes and heard the warmth and assurance in her voice, she
knew that it was the right thing to do. "Bess, you are made to be
married. And you will find no suitable husband anywhere but
London."

"Oh, I shall need so many clothes," Bess fretted, yanking gowns
from the coffers in her bedchamber. "Ruffs. Ruffs are all the rage,
Frances writes—they are growing, like plants it seems, and these
puny things of mine will not do."

"Then ruffs you shall have. My dearest sister, you never lacked
the ability to dress yourself at the height of fashion, and certainly in
Lady Cobham and your other friends you have the most expert
advisors in what is needful."

"You are right," Bess said, yanking off her cap and gazing into the
mirror. "Frances will tell me what is just the thing."

Tenth of August, 1566—Warwickshire

"That," Bess said, as Kenilworth Castle loomed ahead, "is a very fine
place indeed."

"It should be," Frances Brooke replied. "Robert Dudley has been
carrying out building works since the queen gave him the place, in
anticipation of this visit."

"And it was almost for naught."

The queen had nearly decided not to take the court to Kenilworth on the summer progress as originally planned when she got wind that rumors were flying that the visit presaged an announcement that she would marry Robert Dudley, but in the end he had convinced her to come.

"I will welcome a few days' respite from traveling," Bess said. "And I hear that Dudley has some exquisite entertainments planned."

Bess was once more attending Elizabeth, in company with Frances Brooke, Blanche Perry, and Dorothy Stafford. She was happy to be among her old friends, but the court's sojourn could not help but remind her of the idyllic days she had spent with Will during the progress five summers before. At least, she thought, it had been idyllic before Kate Grey had thrown a grenade into her face with the disclosure of her secret marriage and pregnancy.

How much had changed since then and how little, she mused. Then she had been newly married and had thought to spend the rest of her years with Will. Now she had lost him. She was flattered that she was receiving attention from several gentlemen of wealth and standing, but meant to weigh her opportunities carefully before she committed herself to another marriage.

The matter of the queen's marriage was no more settled than it had been five years earlier, nor was the question of who would succeed her. And the queen was now almost three and thirty. Time was running out, Bess thought. But perhaps that was what Elizabeth intended.

Robert Dudley was waiting before Kenilworth Castle as the queen's entourage arrived. He bowed low and the ranks of his household ranged behind him sank into bows and curtsies to the ground.

"Your Majesty, I bid you welcome," Dudley said, and then stepped forward to help the queen from her litter.

"You spoke the truth when you said you had been busy with improvements, Robin," she said, gazing at the towering walls of the gatehouse. "This is new since I was last here."

"Yes, Your Majesty, and much more." He took the queen's arm. "Allow me to lead you to your apartments."

They made their way through the gatehouse and courtyard and into a fine Italianate building of sand-colored stone, tall windows sparkling in the sun.

"Beautiful," Bess said to Frances as they followed behind. "I shall be quite happy here, I think."

The queen's bedchamber and withdrawing chamber were flooded with sunlight, breaking into bright shards on the gleaming honey-colored planks of the floor. Bess admired the high ornamented chimney pieces rising from the mantels above the fireplaces to the brightly painted panels of the ceiling. The plasterwork was lovely, she thought, and decided she would speak to Smythson about adding something similar to the best chamber at Chatsworth.

"You have outdone yourself, Robin," the queen said, turning to inspect the furnishings. "You know just what I like, better than I do myself, I think."

THAT EVENING, THE GROUNDS OF THE CASTLE WERE ILLUMINATED by hundreds of torches and candles flickering in the shadowed depths of the summer night. Supper was followed by a masque, with a faerie queen rising out of the small lake, and then by music and dancing. Bess thought she had never seen anything so enchanting. She loved Chatsworth, but oh, to have such a house as this!

The queen appeared to be as enthralled as she, smiling up at Dudley as they danced and laughing at something he leaned close to whisper in her ear.

Henry Brooke, the brother of Lizzie and brother-in-law of Frances, appeared at Bess's elbow.

"A magical night, is it not?"

He was resplendent in a new doublet of cream-colored satin sparkling with gold embroidery, an ostrich plume curling down from his hat. He was a most handsome man, Bess thought, somewhat of the appearance of Robert Dudley, and she did enjoy his company very much.

"Like nothing I have ever seen," she replied. "The Earl of Leicester has shown himself to be a master at entrancing queen and court. Look, not a sour face in sight."

"You're right." Henry smiled. "Will you increase my enjoyment of this night and favor me with the next dance, my lady?"

The volta was next. It allowed the gentlemen the opportunity to show off their athletic leaps and to hoist their partners high into the air, to the delighted cries of the crowd. The Earl of Oxford, just turned sixteen, kicked high as he capered, his cape flying out behind him. Bess had taken note of him over the weeks of the progress and observed him to be courtly, bright, and witty as well as handsome. Yes, he would make an admirable husband for Bessie, she thought. She would have to speak to Cecil. But not just now; Cecil's daughter was ill with smallpox, preventing the court's planned gest at his home.

"Excellently done, sir!" the queen cried as Henry Brooke circled Bess and lifted her, laughing, above his head.

Bess felt giddy with the dancing and the aura of love and possibility in the air. She danced on and on, with Henry Brooke, with Robert Dudley, with the Earl of Shrewsbury, with Lord Darcy. She couldn't recall when she had enjoyed herself so, or felt so young.

At last the party broke up and Bess and the queen's other ladies attended her as she prepared for bed. Bess, standing behind the queen, unpinned the ruff from around her neck and was about to turn away when the queen spoke.

"I declare, Lady St. Loe, you were much at the center of the gentlemen's attention this night. It appears that you will have a fourth husband e'er I have one."

Bess was startled and glanced into the mirror before which Elizabeth sat. Had there been an edge to the queen's voice, or was she in a good humor?

"No, surely, Your Majesty," she protested, "you might have any man in the world for the asking."

"Think you so?" The queen's eyes met Bess's in her reflection. She pulled off her earrings and dropped them onto the table before her. "Perhaps. But look what it profits a woman to have a husband. The Scottish queen defied me to marry Henry Darnley, and now, how soon after, he has murdered her poor friend and secretary before her eyes. I hear that she bitterly regrets the marriage and wishes to be rid of him. Might I not suffer the same thing were I to marry?"

Bess could not quite read the queen's mood. She longed to glance at Frances, who stood nearby, but the queen's gaze held hers, hawklike.

"Not if you chose the right man, Your Majesty."

"But is there one in whom I could find all that I seek? Tell me, Bess, could you make a perfect man by combining the best qualities of your three husbands?"

Bess thought of Will, who she still missed every day. His humor, his vitality, his ardor. William Cavendish, who had been her rock for the many years of their marriage, always wise, always steady. And poor Robbie Barlow. She could scarcely call his face to mind now sometimes, so many years after his death. But she could well remember his sweetness and gentleness, and the feeling she always had that she wished to make his world a safe and comfortable place.

"And what would you seek in a husband now, madam?" the queen persisted.

What would she like? Passion, such as she had found with Will. But surely that burned out over the years of a long marriage. Serene companionship and mutual respect. Those would be excellent qualities for another partnership. Children? No, she was past that now, and would have no more. But for those she had, she wanted the best life possible.

"What do you advise, Your Majesty?"

"Hold out, Bess. Hold out until you find the man you want." The queen's eyes were sad now. "And what do you advise me?"

"You wish my advice, Your Majesty?" Bess faltered.

"Certainly. There is no lady who I better love or like than you, Bess."

"I . . ." Bess had been going to parrot the advice that she knew Cecil and the rest of the council gave the queen—marry a worthy foreign prince. But all the objections that the queen had raised to the various prospective husbands presented to her were valid. Marrying the Archduke Charles or another Papist would cause fear and hostility among much of the populace. Marrying any foreigner carried the risk that England's power would be lost. Who would Elizabeth wed within England but Robert Dudley, and yet what storms of opposition she had weathered—nay, continued to weather—at the prospect of her marrying the only man whom she seemed truly to love. And whether her husband be foreigner or Englishman, marrying any man would surely mean that she would lose some of her power, for certainly no woman, not even a queen, could really rule a man.

And what harm could come if the queen did not marry? She had been on the throne for near eight years now, and the sun and moon had not fallen from their place in the heavens. Maybe she should not marry. After all, the only reason for her to do so would be to produce an heir, and even if she married soon, it was by no means certain that she would bear a child. She might be past the age. She might have a girl, and then suffer a stillbirth, as had her mother, and countless other women. And how old would she be then? What if she proved barren, like her sister? No, there were heirs aplenty if she would but name them—Mary Stuart and her boy James, or Kate Grey and her two sons—Elizabeth did not need to produce an heir out of her own body.

"What would I advise you, Your Majesty? Why, to do just what you want," Bess said, meaning it with all her heart.

"I think you advise well," the queen said. And then—did Bess really see it, or had she imagined it?—she winked.

"Come," Elizabeth said, turning to Dorothy Stafford. "Unpin me. For I am weary and would be abed."

Twenty-fifth of May, 1567—Greenwich Palace

"I would not be Mary Stuart for all the world," Bess said to Frances Brooke.

"Nor I," Frances agreed. "All of Scotland is mad, it seems."

The court had been rocked in February by the news from Scotland that Lord Darnley, the Scottish queen's husband, had been murdered. An enormous explosion at Kirk o' Field, the house where he lay, was apparently not the cause of his death—it appeared that he and his manservant had been strangled. Queen Elizabeth had released his grief-stricken mother, the Countess of Lennox, from the Tower into the care of Sir Richard Sackville.

Suspicion for the murder had soon settled on the Earl of Bothwell, but after a short trial he had been acquitted. Only a fortnight later, he had abducted the queen, who had inexplicably refused an offer of rescue.

Now, the court was scandalized to learn, Mary had married Bothwell.

"Three husbands, each worse than the last," Frances said.

"How could she have married him?" Bess wondered. "He raped her, they say. Never mind killing her husband."

"Perhaps he did that at her bidding."

"Perhaps. But it's hard to imagine Her Majesty making Mary her heir now."

"You would think," Frances said, "that the prospect of eventually gaining the throne of England would be enough to make a person behave well, wouldn't you? It would certainly make me think twice before I acted like a fool."

"Yes." Bess's thoughts went to Kate Grey and sadness swept over her. Although Kate had wanted love and happiness more than she had wanted to be queen, Bess reflected.

"What's the news of Kate Grey? And Mary?" Frances asked, as though reading Bess's mind.

"Of course Kate's supporters are using the developments in Scotland as reason to raise her claim to the succession anew, so the queen regards her as more of a threat than ever. She is still in Essex, in the care of Sir John Wentworth. And poor little Mary is at Chequers. They both write to me. Kate is kept without company. Mary still holds out hope that the queen will forgive her and let her out. She is most concerned for her husband. She says he is fed meat that is bad and tainted with poison, and fears it may kill him."

Bess covered her eyes, as if that would put out of her mind the heartbreaking images of the girls she loved so well.

CHAPTER FORTY-EIGHT

Twenty-eighth of July, 1567—Greenwich Palace

THIS MATTER OF THE SCOTTISH QUEEN GROWS WORSE AND worse." George Talbot, the Earl of Shrewsbury, leaned close to Bess as he spoke. Glancing up at him, she observed that his green eyes had gold flecks and were ringed by long, dark lashes that any lady would envy. Why had she never noticed that before, she wondered? Or the bold angle of his jaw, or the width of his shoulders, set off with a cape draped to one side?

They were walking along the riverbank, the peaceful scene a stark contrast to the wild scenes that were the latest talk of the court. "The Scots hold her prisoner like a common criminal," Shrewsbury continued, "and she has lost the love of her people. Throckmorton writes that when she was captured, the crowds cried out, 'Burn the whore! Drown her!' And it is said her husband has fled to Denmark. He can never help her now."

Shrewsbury seemed to know more about what was happening than anyone else Bess spoke to. He had many friends, she knew, both in London and abroad.

"Is it true that Cecil dissuaded Her Majesty from sending troops to Mary Stuart's aid?" she asked.

"Yes, most true. For he believes that any attempt to rescue the queen would only lead to her death. And, indeed, when she refused to abdicate in favor of her infant son, Lord Lindsay swore that if she did not do it, he would cut her throat himself. And so she gave in, and the baby is now king of Scotland."

"Her Majesty has seemed beside herself these last few days," Bess said. "She ordered that the keys to all of the doors leading to her chambers be hidden, except for only one, but who holds that I do not know. She is terrified, I think."

"And who can blame her? For if one queen may be so roughly bereft of a crown, why may not another?"

Shrewsbury stopped to gaze out over the water. A small wherry was approaching the landing stairs of the palace, bearing a gentleman whose face Bess could not make out.

"I can scarcely recall such a beautiful day," she said.

Shrewsbury turned to her and she was surprised to feel a sudden thrill of desire as his eyes met hers. She had known him for years and never thought of him as other than a friend, probably because then she had been married, and so had he. But his wife Gertrude had died in January. Bess knew their match had been a dynastic arrangement, made when George Talbot was only eleven, and she wondered if the marriage had been happy. She had always thought that Gertrude had seemed of too bland a temperament to match the vivid character of the outspoken earl.

"It would be a shame to waste such a lovely afternoon," he said, smiling down at her. "We could ride—to Eltham perhaps, and still be back for supper."

"I would like that," Bess said, feeling that the world was suddenly alive with possibilities.

"HE IS COURTING ME," BESS TOLD FRANCES THE NEXT DAY.

"And why should he not? You would make him an admirable wife."

"Surely he must have other ladies in mind, though."

"Bess! You will be the death of me. You are a jewel that any man would be happy to have adorn his life. If you marry Shrewsbury, you'll break the heart of my poor brother-in-law."

Bess laughed. "Hardly that."

"And that reminds me," Frances said. "You heard about the to-do with the Earl of Oxford? Killing Cecil's undercook? Surely that strikes him off your list of possible husbands for the girls."

"He was only practicing his fencing," Bess said. "And the inquest found that Brincknell was drunk and ran onto Oxford's blade." She smiled at the look of amused despair on Frances's face. "But yes, it does give me pause."

"Well, that's something," Frances said. "Now then, let us get back to the matter of Shrewsbury." She jumped up and fetched paper, pen, and ink from her desk. "I am determined to get you married, Bess. So let us make a list of all the qualities of the earl, and see if there is anyone else who can touch him." She dipped the quill in the ink. "Item: only dukes and the royal family are above an earl, and there is only one duke in England just now, and no men in the royal family at all. And our friend George is the premier earl."

"Countess of Shrewsbury," Bess said. "That does have a nice ring, doesn't it?"

Frances quirked an eyebrow at her. "Item," she continued. "He owns Sheffield Castle and Manor, Tutbury Castle and Abbey, Wingfield Manor, Worksop Manor, Welbeck Abbey, Rufford Abbey, Buxton Hall, that lovely house in Chelsea, and when you would like to be in town, Cold Harbour House in Thames Street and another house near Charing Cross."

"He holds more land than anyone else in the country," Bess said. "Great swathes of Derbyshire, Shropshire, Staffordshire, Yorkshire, and Nottinghamshire."

"Very good. Now you are entering into the proper spirit of the thing," Frances said, writing. "Item: he is a Knight of the Garter."

"And Lord Lieutenant of Derbyshire, Yorkshire, and Nottinghamshire, Chief Justice in Eyre, and Chamberlain of the Receipt of the Exchequer."

"Yes, and sundry other offices, too, I believe." Frances looked up from her list. "Now, as to his person. He is tall and well made, with a handsome set of whiskers that has just the merest hint of silver. He has hair."

Bess laughed in delight. "So he does. And he is just my age—in fact a year or so younger, I believe."

"And he has children, Bess. Are you not most determined on making the finest matches for your children that may be? Is this not an opportunity to kill two birds with one stone?"

Bess caught her breath, for this consideration perhaps more than any other exerted a powerful tug on her mind and heart.

"Perhaps. Some of his children are already married. His oldest boy, Francis, is wedded to Anne Herbert, the Earl of Pembroke's girl. And his daughter Catherine is the wife of Pembroke's heir, Henry Herbert."

"Excellent, so we know he has a mind to good matches, as you have."

"His son Gilbert is fifteen, I believe, and Edward a little younger," Bess mused.

"Gilbert is just the age for Bessie then, and perhaps Edward would do for May."

Bess swallowed. Could it really work? Now that the idea was in her mind, she wanted it very much.

"And he has two girls," she said. "Mary and Grace, I believe."

"Excellent. How old is your Harry now?"

"Sixteen. He'll be finished at Cambridge very soon."

"He's a fine boy, Bess, and he'll eventually inherit Chatsworth and your other properties. Any father would think him a good match for his daughter."

"Do you really think it's a good idea?" Bess asked. "All of it, I mean?"

"I do. I feel it in my bones. So when the earl puts his proposal to you—yes, he will, don't argue with me—do yourself the kindness of accepting him."

Fourth of October, 1567—London

Bess draped the ropes of pearls around her neck, careful not to disarrange her hair, and then turned to her mirror. She had feared this day, when she had allowed herself to think of it, for today she was forty years old. But the reflection that gazed back at her was not displeasing to her. She was sound and healthy in body, thank God, and stood straight and slender. Her skin was still smooth and white, little marred by wrinkles, and glowed alabaster against the black velvet of her gown. Her hair, its curls restrained beneath the gold and pearl of her cap, retained its copper vibrancy.

Yes, she had weathered her life well thus far, she thought, and today she had reason to expect that her future would be even brighter. For George Talbot, the sixth Earl of Shrewsbury, was coming to supper, and she believed he was going to ask her to marry him.

"He's here, Bess." Bess turned to see Jenny, smiling in the door of her bedchamber.

"How do I look?" Bess asked, suddenly anxious for the opinion of a pair of eyes other than her own.

"You have never looked more beautiful." Jenny came to Bess's side. "Truly."

"Thank you, dear heart. Then I had better not keep his lordship waiting."

EPILOGUE

Twenty-fifth of March, 1603—Hardwick Hall, Derbyshire

BESS RAISED HER EYES FROM THE LITTLE RED SHOE IN HER HAND to find Crossman gazing at her.

"Well, it's late," she said. "If I'm to make you work, I suppose I'd best get on with it."

She pulled each of the items from the box before her and ranged them on the table. The delicate handkerchief that Robbie Barlow had given her on the morning of her first wedding day. A little cap, worn so few times before poor baby Temperance had let go of her little life with a gentle sigh, and the tiny gown in which Lucres had been christened. A little book, a spelling primer, that had belonged to her son Harry, when she had still had such hopes for him. A heavy gold ring, far too large for her fingers, that had adorned the hand of William Cavendish. A rose, pressed and flat but still redolent of summer, that Will St. Loe had given her during that summer progress when they had been so happy together. A lock of red-gold hair, tied with a bit of blue ribbon—Jane Grey's hair, enclosed in that last letter. The gloves she had worn at her fourth wedding, to

George Talbot, the soft ivory kid still giving off a faint scent of perfume.

Astonishing that these few little items held such a weight of memory and meaning. She took up each again, memorizing their contours, their colors, the feel of each in her hands, for she would never see them again.

A log on the fire gave a sharp crack and shifted, sending a shower of sparks upward. Bess glanced at the westward-facing windows, black now in the wintry darkness. And yet—surely not blank, for something caught her eye, a flash of color, of movement. It seemed to Bess that it was her mother she had glimpsed there. And there, in another window, another fleeting image—William, and beside him Will. There was a ripple of light in the diamond panes of the next window over, and Bess saw the face of Jane Grey. The firelight must be playing tricks on her eyes. She glanced sharply to the windows on the northern wall and drew in her breath, for from the expanse of glass a crowd of faces gazed out at her—Robbie Barlow, George Talbot, Lizzie Brooke, Frances Grey, the angelic countenances of Temperance and Lucres, Cat Howard, Doll Fitzherbert. And Elizabeth, eyes like jet sparkling in the crystal panes.

Bess turned back to Crossman. He must think she was mad. But his eyes were warm and grave and there was a half smile on his face as he gave a minute nod.

"Have you changed your mind, my lady? I can return in the morning."

Crossman shifted his cap in his hands and Bess was tempted to send him away.

"No, let us not wait," she said. She let her fingers caress Temperance's tiny cap. "Let us do it now, for otherwise I might change my mind. We brought nothing into this world, neither may we carry anything out of this world, we are told, and I have carried these things long enough. Let the walls of Hardwick hold them now, for it will still be here when I am no more. And that is really what we crave, is it not, Rob? To know that we are not truly gone."

Crossman nodded gravely, as if weighing her words.

"It is. But you of all folks should have no fear, your ladyship. It would take a bigger world than this to forget such a lady as you."

ACKNOWLEDGMENTS

There are many to people to thank for their help in making this book come into the world:

My agents, Kevan Lyon, Arabella Stein, and Taryn Fagerness.

My editor, Kate Seaver.

Pat Bracewell and Melanie Spiller, my wonderful writing group mates, who provided thoughtful and supportive criticism week after week, and encouragement when I thought it couldn't be done. Pat deserves special thanks for a reading and critique of new scenes added at the last minute.

Diana Gabaldon, Bernard Cornwell, Margaret George, Leslie Carroll, and Patricia Bracewell took time to read the not-quite-final draft of the book on tight deadline and provided me with lovely quotes for the cover.

Helen Hollick, Elizabeth Chadwick, Linda Collinson, Susan Keogh, Jenny Quinlan, Richard Spillman, and Joan Szechtman responded to my query on the Facebook page of the Historical Novel Society about the use of curry combs. With her permission, I have used a couple of sentences that Helen Hollick wrote describing how Bess might have felt herself grow calmer as she groomed her colt.

My father, Dick Bagwell, came up with a great selection of songs for me to choose from to give Bess something to sing to Moth as she groomed him, and provided information about music at court.

Noel Gieleghem and Elspeth Golden provided advice about clothes and fashions of the period.

Alice Northgreaves provided useful information about the Letters of Bess of Hardwick project under Dr. Alison Wiggins, which is digitizing Bess's letters—though, alas, not in time for me to have made use of them. Alice also put me in touch with Polly Schomberg of the National Trust, who arranged for me to visit Hardwick Hall out of season, although I wasn't ultimately able to make that visit.

J. D. Davies kindly took many pictures of Hardwick Hall and Old Hardwick Hall for me, as I was unable to go, and gave me words I could quote to convince my editor that I couldn't write a novel about Bess of Hardwick and not have Hardwick Hall make an appearance.

There are others, I know, whose indulgence I crave in advance for their omission.

AUTHOR'S NOTE

This novel covers only the first half of the very long and very eventful life of Bess of Hardwick. All of the major characters and most of the minor ones are real people. The further Bess rose in prominence and power, the more documentation there was of her life, but much less is known about her early years. David N. Durant's biography, *Bess of Hardwick*, begins with her second marriage, when she was nineteen. Maud Stepney Rawson's *Bess of Hardwick and Her Circle* dispenses with her first two marriages and the first thirty years of her life in ten pages. Another twelve pages takes Bess to the age of thirty-seven and the death of her third husband. Even Mary Lovell's *Bess of Hardwick: Empire Builder*, the most recent biography, takes only two hundred pages of almost five hundred to bring Bess to the age of forty in the autumn of 1567, where my book ends.

So I have used what facts are known about her younger years, but of necessity have had to make some suppositions and also to invent, based on what seems possible or likely. I have chosen to put Bess in places and situations in which she could have been when it made the story better. For instance, she was in the household of Lady Zouche from about 1539, and since Lady Zouche's husband became one of Henry VIII's gentlemen pensioners around that time, Bess could easily have been at court to observe the king's last three marriages, and so I have put her there, though I don't know if she was.

I've taken some small liberties with other real people. Bess certainly knew Elisabeth Brooke, who was eventually the wife of William Parr and the Marchioness of Northampton, but I don't know when they met. Elizabeth Brooke was just Bess's age and was first noted at court at the age of fourteen when she became a maid of honor to Catherine Howard. I have placed her in the household of Lady Zouche with Bess a couple of years earlier, rather than writing a fictional character who drops out of sight. Her presence also creates a plausible bridge to Bess's acquaintance with Catherine Howard and with Catherine Parr, who Elisabeth Brooke also served. Similarly, one of Bess's friends in London was Dorothy Fitzherbert, later Lady Port, who also grew up in Derbyshire, so it didn't seem too much of a stretch to also place her in Lady Zouche's service.

I didn't need to invent Bess's close connection to the Greys. Bess did serve in the household of Henry Grey and Frances Brandon, and her second wedding, to their friend Sir William Cavendish, took place at their home, Bradgate Park. Bess was very close to Jane Grey, and kept Jane's portrait near her all her life. The scenes in which Katherine Grey discloses to Bess her secret marriage and her pregnancy really did take place, as well as all that happened as a result, including Bess's questioning in the Tower. And when Mary, the youngest of the Grey girls, died, she was buried at St. Botolph without Aldersgate, next to Bess's second husband Sir William Cavendish.

I've used bits of real letters and quotations from people, woven into fictional letters and dialogue.

Read on for a special preview of
Gillian Bagwell's novel

THE DARLING STRUMPET

A novel of Nell Gwynn, who captured the heart
of England and King Charless II

CHAPTER ONE

London—Twenty-ninth of May, 1660

THE SUN SHONE HOT AND BRIGHT IN THE GLORIOUS MAY SKY, and the streets of London were rivers of joyous activity. Merchants and laborers, gentlemen and ladies, apprentices and servants, whores, thieves, and grimy urchins—all were out in their thousands. And all with the same thought shining in their minds and hearts and the same words on their tongues—the king comes back this day.

After ten years—nay, it was more—of England without a king. Ten years of the bleak and gray existence that life had been under the Protector—an odd title for one who had thrown the country into strife, had arrested and then beheaded King Charles. What a groan had gone up from the crowd that day at the final, fatal sound of the executioner's axe; what horror and black despair had filled their hearts as the bleeding head of the king was held aloft in triumph. And all upon the order of the Protector, who had savaged life as it had been, and then, after all, had thought to take the throne for himself.

But now he was gone. Oliver Cromwell was dead, his son had fled after a halfhearted attempt at governing, his partisans were scattered, and the king's son, Charles II, who had barely escaped with his life to years of impoverished exile, was approaching London to claim his crown, on this, his thirtieth birthday. And after so long a wait, such suffering and loss, what wrongs could there be that the return of the king could not put right?

NELL GWYNN AWOKE, THE WARMTH OF THE SUN ON HER BACK IN contrast to the dank coolness of the straw on which she lay under the shelter of a rickety staircase. She rolled over, and the movement hurt. Her body ached from the beating her mother had given her the night before. Legs and backside remembered the blows of the broomstick, and her face was bruised and tender from the slaps. Tears had mingled on her cheeks with dust. She tried to wipe the dirt away, but her hands were just as bad, grimy and still smelling of oysters.

Oysters. That was the cause of all this pain. Yesterday evening, she'd stopped on her way home to watch as garlands of flowers were strung on one of the triumphal arches that had been erected in anticipation of the king's arrival. Caught up in the excitement, she had forgotten to be vigilant, and her oyster barrow had been stolen. She'd crept home unwillingly, hoped that the night would be one of the many when her mother had been drinking so heavily that she was already unconscious, or one of the few when the drink made her buoyant and forgiving. But no. Not even the festive mood taking hold of London had leavened her reaction to the loss of the barrow. Replacing it would cost five shillings, as much as Nell earned in a week. And her mother had seemed determined to beat into Nell's hide the understanding of that cost.

Nell had no tears today. She was only angry, and determined that she would not be beaten again. She sat up and brushed the straw out of her skirt, clawed it out of the curls of her hair. And thought about what to do next. She wanted to find Rose, her dear older sister, with whom she'd planned so long for this day. And she was hungry. With no money and no prospect of getting any.

At home there would be food, but home would mean facing her mother again. Another beating, or at least more shouting and recriminations, and then more of what she had done for the past two years—up at dawn, the long walk to Billingsgate fish market to buy her daily stock, and an endless day pushing the barrow, heavy with the buckets of live oysters in their brine. Aching feet, aching arms, aching back, throat hoarse with her continual cry of "Oysters, alive-o!" Hands raw and red from plunging into the salt water, and the fishy, salty smell always on her hands, pervading her hair and clothes.

It was better than the work she had done before that, almost since she was old enough to walk—going from door to door to collect the cinders and fragments of wood left from the previous day's fires, and then taking her pickings to the soap makers, who bought the charred bits for fuel and the ashes to make lye. Her skin and clothes had been always gray and gritty, a film of stinking ash ground into her pores. And not even a barrow to wheel, but heavy canvas sacks carried slung over her shoulders, their weight biting into her flesh.

Nell considered. What else could she do? What would buy freedom from her mother and keep food in her belly and a roof over her head? She could try to get work in some house, but that, too, would mean endless hours of hard and dirty work as a kitchen drudge or scouring floors and chamber pots, under the thumb of cook or steward as well as at the mercy of the uncertain temper of the master and mistress. No.

And that left only the choice that Rose had made, and their mother, too. Whoredom. Rose, who was four years older than Nell, had gone a year earlier to Madam Ross's nearby establishment at the top of Drury Lane. It was not so bad, Rose said. A little room of her own, except of course when she'd a man there. And they were none of the tag, rag, and bobtail—it was gentlemen who were Madam Ross's trade, and Rose earned enough to get an occasional treat for Nell, and good clothes for herself.

What awe and craving Nell had felt upon seeing the first clothes Rose had bought—a pair of silk stays, a chemise of fine lawn, and a skirt and body in a vivid blue, almost the color of Rose's eyes, with ribbons to match. Secondhand, to be sure, but still beautiful. Nell had touched the stuff of the gown with a tentative finger—so smooth and clean. Best of all were the shoes—soft blue leather with an elegant high heel. She had wanted them so desperately. But you couldn't wear shoes like that carting ashes or oysters through the mud of London's streets.

Could she go to Madam Ross's? She was no longer a child, really. She had small buds of breasts, and already the lads at the Golden Fleece, where her mother kept bar, watched her with appreciation, and asked with coarse jests when she would join Mrs. Gwynn's gaggle of girls, who kept rooms upstairs or could be sent for from the nearby streets.

But before she could do anything about the future, she had to find Rose. Today, along with everyone else in London, they would watch and rejoice as the king returned to take his throne.

Nell emerged from under the staircase and hurried down the narrow alley to the Strand. The street was already thronged with people, and all were in holiday humor. The windows were festooned with ribbons and flowers. A fiddler played outside an alehouse, to the accompaniment of a clapping crowd. The smell of food wafted on the morning breeze—meat pies, pastries, chickens roasting.

A joyful cacophony of church bells pealed from all directions, and in the distance Nell could hear the celebratory firing of cannons at the Tower.

She scanned the crowds. Rose had said she'd come to fetch her from home this morning. If Rose had found her gone, where would she look? Surely here, where the king would pass by.

"Ribbons! Fine silk ribbons!" Nell turned and was instantly entranced. The ribbon seller's staff was tied with rosettes of ribbons in all colors, and her clothes were pinned all over with knots of silken splendor. Nell stared at the most beautiful thing she had ever seen—a knot of ribbons the colors of periwinkles and daffodils, its streamers fluttering in the breeze. Wearing that, she would feel a grand lady.

"Only a penny, the finest ribbons," the peddler cried. A penny. Nell could eat her fill for a penny. If she had one. And with that thought she realized how hungry she was. She'd had no supper the night before and now her empty belly grumbled. She must find Rose.

A voice called her name and she turned to see Molly and Deb, two of her mother's wenches. Nell made her way across the road to where they stood. Molly was a country lass and Deb was a Londoner, but when she saw them together, which they almost always were, Nell could never help thinking of a matched team of horses. Both had straw-colored hair and cheerful ruddy faces, and both were buxom, sturdy girls, packed into tight stays that thrust their bosoms into prominence. They seemed in high spirits as they greeted Nell; it was apparent that they had already had more than a little to drink.

"Have you seen Rose?" Nell asked.

"Nay, not since yesterday," said Deb, and Molly chimed her agreement.

"Aye, not since last night." She looked more closely at Nell.

"Is summat the matter?"

"No," Nell lied. "Only I was to meet her this morning and I've missed her." She wondered if the girls' good spirits would extend to a loan. "Tip me a dace, will you? I've not had a bite this morning and I'm fair clemmed."

"Faith, if I had the tuppence, I would," said Deb. "But we've just spent the last of our rhino on drink and we've not worked yet today."

"Not yet," agreed Molly. "But the day is like to prove a golden one. I've ne'er seen crowds like this."

"Aye, there's plenty of darby to be made today," Deb nodded. Her eyes flickered to a party of sailors moving down the opposite side of the road and with a nudge she drew Molly's attention to the prospect of business.

"We'd best be off," Molly said, and she and Deb were already moving toward their prey.

"If you see Rose . . . ," Nell cried after them.

"We'll tell her, poppet," Molly called back, and they were gone.

The crowds were growing, and it was becoming harder by the minute for Nell to see beyond the bodies towering above her. What she needed was someplace with a better view.

She looked around for a vantage point. A brewer's wagon stood on the side of the street, its bed packed with a crowd of lads, undoubtedly apprentices given liberty for the day. Surely it could accommodate another small body.

"Oy!" Nell called up. "Room for one more?"

"Aye, love, the more the merrier," called a dark-haired lad, and hands reached down to pull her up. The view from here was much better.

"Drink?"

Nell turned to see a red-haired boy holding out a mug. He was not more than fourteen or so, and freckles stood out in his pale, anxious face. She took the mug and drank, and he smiled shyly, his blue eyes shining.

"How long have you been here?" Nell asked, keeping an eye on the crowd.

"Since last night," he answered. "We brought my father's wagon and made merry 'til late, then slept 'til the sun woke us."

Nell had been hearing music in the distance since she had neared the Strand. The fiddler's music floated on the air from the east, she could see a man with a tabor and pipe to the west, only the top notes of his tune reaching her ears, and now she saw a hurdy-gurdy player approaching, the keening drone of his instrument cutting through the noise of the crowd.

"Look!" she cried in delight. A tiny dark monkey capered along before the man, diminutive cap in hand. The crowds parted to make way for the pair, and as the boys beside her laughed and clapped, the man and his little partner stopped in front of the wagon. He waved a salute and began to play a jig. The monkey skipped and frolicked before him, to the vast entertainment of the crowd.

"Look at him! Just like a little man!" Nell cried. People were tossing coins into the man's hat, which he had thrown onto the ground before him, and Nell laughed as the monkey scampered after an errant farthing and popped it into the hat.

"Here," the ginger-haired boy said. He fished in a pocket inside his coat. She watched with interest as he withdrew a small handful of coins and picked one out.

"You give it to him," he said, holding out a coin as he pocketed the rest of the money. Nell could tell that he was proud for her to see that he had money to spend for an entertainment such as this.

"Hist!" she called to the monkey and held up the shiny coin, shrieking with laughter as the monkey clambered up a wheel of the wagon, took the coin from her fingers, and bobbed her a little bow before leaping back down and resuming its dance.

Laughing, she turned to the boy and found him staring at her, naked longing in his eyes. He wanted her. She had seen that look before from men and boys of late and had ignored it. But today was different. Her stomach was turning over from lack of food, and she had no money. Molly and Deb had spoken of the wealth to be had from the day's revelries. Maybe she could reap some of that wealth. Sixpence would buy food and drink, with money left over.

She stepped nearer to the boy and felt him catch his breath as she looked up at him.

"I'll let you fuck me for sixpence," she whispered. He gaped at her and for a moment she thought he was going to run away. But then, striving to look self-possessed, he nodded.

"I know where," she said. "Follow me."

HALF AFRAID THAT SHE WOULD LOSE HER PREY AND HALF WONDER-ing what had possessed her to speak so boldly, Nell darted through the crowds with the boy after her to the alley where she had spent the night. Slops from chamber pots emptied out of windows reeked in the sunshine, but the passage was deserted, save for a dead dog sprawled in the mud. Nell dodged under the staircase beneath which she had slept. The pile of straw was not very clean, but it would do. The boy glanced nervously behind him, then followed her.

With the boy so close, panting in anticipation, Nell felt a twinge of fear. For all the banter and jokes she had heard about the act, she had no real idea what it would be like. Would it hurt? Would she bleed? Could she get with child her first time? What if she did it so poorly that her ignorance showed? She wished she had considered the matter more carefully.

Her belly rumbled with hunger again. Why had she not simply asked the boy to buy her something to eat? But it was too late now, she thought. She pushed away her misgivings and flopped onto her back. The boy clambered on top of her, fumbling with the flies of his breeches, and heaved himself between her legs, thrusting against her blindly. He didn't know what to do any more than she did, she realized. She reached down and grasped him, amazed at the aliveness of the hard member, like a puppy nosing desperately to nurse, and struggled to help him find the place.

The boy thrust hard, groaning like an animal in distress, and Nell gasped as he entered her. It hurt. Forcing too big a thing into too small a space, an edge of her skin pinched uncomfortably. Was this how it was meant to be? Surely not. Yet maybe to him it felt different.

She had little time to consider, as the boy's movements grew faster, and with a strangled moan, he bucked convulsively and then stopped, pushed as far into her as he could go. He stayed there a moment, gasping, and then Nell felt a trickle of wetness down the inside of her thigh, and knew that he must have spent.

The boy looked down at her, with an expression that mingled jubilation with shame and surprise. He withdrew and did not look at Nell as he buttoned up his breeches and straightened his clothes. She grabbed a handful of straw to wipe the stickiness from between her legs. The smell of it rose sharp and shameful to her nose, and she wanted to retch. The boy reached into his pocket and counted out six pennies.

"I must go," he said, and almost hitting his head on the low stairs, he ducked out and scurried away.

Nell looked at the coins. Sixpence. She felt a surge of power and joy. She had done it. It had not been so bad. And now she had money. She could do as she liked. And she decided that first and immediately, she would get something good to eat.

She used her shift to wipe as much of the remaining mess as she could from her thighs and hands, and then knotted the coins into its hem. She hurried back toward the Strand, her new wealth banging pleasantly against her calf.

The smell of food hung heavy in the air, and her stomach felt as if it was turning inside out with hunger. Earlier, she had noted with longing a man with a cart selling meat pies, and she sought him out, her nose leading the way. She extracted one of her pennies and received the golden half-moon, warm from its nest in the tin-lined cart. The man smiled at her rapturous expression as she took her prize in both hands, inhaling its heady aroma.

Voraciously, she bit into the pie, the crust breaking into tender shards that seemed to melt on her tongue. The rich warm gravy filled her mouth as she bit deeper, into the hearty filling of mutton and potatoes. She thought nothing had ever tasted so good. The pie seemed to be filling not only her belly, but crannies of longing and misery in her heart and soul. She sighed with pleasure, so hungry and intent on eating that she had not even moved from where she stood.

The old pie man, with a weathered face like a sun-dried apple, laughed as he watched her.

"I'd say you like it, then?"

Nell nodded, wiping gravy from her lips with the back of her hand and brushing a few crumbs from her chest. She was tempted to eat another pie right then, but decided to let the first settle. Besides, there were other things to spend money on, now that she had money to spend.

She again heard the call of "Ribbons! Fine ribbons!" The

rosette—her rosette—cornflower blue intertwined with sun gold, its silken streamers rippling in the breeze—was still pinned to the woman's staff. Waiting for her.

Nell raced to the woman, her face shining. "That one. If you please." The woman gave her a look of some doubt, but as Nell pulled up her skirt and produced a penny from her shift, she unpinned the rosette from the staff.

"Do you want me to pin it for you, duck?"

Nell nodded, feeling grown up and important as the ribbon peddler considered her.

"Here, I think, is best." The woman pinned the rosette to the neckline of Nell's bodice and nodded approvingly. "Very handsome. The color brings out those eyes of yours."

Nell looked down and stroked the streamers. Even hanging on the rough brown wool, the gleaming ribbons were beautiful, and she wished that she could see herself. At home she had a scrap of mirror that she had found in the street, but she would have to wait until she went home to have a look. If she went home.

That brought back to mind her next task—finding Rose. The street was becoming more crowded, and she would have a hard time seeing the king when he came by, let alone her sister. She needed to find a perch from which she could view the road. But not the wagon with the red-headed lad. Given his urgent flight, he might not relish her company. And in truth, she did not think she would relish his. He had served his purpose. Now, perhaps, there were bigger fish to fry.

She considered the possibilities. The carts, wagons, barrels, and other vantage points at the sides of the road were packed. The windows of upper stories would provide a superior view, if she could find a place in one.

She made her way eastward, searching windows for familiar faces but found none, and felt herself lost in a sea of strangers. She was almost to Fleet Street now. Surely Rose would not have come this far. She would go just as far as Temple Bar, she thought, and then turn back.

"Oy! Ginger!" The voice came from a window three floors up,

where several lads were crowded. A stocky boy with close-cropped hair leaned out the casement and regarded her with a wolflike grin.

Maybe she didn't need an old friend. Maybe new friends would do.

Nell put a hand on her hip and raked the lad with an exaggeratedly critical glance, drawing guffaws from his mates.

"Aye, it's ginger, and what of that?" she hollered. "At least I've got hair. Unlike some."

The lads howled with delight, one of them gleefully rubbing his friend's cropped poll and drawing a shove in response.

Playing to his audience, the boy took a deep swig from his mug and leered down at Nell. "You have hair, do you? I'd have thought you was too young."

"Too young be damned," cried Nell. "It's you who must be too old, bald-pated as you are." The lads set up a raucous cry at that, thumping their friend from all sides. Nell grinned up at them, gratified at their reaction and the laughter from the crowd around her. In her years selling oysters, she had found that a little saucy humor helped her business, and made the time pass more quickly.

"Come up and join us!" shouted another of the lads, a cheerful-faced runt with bright blue eyes.

"Aye, come aloft! Let me get a look at you up close!" cried Nell's original sparring partner.

"And why should I?" Nell called back. "What do I want with the likes of you?"

"Come up and I'll show you!"

"We've plenty to drink!" promised the thin lad, waving a mug. "And a view better than any in London!"

"Well, I could use a bit to drink," Nell twinkled up at her admirers. There was a scramble at the window, and a few moments later, the door to the street-level shop flew open and one of the lads beckoned. He was gangly and sandy haired, and he giggled as he ushered her inside. She hesitated a moment, wondering if she was courting danger. But she followed him up the narrow stairs, finally arriving at the room where the boys were gathered.

"Here's the little ginger wench!" The first lad swaggered over, chuckling as he eyed her. Behind him were the boy who had let her in, the scrawny lad, and a boy with dark brown hair and snapping dark eyes. They crowded around Nell, and she suddenly felt very small. But it would never do to seem shy, so she gave them a cheeky grin and chirped, "Pleased to meet you, lads. I'm Nell."

They were all about sixteen years old, probably nearing the end of their apprenticeships, and it looked as if their master was nowhere near, for a barrel had been tapped and stood on a table at one side of the room. Each of the boys held a mug, and from their red faces and boisterous laughs, Nell guessed they had been drinking for some time.

"I'm Nick," said the first boy. "This is my brother Davy, and Kit and Toby."

The boys nodded their greetings, and Nell took the mug Kit handed her and drank. The dark stout tasted full and bitter, much heavier than the small beer she was accustomed to drinking, but she swallowed it down as the boys looked on, grinning. Feeling their eyes on her a little too keenly, she went to the window.

From this height, the view stretched eastward down Fleet Street toward St. Paul's, and southwest past Charing Cross to Whitehall Palace. Across the road to the south, she could see over the walls of the grand houses along the Thames, their imposing fronts facing London and their capacious gardens sloping down behind to the river. Every wall, window, and rooftop was occupied, and the streets as far as she could see were aswarm. The noise of the crowd was growing louder. Nell heard drumbeats and the tramp of booted feet.

"Here they come!" Kit shouted, and the lads crowded to the windows around Nell. A shimmering wave of silver moved toward her, and she saw that it was a column of men marching. At the front was a rank of soldiers in buff coats with sleeves of cloth of silver, a row of drummers to the fore, rapping out a sharp tattoo as they swung along. Behind them marched hundreds of gentlemen in cloth of silver that flashed and shone.

Toby whistled. "Lord. Never knew there was so many gentlemen."

"There wasn't, a month since," laughed Nick. "They was all lying quiet in the country or somewheres. Only now the king is come and it's safe again. . . ."

The silver swarm was followed by a phalanx of gentlemen in velvet coats, interspersed with footmen in plush new liveries of deep purple and sea green.

"I didn't know there was so many colors," Nell breathed, awed by the beauty of the rich reds, greens, blues, and golds. "I didn't know they could make cloth like that."

"They can if you can pay for it," said Davy.

"Aye," Nick agreed. "I'll wager Barbara Palmer has a gown of stuff like that." He turned to Nell with a wink.

"Who's Barbara Palmer?" she asked, not wanting to seem ignorant, but desperate to know.

"Why, the king's whore!" Nick cried. "They do say she's the most beautiful woman in England. Nought but the best for the king!"

Nell took this in with interest. The king's whore. Wearing fine clothes. The whores she knew made themselves as brave and showy as they could, but she had never seen anything like the finery on display today.

The Sheriff of London and his men, all in scarlet, passed and were succeeded by the gentlemen of the London companies—the goldsmiths, vintners, bakers, and other guilds that supplied the City, each with its fluttering banner.

"There he is!" cried Kit. "Our master," he explained, pointing to a beefy man in deep blue who strode along with his brothers in trade.

After the guilds came the aldermen of London, in scarlet gowns, and then more soldiers with tall pikes and halberds. But unlike the grim-faced soldiers who had patrolled the streets throughout her life, these men did not strike fear into Nell, for they couldn't help smiling at the ringing cheers.

The roaring of the crowd exploded into a frenzy. Nell scrabbled for a hold on the windowsill and craned to get a better view.

The king was coming. Three men on horseback rode through Temple Bar, but the king could only be the one in the middle, in a cloth-of-silver doublet trimmed in gold, his saddle and bridle richly worked in gold. He turned from side to side to wave as blossoms showered down upon him. The throngs pressed forward, waving, throwing their hats into the air, calling out to him—"God save the king," "God bless Your Majesty," "Thank God for this day!"

"Those are his brothers," Toby shouted to Nell. "The Duke of York and the Duke of Gloucester." They were a dazzling sight, all in silver, riding side by side on three enormous dark stallions, radiant as angels in the noonday sun.

The king was close enough now that Nell could see him clearly. Big and broad shouldered, he sat tall in the gilded saddle, long booted legs straightening as he stood in the stirrups, as if he could not stay seated in the face of his people's adulation. His long dark curls cascaded over his shoulders as he swept his hat from his head and waved it, turning to either side to acknowledge the cheers.

He smiled broadly, laughing with exuberance at the tumultuous welcome. "I thank you with all my heart," he called, his deep voice ringing out amidst the clamor and cries.

"God save King Charles!" Nell realized it was her own voice. The king looked up, and Nell caught her breath as he looked her full in the face. He grinned, teeth showing beneath his dark mustache, eyes twinkling in his swarthy face, and called back to her, "I thank you, sweetheart!" Impulsively, Nell blew him a kiss and was immediately overcome with horror at the audacity of her act. But the king threw his head back and laughed, then blew a kiss to her, waving as he and his brothers rode on.

Nell giggled and bounced off the windowsill. "Did you see? He blew me a kiss!"

"Aye, and from what I hear of him, he'd offer you more than a kiss, was you close enough for him to reach you!" Nick guffawed.

"He's got a mistress who's another man's wife, and two or three merry-begotten brats by other women, they say. For who will say nay to the king?"

Not I, thought Nell.

The procession continued below, but once the king had passed, Nell's attention was no longer focused exclusively on the street. Nick refilled her mug, and the other boys drifted away from the window to drink.

Nell was in high good humor, awed by the glamour of the procession and her exchange with the king. Her head swam a bit from the stout and from the excitement at being out on her own for the first time, in company with these older boys, almost men.

"What think you of the king, Nelly?" Kit asked.

"Oh," she cooed, "he's fine as hands can make him."

"Not finer than me, surely?" cried Nick.

"Oh, no," Nell shot back. "No more than a diamond is finer than a dog turd." The boys roared and moved in close around her. At the heart of this laughing group, she felt worldly and sophisticated. She had been silly to doubt that she could handle the lads. They were eating out of her hand.

"Ah, Nick, you're not good enough for Nell," Toby chortled. "Mayhap you'd have better luck with Barbara Palmer."

"Well, Nell?" Davy laughed. "Do you think she'd have him?"

"Aye, when hens make holy water," Nell answered tartly.

"What?" Nick gawped at her in mock amazement. "How can you say such a thing? When you've hardly met me! Why, I have qualities."

"Aye, and a bumblebee in a cow turd thinks himself a king," she retorted. "Is there no end of your talking?"

"I'll leave off my talking and set you to moaning," Nick leered, sidling closer. "Once a mort is lucky enough to feel my quim-stake, she's not like to forget it."

Nell gave him a shove in the belly.

"Enough of your bear-garden discourse."

"Aye, speak that way to Barbara Palmer, and you're like to be taken out for air and exercise," Toby grinned.

"No, you'd get worse than a whipping at the cart's arse for giving her the cutty eye." Kit shook his head. "Look the wrong way at the king's doxy and you'll piss when you can't whistle."

"How say you, Nick?" Davy asked. "Do you reckon there's a woman worth hanging for?"

"If there is," Nick said, "I've yet to clap eye on her."

"Don't lose hope yet." Nell batted her eyes at him. "The day is young."

Eventually the last of the king's train passed, followed by a straggling tail of children and beggars, but the crowds in the street below did not disperse. Drink flowed and piles of wood were being stacked in preparation for celebratory bonfires. The party would continue through the night.

"Come on, who's for wandering?" Nick turned from the window. "To Whitehall!" he bellowed, once they were in the street. "I want to see this trull of the king's."

Their progress was slow, as the way toward Whitehall was packed with others wending their way there, and there were constant diversions. Musicians, jugglers, stilt walkers, and rope dancers performed, as if Bartholomew Fair had come early.

Before the palace, the gang crowded with others around a roaring bonfire. The windows of the Banqueting House glowed from the light of hundreds of candles. Carriages clogged the street, the coachmen and footmen gathered in knots to talk as they waited for their masters.

"The king's having his supper now, before the whole court," Nick said. "I reckon he's got that Barbara Palmer with him." He moved closer to Nell and she felt his eyes hot on her. He was quite big and the intensity of his gaze made her heart race.

"I know I'd have her," he continued, "wherever and whenever I wanted, was I king." The boys hooted their agreement, but Nick's attention was on Nell now. He pulled her to him roughly and ran a hand heavily over her small breasts. She felt a surge of fear and tried to pull away.

Someone nearby cried out, the crowd stirred and buzzed, and Nell saw that the king had appeared at one of the windows of the Banqueting House. Nick loosened his hold on her and turned to gawk. The light blazing behind the king created a golden aura around him. The bonfires illuminated his face and made the silver of his doublet shine. He raised a hand to salute the crowds below, and they roared their approval and welcome.

Then a woman appeared next to him, and Nell knew that this must be the famous Barbara Palmer. She was darkly beautiful, her hair dressed in elaborate curls, and she wore a low-cut gown of deep red that set off the pale lushness of her bosom. As she leaned close to the king, sparkles and flashes of light from the jewels at her ears and throat cut through the shadows.

Nell had never seen a woman so stunning. She looked carefully, memorizing every detail, and longed to be like her—gorgeously dressed, elegant, and at ease before the adoring crowds.

Barbara Palmer disappeared from view. The king gave a final wave to the crowds and followed her.

"Aye, just give me half an hour with her," crowed Nick. "I reckon she'd be worth the price."

"You'll not earn the cost of her in your lifetime!" Davy gibed.

Nell felt a rush of envy. She didn't want to lose the delicious new sensation of feeling admired and special.

"She may be beautiful," she announced, tossing her tangled curls, "but she's not the only one worth her price."

This pronouncement produced a ripple of some indefinable undercurrent and an exchange of meaningful glances among the lads. Nick moved close to her, and she could not breathe for the nearness of him and his size. The firelight flickered orange on his face, and on the faces of the other lads, who stood flanking him and regarding her with new interest.

"Is that so?" Nick asked, taking a lazy drink. His eyes gleamed in the dark. "And just what might your price be?"

Nell's stomach heaved with nervous excitement, but remembering Barbara Palmer's easy confidence, she managed an inviting smile as she looked up at him. She thought of what Deb and Molly had said—was it only this morning?—about the riches to be made this night.

"Sixpence," she said to him. And then, taking in the others with a flicker of her eyes, "Apiece."

"Well, then. Time's a-wasting," said Nick, with a canine grin. He glanced toward the blackness of St. James's Park, grabbed Nell by the wrist, and pulled her along, the other boys in tow.

The park was scattered with revelers, but there were secluded dens amidst the darkness of the spreading trees and tangled shrubbery, and in any case, no one was likely to ask questions, tonight of all nights. Nick drew Nell into a thicket of trees, and the others crowded in behind him.

This felt very different from the morning's hasty coupling with the red-haired apprentice, and facing the four lads, panic rose in Nell's throat. But there was nothing really to be afraid of, was there? A bit of mess and it would all be done. And she would be two shillings the richer. Best to get it over with. She turned to find the driest spot on which to lie, but before she could move farther, Nick shoved her down and onto her back, pulled her skirt up to her waist, and was on top of her.

He leaned on one forearm as he unbuttoned his breeches, his weight taking Nell's breath away, then spit on his palm, guided himself between her legs and entered her hard. Her nether parts were tender, and his assault made her gasp in pain. She bit her lip and struggled not to whimper.

Nick lasted much longer than the young apprentice had, and finished with a low growl and a deep sustained thrust that made Nell cry out. He looked down at her for a moment, vulpine triumph in his eyes, then, grunting, heaved himself off her, put his cock back in his breeches, and buttoned his flies.

"Who's next?" he asked. There was a moment of hesitation, and he turned in irritation to his mates. "What ails you? I said who's next?"

Toby came forward. He was faster than Nick, and Nick having spent within her made his entry easier, but still it was painful. Nell turned her head so that she would not have to look him in the eyes. The other boys needed no urging now. Davy and Kit hovered on either side of her, watching, eager for their turns, and Davy knelt between Nell's thighs as soon as Toby was done. He hooked his arms under her knees, and he looked down at her keenly as he moved inside her, snarling like an animal.

The other boys laughed and called out their encouragement. Nell shut her eyes. Rocks and twigs pressed into her back, and the damp earth was soaking through her clothes. She didn't feel elegant and enchanting, only uncomfortable and frightened. But it would soon be over. And the money would make it all worthwhile.

Kit nearly knocked Davy aside in his haste to get on top of Nell. She was so sore now that she could barely keep from crying, but managed not to let more than a stifled moan escape.

Finally, Kit finished, and sat back to fasten his breeches.

"Come on!" Nick ordered, yanking him to his feet.

"My money!" Nell cried, struggling to get up. "Two shillings." Nick shoved her onto her back with a foot.

"Two hogs?" he sneered. "For that? We'll not pay a farthing. You're not only a whore, you're a stupid whore, at that."

Nell scrambled to her feet and caught at him. They couldn't. After all she had suffered.

"You said—you agreed!" But Nick just flung her away, and she tripped sideways and fell to her knees as the boys ran, crashing away through the branches.

It was hopeless. She gulped, fighting back sobs. Every part of her ached; the insides of her bruised thighs were clammy; she was covered in mud. She tried to straighten her clothes, and cried out as she realized that her rosette was gone. In a panic, she looked and felt around her. And there it was. It must have come off when Nick first pushed her down and been crushed beneath her. It lay crumpled in the muck, its beautiful bright colors sodden gray.

The tears Nell had held back flowed now, and she wept, her body shaking, as she clutched the precious knot of ribbons in her hand. Nick was right. How stupid she had been, to think that she could ever be like the glorious Barbara Palmer. She was just a shabby little ragamuffin, fit for nothing better than selling oysters. Her dreams of freedom had been so much foolishness. She would have no choice but to go back to her mother, to endure the beating that she knew awaited her, and resume her life of drudgery.

When she had finally cried herself out, Nell pushed herself up, wincing in pain, and wiped her nose and eyes on her shift. Her fingers closed around the lump in the hem. Her remaining pennies were still there. One shred of consolation. But the money would not buy her lodging for the night, and she longed to lie herself down. She could go home. Or spend a second night on the street. Unless she could find Rose. That thought brought her to her feet. Rose would surely be at Madam Ross's.

She emerged from the trees. There were still crowds gathered around the bonfires before the palace. She hurried toward Charing Cross, spurred on by hunger and weariness and the hope of comfort. Fires burned in the Strand and music drifted toward her on the warm evening breeze. She turned into the warren of narrow lanes that lay to the north of Covent Garden. She was near home now, and it felt odd to bypass the familiar close. But, resolutely, she made toward Lewkenor's Lane.

"Nell!" Rose's voice called her name. Nell rushed toward Rose and clung to her.

"I've been looking for you all the day," Rose exclaimed, and then took in Nell's state of dishevelment. "Wherever have you been?"

Nell's tears burst forth again, and Rose guided her to a step, sat her down, and listened as the whole story came out in a rush. After she finished, Nell sat sobbing, overcome by humiliation and shame. Rose stroked her hair and kissed the top of her head.

"Oh, Nelly," she said. "I wish I had found you this morning. If I had only known what was in your mind. . . ." She shook her head, considering, then put a finger under Nell's chin and tilted Nell's face to hers. Nell looked into her sister's eyes, and Rose's voice was gentle.

"I cannot make the world a different place than it is. But I can tell you this: Get the money first. Always."